24: **TRIAL BY FIRE**

Also available from Titan Books:

24: Deadline by James Swallow

24: Rogue by David Mack

as their own. It was an agreement both sides had honored for decades. So far as Jimura knew, his organization had done nothing to offend the *Kyokuryū-kai*. Even if that was the case, it was unlike the yakuza to retaliate in this manner.

As though reading his thoughts, Yeager said, "I don't think it's them. They wouldn't send a message to you like this. They'd want to meet face to face." He shook his head. "No, this is somebody else, and I think I have a pretty good idea who."

Now it was Jimura's turn to anticipate the other man's thinking. "Kanashiro."

"Exactly."

Aside from the obvious threat of disruption by any of the various law enforcement agencies, Jimura knew that his main concern was competition from rivals. When it came to dealings with other organizations headed by men closer to his own age, an honor system had developed over time whereby territorial boundaries were respected, and poaching business from another group was discouraged. However, in recent years, younger, more contentious challengers to the status quo had attempted to move in and stake their own claims. In most of these cases, the interlopers soon learned either the virtues of working and living in harmony with their established counterparts or else they opted to seek life and opportunity elsewhere. Only on rare occasions had more extreme measures been required. Those tended to serve as object lessons for anyone else contemplating similarly ill-advised actions.

It remained to be seen whether such a lesson might need to be imparted to Edoga Kanashiro.

"He's been playing it cool for a while, now," Yeager continued, "but I think he's just been biding his time. A guy like Kanashiro doesn't want to be hemmed in, and we know he's already pushed out a couple of the smaller groups."

"Yes," replied Jimura. Upon arriving on Okinawa from the mainland, Edoga Kanashiro had made no secret of his desire to carve out a slice of the action enjoyed by Jimura and other established groups. Only the *Kyokuryū-kai* seemed deserving of a wide berth in the eyes of the young, ambitious "entrepreneur," and even they had communicated their displeasure with

Kanashiro's apparent lack of regard and respect. The one thing upon which all of the groups, gangs, and families agreed was the desire to avoid the attentions of law enforcement, and a few of Kanashiro's business dealings had threatened that goal. Among the elder heads of the established groups now facing this encroachment, Jimura had been the most outspoken, earning him early disdain from the younger opportunist. It was easy to believe that Kanashiro might finally be making a move to advance his cause, with Jimura as his first target.

"If you're right," he said, "then he's picked an unfortunate time to launch his campaign." The deal he had brokered with Tateos Gadjoyan to sell the consignment of M16s was by itself of only minor consequence to Jimura. The weapons and even the money lost could be absorbed or replaced, but if Kanashiro had chosen today to begin serious disruption of his other interests, then it was a problem demanding immediate attention.

"Find out for sure if Kanashiro is behind this," he said, gesturing toward Yeager. "If he is, then we deal with him, today."

Yeager nodded. "Understood, Jimura-san. I'm on it."

His subordinate turned and left, leaving Jimura alone in his office. Leaning back in his chair, he stared through the window overlooking his garden, and sighed as he shook his head.

Today, of all days.

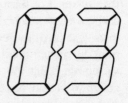

Dale Connelly was up before the alarm went off.

Of course, he had only been awake for less than a minute, lying on his side and staring at the digital clock as it changed from 5:59 to 6:00. The occasion was marked by a shrill beeping which Connelly silenced with a well-practiced slap, hitting the clock's snooze button. This prompted the day's first decision: Should he get out of bed and on with his day, or lie here for nine minutes until the alarm sounded again?

Then he felt a soft hand slide over his hip, and forgot about the clock.

"Morning," said a quiet voice behind him. Connelly felt the covers shift and the warmth of the bed's other occupant pressing into his back.

"Good morning," he replied, rolling over to face his wife. Jessica Connelly, in defiance of all reality, laws of physics, or whatever the hell governed such things, looked beautiful even freshly roused from sleep. It was a safe bet she'd been up for a while. After all, it was their last full day on the island, and tomorrow they were homeward bound. For him, the day carried additional weight, because for all intents and purposes, it marked the beginning of the end of his military career.

"You better get a move on, Top," said Jessica, pushing closer and planting a kiss on his nose. "Lots to do today, and you don't want to keep the boys waiting."

"Tell me about it." Connelly sighed. So far as his family was concerned, most of the hard work was done. Their household effects had been packed and taken away for shipment back to the United States, and they had moved out of their home of the past three years. For four days, the Connellys had taken up residence at the motel-like temporary housing while waiting for his orders to be finalized. Jessica and their two children would spend their final day saying good-bye to friends and doing some last-minute shopping, while he went to work. Most of his day's official activities would involve completing his transfer documentation and other administrative hurdles standing between him and his plane ticket. Once that was completed, there would be the traditional going-away party with his unit and a few hours' sleep before he and the family—with him nursing an inevitable hangover—began the eighteen-hour flight home.

Screw it. I'll sleep on the plane.

Where had the last three years gone? For that matter, where had the last *twenty-six* years gone? It seemed like just a few days ago that he and his family had arrived on Okinawa, where he had reported for duty as an aviation ordnance chief with Marine Aircraft Wing 36 at the Futenma Marine Corps Air Station. It was his third tour on the island, the first two having been one-year stints early in his career and before Jessica and the kids were in the picture. His first assignment here had been right after completing boot camp and his aviation specialty school in Florida; he had even requested the overseas duty.

Growing up in a small town in central Kansas, Connelly had never traveled beyond the borders of his home state, let alone to the other side of the planet, and he had been anxious to see what the world offered. Average grades in high school and limited funds for college made a hitch in the military an enticing proposition, and it was with that outlook that he had walked into the Marine Corps recruiting office in Salina, Kansas, one day after school. The recruiter—a grizzled veteran with a high and tight haircut and rows of multicolored ribbons offering testimony to a glorious career spent in uniform—tried to convince him that a tour in the infantry was the way to go, but Connelly had always loved airplanes and wanted something aviation-related. Anything would do, he told the recruiter, who had wasted no time selling him on the virtues of aviation ordnance and the need to help pilots be ready to, in his words, "blow shit up real good." That was enough for Connelly, and the seeds for growing a brand new aviation ordnance man were born that day. His choice of specialization saw to it that he would serve at bases and aboard ships around the world, in peace and wartime. As for the college education he had planned to pursue following a single four-year enlistment in order to qualify for the G.I. Bill? Connelly ended up earning his degree via night courses at whatever schools were near the bases where he worked.

It was while attending one such class during a stint at Camp Pendleton that he met Jessica, who likewise was completing her degree while working as a payroll clerk at a civilian hospital in Escondido, California. "Lust at first sight" was the kindest way to explain their immediate attraction to one another, but it had taken little time for them to figure out that they were meant to be together. They were married less than eight months after that first meeting, and sixteen years later, here they were, still crazy for each other.

"You're going to be late," said Jessica, her words teasing as her hands began to wander.

Connelly chuckled. "You're going to make me late."

"What are they going to do? Shave your head and ship you overseas?" It was a common joke, uttered by some Marine somewhere perhaps every day of the Corps' existence, but it was funnier coming from her.

Behind him, the alarm sounded. Nine minutes.

"Hit it again," Jessica said, her hand slipping beneath his T-shirt. "Let's see if we can beat it."

Before he could retort, other voices sounded through the wall separating their room from the one occupied by their kids. Though he couldn't make out any words, Connelly could tell from the tone that all wasn't cheerful next door.

"Uh-oh," he said. "The war's starting early today."

"It's been like this the last couple of days. I can understand it, at least a little. Saying good-bye to your friends is always hard."

Connelly nodded. "Yeah, I know, but they'll be okay. Moving is part of the job, after all, and this is the last time we're doing it." As a family, they had discussed and agreed that returning to Southern California was the best option for everyone. His children would reunite with at least some of the friends they had left behind before coming here, and Jessica's parents were an hour's drive away. Even his mother had considered the idea of moving out from Salina in order to be closer. With his father having died five years earlier, she had no other family in Kansas, and she was still young enough to enjoy retirement and doting on her grandchildren. He had already received interest from several aviation firms in San Diego, and interviews with the first of them were scheduled for next week. Life all around was looking good for the Connelly family. It would be an interesting transition, and one he welcomed, at least in most respects.

"There's that look again," said Jessica as she studied his face. "You're going to miss this, aren't you?"

"I'm not going to miss getting out of bed at dawn to go running," he replied, rolling over to a sitting position and swinging his legs out of the bed. Today would begin with his unit's normal weekday physical training routine, consisting of calisthenics and a formation run around the base. At age forty-four, Connelly still ran at least five miles three or four times a week, and his physical fitness scores remained in the top bracket for his age group. He was helped along in this endeavor by his daughter, Brynn, who had taken an interest in jogging and even joined her school's track team. Thanks to this extra motivation, Connelly had no plans to abandon his exercise regimen. Still, there was something to be said for doing such things at a more civilized hour.

Stretching across the bed, Jessica gave him a shove to send him on his way. "Last call for morning PT. Hop to it, Top," she said, employing the unofficial appellation traditionally reserved for master sergeants and master gunnery sergeants, particularly if that Marine occupied the senior enlisted billet in a given unit. Some holders of that rank or position disdained the informal moniker, but Connelly had never minded what he considered a term of endearment bestowed upon him by officers and subordinates who respected him. Then there was Jessica, who tended to use it when she was feeling playful.

Rising from the bed, Connelly reached for his watch on the nightstand before looking to see where he had put his running shoes, shirt, and shorts. He was pulling on the shorts when he caught sight of Jessica, lying on her stomach and watching him while propping her chin atop the heel of her left hand. Bobbing her eyebrows, she offered him one of her trademark smoldering smiles.

"You coming back to clean up, or are you just going to shower there?"

"I'll probably just shower there." His reply earned him a look of mock disappointment.

"Your loss, Top."

• • •

Scanning the area around the building to ensure they hadn't been observed, Jack pulled the garage door closed and engaged its lock. He glanced at his watch. Traffic and pedestrian activity was already on the increase now that daybreak had arrived. After stealing a car from a parking lot adjacent to the warehouse district, they had made their way through the backstreets of Naha. The abandoned building they had found was one of several on the city's outskirts. It was a dilapidated structure that to Jack looked as though it had stood here for decades, perhaps predating the massive amphibious assault and subsequent campaign carried out by Allied Forces in the spring and summer of 1945. That battle, the bloodiest of the Pacific War, had inflicted massive damage on Naha and the surrounding region, and evidence of the conflict was still visible even all these years later.

"We can't stay here long," he called out, remembering his Russian inflections. Getting to the safe house was still their plan, but he and Banovich would first have to deal with a more pressing issue.

After peering once more through the dirty window set into the door and seeing no signs of movement or other activity outside, Jack moved from the entrance and made his way deeper into the garage. The air here was stale, and fused with the odors of animal waste and decomposition. He ignored all of that as he crossed to where Banovich had secured their hostage in the middle of the room.

"We're sure as hell not taking him with us," replied Banovich from where she knelt behind the Okinawan man she had bound to a straight-backed chair. She had used his belt to secure his wrists, and the laces from his shoes to fix his ankles to the chair's front legs. His chin rested on his chest, his eyes closed, and even after studying his breathing, Jack couldn't tell if the man was still out, or merely feigning unconsciousness. Banovich didn't care, as she moved to stand in front of him before grabbing his hair and pulling his head up before slapping his face.

"Wake up."

It took two more strikes before the man coughed and blinked. Yanking his head free of Banovich's grip, he looked around the room before his eyes came to rest on the woman before him, after which he mumbled something in his own language.

"Save it," said Banovich, her tone hard. "You already spoke English, remember?" When the man stopped talking and glowered at her, she asked, "Do you work for Jimura?" She gave him only two or three seconds before she punctuated her question with another slap to his face. "I asked you a question." When the man didn't respond, she struck his temple with her fist. His head rocked back and forth and he grunted in pain, his mouth tightening and his left eye squeezing shut from the impact. As he recovered from the strike, Banovich stuffed one of her gloves into his mouth and secured it with a handkerchief she had pulled from a pocket of her jacket. That completed, she stepped back, glaring at him.

"This is only going to get worse, you know." To emphasize her point, she drew a folding knife from her pocket, but rather than opening its blade, she instead extracted a marlinspike from the handle's opposite end. The click from the spike locking into place echoed in the garage. "I don't have time to screw around waiting for you to feed me a line of crap, so we're just going to cut to the end of the story."

Without another word or hint of warning, Banovich stepped

forward and jammed the marlinspike into the man's shoulder.

Jack flinched as the spike sank into the soft flesh between the man's arm and his chest. Even with the makeshift gag, Jack was certain their prisoner's scream would be loud enough to wake the dead, let alone anyone who might be nearby.

"Amorah!" he hissed, stepping closer. "Someone will hear us!"

Ignoring him, Banovich kept her focus on their hostage. Her right hand twisted and the spike, buried to the hilt in the man's shoulder, moved within the puncture wound it had inflicted. The Okinawan growled yet again in obvious agony, his eyes watering as he struggled to withstand the impromptu torture.

"Are you ready to tell me what I want to know?" asked Banovich, and this time the man nodded in reply. She pulled the improvised gag from his mouth while leaving the spike in his shoulder. "Start talking."

"Not Jimura," the man said, his voice hoarse and racked with pain. "I don't work for him." He paused, swallowing. "Undercover."

It required physical effort for Jack not to react to the unexpected statement. When Banovich turned to look at him, her expression one of shock, he schooled his own features into what he hoped was a convincing frown.

"Undercover?" Jack repeated. "With who? Intelligence Command?"

When the man nodded, Banovich's eyes narrowed. "How do you know about that, Stefan?"

"My unit once ran covert ops with Chinese special forces," Jack replied, falling back on elements of Stefan Voronov's cover story that had been left vague and allowing him to fill in blanks as needed to adapt to unexpected developments. "One of the things we studied was infiltrating Japan to sabotage military and government targets. The Japanese Self-Defense Forces have their own intelligence agency, so dealing with them was part of our simulations and planning." He shrugged. "Never got a chance to do it for real, though." Turning back to their prisoner, he indicated for Banovich to remove the marlinspike. She did so with reluctance, and Jack almost winced when the man groaned in a mixture of pain and relief.

Jack asked, "What's your name?"

"Tadashi Enogawa," the man replied, drawing deep breaths. "I've been undercover inside Jimura's organization for nearly a year. We've been working with the American military to expose his operations."

"American military? NCIS?" Jack looked to Banovich. "If that's true, we could be in deep trouble." It made sense for the Naval Criminal Investigative Service to be investigating Jimura if the arms dealer was trafficking U.S. military weapons and equipment. To Enogawa, he asked, "Why?"

The Okinawan grimaced, swallowing yet another lump in his throat. "Both our agencies have been tracking weapons theft for years. Jimura's been a prime suspect, but he's been impossible to pin down. When I found out he was setting up an exchange for American military weapons, I alerted my contact and they started focusing on his operations. At the time, we still didn't have anything actionable from the American side, but NCIS was willing to support us." He drew another breath. "We were hoping this deal might give us a line to Jimura's sources within the American military and the JSDF, but all that was flushed when we were hit."

Once again, Jack forced himself not to give away any hint of what he now was feeling. JSDF members undercover within Jimura's organization? Had Bill Fields known about this? Jack was aware that his partner, the senior agent on this investigation, had possessed information he had kept to himself, but did that include the involvement of other agencies? Had any of those agents been at the exchange? What about the men who had attacked him and Banovich? Had any of those been Jimura's, or perhaps support personnel?

Dear God, did I kill . . . ?

"So, who hit us?" asked Banovich. "If it wasn't Jimura or the military, then who?"

Enogawa seemed to ponder this before shaking his head. "I don't know."

"Come on," said Jack. "You have to have some idea. Traitors within Jimura's organization, or maybe a rival?"

"If I had to guess," replied Enogawa, "I'd bet on a rival.

Jimura has a handful of enemies, but I don't know which one it might be." He stopped, groaning in pain as his head drooped. The front of his shirt was stained from the marlinspike's puncture wound, which was still bleeding. "I've told you everything I know. Cut me loose and I'll find my way to a hospital. You can be long gone before . . ."

The rest of his sentence was drowned out by the single shot of Banovich's pistol, the weapon's report muffled thanks to the suppressor still threaded onto its barrel, and the lone bullet struck Enogawa above his right eye. Blood and tissue exploded from the back of the man's head as the force of the round's impact pushed his body and the chair backward to the garage floor. Banovich had moved so fast that Jack had no chance to attempt stopping her, and for the first time his expression betrayed him as he watched Enogawa's body coming to rest on the dirty floor.

"You didn't have to do that," he snapped, scowling at Banovich in genuine anger as she returned the pistol to its holster inside her jacket.

"Why do you care? He had nothing else of value to offer."

Jack pointed at him. "He's JSDF. Once they figure out he's missing, they'll launch a full-scale manhunt to find him and whoever killed him. They might even seal off the entire island if they think they can catch us."

Somehow, Jack had to find a way to make contact with his own handler. The situation was threatening to spiral out of control, and he was unsure of his footing here. He wasn't afraid to ask for help, and he knew Abigail Cohen was at the CIA field office on Kadena Air Force Base, standing by to send in the cavalry at the first sign of trouble. Cohen would know what to do, but only if Jack could reach her. If nothing else, Jack had to warn her that there were other players in the game, in the hopes that more agents didn't suffer the same fate as Tadashi Enogawa. It was possible, even likely, that Cohen had no clue that NCIS and JSDF also had an operation active against Jimura. Knowledge of any mission requiring such stealth would be restricted only to essential personnel, and United States intelligence agencies had a nasty habit of not working and playing well with each other.

Damn it.

With a final look to Enogawa's body, Jack reached for Banovich's arm and pulled her after him. "Come on, we've got to move." The safe house. They had to get to the safe house. Once there, Jack would figure out his next steps.

One thing at a time.

• • •

Surveying the scene, Christopher Kurtz sipped coffee from a Styrofoam cup and shook his head. "It's going to be one of *those* days, isn't it?"

A voice from behind him called out, "You didn't want to go on vacation, anyway."

Kurtz turned to see his junior partner, Special Agent Jordan Aguilar, walking toward him. Dressed in khaki pants, a maroon top, and black running shoes, her lithe figure and dark hair pulled into a ponytail attracted various looks from other cops and agents on scene. She ignored most of the eyes directed her way, though a few of the more intense observers earned a scathing glare from her as she walked past. A uniformed Okinawan police officer held up a hand at her approach, but Aguilar directed his attention to the Beretta pistol holstered on her hip and the NCIS badge clipped to her belt. He waved at her to proceed.

"No vacation could ever be more fun than this," said Kurtz, using his coffee cup to indicate why they had been summoned at such an unholy hour to this place. The sun had turned the sky from black to gray, but the brilliant pink-orange hue on the horizon promised another day of clear blue skies. Of course, that would come with the requisite summer humidity lessened only by the constant breeze from the East China Sea.

Moving to stand next to him, Aguilar said, "All I've got is the preliminary report when they called us. Anything new?"

Kurtz shook his head. "Not yet. We're still sorting it all out." He pointed to where bodies still lay as they had been found, awaiting initial inspections from the medical examiners from NCIS and the JSDF. Local law enforcement agencies had already been apprised of the situation and that their assistance would only be needed for traffic control and access to and from the scene.

"Have we verified that any of these are Jimura's men?" asked Aguilar as she and Kurtz began walking toward what had been designated as the focal point of whatever had taken place here mere hours earlier.

"A couple look to be people we've previously suspected as being on his payroll," replied Kurtz, listening to the sound of his boots on the gravel. Like Aguilar, he preferred casual working attire, opting today for jeans and a pullover shirt along with a pair of low-rise hiking boots he had purchased at the Post Exchange on Camp Foster. The shirt—a blue one, today—was large enough to conceal the Colt .45-caliber pistol in its ballistic nylon holster at the small of his back. He wore his NCIS badge on a chain around his neck, as was his habit for crime scenes like this one.

Around them, NCIS and JSDF intelligence agents were taking pictures and talking into radios and mobile phones. Two vehicles—one a Toyota sedan, the other a garden variety cargo truck, formed the epicenter of a bloodbath. Bodies lay scattered about the open dirt and gravel lot separating several warehouses, the walls of a few of which had been damaged by gunfire. Watching the crime-scene analysts work, Aguilar pointed to one of the dead Okinawans.

"I think I recognize this one. He's one we'd marked as being a courier for Jimura." She eyed Kurtz with a sidelong glance. "And when I say 'courier,' I really mean, 'guy who will do anything up to and including disappearing a body on his way to get pizza.' I can run his prints when we get back to the shop."

Kurtz finished his coffee, realizing as he did so that there was no place for him to dispose of the cup.

Very smooth, Special Agent.

"What about these other guys?" asked Aguilar. "Any ideas?"

Shaking his head, Kurtz replied, "Not a clue. None of them are carrying ID, but their clothing labels indicate European: German or Russian, maybe." He gestured to the cargo truck parked next to the Toyota. "We found four crates of M16A2s in the truck, so I'm guessing it was an arms deal gone bad, but we're only talking a couple of dozen rifles altogether. Seems like an awful lot of risk for such a small batch."

Aguilar shrugged. "Depends, I guess. Given how strict Japanese gun laws are, maybe fewer is better. It wouldn't be the first time we've seen it. Then again, those were usually small-time idiots."

Firearms—and swords, interestingly enough—were strictly controlled in Japan and the Ryukyu Islands. With few exceptions, civilians were not permitted to possess such weapons, and those which were allowed—such as hunting rifles—were regulated to an exacting degree. Approvals were contingent upon passing an annual weapon inspection, drug test, physical exam, and a range certification to determine the owner's capacity to safely operate the firearm. Violation of the gun laws here carried with it a range of possible penalties, up to and including life in prison. While firearm ownership by American military members was a small concern, a more common issue was young servicemen and women running afoul of local law enforcement after purchasing what they at first believed to be a decorative sword, bound for the wall of their barracks or to be shipped home to the United States. Kurtz had dealt with various flavors of that misunderstanding more times than he cared to count. For someone like Jimura to be involved in an arms deal, there had to be substantial reward to offset the obvious risk.

"Jimura's too smart to do something like this half-assed," said Kurtz, pointing to the cargo truck. "If he was involved, then you can bet there were a hell of a lot more guns in there. This smells like a major deal gone sideways, and maybe whoever popped these guys had to beat feet. According to the report I got, police units were here within ten minutes of shots being reported."

Before Aguilar could reply, both agents turned at the sound of approaching footsteps, and Kurtz saw one of their junior agents, Carol Oliver, walking toward them. Dressed in jeans and a faded black T-shirt bearing the logo for some rock band Kurtz thought had broken up or died out a decade earlier, Oliver wore a blue windbreaker that sported a gold silkscreen image of an NCIS badge. A black baseball cap kept her blond hair at bay as she worked the scene, and a Nikon 35mm camera hung from a strap around her neck. She was carrying a clipboard in one hand, and no sooner did she walk up to them than she began tapping it with a cheap government-issue ballpoint pen.

"Good news," she said by way of greeting. "Well, good news and bad news, I guess. Good for somebody, bad for somebody else. I suppose it depends on . . ."

"Morning, Carol," Kurtz said, knowing that left unchecked, Oliver would continue her introductory litany until a lack of oxygen forced her to pause for breath, which could be a while. "What's the good news?"

Oliver gestured with her pen over her shoulder toward the truck. "We're cross-checking the serial numbers on the weapons we found in the truck, and so far every one of them matches a list of M16A2s that were stolen a year ago from the armory at MCAS Iwakuni. The bad news is that there's only forty of them, out of a batch of five hundred."

"I wondered if these might be part of that," said Aguilar, crossing her arms. "If I remember right, the base CO was even relieved of his duties."

"Yep," replied Kurtz, recalling the incident. One of only two Marine Corps installations on the Japanese mainland, Air Station Iwakuni had been a vital component of the Corps' fixed and rotary flight operations since the Korean War. Thousands of military and civilian personnel were employed at the base, which also supported many dependent family members with a variety of services. The loss of the M16s, while just the latest in an infrequent string of similar thefts the base had suffered over its history, was the first time weapons in such quantities were stolen. The incident hadn't been made public, but it still counted as an embarrassment for the Corps. Aguilar was correct in that the air station's commanding officer had been relieved of his duties and shipped stateside. He, of course, was allowed to quietly retire, while those closer to the incident suffered varying degrees of disciplinary and career-damaging reprimands and other punishment. As for the weapons themselves, they had vanished without a trace. Both the Marine Corps and NCIS suspected help from someone on the inside, but neither group had ever been able to find evidence to support that theory.

"Five hundred rifles, missing for a year," said Aguilar. "That sounds like something Jimura would do. Sit on them for a while, until the right opportunity comes along to move them when he hopes nobody's looking."

Kurtz nodded. "Definitely. Of course, it begs the question of what else he might have." Reports of other equipment turning up missing had always plagued the service branches, and black market dealings were usually high on the list of suspected reasons. Of course, while most of the criminal organizations operating in Japan were keen to get a slice of the enormous pie that was American military hardware, only a handful had the necessary resources and audacity to make such an attempt.

Looking to Oliver, he asked, "Okay, so do we have any thoughts on who hit these guys?" He gestured to the dead Caucasian men. "And who these belong to?"

Oliver shook her head. "We're still collecting evidence, but the reports were right; there was a hell of a lot of gunplay. Somebody was serious about taking out everybody here."

"Okay," said Aguilar, "so if we go with the notion that this was Jimura's deal and these other guys were the buyers, then we're probably talking about a rival. Assuming it's somebody who doesn't like Jimura, anybody want to take a guess?"

Holding up her hands, Oliver shook her head. "I'm just processing the scene. You two handle all the detective stuff, remember?"

"None of the older groups," replied Kurtz. "They've all got their honor code or peace treaty or whatever you want to call it, but they agree not to step on each other's toes or muscle in on each other's turf." He looked around the compound. "This place isn't in any of Jimura's supposed haunts, but so far as I know, nobody else has claimed it, either. So, neutral ground, maybe?"

Aguilar said, "Could be. As for who? Smart money says it's one of the younger bosses; somebody who doesn't care about the old codes and manners and all that, and we know one in particular who's got a beef with Jimura."

Sighing, Kurtz shook his head. "Edoga Kanashiro."

Yes, he reminded himself. It definitely was shaping up to be one of *those* days.

"Well, look who decided to show up for his last day."

Stepping into his office while carrying a red nylon gym bag and a hanger supporting his uniform for the day, Dale Connelly smiled as he beheld his friend, Gunnery Sergeant Thomas Wade. Already dressed in his own camouflage uniform and sitting with his feet up on Connelly's desk, Wade was holding what Connelly figured was likely his third or fourth cup of coffee of the day. A cigarette dangled between the first two fingers of the hand Wade was using to hold the cup, in unapologetic defiance of Department of Defense regulations banning smoking in workspaces.

"I thought I told the bouncers to throw you out of here," said Connelly as he tossed his PT bag onto the chair behind his desk and moved toward the wall locker occupying the far corner of his office.

"They love me too much," Wade replied. "Everybody loves me."

"I know two ex-wives who'd probably argue that." Opening the locker's double doors, Connelly hung his uniform inside. The camouflage utilities, including the matching cover, were freshly pressed and with rank insignia affixed in their proper positions. His black leather combat boots were polished to the point that he could see his reflection in them. Such preparations before each day's duty had long ago become second nature.

Not for the first time, he wondered if he would miss going through these daily rituals after his retirement.

Hell, no.

Connelly eyed Wade as the other man drank his coffee and took a drag from his cigarette. "How are you not dead yet?"

"What, this?" Wade asked, holding up the cup and cigarette. "I use bourbon to cancel these out."

For as long as Connelly had known him, Tom Wade had been a smoker, drinker, and relentless connoisseur of coffee, even going so far as to have his own brewing pot in his office, which was on and active at all hours of the day. Connelly, who had given up smoking a decade earlier, still liked his coffee and a moderate alcohol intake, but as the years added up, he knew he wasn't doing his body any favors. To that end, he had increased his personal exercise regimen so that he ran every morning and hit the gym a few times a week. Meanwhile, Wade with his smokes and coffee and booze had owned the highest physical fitness scores in the entire unit since the moment he stepped off the plane. He never failed to achieve a perfect score on their required semi-annual physical fitness tests, which included completing the prescribed three-mile run two minutes faster than the eighteen minutes needed to earn full points for that portion of the test. Once, just to make a point to the rest of the unit, he had smoked a cigarette within minutes of beginning a run, only to complete the exercise with a personal best record.

"No excuses," Wade had proclaimed upon crossing the finish line.

Damned showoff.

Walking toward his desk, Connelly glanced through the doorway and into the main room of the armory building. Rows of cargo containers, embarkation crates, and storage shelves crowded the floor, along with a cluster of desks where Marines assigned to this area of the armory worked. None of the desks were occupied, and it took Connelly an extra moment to realize that he heard no voices coming from the floor.

"Where is everybody? Already outside?"

Wade drained the last of his coffee and pushed himself from his chair. Glancing at the military-issue watch strapped to his left wrist, he replied, "Most of them are getting ready, but I put a few of them to work." He grinned. "You know, trying to get a jump on things for later."

"Right. Later." Connelly shook his head. "So, it's official, then. Not a damned thing of any importance is going to get done around here today?"

"Pretty much the size of it," replied Wade. "Okay, that's not entirely true. There's some paperwork and other crap that has to get sorted out after our last inventory, and the usual maintenance schedule. I'll get on that while you're out with the gang. The skipper also wanted a couple of random spot checks of the ammo bunkers, and we've got some supplies to be stored once they get here from Foster later this morning. Nothing critical, though." He gestured to the cork bulletin board on the office's front wall, which was home to a *Sports Illustrated* swimsuit calendar and assorted memos and flyers, including the weekly unit schedule. "Skipper's already authorized all nonessential folks to secure early for the party, and Sergeant Lucas will make sure the folks stuck back here will get spotted or at least fed."

Connelly knew that his going-away party had been the subject of much discussion and planning for the past two weeks. He had been insulated from much of it, but he still had managed to pick up a few clues, here and there. In addition to his people assigned to the aviation ordnance armory, invitations had been blasted to his friends and colleagues at units all across the Futenma Air Station. It was going to be a fun day, even more so because he would spend it in the company of men and women with whom he had served these past few years, as well as a handful of guys he had known since his earliest days in uniform. The camaraderie fostered by a military life was one of the very real things he would miss when he retired, and he hoped he would be able to maintain connections with the closest of friends.

"Okay, then," Connelly said as he headed for the door. "Let's try to be productive for a few hours before we call it quits for the day."

Wade replied, "I'm on it. We'll have the important stuff wrapped up by noon chow." Tossing a mock salute in Connelly's direction, the other Marine headed off to his own office, content to mind the store while the rest of the unit was out running.

When Connelly exited the building, it was to find a group of thirty or so Marines—mostly males but also a half dozen females—milling about the parking lot. Each was dressed in the usual PT uniform of green T-shirt, shorts, and running shoes. A few were already sweating in the morning humidity after going a few rounds with the set of four pull-up bars installed in the grass next to the armory. Upon seeing Connelly, one Marine, Sergeant Mark Lucas, ordered the unit to form up, and everyone quickly assumed their proper positions, standing in four rows of seven with the two extra Marines at the rear of the first two squads. Once everyone was in place, Connelly eyed his people and smiled.

"I hear there's a party today," he said, eliciting a chorus of cheers. After they faded, Connelly continued, "I know we're anxious to get on with the really important stuff, but we've also got a few housekeeping items on the schedule. So, let's get on with that, do everything the way it's supposed to get done, and then we can all go and get stupid with a clear conscience. I promise you the party will still be there this afternoon. Any questions?"

When no one responded, Connelly looked to Lucas. "All right, Sergeant. Let's go for a run. Take the scenic route," he said, which was his way of telling the NCO to lead the group on a route that would take them along the service road encircling the base's relatively small perimeter. Surrounded as it was by the Okinawan city of Ginowan, the run provided views of the city and the ocean to the west of the island. It was his favorite course, not just for unit PT but also his own jogging.

Last time, Connelly reminded himself, realizing he was going to be thinking and saying that a lot today.

• • •

"Stefan."

Only when Amorah Banovich said the name for a second time did Jack realize she was talking to him, and he jerked himself straighter in his seat. Had he fallen asleep? Blinking several times, he looked to his right where Banovich was dividing her attention between him and the road in front of them. Her left hand rested on the gearshift between them, while her right rested on the center spokes of the steering wheel.

"Sorry," Jack said, reaching up to wipe his face. Holding up his left arm, he looked at the dial of the Raketa watch he wore on the inside of his wrist. It was coming up on 8:00. Like his clothing, the watch was yet another component of his Stefan Voronov persona, being a model favored by Soviet military personnel for decades. It bore Russian markings and had been fitted with a worn leather band, and its face and casing were dulled and scratched, suggesting years of use and abuse.

"Traffic's getting heavier," he noted, looking through the windshield at the cars crowding them on all sides. The streets of Naha were filling up with morning commuters, Okinawan and American. Jack recalled from previous visits and the briefing provided by Grisha Zherdev before their arrival here that traffic congestion was a constant and increasing problem. National Route 58, the highway running the length of the island from Naha north to the village of Kunigami, was a particular source of ongoing headaches for traffic management and law enforcement.

"It'll thin out once we're out of the city," replied Banovich, who had returned her attention to the road in front of them. She used the back of her left hand to wipe perspiration from her forehead before returning it to the gearshift. The sedan they had stolen featured no air conditioning, and with the morning humidity already climbing toward uncomfortable levels, she and Jack had rolled down the sedan's side windows in an all-but-futile effort to cool the car's interior. The air was thick with exhaust from the numerous cars jamming the road, too many of which were too close for Jack's comfort. Checking the sideview mirror, he saw another sedan, white like theirs and so many others but missing its passenger-side headlight, and there was a patch of paint scraped off the car's front quarter panel.

Settling back in his seat, Jack noted Banovich glancing at him. "What?" he prompted.

"Are you all right, Stefan? You seem like something's bothering you."

Jack shook his head, shifting as though trying to get more comfortable. "I'm fine. Just tired, I guess. We've been going for a while now." Aside from two brief cat naps, he had been awake for close to twenty-four hours, thanks to the preparations leading up to the busted deal. His stomach opted for that moment to chime in, producing an audible grumble. "And hungry."

"There's food at the safe house," replied Banovich. Then, her voice changed, losing some of the seriousness of the past few hours. "And a bed."

It wasn't the first time she had made such a comment, subtle or otherwise. Indeed, Amorah Banovich had made her desires known to him within the first month of his coming to work for Tateos Gadjoyan. It had required some fast, creative talking to keep her at bay while feigning interest in her advances, figuring that the closer he could get to individuals within Gadjoyan's organization, the better his chances for gathering intel on the man himself. To this point, their reciprocal flirtations had been a game, but Jack knew Banovich was aiming to take things further.

He had wrestled with the issue more than once, struggling to balance the need to maintain his cover, and even protect his very life, against more personal concerns. Far away from here, his wife, Teri Bauer, and their daughter, Kim, were going about their lives, coping with yet another of his prolonged absences because of his job. Deployments during his time with the Special Forces were common, followed by long duty shifts, stakeouts, and undercover assignments while working for the LAPD. Now there was the secretive nature of his job with the CIA, which was inflicting tremendous stress on his marriage, and this latest mission had only served to make matters worse. Adding to that burden was his daughter, his and Teri's only child, all of eight years old but possessing a spirit and force of will equal to his own. Kim Bauer carried within her the best qualities of her parents, combining Teri's gentle strength and compassion with his own fierce drive to succeed at any task. Jack knew without doubt that with the proper guidance to help channel her energy and determination, Kim would blossom into a strong, independent woman the world would have no choice but to respect.

You can't think about any of that right now. Focus on your job.

Even with a career that demanded it, compartmentalizing his feelings was a skill Jack had only grudgingly acquired. He acknowledged it as a necessary survival skill, along with burying his real life in order to inhabit the role his mission required him to play. Jack Bauer might not have any desire to sleep with Banovich, but there was no real reason for Stefan Voronov to pass up such an opportunity. With that in mind, he had played the game, returning her teasing and innuendoes and hoping he could keep her interested long enough to get the information he needed to complete his mission.

"Is there a phone at the house?" he asked. "We should contact Gadjoyan, and tell him what happened and ask him what to do next."

Banovich replied, "There should be a satellite phone with the rest of the cache." Then she laughed. "Do you want to be the one to tell Gadjoyan his money and his weapons are gone?"

"Not particularly, but except for you, pretty much everyone who outranked me on this job is dead, so I guess I'm open to ideas. If nothing else, Gadjoyan needs to know that NCIS and JSDF might be on to him and Jimura."

More important to Jack than contacting Gadjoyan, itself only an act to maintain his cover, was getting in touch with Abigail Cohen. If American assets were investigating Miroji Jimura and—by extension—Tateos Gadjoyan, they might be poised to drop the hammer on both men and their respective organizations at any moment, with Jack caught in the middle of it all. Cohen, as the agent watching his back, needed to be in the loop. She also needed to know about Bill Fields, assuming she didn't already know.

Sorry, Abby.

Guiding the car as she changed lanes, Banovich said, "You make a good point. Gadjoyan will at least want to know if American intelligence agencies are tracking him." She sighed. "He definitely won't be happy with our coming back empty-handed."

"Maybe we don't have to," replied Jack, at once regretting the words.

Damn it! Too soon.

He had already considered the idea of convincing Banovich

to reach out to Jimura, explain that Zherdev wasn't at fault for the deal going bad, and ask what could be done to set things right. It was a dangerous tactic, he knew, considering his place on the late Zherdev's team and Gadjoyan's organization. Making such a suggestion, if not done with care, might come off as too pushy, or even hinting at a hidden agenda.

"What do you mean?" Banovich eyed him, confirming his suspicion that he may have played that card too quickly, before returning her attention to the road in time to avoid slamming into the back end of a taxi. Jack saw the cabbie throw up a hand, gesturing toward them as he glared in his rearview mirror. Easing off the accelerator, Banovich allowed the taxi to put some space between them. Jack exhaled, watching the other vehicle pulling away as another car moved into the new gap in traffic, then glanced again to his sideview mirror.

The white car that had been riding their rear bumper was still behind them. It was traveling behind another car, but as Jack watched it, he noted how it maintained pace with their sedan. Either speeding up or slowing down as it moved past other cars, the vehicle's driver was obviously working to maintain a respectable yet still consistent interval. He just wasn't very good at it.

"We've got a tail," he said, reaching for the Glock pistol inside his jacket.

Frowning, Banovich looked at the rearview mirror. "You're sure?"

"Yeah."

• • •

With half of his attention focused on the line of shrubs he was trimming with a pair of manual hedge clippers, Saburo Genko checked his watch. It had been almost fifteen minutes since the unit of Marines had jogged through the gate of the tall fence encircling the armory building, heading off to other parts of the base for their morning run. An older man, their leader, ran alongside the group, singing portions of a chant that his subodinates repeated.

Genko was amused by the choreography of it all. Four of the Marines, each wearing a reflective vest over their green shirts and shorts, broke away from the group and moved into positions that would allow them to alert and halt oncoming traffic as the unit maneuvered into the road. Once that was accomplished, one of the four Marines closed and locked the gate before they ran to catch up and retake their positions in the group. The group had jogged up the street and around a corner, the sounds of their chanting fading after a few moments.

"It's time," said Kioshi Jahana from where he stood a few meters to Genko's right, tending to some of the tools they had brought with them on a motorized cart and its connected trailer as part of their cover. "We have thirty minutes before they get back."

Genko nodded in agreement. Posing as groundskeepers and delivery drivers, they and other men working for Miroji Jimura had been studying this target for months, learning the schedules and routines of the armory and those who worked inside it. In particular, they had observed the older Marine's daily habits along with those of his family, both here and at his home. They could anticipate the movements of nearly everyone assigned to this facility, and knew that this window of opportunity was their best chance at executing the next step in Jimura's larger plan.

"Let's go," said Genko as he returned the clippers to a basket in the cart's rear cargo area before ensuring the trailer's tailgate was locked in place and the mower it carried was secure. When Jahana stored his tools back in their box and climbed into the passenger seat, Genko took an extra moment to inspect the area around them. As usual, none of the Marines or civilians working at or moving through this part of the base took any notice of them. He smiled. Okinawan groundskeepers and landscapers were ubiquitous here, employed by the American military to work on all but a few bases and other installations scattered across the island. Each worker was vetted, of course, but even those checks were cursory in most instances. For a time, there had been a heightened state of alert at American military installations here and elsewhere around the world, brought about by the war the United States and other countries had taken to the Middle East a few years earlier. With Kuwait and its rich oil fields liberated from the rule of Iraqi dictator Saddam Hussein and the country returning to whatever passed for stability in that region, the increased state of vigilance that had characterized U.S. military bases began to ease. Here on Okinawa, far from the turmoil that now looked to be America's focus for the foreseeable future, the confidence and superiority so often exuded by the American soldiers and their leaders had returned.

Complacency is the enemy of security. This simple bit of wisdom, uttered on more than one occasion by Miroji Jimura in the course of the elder man's dealings with his employees, was one that had stuck with Genko since he had first heard it. Jimura, as well-read a person as any Genko had met, often provided such reminders and other fragments of insight. Sometimes, they were offered as a means of motivating or comforting an individual for one reason or another, but more often they accompanied discipline for some transgression. For Genko, his interactions with Jimura had always been of the more positive variety, and he was in no hurry to see that change.

Maneuvering the cart and its trailer across the narrow street, Genko brought the vehicle to a stop before the gate. Mounted on a pole to the left of the gate was a speaker with a call button, which Genko pressed. After a moment, a brief burst of static accompanied a male's voice.

"Good morning. May I help you?"

Genko cleared his throat. "Yes. We are here for cutting grass," he said, affecting a halting delivery, as though his command of the English language was incomplete. He had done this for the past two months when interacting with personnel on the base as part of his cover.

There was a pause before the man on the other end of the connection replied, *"Okay, I'll be right out."*

From their study of the armory, Genko knew that with the bulk of the unit out running, there would be one or perhaps two Marines working in the building at this time of morning. Once he and Jahana were inside, they should have the place to themselves for the brief interval required to complete their task.

Resting his left hand on the cart's steering wheel, Genko glanced to his companion as both men did their best to present the appearance of simple groundskeepers.

Avoid attention by not attracting attention.

Yet another of Jimura's discerning observations rang in Genko's ears as the armory building's front door opened and a single Marine dressed in a camouflage uniform stepped outside, pausing to close the door behind him. He walked to the gate and unlocked it with a key retrieved from his pocket. Genko recognized him as one of the older, more experienced Marines assigned to this unit and one with whom he had interacted on previous occasions while pursuing his cover.

"How's it going?" asked the Marine as he pulled open the gate and made room for the cart to enter the fenced compound. The embroidered label over his right pocket read WADE.

Genko nodded as he guided the cart through the opening. "We are fine, thanks." He pointed to the grass in front of the building, at the far end of which was a concrete slab with a basketball goal mounted on a metal pole. Running adjacent to the building along the yard's one side was a row of waist-high evergreen bushes. "We start there."

The Marine, Wade, waved. "Works for me." The man had repeated this routine numerous times over the past few months, since Genko and Jahana had begun their covert surveillance. Already disinterested in the lawn work, Wade relocked the gate before putting the key ring in his pocket and then gesturing toward the armory's front door. "You know the drill. Hit the buzzer if you need anything or when you're done."

"Hai," replied Genko, nodding in understanding while moving to the cart's rear section and opening the tool bag stored there. Glancing around the area, he saw no one who might observe what was to happen in the next few seconds. As he grabbed the hedge clippers from the cart, his free hand dipped into the tool bag and extracted a long combat knife. It was a copy of the knife carried by Marines, which Genko had acquired in a shop near another of the bases in the island's northern region. Carrying a firearm onto the base was out of the question, of course, owing to military restrictions and

Okinawa's own harsh gun possession laws.

Besides, guns make noise.

Hiding the knife in his belt and under his shirt, Genko moved toward the bushes, which put him less than five meters from the armory's door just as Wade walked back from the gate. With Jahana still at the cart, Genko began clipping errant leaves and branches from the first of the bushes, watching as the Marine keyed a four-digit code into a keypad mounted on the wall next to the door. There was an audible click as the lock disengaged and Wade opened the door to step inside. Hearing Jahana hiss between his teeth—their signal that all was clear and no one was observing them—Genko made his move.

As Wade moved into the building, Genko caught the door's edge and pulled it open far enough to slip inside. He heard Jahana on his heels but kept his focus on the Marine, who was just now realizing that something behind him was amiss. The man's expression turned to shock in the instant before Genko struck his throat with the edge of his hand. Choking around a cry of pain, Wade staggered backward, reaching for his throat and trying to distance himself from Genko, who pressed his attack. With practiced ease, he dropped and swung out with his right leg, catching the other man behind his knees and sweeping his feet out from under him. Still gagging from his injured throat, Wade dropped to the tiled floor, hitting his head on the edge of a nearby table. He never even had a chance to roll onto his side or regain his feet before Genko was on him.

"Don't," he warned. With the combat knife now in his hand, he knelt across the man's chest, pinning his left arm to the floor beneath his boot as he pressed the weapon's edge to the Marine's neck. Behind him, Genko heard Jahana closing and locking the door. Returning his attention to Wade, who with a reddened face was still coughing, he asked, "Are you alone?" Attempting to forestall any attempt at deception, he pressed the knife's blade harder against the man's neck.

Wade offered a frantic nod. "Yes."

"You're sure?" Genko's expression hardened as he posed the question, and the Marine again nodded. "Fine." He gestured to a desk pushed against a nearby wall, where Jahana had situated himself in front of the personal computer perched there. "That computer, it contains inventory information, yes?"

Now, Wade's eyes widened as he realized what was being asked of him. "Wait," he began, his voice hoarse thanks to his injured throat.

"A password is required," called Jahana over his shoulder.

Genko stared down at the Marine, once more pressing harder with the knife's point. "Well?"

Wade's eyes shifted so that he looked toward Jahana and the computer. "Under the keyboard."

Lifting the computer's keyboard from the desk, Jahana turned it over, and Genko saw a piece of yellow paper taped to its underside. On the paper were several scratch marks in different shades of blue, black, and even red ink. Only one string of unmarred letters and numbers was not scratched out: USMC1775.

"Really?" asked Jahana, shaking his head while entering the password into the PC. A moment later, Genko watched as his companion worked the machine like a musician playing an instrument. "I think I found it," he said, a moment later. "Their inventory is in a database, and I can make a copy of it."

For the first time, Genko felt Wade's body tensing beneath him. Sensing an attempt at escape or preventing them from stealing the computer's information, Genko looked down at the other man just as the Marine made his move. His right hand clamped around Genko's wrist but it was a slow and clumsy maneuver, easily deflected. Twisting his arm up and away, Genko punched Wade in the face, the knife still in his hand. The force of the blow knocked the man unconscious, and the blade just caught the side of his face. A razor-thin line of blood formed on the Marine's cheek.

Grunting as he switched the knife to his other hand and shook off the punch, Genko looked up to see Jahana copying whatever he had found to a computer disk they could take with them. "Print that, too," he said. "Not all of us are as gifted as you are with those things." Whereas Genko had no proficiency with such technology and even less interest in acquiring such skills, Jahana delighted in learning about the devices. He had one of his own in his apartment, and he often stayed up until the early morning hours playing computer games and communicating with other computer owners from around the world in something he called "chat rooms." None of that appealed to Genko, but he was grateful for his friend's expertise.

After another moment, he heard the sound of the printer coming to life from where it sat next to the computer, and several pages of information were spit out. Once that was done, Jahana grabbed the pages and retrieved the blue plastic computer disk from the PC.

"That's it," he said, pushing himself out of the chair. "Let's go." He gestured to Wade. "Do it."

It was with a look of momentary sadness that Genko looked down at the Marine. The man was a simple victim of unfortunate happenstance. Did he deserve to die? No, but sparing him meant jeopardizing the task Jimura had given Genko. There was no other choice.

Without further hesitation, he reached for Wade's head and applied only the pressure that was necessary to break the man's neck.

"Son of a bitch. Here they come."

Jack heard Banovich's warning to hang on mere heartbeats before she stomped on the gas and jerked the steering wheel to the right. Whipping into the oncoming traffic lane, she maneuvered the sedan around a cargo van, close enough that Jack could have reached out and opened the vehicle's driver-side door. The car edged past the van and Banovich guided it back into the proper lane, ignoring the protests of blaring horns.

"They're still coming," Jack called out. He had shifted his position so that he now leaned sideways in his seat, looking through the sedan's rear window and watching as the tail weaved between other cars and their oblivious drivers. After several minutes spent trying to act like anything except a tail, the driver of the other car had fallen for one of Banovich's feints as she maneuvered through traffic. He had given himself away when she made a sudden left turn, and he opted to cut his own turn too hard and fast in the hopes of maintaining pursuit.

Checking his Glock, Jack verified that the magazine was full and a round was chambered. He had left the sound suppressor threaded to the pistol's barrel in the hope of avoiding too much attention should he be forced to use the weapon.

You know, like any time now.

Taking another look through the car's back window, Jack saw that the other vehicle's driver- and passenger-side windows were down, but no guns appeared. With the other cars and pedestrians on the crowded street at this time of morning, it was unlikely their pursuers would start shooting. That might change once they got out onto open ground. He and Banovich needed a way to shake loose of the other car before that happened.

Wait a minute. Something's not adding up.

"They were following us at a distance," he said. "The only way they could be doing that is if they'd been following us all along."

Her attention focused on the road in front of her, Banovich frowned. "So?"

"So if they've been following us since the shootout, then it can't be the Americans or the Japanese police. They would've moved on us when we stopped at the warehouse." That, at least, was a scenario with which he might have been able to deal, and it may well have saved Tadashi Enogawa's life.

Damn it.

Banovich guided the sedan around another car, her focus shifting between the road and her mirrors. As they approached an intersection, and again without any sort of forewarning, she jerked the steering wheel hard left, guiding the car into a quick turn at the corner. She jammed the accelerator into the floorboard and the sedan jumped forward, its four-cylinder engine whining in protest. Looking through the back window, Jack saw the other car trying not to overshoot the intersection. Its tires were squealing as its driver had to confront another vehicle that now was blocking his way.

"Hell of a move," he said, just before Banovich executed another left turn and guided the car into a narrow alley between two three-story buildings. The passage was littered with trash cans and other detritus, all of which Banovich ignored as she gunned the engine once more. Jack felt himself pressing into his seat, waiting for someone to make the mistake of stepping into their path. Seconds later, they came to the end of the alley, and she slowed the car enough to make sure they wouldn't hit anyone before emerging back onto a two-lane street. Jack surmised that they now were running parallel to Highway 58 while blending into the rest of the morning commuter traffic.

"Do you know where you're going?"

Banovich nodded. "Yes. I've been here a few times before, remember?" After another moment spent checking her mirrors, she asked, "So, if it's not the Americans or the Japanese authorities following us, then who? Jimura, or perhaps this rival Enogawa mentioned?"

"Could be either." Jack braced himself with his free hand against the dashboard as Banovich made a quick, jerking maneuver between two other vehicles. A look back through the rear window revealed no sign of the other car. "If these guys are Jimura's, then they might be trying to track us to our rally point so they can hit us again."

Banovich countered, "A rival might be acting for the same reasons. That, or they have something against Gadjoyan. There are many who compete for his attention and money. It's not always a friendly business, Stefan."

"Yeah, tell me about it."

There was another scenario, one that Jack couldn't share. What if Tateos Gadjoyan somehow had learned the truth about him and Bill Fields? If the arms dealer knew that Jack and Fields were plants, he would waste no time settling that score. Could this entire operation have been a ruse with the sole purpose of flushing out turncoats within his organization? It seemed a bit unlikely for Gadjoyan to go to such trouble when he could address the issue back in Kiev and exercise greater control of the situation.

Jack glanced at the passenger-side mirror, noting the cargo truck a few car lengths behind them. Then the truck slowed and he saw another vehicle weaving behind it. He caught a glimpse of the vehicle's front and noted its missing headlamp.

"Damn it," he hissed. "It's them." He turned in his seat in time to see the white sedan weave into the oncoming lane and begin passing the truck.

"How the hell did they find us?" Banovich asked, and Jack heard the tension in her voice.

Jack shifted in his seat, his grip tightening on the Glock. "If they've been following us since this morning, they may have had a chance to plant a tracking device on us." Could that have happened while he and Banovich were interrogating Tadashi

Enogawa? Before joining the CIA, Jack might have considered it farfetched, but his current employer and the methods and tools it utilized to carry out its various missions had disabused him of such naïve notions.

"We're not going to shake them," Banovich said. When he looked through the car's windshield, he saw that they were leaving the town behind in favor of rice paddies on either side of the narrow road. Their pursuers knew this, too, and they used the opportunity to close the distance. A head and arm appeared from the left side window as the white car accelerated, and Jack saw the pistol.

"Gun!" he warned, shifting his position so that he now knelt on his seat while readying the Glock in his right hand.

Banovich swerved into the oncoming lane, forcing the shooter behind them to lean farther out of the car in order to shoot across its hood, spoiling his aim. They passed a taxi and she jerked the wheel to the left, putting the car back in their own lane. Behind them, the other sedan's passenger was lining up for another try, but Jack beat him to it. Thrusting his arm through the car's open window, he took aim with his Glock and fired two quick shots. A single hole appeared in the center of the other car's windshield and the car veered into the oncoming lane.

"Nice," said Banovich, "but they're still coming."

Jack lifted his arm so that the Glock rested atop the car's top and fired twice more. Not expecting to hit anything, he was hoping to force the driver to take evasive action. The ploy worked, at least for a few seconds, as the other car slowed and was forced to maneuver back into the proper lane. Then Banovich made a bold move to pass another car. Her action was sufficient to force an oncoming car to its left, giving her enough space to thread between both vehicles, and Jack saw the pursuing car's nose dip as its driver hit the brakes to avoid rear-ending the car ahead of it.

"We've got to finish this, before a cop sees us," he said. Leaning through the passenger-side window so he could grip the Glock with both hands, Jack watched as their pursuers accelerated once more. The instant the other car maneuvered into the oncoming lane to pass the vehicle between them, Jack emptied the pistol's magazine. Multiple fractures appeared in the sedan's windshield and he knew he had hit the driver when he saw the car jerk to its right, careening across the road and down the short embankment into a rice paddy.

"Go," Jack said, shifting back into his seat. Banovich responded by hitting the gas and passing two more cars. Now with open road ahead of her, she kept up the speed until she was well ahead of the other vehicles. At the first side road to present itself, in this case a narrow dirt path separating two rice paddies, she slowed just enough to make the turn before accelerating again. A cloud of dust kicked up as she guided the car away from the road.

"Definitely not the Americans or Japanese police," she said, after a moment spent navigating the uneven, poorly maintained trail. "So, Jimura or a rival."

Jack nodded. "We need to get away from here. Somebody has to be calling whatever passes for cops around here." Dropping the Glock's spent magazine, he replaced it with a fresh one from his jacket pocket. He braced himself as the car hit a divot in the dirt path. "What do we do now?"

Banovich, her eyes fixed on the trail ahead of them, replied, "Stick to the plan. Get to the safe house."

• • •

Abigail Cohen wanted to crawl back into bed.

At this moment, the idea of burrowing under the covers and telling the entire world to go to hell was an appealing proposition. There was no way that was going to happen, of course. Not now, with everything else that was still in play. Sleep had been taken from her hours earlier, and there was no immediate sign that it would be returned any time in the near future.

At least you're not dead. Maybe you should quit whining. For Bill's sake, if nothing else.

The self-inflicted reprimand echoed in her mind, making Cohen feel even guiltier as she stifled a yawn. When had she become so soft that a single night's lost sleep affected her this much? Opting against exploring possible answers to that question, she pushed away from the scuffed, dented gray metal desk that was a standard furnishing for government and military offices and rose from the equally dilapidated gunmetal chair that went with it. From the edge of her desk, she retrieved a stained, well-worn coffee mug, which was all but buried underneath folders, photographs, scraps of papers bearing notations, and other reminders. There also were the remnants of a bagel with cream cheese she had forgotten before the sun had risen. She dreaded the prospect of yet another cup of the sludge that passed for coffee here, but at the moment, it was the only thing keeping her awake and functional.

For now, anyway.

The yawn that came as Cohen poured coffee into her mug wouldn't be denied. She was in the act of covering her mouth when her cup ran over and spilled onto the table where the coffeemaker and other coffee-related claptrap resided.

"Damn it," she hissed, returning the coffeepot to its cradle while just managing to avoid breaking the thing. She reached for the drawer that should have contained napkins or paper towels and instead found nothing. "Again with this crap? Am I the only one who knows where the damned closet is around here?" Cohen's outburst evoked several quizzical stares from other agents working in the oversized room, but no one appeared willing to offer any reply to her question.

"Here," said a voice behind her, and she turned to see a hand holding several paper napkins. The hand belonged to her friend and fellow agent, Miles Warren, who offered her a small, understanding smile.

Taking the napkins, Cohen made a halfhearted attempt to clean up her spill before throwing the whole mess in the nearby trash can. Even the coffee had lost its appeal, and she turned her back on it before heading back to her desk.

Hell with it.

"How are you holding up?" asked Warren. He followed her to their desks, which faced one another along the wall of the open room she and the rest of her team were already calling "the bullpen." He plopped into his government-issue black metal chair and its ancient springs groaned in protest. Frowning at the odd noise, his expression softened as he regarded her. "I know you two were close."

Cohen sighed, returning to her own seat. "Yeah. We've been partners longer than I was married." She felt moisture in the corner of her eyes and reached up to wipe them, irritated with herself for the momentary lapse. "I'll be okay."

"You sure?" Warren leaned forward in his chair, resting his elbows atop the desk. "Nobody would think less of you if you needed to take a break."

"Somebody would." Realizing her retort sounded harsher than she intended, she added, "Sorry. That wasn't aimed at you." She cast a look around the room. "You know what I mean."

Warren nodded. "Sure thing."

It wasn't an exaggeration for Cohen to say that her relationship with William Fields had been of greater benefit to her than the shaky, ill-advised marriage she had terminated after three years. Her former husband, Rick, was not a bad person, but he had never truly accepted her job and the toll it could take on relationships. The mission came first, always. Not all spouses or romantic partners figured out a way to weather the demands placed upon someone who was at the continuous beck and call of the United States government, and in her specific case the Central Intelligence Agency.

The requirement that she not reveal much of anything to her husband about her work, coupled with her frequent trips to destinations she couldn't discuss, only compounded the strain. Add to that her male work partner, with whom she often traveled to these secret locations, and resentment was soon followed by jealousy and accusations. Though nothing had ever happened between her and Fields, she could understand Rick's feelings, and she didn't fight when he filed for divorce. Leaving the agency had never been an option for her, but neither did he deserve to continue living this way. At last report, Rick had found someone else—someone with a normal job and life—and he was happy. That was good, Cohen had decided long ago; he deserved that much.

Casting a forlorn gaze upon the administrative flotsam covering her desk, she asked, "Do we have anything new?"

Warren cleared his throat, turning his attention to one of the folders cluttering his desk. "Nothing since the last update from the scene. Our guys down in Naha are still trying to piece together what happened."

"Yeah, along with everybody else."

"All we know is that the exchange went sideways. Based on what our guys observed the NCIS and JSDF agents doing at the crime scene, it looks like an ambush. Somebody got to them from concealed positions around the warehouses, and caught everybody in a crossfire." Warren blew out his breath. "Bill never had a chance."

Not realizing she was clenching her jaw until her teeth started to hurt, Cohen tried to relax. Retrieving a pencil from atop the stacks of papers in front of her, she began tapping it on the desk. "The big question is, who hit them? Jimura's not above whacking one of his own people if it's convenient, but this doesn't smell like that."

"My money's on a rival."

"That's what I'm thinking, too." Pushing herself out of her chair, she headed across the bullpen to the conference room. Aside from the scratched and dented rectangular wood conference table and its haphazard collection of chairs, the room's prominent feature was the corkboard wall at its far end. A large map of Okinawa was tacked to the board's center, with smaller maps depicting various areas of the island.

"What about Bauer?" she asked by way of greeting.

Standing at the board, Agents Gerald McCormack and Laron Williams turned away from the maps. Both men were young—in their mid-thirties, as Cohen recalled from their personnel jackets—and each possessed the sort of trim, athletic physiques that the CIA approved of for its field agents. Cohen found that amusing, given that neither man had ever worked outside an office.

"Still nothing," replied Williams, turning back to the board and pointing toward a map that illustrated a detailed city view of Naha. Cohen saw that two areas were circled in red marker: Naha Port, and the warehouse district. "Our spotters tracked him and Agent Fields from the port to the site for the exchange, but once everything went to hell, we lost him and at least three of Zherdev's men."

Cohen knew that Grisha Zherdev had been killed along with Bill during the firefight. Losing Zherdev, the man the agency had been able to turn inside Tateos Gadjoyan's organization, would be costly. It had taken another covert operative, Daniel Boyce, more than a year of working within Gadjoyan's organization to cultivate Zherdev as an asset. Duplicating that kind of effort would be a prolonged affair, assuming it was even possible and Gadjoyan hadn't discovered the mole in his midst before instituting even more stringent methods to cover his tracks. The Armenian wasn't an idiot. If he suspected his inner circle was compromised, he would execute a scorched earth policy to smoke out any other spies or traitors. A low-level worker like the one Jack Bauer was supposed to be playing as part of his cover would stand no chance.

"We should've had people closer to the exchange," said McCormack, shaking his head as he stepped away from the board. "We could've had people in place, maybe done something to help Bill."

"It was too risky," Cohen countered. A preliminary analysis of the scene had shown that Zherdev had deployed men at elevated positions around the warehouses, and that whoever hit the exchange also engaged some of those people. "Even tracking them this far was dangerous. This wasn't supposed to be anything more than a simple deal between Gadjoyan's people and Jimura." The mission had never called for the CIA to move in now; not for a simple small arms deal. Bill Fields and Jack Bauer had been working undercover for months to get close enough to expose Gadjoyan's brokering of nuclear weapons stolen from American military units. Daniel Boyce had been embedded there even longer. The plan developed by Cohen and other senior case officers called for moving on Gadjoyan in Kiev upon obtaining proof of his dealings and any ties he might have to international terrorist organizations, and then only after Boyce, Fields, and Bauer were extracted. If the Armenian was tipped to the net about to be dropped on him, he would disappear.

"Fields was dead the moment they drove in there," said Warren, who had entered the room behind Cohen. "The whole thing went down in seconds." Walking to the map, he tapped two points within the circled area indicating the warehouses. "NCIS and JSDF found shell casings at these locations, both of which make good points of cover for anything happening down on the ground. So, whoever hit these guys knew about their backup." He turned to Cohen. "I'm liking the rival theory a lot right now."

"What about Bauer?" asked McCormack, adjusting the holster on his left hip and moving his Beretta pistol out of his way. "He and Fields had instructions for what to do if things went bad, so where the hell is he?"

"That's what they're paying us to find out," replied Cohen. That Bauer's whereabouts remained unknown was troubling, but it had only been a few hours since the shootout. There was no way to know his current situation, or if any attempt at making contact would jeopardize his cover.

"Assuming he's alive," repeated Agent Williams. "Look, Abby, I know you're keen on this guy, but it's his first field op where he's got no backup. Now that things have gone sideways, and he's on his own, are we sure he can handle it?"

Cohen crossed her arms. "I'm sure." When Williams began to respond, she held up her hand. "This isn't some fuzz-nuts rookie, Laron. He's ex-Army Special Forces and LAPD SWAT, with more time in the field and under fire than anybody in this room, myself included."

She and Bill Fields had seen Jack Bauer's potential from the moment they began reviewing his personnel files from the Los Angeles Police Department and the Army as part of the recruiting process. The latter dossier, complete with its long list of classified notations and citations, described not simply an accomplished soldier with all of the skills that implied, but also an adept leader with a capacity for innovative, unconventional thinking and decision making that made him the ideal candidate for training as a clandestine agent. As Bill Fields had put it during their review, "Jack Bauer's a born operator."

"Paquette's already getting calls from Langley," said Warren, referring to their superiors at CIA Headquarters in Langley, Virginia, and their immediate supervisor here on the island, Mark Paquette. "They want updates on everything, including Bauer. What do we tell them?"

Cohen knew that whatever authority and latitude she enjoyed for this operation would start to be curtailed, if not rescinded, the longer things dragged on. She also was sure that Paquette would be in her corner until his own superiors overruled him, especially if there was no contact from Bauer soon. Still, she was unwilling to take premature action. If Bauer was out there, he would find a way to reach her. She and her bosses just needed to give him that time.

"Tell them we're sticking to the plan, at least for now."

Warren eyed her with skepticism. "They're not going to like that."

Shaking her head, Cohen was unable to stifle a chuckle. "They never like anything."

• • •

Christopher Kurtz looked up as Jordan Aguilar dropped her phone's receiver back into its cradle. From the look on her face, Kurtz knew he wasn't going to like what she had to say.

"That was JSDF," she offered, leaning back in her chair. "Their crime scene people are still waiting on fingerprints and a few other things, but we've got a hit. One of the victims was Kenta Sashida."

"That's one," replied Kurtz. "Sashida was one of Jimura's go-to guys for all sorts of errands and dirty deeds." NCIS had suspected the man's involvement in a number of illicit activities including gunrunning, prostitution, and human trafficking. Then there were the other, more mundane offenses such as assault, theft, and even a murder or two. The official case file maintained for this mid-level employee in Jimura's organization was almost an inch thick.

"What about the others?" asked Kurtz.

Aguilar shook her head. "Nothing that can definitively link any of them to Jimura, at least not for anything useful. Other than Sashida, we're still stuck with a big 'maybe' so far as whether any of these clowns are working for him."

"Sashida's a start, but I kind of figured it was going to go that way," replied Kurtz. "There wasn't a single wallet or piece of ID found on any of them. No phones or pagers, nothing." He tapped one of the papers on his desk. "Two cars had cigarette lighters missing from the dash, indicating something like a car phone may have been plugged in there." Mobile phones for vehicles and even models small enough to be carried in a pocket or purse were becoming more common in the United States and other countries, but older people hadn't yet embraced such technological advances. Such things also were slow coming to Okinawa, given that the island lacked the infrastructure to support a cellular phone network. At least two were in the planning stages, but it would be a while before service was available.

It also was likely that someone like Miroji Jimura, being of a generation who still turned up their noses at all the electronic gadgets that seemed to capture the attentions of their children and grandchildren, didn't trust such devices from a security or privacy standpoint. Kurtz could understand that, even if carrying a pager or cellular phone, or using a desktop computer instead of digging through rooms of file cabinets, made him better able to do his job.

Aguilar said, "So, best guess is that somebody tried to sanitize the scene before the law got there. Question is, who? Some of Jimura's people, trying to cover tracks?"

"Safe bet, especially given everything else that was left behind. That, or they left all that crap at home to avoid being identified." In addition to dozens of shell casings recovered from the warehouse lot and the hills above the primary scene, crime scene investigators from the Okinawa Prefectural Police working with agents of the Japanese Self-Defense Force had also found two dropped or discarded pistols and one rifle. "If the weapons found at the scene can be traced back to Jimura in any way, that's all she wrote for him. JSDF will drop on him like a hammer."

Aguilar offered a mock frown. "That'd be a damned shame, wouldn't it?"

Lifting his legs, Kurtz rested his feet on the corner of his desk. The action dislodged one of the file folders cluttering that area and sent it dropping to the floor, but he ignored it. "Okay, so what about the other guys. European? American?"

"No ID on any of them, either," replied Aguilar. "We're still waiting on fingerprints for them, too, and whatever else Carol's been able to dig up, once she comes up for air." Carol Oliver, the NCIS crime scene analyst upon whom Kurtz and Aguilar normally relied, had been neck deep in the case since daybreak, and both agents knew better than to disturb her when she was "in the zone."

Kurt asked, "You still like the rival idea, moving in on Jimura's action, along with whoever was there to make the deal for the weapons?"

"Right now, it's what makes most sense. Edoga Kanashiro's the one with the balls big enough to try something like this." Aguilar shrugged. "On the other hand, he's also smart enough not to get himself into trouble over something stupid. Maybe this was a double cross, by either side. Hell, it could've been both sides. It's not like we're talking about choir boys, here."

Shaking his head, Kurtz replied, "Maybe we're overthinking this a bit." He looked to the bulletin board mounted on the squad room's far wall, and the pictures pinned to it. Arrayed in a series of pyramids, the photographs depicted known Okinawan organized crime leaders and identified associates or employees. The two largest pyramids belonged to Miroji Jimura and Edoga Kanashiro. A large red X had already been crossed through the picture of Kenta Sashida under Jimura's group.

One down. Who the hell knows how many more to go?

Kurtz's phone rang and he grabbed its receiver. "Kurtz."

"It's Nick," said the voice of Special Agent Nick Minecci, who among other things was the NCIS liaison officer to Okinawa's local law enforcement agencies. "I just got a heads-up from local PD. There's been some kind of car chase and shoot-out down in Naha."

"Naha? Again?"

"Yeah, but away from the warehouse district. PD has a couple of witnesses who say the people in the car being chased weren't locals; maybe Americans."

"Or European," replied Kurtz.

"Could be. Local uniforms are on the scene, taking statements and all that jazz. Somebody will be there if you want to give it a look."

Writing down the address information Minecci provided, Kurtz said, "Okay, we're on it. Thanks." He hung up the phone, pushing himself from his chair. "Let's go."

"Back to Naha?" Aguilar rolled her eyes as she stood. "It's forty-five minutes back there, this time of morning." Even with the relatively straight commute down Highway 58 from the NCIS field office at Camp Foster to wherever they were going in Naha, the streets would be clogged with commuter and American military traffic.

Kurtz smirked. "Come on. I'll buy you breakfast."

"I already ate breakfast."

"Then you can buy me breakfast."

The rice was soggy and the dumplings were cold. Jack ate everything without tasting any of it, pushing it all down with as much water as he could swallow. How long had it been since his last meal? Beyond some vague recollection of a flavorless meat and vegetables concoction on the *Konstantinov* prior to their departure for the meeting in the port district, he couldn't remember.

"I didn't think you liked my cooking, Stefan," said Banovich, eyeing him as he grabbed another clump of rice with his fingers and ate it.

"No complaints from me," Jack replied before draining his water glass. Stepping away from the compact kitchen's sink, he surveyed the small, modest home serving as the group's safe house. There was just enough room for him and Banovich, along with Rauf Alkaev and Manish Pajari, who had found space on the floor or couch in the main room. Both were big and brawny, wearing military-style field jackets over jeans and tight-fitting muscle shirts. Whereas Alkaev was bald—or at least shaved his head smooth—Pajari wore his dark hair cropped close and flat on top, much like a stereotypical hard-charging, cigar-chomping drill sergeant.

Beyond the fact that they had worked for Grisha Zherdev, and by extension Tateos Gadjoyan, Jack knew nothing about the two men. Still, they had to be at least somewhat trustworthy for Zherdev to have selected them for this assignment. Neither said much, though Jack had watched them study any room, vehicle, or outside area with critical eyes, searching for points of possible attack and retreat. They were dangerous. He would have to remain mindful of their whereabouts at all times, which for now was on the couch. Their snores reverberated through the shoji screens dividing the house's living spaces. Unlike him and Banovich, they had managed to make their way here without incident, at least according to the terse report they had given her after she had kicked them awake.

The safe house had been just one facet of the preparations ordered by Grisha Zherdev prior to meeting with Miroji Jimura's men. Banovich, Alkaev, and Pajari had been part of the advance team that had flown into Naha days prior to the *Konstantinov*'s arrival in port. In Jack's observations, Zherdev was the sort of person who left very little to chance, preferring instead to plan for the worst possible outcome of any given situation. Thanks to his zealous provisioning, which included stockpiles of food and water, weapons and ammunition, and even clean clothes, Jack and other survivors of the botched exchange had a place to lay low while they regrouped.

Banovich had chosen to err on the side of caution and leave their stolen car some distance from the safe house. A cursory check of the vehicle revealed no tracking device, but they had opted to steal another car—white and nondescript like the majority of vehicles on the island—to get them to the safe house. The first thing Jack had done upon their arrival was turn on the television, where he found local news broadcasts offering only surface information about a car chase outside of Naha. The reporters were speaking Japanese, but Jack was able to infer bits and pieces of the offered narrative, which seemed to consist largely of vague descriptions of the vehicles involved. Still, he winced when Banovich translated one witness's mentioning of gunfire and the Caucasian man and woman in the car being chased. News camera footage of the wrecked sedan being pulled from the rice paddy also dominated a couple of the reports, including one telling angle revealing bullet holes in the car's windshield.

How much did they know? There was no way to be certain,

but Jack was worried that a lucky or attentive witness might have been able to provide a license plate or perhaps descriptions of him or Banovich to the police. So far, nothing was showing up on TV, but Jack knew that could mean the authorities were being careful with whatever information they might receive.

For the sake of completeness, Jack also spent a few moments listening to the Armed Forces Radio station, but the only news there centered around topics of interest to the American military personnel and civilians living on the island. According to one report, the final remaining Russian ground troops were preparing to depart Germany, yet another in a long series of steps that had seen to the formal ending of the Cold War. The collapse of the Soviet Union had ushered in an ongoing wave of changes in the American military and intelligence establishments, as those embroiled in the decades-long standoff with Russia now wondered who or what they would fight next. Of course, the USSR's dissolution actually caused as many if not more problems than it solved, at least from a security and intelligence-gathering perspective. After all, there were scads of parties out there eager to get their hands on neglected or abandoned Soviet military hardware, in particular nuclear weapons. The intelligence agencies of countries around the world were scrambling to deal with these and other new threats. This, of course, was proving far more challenging than simply preparing for conventional warfare against an enemy that was no longer capable of engaging in such a fight, and who now was leaving the door open for people like Tateos Gadjoyan, Miroji Jimura, and thousands of other opportunists.

Which is why you have a job.

"What do you want to do now?" Jack asked, talking around one last mouthful of rice that he chased with a long pull of water from a plastic tumbler.

"We'll wait until dark," Banovich replied, filling her own glass with water from a bottle perched on the small kitchen counter. "Then head for the port." She sighed, shaking her head.

Jack asked, "You all right?"

"I was just thinking about Grisha." She reached up to wipe the corner of her left eye. "Gadjoyan was very fond of him."

Her mention of Grisha Zherdev also triggered an image of Bill Fields, and Jack forced himself not to dwell on memories of his friend and mentor. Had his wife and family been notified yet about his death? Would the CIA even be able to tell the truth about what had happened, or would it be forced through necessity to concoct a story to conceal where, when, and how he had died? Jack guessed the agency would do the latter, if for no other reason than to preserve his own cover for however long his mission required him to maintain a foothold within Tateos Gadjoyan's organization.

"Stefan?" Banovich asked, shaking him from his reverie. "Are you all right?"

Nodding, Jack took another drink of water. "Sorry. I was thinking about Grisha and the others, too. I only knew Grisha and Levon well, and they were friends. I feel badly for their families."

"So do I," Banovich replied, "and we can mourn them later, but right now, we need to get away from here and back to the ship."

Jack glanced at his watch. There were still nearly fourteen hours before the *Konstantinov* was scheduled to leave Naha Port. He and the others could wait here until nightfall and still have plenty of time to get back before the ship's departure, assuming NCIS, JSDF, or another law enforcement agency didn't lock down ports, airports, and any other means of leaving the island. He suspected the authorities wouldn't make such a play just yet; not if they were still trying to piece together what happened in the warehouse district. The looming question in his mind was whether they knew about the transfer of American weapons. Whoever had conducted the ambush likely had taken the consignment, but if by chance NCIS had learned of the botched exchange, they might be moving with caution in the hopes of pursuing leads to those responsible.

"If the Americans figure out that it was their weapons being sold," said Jack, "they'll be watching the ports and airports. They'll be looking for foreigners. For all we know, they have all of our pictures. We need to be careful." He paused, deciding that if he was going to broach this next topic, now was the time. "And shouldn't we at least try to contact Jimura's people?" He gestured to the satellite phone Banovich had retrieved from the bedroom and placed on the kitchen counter. "If he thinks we double-crossed him, and those were his guys who were chasing us, then he won't stop. Plus, he might opt to go after Gadjoyan." Banovich had already used the phone to make a very brief call to Kiev to notify Gadjoyan about the failed exchange, and her concerns about not knowing who was responsible for the hit. Gadjoyan himself had not been on the other end of the phone, requiring her to relay the information to one of the arms dealer's many underlings. Now she was waiting for him to call back with instructions.

"That would be stupid," countered Banovich. "Even if he wanted to do something like that, Jimura doesn't have that kind of reach."

Jack shook his head. "That doesn't matter. If Jimura thinks Gadjoyan screwed him, he's going to tell others who might deal with Gadjoyan. It could derail every contact Gadjoyan has in this part of the world." He was spinning this hypothesis from nothing, and he forced himself not to talk too fast. In truth, it was a plausible development based on the morning's events, but Jack—or, rather, Stefan Voronov—would have little to no knowledge of any such relationships. He had to be careful not to overstep his place here.

He raised his hands, as though gesturing that he didn't want to upset or offend Banovich. "I'm sorry, Amorah. I'm not trying to tell you your job. I've never been involved in something like this, and I think I'm just scared. And I can get carried away with worst-case scenarios." He forced a smile. "Too many American movies, I guess."

Banovich actually laughed at that. Brushing a lock of brown hair from her forehead, she said, "All right, Stefan, what do you suggest we do?"

"Call Jimura. Tell him it wasn't us who hit him. Even if he already knows or suspects that, he'll think it's an honorable gesture on your part to reach out. Remember, older men like him value integrity and courage, particularly when the other party thinks they've given offense."

Eyeing him with open curiosity, Banovich said, "Who told you that?"

Jack shrugged, attempting to affect a casual air. "Grisha. We talked a lot on the ship." That wasn't a lie, as he and Grisha Zherdev had shared several conversations following evening meals. Bill Fields had been a part of some of those discussions, which Zherdev had treated as similar to holding court while educating the junior, less experienced members of his group. Jack had been content to sit in silence and let the older man pontificate, as the vodka-fueled rantings provided the occasional morsel of useful insight into Tateos Gadjoyan and the inner workings of his organization.

"Perhaps you're right," said Banovich after a moment. "Maybe we should call him."

"Besides," Jack replied, "coming away from here with any kind of deal instead of a total loss is in everybody's best interests, particularly for Gadjoyan. We've still got time to get something together before the ship leaves tonight."

Saying nothing for a moment, Banovich seemed lost in thought, no doubt considering the pros and cons of making contact with Jimura. When she nodded, Jack could see she hadn't quite succeeded in convincing herself.

"All right, I'll make the call." Her words lacked real conviction, but he figured she would rather do anything than sit around here for the rest of the day, waiting for darkness and their opportunity to return to Naha Port, or for another batch of men—Jimura's or someone else's—to find them.

She picked up the phone and left the kitchen, and Jack heard her footsteps retreating to the bedroom before the door closed. Standing alone in the kitchen, Jack drank more water as he weighed his options. Jimura and Gadjoyan could go to war with each other, for all he cared. What he needed was an opportunity to make contact with Abigail Cohen. Jack needed only a few minutes to alert her that he was alive and that his cover was intact, but he also needed to tell her what he knew about the aborted weapons exchange and that another player likely had entered the game. How was he supposed to do that? The phone on the wall in the safe house's living room was out of the question, of course, as was the satellite phone.

Even if he was able to make contact, how much did Cohen

even know in the wake of the morning's developments? Further, how much would she share with him, a relatively junior agent with limited need to know? Jack could argue that this need had grown significantly during the past few hours, but he guessed his and Cohen's superiors wouldn't see things in similar fashion.

As for his own situation, he had considered just finding a way to separate himself from Banovich and her companions, contacting Cohen from the first phone he found, and allowing himself to be brought in by agency assets. It would remove him from the danger of continuing with this mission, and might even be an expected decision from an agent of his tenure and experience. On the other hand, there was still a need to obtain information on Gadjoyan's arms dealing, particularly if it involved American weapons, as was the case with the exchange this morning. That extended to Miroji Jimura, whom Jack suspected was a person of interest to law enforcement agencies here on Okinawa. If he played his cards right, Jack possessed an opportunity to gather information and perhaps even take direct action against Jimura's organization while furthering the case against Gadjoyan.

What would Bill do?

Jack was sure his partner would attempt to stay in play here, for the good of the mission. The question was whether Jack could carry on in his friend's stead, or would he somehow screw up everything, compromise the mission, and get himself killed?

There was only one way to find out.

A hand fell on his arm and he started, turning from the kitchen counter to see Banovich standing behind him, the satellite phone in her hand. Blinking several times, Jack realized he had been so lost in thought that he hadn't heard her return from the bedroom.

Need to watch that, rookie.

"Sorry," he said, almost stumbling over the single word as he nearly tripped himself remembering to employ his accent. To cover his awkwardness, Jack put one hand to his mouth and faked a yawn. "I think I was starting to doze, there."

Banovich held up the phone. "I just talked to one of Jimura's people, an American named Yeager. Apparently he handles much of the organization's business dealings."

"How'd it go?"

Shrugging, she replied, "Jimura doesn't seem to think we were responsible for the ambush at the port, and he has a good idea who was."

Jack considered this. "A rival."

"Right." Banovich placed the satellite phone on the counter. "So, Yeager says Jimura's already talked to Gadjoyan, and they've worked out an alternative deal, and it has two parts. Jimura will provide another cache of weapons, but that won't be happening today."

"So, what do we do?" Even as he asked the question, Jack's instincts were telling him he wasn't going to like the answer.

Banovich reached up to run a hand through her hair. "Jimura wants us to help his people put a hit on this rival."

Yeah, Jack mused as he pondered how much farther he was being drawn into this increasingly chaotic situation. *This deal's just getting better by the minute.*

• • •

The taillights on the van in front of her flashed red, and Jessica Connelly stomped on the clutch and brake pedals. She felt the car's nose angle downward as the vehicle shed its speed at the same time she heard its engine protest the abuse to which it was being subjected. For one anxious second, she thought the car might stall.

"Son of a bitch," Jessica hissed as she reached for the Toyota's gearshift and moved it back to first, easing the car forward once more.

"Mom," said her eight-year-old son, Dylan, from where he sat in the car's rear seat. "You're not supposed to say stuff like that."

Jessica grunted. "No, *you're* not supposed to say stuff like that."

Sitting to her left in the front passenger seat, her running shoes perched on the car's dashboard, Brynn Connelly offered her own commentary in the form of a derisive snort. "That's not what Dad says."

"You've met your father, right? And get your feet off the dash." A glance in the rearview mirror showed her nothing but the front grill of a black Mitsubishi SUV. How close had it come to smashing into her car's rear end?

That's all I need, she thought, letting the car accelerate before shifting into second. She had no idea what had caused the van to brake, as the traffic around them appeared to be resuming speed. Highway 58 between Camp Foster and Kadena Air Force Base to the north was always congested at this time of day. She wished she'd waited at least another hour before leaving the temporary lodging facility, but time was running short on this, the Connellys' last full day on the island. There were last-minute errands to complete, and final farewells to convey to friends they had made during these past three years. As part of those preparations, the Connellys had already sold one of their two cars. The Toyota was a loaner from their neighbors, the Lathams, who had been of tremendous help all through the process of packing and getting ready to return stateside.

Former neighbors, Jessica reminded herself. When she arrived at the Lathams' in Camp Foster's family housing area, a truck was in the driveway of what had been the Connellys' home, with a maintenance crew already inside and in the process of installing new carpeting and linoleum flooring, and cleaning or replacing bathroom tiling and fixtures. Interior and exterior paint would follow in the next few days, and within two weeks it would be ready for one of the many families on the always crowded waiting list for on-base housing.

The van ahead of her hit its brakes again and Jessica slowed the car. A glance over her right shoulder told her that the inside lane of northbound traffic was just as packed as the one she occupied, while cars in the oncoming lanes whipped past on her right. It had taken Jessica months to get used to driving cars with right-hand drives on the left side of the road, and she wondered how long it would take to readjust to driving "normally" once they returned to the States.

Probably three years.

"This car smells," offered Dylan from the backseat. "I think somebody spilled milk on the floor back here." Glancing over her shoulder, Jessica saw that his features were scrunched up in disapproval in a way that made him look like the spitting image of his father. The illusion was furthered by her son's choice to wear an olive-green T-shirt with a yellow silk-screened Marine Corps logo of the sort Dale might wear for his daily runs.

Brynn made a show of fanning herself with a magazine. "And why didn't we borrow a car with air conditioning?"

"Because we don't get to be choosy when somebody's doing us a favor," replied Jessica, eyeing a growing gap between two cars in the left lane as the Toyota accelerated again and she shifted up to third gear. She might have a chance if she timed it right.

"Why couldn't we have taken Dad's car?" her daughter asked, making sure to punctuate the question with a sigh.

"He needs it for work." Her husband's car would change hands with a friend later today, as Dale had his own running around to do while completing the process of check-out procedures that were part and parcel of changing duty stations. It was no less a bureaucratic headache when one was on the way to retirement. If anything, there was even more paperwork involved, as though the Marine Corps was doing its level best to annoy Dale one final time before he finally was free of its hold on him.

Who are you kidding? The man will never bleed anything but scarlet and gold.

It was true, of course, the same way it was true for just about every person who had made a career of the military as her husband had done. Leaving the service brought with it a cascade of paperwork and a change of address, but it would be many months, if not longer, before Dale Connelly weaned himself of uncounted habits and quirks ingrained over nearly three decades. He had already been a Marine for ten years when Jessica first met him. The ensuing sixteen years had brought with them prolonged separations, frequent relocations, and accepting the fact that so far as the Marine Corps was concerned, a wife and family were secondary considerations when it came to duty and the mission.

Though Dale had tried to explain all of this well before their wedding, the reality of life as a military spouse was something that had to be experienced to be believed. It was a situation that grew more complicated in short order, once Jessica learned she was pregnant with Brynn, and her arrival expected five months into a six-month deployment for Dale to the Mediterranean Sea. Her mother had been on hand to help through that difficult period and the following weeks before his return, but Jessica had never quite forgiven the Marine Corps for seeing to it that her husband missed the birth of his first child. She had never shared this resentment with him, of course; nothing good would have come from that.

Besides, it's all behind us by this time next week.

"Mom!"

Jessica heard Brynn's warning shout an instant after the van's taillights flashed yet again, and this time it was too fast for her to react. She jammed the brake pedal to the floorboard and felt the Toyota's tires lock and then begin skidding along the asphalt. She had but a second to release and then pump the pedal, feeling the brakes trying to take hold. The car's speed dropped to thirty kilometers per hour before its front bumper slammed into the back of the van. Jessica grunted more in shock than pain as she was thrown forward, her seat belt cutting into her shoulder in the midst of preventing her from being slung through the windshield. The car's hood crumpled and she heard its engine sputter and die. Muffled shouts were coming from somewhere outside but Jessica ignored them, shaking away cobwebs from her brain as her left hand shot out toward Brynn.

"You okay?" she shouted, her voice echoing inside the car. Jerking her head around, she saw Dylan grimacing in obvious discomfort, but he appeared uninjured. "Dylan?"

Both of her children responded that they were uninjured. Jessica glanced through the car's rear window to see the black SUV still behind them, now stopped on the road, as well. Two men emerged from the vehicle's front seats, running down either side of the Toyota. An Okinawan man with dark hair and wearing dark sunglasses came abreast of the driver's side door, and he bent low to peer inside.

"You all right, lady?" he asked in broken English. He was

reaching for the door's handle as his companion did the same on Brynn's side of the car.

Nodding, Jessica allowed the man to help her out of the Toyota and then gripped his arm when her legs felt wobbly. The other Okinawan had already helped Brynn from her seat. Now he was assisting Dylan, and Jessica used the car itself to maintain her balance as she made her way around to him. Throwing one arm around him, she reached for Brynn and pulled her close.

"You're sure you're okay?" she asked, gripping her children and giving serious thought to not letting them go.

Dylan was the first to give the moment perspective. "It's cool, Mom. You only tapped that guy's bumper."

"The Lathams are going to be pissed," said Brynn.

It was enough to make her laugh, and she sighed with relief. The pain in her shoulder from the seat belt was already fading, though she suspected her muscles would be protesting all of this by tomorrow morning. Footsteps behind her made her turn, and she saw the man who had helped her gesturing toward them.

"Not safe in street," he said, waving them to the sidewalk.

With his friend following them, Jessica led Dylan and Brynn away from the car and onto the curb. Other cars were slowing to inspect what had happen, though no one else was stopping. Looking toward the van, she saw another Okinawan man dressed in gray coveralls and sunglasses being assisted from the driver's seat by a pair of onlookers, while others had emerged from nearby stores to see what was happening.

"Thank God," Jessica said, offering a weak smile and what she hoped was an expression of guilt and relief to the van's driver as he moved toward them. In a louder voice, she called out, "I'm so sorry about this." She looked around, eyeing the establishments facing the street. "We need a phone. Can someone call the police?" She wondered if she should call Dale, but thought that could wait for a bit. He was busy enough without being distracted by this, especially since no one appeared to have been hurt.

The Okinawan waved toward one of the stores north of where they stood. "Phone this way," he said.

Remembering her purse at the last second, Jessica returned

to the wrecked Toyota. She surveyed the damage to the car and the van before casting another regretful look at the other vehicle's driver. "Maybe we should just stay here until the police arrive." To her surprise, the driver motioned toward her.

"It's okay. We call police."

Jessica smiled, relieved that the driver looked to be uninjured and that he seemed to be taking the incident in stride. She reached out and placed a hand on his arm. "Are you sure you're all right?"

The driver nodded, adjusting his sunglasses. "Yes. Come. We call police."

Brynn and Dylan were waiting for her on the sidewalk, and they, along with the van driver and their Okinawan benefactors, began moving toward the store the one man had indicated. It occurred to Jessica that she hadn't even had the wherewithal to ask the men their names, let alone thank them for their assistance. She increased her pace to catch up with the man who had pulled her from the car, coming abreast of him as they began to pass an alley between two buildings.

The Okinawan shoved her into the alley.

"Hey!"

Stumbling to her right and toward an SUV parked in the narrow passage, Jessica tried to maintain her balance at the same time she heard the sounds of struggle behind her. She glanced over her shoulder to see the other Okinawan and the van driver grabbing Brynn and Dylan. Each of them clamped a hand over her children's mouths at the same time they lifted them off their feet and carried them into the alley. Jessica tensed when she heard the SUV's rear door open to reveal another man, holding a pistol and aiming it at her face.

"No!"

Turning toward the man who had pushed her, Jessica shifted her feet, preparing to kick or punch as she had learned at the self-defense classes offered by the base gym. A hand on her mouth stopped her as the man pushed her backward. She swung a fist at him but missed, and something struck her in the side of her head. A muffled shout of terror echoed in her ears, but then she was being pushed into the SUV's rear cargo area.

Something landed beside and on top of her, and when she looked up it was to see Brynn and Dylan lying next to her. The SUV's doors closed, and Jessica felt the vehicle lurch, and it began moving, accelerating as its driver navigated the narrow alley. She started to sit up but stopped when the muzzle of a pistol materialized, inches from her face.

"Don't," warned the weapon's owner, yet another Okinawan male wearing dark sunglasses. He was bald and bulky, and sweat beaded on his oversized forehead. "Stay where you are. Do what you're told, you don't get hurt."

The sounds from the squad bay where the rest of her team was working were subdued as Abigail Cohen closed the office door.

"How are you holding up?" asked her supervisor, Mark Paquette. A bald, burly man in his early fifties, he sat with his muscled forearms resting atop his gunmetal gray desk. His white dress shirt's sleeves were rolled up just enough to reveal the faded tattoo of a skull wearing a military helmet on his left arm. His dark blue tie was loosened and his top button was undone, and a tuft of black hair peeked above the collar of his white undershirt. "You look tired."

Cohen forced a smile. "I'm doing okay, but thanks for asking." She had been standing outside Paquette's office, having come at his summons but listening through the door to fragments of the animated conversation he was having with someone on the phone. It was easy to deduce that he had been talking to a supervising case officer back at CIA Headquarters in Langley. Though she had heard no yelling, it was obvious that the person on the other end of the line wasn't happy.

"I couldn't help hearing you on the phone," she said. "What's the word?"

A white ceramic coffee cup bearing the emblem of the United States Marine Corps, its insides stained brown after undetermined years of buildup, sat on the desk near Paquette's right hand. He reached for the cup and drained its contents before replying, "You'd think after all these years, I'd learn to like getting my ass chewed. Turns out I still hate it."

Cohen grimaced. "That bad?"

"I've had worse." Paquette set the now-empty cup back on his desk blotter, pushing aside several of the uncounted papers arrayed before him. "Folks back in Langley are getting a little edgy, Abby." He gestured toward the pair of decrepit gray chairs positioned before his desk. "You know how they get when things don't follow their cute little color-coded and indexed op plans."

Cohen dropped into one of the chairs. "It's field ops, Mark. Things happen." She knew he understood this, of course. Mark Paquette was a combat veteran with two tours in Vietnam, and a battle-tested disciple of Murphy's Laws of Close Combat. One of those laws stated that few if any operations plans, regardless of the effort put into conceiving them, survived initial contact with the enemy. "We need to give Bauer time to make contact, and we need to get people out there, looking for him."

"I agree." Paquette pushed his chair to one side and leaned back, lifting his legs and resting them on the corner of his desk. "And that's what I told them. They're not happy, but for the moment they're leaving it in my hands."

Cohen rubbed her temples. "I know they're worried about Gadjoyan running for a hole somewhere, but has there been anything to suggest he's getting antsy?"

"No. Our people in Kiev say everything looks to be business as usual. One of our contacts reports that Gadjoyan took a sat-phone call an hour so ago from an unknown party. There aren't a lot of details, and it was too short to run a trace. However, the contact did say that she heard the names 'Jimura' and 'Zherdev,' so make of that what you will."

"My first guess? Gadjoyan knows about the weapons exchange," replied Cohen. "Which means the call likely came from one of his people on the ground here."

Paquette tapped a finger on his desk before aiming it at her. "Bingo."

"But we don't know who that might be. Hell, it could've been Bauer, maintaining his cover."

For the first time, Paquette offered a grim smile. "I like the way you think. That's exactly what I told Langley. Somebody did a damned fine job training you, Agent Cohen."

It was an old joke between them, dating back to Cohen's first weeks as a rookie assigned to Mark Paquette's team. Fresh out of college and agency training, she had arrived at a time when the Cold War was in its death throes. Eyes and ears and whatever state-of-the-art surveillance equipment that could be found was being directed at new and emerging threats, namely the ongoing concern of international terrorism and "rogue states." The president's national security advisor had recently bestowed that designation on Cuba, Iraq, Iran, Libya, and North Korea. Each of these countries had expressed an apparent willingness to exist at odds with most of the world's democratic nations while committing human rights violations against its own citizens, sponsoring terrorism, and attempting to acquire weapons of mass destruction. Attention also was being directed at Afghanistan, Sudan, and Yugoslavia to name other potential players, any one of which was enough to give a CIA case officer chronic heartburn and migraine headaches.

It was into this evolving climate that Abigail Cohen had waded, her head spinning with certainty of purpose and doubt as to whether she might ever make a meaningful contribution toward keeping her country safe. Paquette had wasted no time picking her up and throwing her into the deep end of that metaphorical pool, and it hadn't taken him long to assess her strengths in data and threat analysis. Though she had envisioned herself one day becoming a field agent, Cohen had come to realize that her true talents lay in making sure field agents had the best, most complete information available to them as they undertook dangerous assignments around the world. This hadn't precluded her from the occasional field operation, but she knew that any career she hoped to enjoy with the agency would be due to the talents she possessed in this vital area of logistics and support.

Shifting his feet on the desk, Paquette said, "On the other hand, it's very possible Bauer's dead. All we know is that his wasn't one of the bodies recovered from the warehouse shootout."

Feeling emotions welling up within her, Cohen forced her

voice to remain level as she asked, "What are we doing about Bill?"

Paquette sighed. "All of the bodies recovered from the scene are currently in NCIS custody down at Camp Foster, and are being prepped for transport to their field office in Yokosuka. Once they get to mainland Japan, we'll coordinate with them to get Agent Fields sent home."

It wasn't the best answer, but Cohen knew the actions being undertaken were necessary to preserve the sensitivity of the current mission and the cover identities used by Bill Fields and Jack Bauer, as well as Daniel Boyce, who was still undercover in Kiev. As for Fields, Cohen also knew that his family would be provided with a plausible explanation for his death that would protect the mission's secrecy. They likely would never know the truth about the numerous sacrifices he had made in service to his country over a lengthy, distinguished career.

"Depending on how far NCIS wants to dig," said Cohen, "this could become a problem. They're investigating weapons thefts from our military bases and sales of those goods on the black market. They've got files on all the major players in this part of the world, and they're going to want to know who these potential buyers are." She paused, swallowing a lump that had formed in her throat. "Or were. Bill's cover ID is good enough to fool most of these gunrunners and even the JSDF, but NCIS? Give them enough time, they're going to figure something's up. That could be dangerous for Jack."

"If he's still alive," Paquette countered.

"Right. If he *is* still alive, then he's our best bet for preserving a link into Gadjoyan's organization. Informants are one thing, but we need an active agent in there. For the moment, Jack's our man, but even if Langley shuts us down, we still need to be in a position to bring him in."

Paquette reached up to rub his hairless dome. "As things stand now, we're to stand fast and wait for Bauer to make contact, but the clock's ticking on this, Abby. If Langley thinks Gadjoyan might start to smell something off about this, they're going to make me pull the plug. They're looking at the bigger picture." He sighed, his lips tightening. "But I'm looking at the picture that shows me I've still got a man out there, somewhere."

Pushing his feet from the desk, he shifted his bulk so that he once more was resting his elbows atop the scattered papers. "Keep a close eye on what NCIS is doing with JSDF. I don't want them making a move we don't know about."

"You're not suggesting we interfere with their investigation?"

Paquette scowled. "You know me better than that. Once we approach them about recovering Bill, they're going to know we're here and have been poking around. I'm not interested in jurisdictional pissing matches or who gets credit for what. Whether we like it or not, we're all connected, somehow. If we can help them with their investigation while we search for Bauer, that works for me. If we can do all of that while not blowing a hole in this mission, that's even better."

"Langley's not going to like this," said Cohen.

"Then they can put somebody's ass on a plane and have them come over here to tell me that. For now, we keep supporting Bauer. If he's as good as you say he is, he'll find a way to contact us."

A knock on the door made Cohen look over her shoulder as Paquette shouted for whoever was there to enter the office. The door opened to reveal Agent Laron Williams, his expression serious as stepped into the room and extended to Paquette a set of papers in his right hand.

"I think we've got a lead on Bauer. There was a car chase outside of Naha a couple of hours ago. The car being chased was driven by a Caucasian woman and the passenger was a Caucasian male who was shooting at the other car."

"Bauer?" asked Cohen. "The woman might be Amorah Banovich. She's the only female on Zherdev's crew."

Williams shrugged. "Maybe. The car doing the chasing ended up in a rice paddy with two dead Okinawans inside. Local cops are still trying to figure it all out."

"Any sign of the other car?" Paquette asked, his attention focused on the papers Williams had given him.

The other agent shook his head. "Nobody saw where it went. Cops are doing a sweep, but it's a white Toyota sedan."

Rolling his eyes, Paquette replied, "Yeah. Those are pretty rare."

"If it is Bauer," Williams said, "then who the hell was chasing him?"

"The same people who ambushed the weapons exchange?" offered Cohen.

Looking up from the papers, Paquette pointed to her. "Keep tabs on NCIS and JSDF. See if they're working this angle."

Cohen pushed herself from her chair. "On it, boss."

What the hell are you into, Jack?

• • •

Crystal blue waves crashed against rocks below him. The sound was hypnotic, and when Jack closed his eyes, his mind conjured images of another beach far from here. It had been a small stretch of sand on Molokai's south shore adjacent to the condo he had rented after setting aside money for nearly two years. Ten blissful days that would end up being their last vacation before his wife announced her pregnancy. Just him and Teri, thousands of miles from the demands and pressures of his job, and her wearing the smallest bikini he had ever seen on another living being, at least until she had opted to go without it.

"Don't fall, Stefan."

Opening his eyes, Jack turned to see Banovich, who stood with Rauf Alkaev and Manish Pajari near the car they had used to travel from the safe house. The observation point overlooked the Pacific Ocean, though he had only to turn to his right to look past the island's southern tip and the East China Sea that stretched toward the horizon. Less than three hundred miles to the northwest lay the Korean peninsula, and Jack knew that there was ferry service from a nearby port to Busan on the South Korean coast. Grisha Zherdev had mentioned that as one possible avenue of escape in the event it was necessary to depart the island without being able to return to the *Konstantinov* at Naha Port.

Another alternative was here, where he and the others now stood. According to the guidebook Jack had read on the ship, Itoman and its attending port thrived on fishing, which was the small city's primary industry. Hundreds of boats of all sizes could be found here, any number of which could be commandeered if the need arose. Jack knew from history studies that the town also had been one of the final fronts in the waning months of World War II and the battle to take Okinawa, as American and allied forces continued their push toward Japan during the Pacific "island-hopping campaign." The nearly three-month crusade to secure the island was one of the most ferocious, bloody battles of the entire war, with tens of thousands of military personnel on both sides killed or wounded, and an estimated one hundred fifty thousand civilian deaths recorded. The Okinawa Prefectural Peace Memorial Museum was just across the road, a sanctuary commemorating the lives on both sides lost to the conflict, and Jack had seen a posted sign informing visitors about an upcoming annual ceremony in remembrance of the battle's end.

Glancing at his watch, Jack looked around but saw no sign of other vehicles or activity. "They should be here by now."

"Not much we can do about it," replied Banovich. After her phone call with Miroji Jimura's point man, she had informed him and the others about the instructions to meet here in Itoman, at this observation point near the entrance to the peace park. The adjacent road was lined with homes and other buildings, making this an interesting place for a meeting, but Jack was encouraged by the decision to rendezvous in such an open, public area. Perhaps it had been a subtle way for Jimura's man to communicate that there would be no gunplay or other antics.

I like the sound of that.

The faint sound of first one, then a second car engine caught his attention, and Jack and the others turned toward the road as a pair of black Toyota SUVs rounded a curve. To Jack, they looked identical to those he had seen at the warehouse and ostensibly driven by members of Miroji Jimura's organization. The first vehicle slowed and its counterpart swung to its right before both SUVs came to a halt. Banovich, as the leader of the small group, stepped in front of Jack and the others. All four of them made sure to keep their hands out of their pockets and away from their bodies.

The doors on both SUVs opened and Jack's attention fixed

on the Caucasian man emerging from the first vehicle's front passenger seat. He wore a simple black, collarless long-sleeved shirt tucked into dark jeans, and black tactical boots. Jack could tell from the styled and gelled brown hair and designer sunglasses that the man took pride in his personal appearance. His four companions were Okinawan or Japanese, each dressed in an assortment of civilian clothing and sunglasses. To Jack's surprise, none of the men held a weapon, though he noted that they wore jackets or long shirts which were not quite loose enough to hide bulges beneath arms or along waistlines.

"You must be Mister Yeager," Banovich said by way of greeting.

"I must be, Miss Banovich," replied the Caucasian, and Jack detected the hint of a New England accent in his voice. Was he an American? He carried himself with a military bearing and Jack suspected he had to be a veteran, likely an expatriate who had ended his career here and elected to remain on the island for whatever reason. Maybe he had been corrupted by Jimura or one of his men while still wearing a uniform. Did that make him a traitor?

Could be.

"Mister Jimura sends his regards," Yeager said. "He's been in contact with Mister Gadjoyan, who assured him that you were willing to assist with our little problem."

"You want us to help you hit this other man, Kanashiro," replied Banovich.

Yeager nodded. "That's correct. Consider this a test, of sorts."

Banovich glanced over her shoulder at Jack and the others before saying, "A test? Of what, our loyalty? You're suggesting we work for this other man?"

"I'm not suggesting anything, but sure, we'll go with your version. Mister Jimura would like to have his lingering doubts satisfied." He paused, looking past her at Jack, Alkaev, and Pajari. "There are only four of you?"

"That's right. Everyone else was killed at the exchange." Then, Banovich's voice softened and she added, "You lost men, as well. I'm sorry for that. You suspect this Kanashiro is responsible?"

"We're as sure as we need to be. Kanashiro's been making

noises about moving in on Jimura-san's action for a while now. He's done a few things here and there, but until now, it's been against smaller organizations. Our contacts tell us he's looking to up his game and take us on." He offered a humorless smile. "Jimura-san has decided that can't stand."

Oh, damn.

Jack schooled his features, forcing himself to offer not even the slightest hint of emotional reaction to what he was hearing. Into what fresh hell was he being drawn? A civil war between rival mobs? How big was this? Was the yakuza involved? From what he knew about the infamous Japanese organized crime faction, they preferred to avoid these sorts of situations. Instead, they generally abided by a very rigid code that governed their every move, even those involving enemies. This, on the other hand, appeared to be a spat between two lesser groups, either or both of which had no connection to the yakuza. Whether this was a good or bad thing, Jack couldn't be sure.

What was he supposed to do? The idea of participating in a raid against a gang of Okinawan mobsters was most definitely not part of his mission, but there was no way to extract himself from this without risking his cover. On the other hand, if this Kanashiro was the one responsible for the ambush and who now had control of the weapons stolen during the thwarted exchange, then he was a threat to American military security here on Okinawa. If he was selling such weapons to enemies of the United States, that made him a danger to any number of national interests anywhere around the world.

Cohen. I need to reach Cohen, before this gets completely out of hand.

"Are you in or out?" prompted Yeager, staring at Banovich from behind his sunglasses.

With one last glance to Jack and the others, she nodded. "We're in."

• • •

Lying on the floor of the SUV's cargo compartment, Jessica Connelly watched the tops of trees passing through the vehicle's tinted windows. The going was rougher now, as the car had turned off a paved road some distance back and now seemed to be making its way over a bumpy, uneven path. Jessica could hear the sounds of dirt and small rocks crunching beneath the SUV's tires, and felt the jolt as the driver failed to miss the occasional rut or hole.

How long had they been driving? An hour? Jessica didn't wear a watch, but her son did. She hadn't been able to look at it, as the bald, sweating man sitting in the SUV's backseat and pointing a pistol at them had commanded them to lie still. Dylan's leg lay across hers, while her daughter, Brynn, lay on her side to Jessica's right. All three of them had been too scared to move, leaving her to wonder, and worry.

"Where are you taking us?" Brynn asked. It was the first thing she had said since they had been hustled into the SUV.

"Shut up," replied the Okinawan. He had spoken to them in short, curt sentences throughout the journey, and it was obvious to Jessica that like his companions, he possessed only a marginal grasp of English.

Jessica moved one hand and rested it on her daughter's leg. Their eyes met, and she saw the fear in Brynn's eyes. Shifting her head, she saw the expression mirrored on Dylan's face. He had held her hand from the moment they were tossed into the car. His lips were quivering, and his eyes were puffy and red from crying.

"It'll be okay," Jessica whispered. "I promise." The words sounded hollow to her own ears, but she hoped they might help keep Dylan calm. She waited for some form of reprisal from the Okinawan, but he said nothing. His attention seemed to be focused on something ahead of the SUV, which Jessica noted was beginning to slow. There was another turn, to the left, this time, and then she heard the small squeak of brakes as the vehicle bounced to a halt.

"Get up," said the man, gesturing with his pistol. Without saying anything, Jessica and the kids pushed themselves to sitting positions a moment before the SUV's rear doors opened, and the dark-haired Okinawan who had thrown her into the car back in the city was standing there, gun in hand.

"Out," he snapped.

They exited the SUV and Jessica lifted her hand to shield her eyes. Gone was the city, or anything that might resemble one of the smaller villages situated along the island's better-traveled roads. A pair of buildings sat in a grove ahead of the car, a smaller house and a larger structure behind it that resembled a barn. Both buildings were simple in design, while at the same time featuring many of the exterior aesthetics that so characterized Okinawan homes.

"Where are we?" asked Jessica, keeping her voice low and her tone nonconfrontational.

"Move," replied the Okinawan, who now was flanked by his two companions. The bald, heavyset man was still sweating, but otherwise offered no reaction, whereas the third man, the one who had helped Brynn and Dylan from the wrecked car, was openly staring at her daughter. Swallowing in a feeble attempt to alleviate her dry throat, Jessica gripped her children's hands and began walking toward the house.

"Do you know where we are?" Brynn asked, her voice a whisper Jessica could barely hear.

"No." Jessica tried to think about the route they had taken from the city. She had seen the sun through the SUV's windows, high overhead and to the vehicle's right. It was only mid-morning when all of this had happened, so that meant they had traveled north for a good distance before turning right into what looked to be one of the island's lesser-developed areas. She guessed they had to be closer to Okinawa's eastern coastline. If they had been traveling north for more than thirty minutes as she suspected, that might put them somewhere near Camp Hansen, one of the island's larger Marine Corps bases and training areas. The sun was almost directly overhead now, providing no clue as to which direction they might need to go if an escape opportunity presented itself, but that would change in the next hour or so. East or west would take them to either coast, and in short order if in fact they were near Hansen, as the base lay at one of Okinawa's narrowest points. Once they reached water, and if they didn't find Hansen, heading south would take them toward more populated areas, including several American military bases.

Who are you kidding?

Jessica forced away the thought as they approached the unassuming house. The dark-haired Okinawan moved into view on her left side, gesturing with the pistol for them to head into the house.

"Please," she said, trying to keep her voice calm. "If you just tell us what you want, I'm sure we can . . ."

"Get in damn house!" the man snapped, all but spitting the broken English at her just as one of his friends put a hand between her shoulder blades and shoved. She stumbled forward, almost pulling Brynn and Dylan with her to the ground before she regained her balance, and the first man yelled something in Okinawan or Japanese. Then there were rushing footsteps and she flinched at the sensation of a hand on her arm.

"No more of that," he said, pointing with his pistol toward the house. He seemed genuinely troubled at what his friend had done. "You go inside. Stay quiet, don't make trouble. No one hurt you."

Nodding, Jessica looked at Brynn and Dylan and saw their uncertainty and dread. For the time being, there was nothing for them to do but obey.

Like a portal of unending blackness, the door to the house beckoned.

Watching as the butterfly landed on the newspaper's top edge, Edoga Kanashiro remained still so as not to frighten away the beautiful creature. Late morning sunlight highlighted the insect's green and blue accents and the red spotting at the edges of its wings. Kanashiro had no idea what species the butterfly represented, or whether it was male or female, and neither did he care. All he knew was that it was beautiful, and the perfect addition to the tranquil surroundings of his garden.

After a moment, the butterfly seemed to grow bored with its perch, and pumped its wings. It arced away from the newspaper and toward one of the garden's many well-tended plants, leaving Kanashiro alone.

"I once read that a butterfly is the embodiment of a person's soul," said a voice behind him. Kanashiro lowered the newspaper and looked up to see one of his most trusted employees, Rino Nakanashi, walking toward him. He was dressed in light gray slacks and a rich blue shirt. In his left hand, Nakanashi carried the black leather portfolio that seemed to be an extension of his arm. Narrow reading glasses were perched on the edge of his nose, and along with his lined, tan skin, his short gray hair gave him an air of distinction. Nakanashi had been with the business for years, one of the few people Kanashiro had kept when he took over operations from his father, and with good reason; the man was an accounting genius, and loyal without qualification to the Kanashiro family.

Folding the paper and placing it on the table, Kanashiro replied, "And I read an old tale that states if a butterfly enters your home and perches atop a bamboo screen, the person you love above all others will soon be visiting you."

"I believe both of those come from the same book," replied Nakanashi, moving to stand on the table's opposite side so that Kanashiro could face him directly. When Kanashiro gestured toward one of the unoccupied chairs, Nakanashi offered a nod before taking a seat and laying his omnipresent black portfolio on the table.

"You have something for me?" asked Kanashiro.

"Only updates." Opening the portfolio, Nakanashi proceeded to scan his handwritten notes, which Kanashiro could read upside-down. "I've been on the phone this morning, arranging for buyers to take possession of our new merchandise. You'll be pleased to know that two of our usual buyers are very interested, and have agreed to our prices and terms." Taking a pen from a holder inside the portfolio, the elder Okinawan began making additional notes in the margin of one paper. "I expect to have the deals finalized in the next few hours. All I would need from you is your preferred timetable for the exchange."

Kanashiro considered that for a moment. "Let's not move too quickly. A week, at least. Two would be better. We should allow time for things to calm down after this morning's events." The brash attack he had ordered against Miroji Jimura and his European counterpart, Tateos Gadjoyan, had been effective, more so because Kanashiro believed none of it could be traced back to him or his people. The men he had lost during the ambush, according to Nakanashi, couldn't be conclusively tied to his organization. Jimura and even the authorities might have their suspicions, but without hard proof, the police wouldn't act. If he held to his usual methods, Jimura also would hesitate to retaliate, though Kanashiro suspected even the old man might still have one or two surprises left in him.

As for the clients to which Nakanashi was referring, they were located in the Middle East and Eastern Europe. They wouldn't want to wait long to close their respective deals, but

Kanashiro was confident they could be persuaded to wait an appropriate interval. The weapons for which they were waiting would be worth such a delay, and his clients in turn would enjoy healthy profits from sales to their own customers. Most of the arms in the seized shipment would eventually be channeled into the hands of groups who would use them against American interests, but that didn't matter to Kanashiro. The United States military had been an irritant on Japanese and Okinawan soil his entire life, and he had no problem with Americans or their soldiers dying even as an indirect result of his actions. Such was the cost of business.

"I'll see that it's handled," Nakanashi replied, continuing to make notes. Once he finished with his writing, he laid the pen down before folding his hands and placing them on the table. "There is another matter. Higashi and Fumoto have not reported in for almost two hours, now."

Frowning at this development, Kanashiro asked, "You're sure?"

"At their last call, they were still following two of Grisha Zherdev's people who had escaped the ambush. One of our scouts at the perimeter spotted a white sedan leaving the warehouses some moments later. The car was last seen heading south, perhaps out of the city."

"And Zherdev is confirmed among the dead?" asked Kanashiro.

Nakanashi nodded. "I am afraid so."

"Pity." The death of Grisha Zherdev, one of Tateos Gadjoyan's senior people, was unfortunate, in that Kanashiro had seen the man as being more open to negotiation than his employer. Kanashiro had given thought to eliminating Gadjoyan in the hopes that Zherdev might be elevated within the remaining organization, but that now was a moot point.

Such is the cost of business.

"Higashi and Fumoto tracked this pair to an abandoned building on the outskirts of Naha," Nakanashi continued, "into which they took what we at first thought was one of Jimura's men. It's possible this man was actually a member of the Japanese Self-Defense Forces."

Kanashiro wasn't expecting this. "Intelligence Command?"

"It appears so. We've heard rumors about undercover agents within some of the more prominent organizations on the island, including Jimura's and even our own. Of course, we've never found anything to indicate that's the case with us, but one can't be too careful."

"No, one can't." Every group of any decent size was subject to infiltration by unwanted parties, Kanashiro knew, just as he was aware that his own operation wasn't immune to such acts. "What happened?"

Nakanashi's expression soured. "They apparently interrogated this man. Higashi and Fumoto found his body. There's no way to know what Zherdev's people may have learned before killing him." He shifted in his seat, uncomfortable with the topic. Nakanashi had never been one for violence or confrontation, and Kanashiro had always known him to be a gentle, humble man. It was but one of the many traits he admired about his friend and trusted assistant.

"If they learned he was with the defense forces," Kanashiro said, "that would mean they either hold no concerns about potential repercussions, or they're just stupid." Either possibility invited its own set of problems, he knew. His only regret was that if the dead man actually was a spy working for the defense forces, then he had been denied a chance to get vital information about the inner workings of Miroji Jimura's organization. His rival was a secretive man, and that confidentiality extended through every tenet of his various businesses and dealings. Obtaining information as an outsider was difficult, as Kanashiro knew all too well, but not impossible. He had managed to insert a small handful of informants into Jimura's operations over the past couple of years. Even then, details were hard to gather, given the compartmentalization and insulation of the man's various dealings. There could be no denying that Jimura's methods were very effective, in that they resulted in very few leaks, and often succeeded in exposing moles and spies. One of Kanashiro's plants had been discovered this way. That the man had disappeared and likely met an unfortunate end had troubled Kanashiro for a time, but the risks had been understood by all parties.

The business, he reminded himself.

Kanashiro heard new footsteps behind him and didn't turn as one of Nakanashi's assistants moved into view. He said nothing, but only stopped before the table and offered Kanashiro a bow before handing Nakanashi a piece of folded paper. The older man waved away the assistant and opened the paper, and Kanashiro saw his trusted friend's expression darken as he read its contents.

"What?" prompted Kanashiro.

Clearing his throat, Nakanashi adjusted his sunglasses. "Higashi and Fumoto. Their car was found north of Naha. They apparently were run off the road." He paused, swallowing again. "Both of them are dead. Fumoto was shot in the head."

"Shot?" Kanashiro didn't like to hear about gunplay on the streets. Such incidents without fail attracted the attention of law enforcement, who always were eager to tie any shootings to organizations such as his own. "How?"

"I don't yet have all the details," replied Nakanashi, "but there are reports of a chase through one of the city's outlying districts."

Kanashiro leaned forward in his chair. "What about the other car? Was it Zherdev's men?"

"We think so. They fled the area, so there's no way to know where they are now. As for Higashi and Fumoto, their bodies were recovered by the police. Like the others we lost this morning, neither of them should have been carrying anything which might tie back to us."

Slapping the table with the flat of his hand, Kanashiro pushed himself out of his chair and began to pace the length of the garden's stone pavilion. "Ridiculous." Though the loss of two dependable men was, of course, regrettable, the cold truth was that Higashi and Fumoto could be replaced. Of greater importance was the potential for attracting unwanted scrutiny from the police or the self-defense forces, or even the American military if their investigation into the morning's events led them in this direction. That would be a most unfortunate turn of events, particularly now, as Kanashiro was preparing to take even bolder, more decisive action than what had transpired earlier this morning.

"We didn't have anyone else to send," Nakanashi said. "You had me send ten men to watch after some of Jimura's other people."

Kanashiro, still irritated by the news about Higashi and Fumoto, placed his hands on his hips. "Our woman inside Jimura's house says he's up to something today. All she knows is that she thinks it's another hit to secure more American military weapons. Whatever it is, Jimura's been focused on it for a while."

"It's well known that he has no love for the Americans." Pausing, Nakanashi removed his sunglasses. "You don't think he'd stage a hit or an attack?"

"No," Kanashiro said, gesturing as though waving away the idea. "That is not Jimura's way. He's much too smart to do something like that. Any direct action against American targets, especially their military, would be met with immediate retribution. They would suspect him, me, and anyone else who ever voiced an anti-American sentiment." A list of such people would be rather long, he knew. Still, despite whatever one might think of the slumbering beast that was the American military machine, its reputation for efficiency and destruction once provoked was well known. History had shown that much.

"He's up to something else," Kanashiro said. "We just need to be patient, and let him show us. Perhaps it's another situation where we can benefit once he and his people do all of the hard, dangerous work." As far as he was concerned, Miroji Jimura's time had passed. He and the aged, feeble "business leaders" who were his contemporaries had fashioned themselves a tidy little fiefdom here on Okinawa. Each was content to operate within areas which had been designated via mutual understanding. While that might limit confrontations and feuds between groups, it also served to maintain a status quo that brought with it no real upward mobility.

Along with two or three other younger, more spirited venturers into this well-established realm, Kanashiro wasn't content to subsist on whatever meager slice of the action the elders deigned to give him. He wanted more. In truth, he wanted it all, but he was willing to play a longer, patient game in order to achieve his goals. It was that lack of deliberate strategy that had undermined his other, younger counterparts, who each had tried to go too far too fast. Their unbridled zeal had cost them, but Kanashiro refused to fall into that trap. Still, new blood, new ideas, and new courage were needed if the real money was to be made, and that meant expanding his business beyond the confines of Okinawa. He knew that Jimura and a few of the other, older bosses possessed contacts and business partners around the world. Tapping into that network was vital to Kanashiro's long-term success, but to impress a man like Tateos Gadjoyan he first had to demonstrate to the European arms dealer that his continuing relationship with Jimura was a mistake. The raid Kanashiro had orchestrated should at least set those wheels into motion. Once Jimura's weaknesses were exposed, making a case to Gadjoyan would be a far simpler task.

We shall see.

If Kanashiro could pull off another raid that garnered him more American military hardware, and do so in a way that put Jimura at risk while leaving him free, it would go even further toward solidifying Kanashiro's standing on the island. At the same time, it would do greater, perhaps irrevocable damage to Jimura.

Kanashiro smiled, pleased with this notion.

Such is the cost of business.

• • •

"Where the hell is everybody?"

Walking the length of the armory's open work area and noting the numerous unoccupied desks and general lack of noise or anything else that might signify productivity, Dale Connelly shook his head in amusement.

"You know how it is, Top," said Sergeant Martin Holt, from where he sat at his desk along the far bulkhead. "Give us an excuse to throw a party, and we're going to run with it. If we don't hear about this shindig on the news, I'll be pretty disappointed." Like Connelly, the sergeant wore a smartly pressed green-and-brown camouflage utility uniform. The sleeves of his uniform top were rolled to a point above his elbows, and his trousers were bloused over a pair of shined black leather combat boots.

As he approached the younger Marine, Connelly gestured toward the paperwork on his desk. "What are you working on?"

"The last of the LTI reports," replied Holt, referring to the limited technical inspections the unit had performed the previous day as part of their regular maintenance duties. "Once they're done, I'll give them to you for a final once-over and the captain's signature. Then I can run them over to headquarters before we secure for the day."

Connelly nodded. "Sounds like a plan." The unit's commanding officer, Captain Thomas Blair, was a stickler for procedures and rules, but he as much as anyone wanted to get out of here this afternoon in order to join in the festivities. "Let's make sure everything's covered and aligned," he said, employing the close-order-drill term referring to proper intervals for troops in formation and especially when standing for an inspection. "The skipper promised two bottles of twelve-year-old scotch if we got everything done before the party starts." He smiled. "I'd hate to give him an easy out."

"Aye, aye, Top."

Connelly left the sergeant to his work and turned toward his office. He was halfway there when he heard his phone ring. It had rung a third time before he could reach it.

"Ordnance," he said into the receiver. "Master Gunnery Sergeant Connelly speaking. How may I help you?"

"Is your door closed?"

The question made Connelly frown. "Excuse me?"

"Close your office door," said a man on the other end of the line. "You want privacy." Connelly detected a faint accent. A local?

Unsure of what to make of this, Connelly said, "Look, I don't know who . . ."

"We have your wife and children. Do as I say or they die. Close your door!"

His heart felt like it might crawl into his throat. Connelly complied with the order. The motion made him look out the window that was behind his desk, which gave him a view of the parking lot adjacent to the armory and the supply building next door. Was someone watching him from one of the cars out there?

"Okay," he said. "I've closed the door." He heard the tremor in his voice and scolded himself to remain composed. "Who are you? What do you want?"

"No questions," the voice snapped. "You help us today. Do what we say, we let your family go. Be a hero, and they die. Understand?"

Connelly felt his grip tightening on the receiver. "I understand." Then, in a moment of hope, he asked, "How do I know you're telling me the truth?"

The man said nothing into the phone, but he heard his voice shout something, which was followed by another male voice barking an unintelligible command, and then a female voice crying.

"Dale!"

Oh my god.

There was more barking away from the phone before the man's voice returned. "Happy now?"

"Look, I don't . . ."

"Shut up," the unknown man snapped. "Just listen. Do as you're told, don't make trouble, and nothing happens to them. Otherwise? Not good for them. Maybe not kill them right away, though."

Gritting his teeth at the unspoken suggestion, Connelly forced himself to focus on the man's voice. Definitely Japanese or Okinawan, but who was this person? Did he know him? Was it somebody he had pissed off?

"Why me?"

"Don't worry about that. Okay, time for you to work. First thing? Look in your locker."

"My what?" Had he heard the man right? Connelly squeezed his eyes shut. "I'm sorry. I'm not sure I . . ."

"Your locker."

Connelly maneuvered around his desk to the locker in his office's rear corner and opened it. The two doors swung aside and he stepped back, his eyes widening in horror. Inside the locker, his skin ashen, was the lifeless body of Tom Wade.

"What the hell?"

"Keep your voice down," barked the man on the phone.

"Did you do this?" Stepping forward, Connelly pressed his fingers to the side of Wade's throat. Of course, his friend was dead; that much should have been obvious, if not from his skin then by the sick angle at which his head lolled to one side of his bruised neck.

"Find place to hide him before he starts to smell. Be careful. We don't want you to get caught."

• • •

From where he stood beneath the canopy of trees that served to conceal his position, Jack took his turn with the binoculars and studied the house. At first glance it looked like nothing more than a typical residence: a traditional single-story structure sitting in the middle of a glade, with a small pond just visible on the meadow's far side. The grass around the home was well manicured, as was the assortment of hedges, trees, and other plants and bushes that lined the low cinder block walls—perhaps five feet in height—running behind and to the sides of the house. As for the home itself, thick round wood columns rising from the front porch supported the sloped roof, which was shingled with red clay tiles. Large bay windows dominated the house's front wall, and through the binoculars Jack could see through one or two of the portals and the adjacent windows facing the backyard wall and pond. He also noted the bars that were mounted inside each window's frame.

"They've got some security, at least," he said. From the looks of things. There was no way from this distance to determine the strength of the front door.

"Lots of open ground," said Samuel Yeager from where he stood behind Jack's left shoulder, leaning against a tree. He had donned an olive-drab American military-issue harness over his black long-sleeve shirt. The harness and the belt to which it was connected were festooned with a pair of magazine pouches, two canteens, a first-aid kit, and a large Ka-Bar knife of the sort favored by U.S. Marines.

To Jack's right, Amorah Banovich added, "That wall helps a

bit, if we approach from the sides."

Pondering both observations, Jack considered the possibility of sentries posted at points around the house, or even in the trees encircling the property. There was only one narrow, gravel path leading through the woods from the road, and Jack couldn't believe that was being left unmonitored. Still, he detected no movement or other signs of activity outside the house.

"If they're trying to maintain a low profile," said Yeager, "they'll keep their people close to the house and out of sight. Just because we can't see them doesn't mean they're not there."

Jack opted not to reply to the statement. His own training and experience had already provided him with several scenarios as to how the house might be defended, but he was worried that offering such insights might make him appear as more than the simple former Russian infantry soldier that was in keeping with his cover identity.

"How did you know about this place?" asked Banovich.

Yeager replied, "We've had people watching Kanashiro's operations for a while now. He's got a handful of safe houses and warehouses and whatnot around the island, but this is one of the ones that seems to get used a lot." He shrugged. "It's out of the way, but not too far from Naha, which lets him make use of the port and airport. He has people from both on his payroll. We know he's hoping to make a move against other groups, including Jimura. His problem is that he's young and not as patient. He wants it all and he wants it fast. That makes him prone to mistakes."

Moving the binoculars so that he could look toward the rear of the property, he studied the smaller structure in the backyard, its rear wall resting against the retaining wall running along that area of the plot. The structure was painted and shingled in the same manner as the house. Jack figured it for a garage or similar outbuilding. Backed up to one side of the building was a white cargo van, which to Jack looked identical to the one he had seen hours earlier.

"That has to be the same truck," he said. Another moment's observation yielded no signs of activity around the van or the building, so Jack shifted back to the front of the house. There were two cars parked in front, each a standard-sized sedan.

"Between the cars and the van," said Yeager, "figure on at least a dozen men between the two buildings. Maybe fifteen."

It was a decent estimate, Jack thought. There was no way to know how many men had accompanied the van from Naha, or if other men were already here to meet it. "Okay," he said, looking first to Banovich and then Yeager. "It's your call. What do you want to do?"

Pushing away from the tree, Yeager moved to stand next to them. "We split into two teams, and circle around so that we can approach from the sides." He gestured toward the house. "No windows, but I also figure if we maneuver into position using the trees for cover, we might be able to catch any lookouts off guard."

It wasn't a bad plan, Jack concluded, though it did carry elements of risk. "Shouldn't we wait until dark to try this? We'd have better concealment."

Yeager shook his head. "No time for that. Jimura-san wants this done quickly." He nodded toward the house. "Besides, if the stuff is here, then Kanashiro plans to move it quickly; most likely before nightfall, so we have to go in now." He turned to look at Banovich and Jack. "No survivors."

That gave Jack pause. There had already been at least one unnecessary death this morning. Tadashi Enogawa's face still haunted his thoughts, after all. What if there were other undercover agents embedded within Kanashiro's organization, as was the case with Jimura? How would they react to the assault that was coming? Would they engage, seek cover, or even try to escape? What if, for fear of blowing their own cover, they took up arms and fought alongside the rest of Kanashiro's men?

Then it's them or you.

It was a callous realization, but it also was the only one Jack had

Dale Connelly grabbed the phone on the first ring.

"Ordnance. Master Gunner . . ."

"I know who you are," said the voice Connelly had come to loathe. "Did you finish it?"

Connelly felt his stomach heave at the very mention of what he had been forced to do. "Yes, it's done," he said, biting down on each word.

With no one in the armory, he had been forced to seal the body of Gunnery Sergeant Thomas Wade in plastic trash bags wrapped with duct tape. The task was made even more difficult by the man's body having started to stiffen with rigor mortis, after it had been stuffed into Connelly's wall locker. Also, the poor bastard's bowels had emptied, soiling his uniform trousers and requiring Connelly to douse the locker and his office with disinfectant and air freshener. After preparing Wade's body with the bags and tape, he had hoisted his friend over one shoulder and moved him to the rows of storage crates at the back of the armory. It had taken some doing, but he had found a suitable container to conceal the dead Marine, covering him with foam insulation and other packing materials. He had then stacked a pair of smaller boxes atop the crate.

"It won't take long for someone to find him," he said, gripping the phone receiver hard enough that he felt his fingers beginning to tingle.

"After tomorrow, it won't matter," said the man on the other end. "Now, you go get your car."

"My car? Why?"

"No questions," the man snapped. "You drive. North on fifty-eight."

Connelly frowned. "Where am I . . . ?"

"You find out soon enough. You have two minutes to get in your car." The line went dead, and Connelly pulled the receiver from his ear, looking at it. He returned it to its cradle just as there was a knock on his door.

"It's open," he said, rising from his chair as the door opened to reveal Sergeant Holt. The younger Marine poked his head inside.

"I have the LTI reports for you, Top." He held up a file folder.

Connelly reached for the camouflage uniform cover and car keys sitting in the wooden letter tray positioned at the corner of his desk. "Just throw them on my desk. I have to step out for a bit." He felt a lump forming in his throat, but forced himself to maintain his composure as he exited the office and began walking at a brisk pace for the armory's front door.

"Something up?" asked Holt.

"Admin." Connelly forced a sigh. "Some crap about needing to sign some papers they missed yesterday. It's retirement stuff, so it's now or never." While a weak story, it was the best he could do off the top of his head.

Holt grimaced. "You going to be back for the party?"

Not breaking stride, Connelly tossed a wave over his shoulder. "Count on it."

Assuming I'm not dead in an hour.

The Toyota sedan was sitting in his assigned spot outside the armory, and though it looked undisturbed Connelly saw the unfamiliar object sitting on the passenger seat even before he inserted his key into the car's driver-side door lock. It was a mobile phone, one of those newer model "bag phones" with its own battery and a plug to feed off a car's cigarette lighter. Without turning his head, Connelly tried to examine the surrounding parking lot for signs he was being watched, but saw nothing.

Bastards.

It wasn't until he was away from the armory and through the air station's front gate, traveling north from Futenma along Highway 58, that the phone rang. It took him a moment to fumble with the unit with his left hand while keeping his eyes on the road, but he wrestled the receiver free from its cradle and brought it to his ear, feeling the phone's coiled cord stretching taut.

"Hello?"

"Just keep driving," said the same voice. "I call you again when you get close to where you're going."

"What about my family?" asked Connelly, hearing his voice shake. "Are they all right? I'm cooperating with you. Please don't hurt them." Even as he spoke the words, he thought of his friend Tom Wade. It was obvious these people had no problems with killing, but his wife and children? Would they really go that far?

"Keep doing what you're doing, and they'll be fine. Watch your driving. Don't need you getting in wreck."

Connelly's eyes widened as he realized the implications of the warning. Of course they were following him. He looked to the rearview mirror, seeing at least a dozen cars in the highway's two northbound lanes. Any one of them could be his tormentors. Hell, they could all be following him, for all he knew.

"Can I talk to them?" he asked.

The man grunted something Connelly didn't understand, before replying, "No. And don't try calling anyone else. We'll know. Just drive. We'll call." Then there was a click, and the mystery caller was gone. Connelly returned the phone to its cradle, eyeing the device an extra moment. Then a car horn startled him and he jerked the car's steering wheel back to the left, narrowly avoiding a head-on collision with a cargo truck in the oncoming lane.

Damn it!

"Drive," Connelly told himself, feeling the blood forced from both hands as he held the steering wheel in a death grip. "Just drive."

• • •

Standing on the porch, Yasuo Emura inhaled deeply, enjoying the drag on his cigarette. Holding the smoke in his lungs for an extra moment, he released it in a thin plume and watched it dissipate in the slight breeze. He stifled a yawn, checking his watch and grimacing at the time. The day had begun just after midnight, and after twelve hours it was already feeling long. It would be several more hours yet before he and the rest of the crew could even consider calling their work done. That only made Emura more irritable.

Just get me out of here by six. It was Ladies Night at his favorite bar in Okinawa-shi, which was also a popular hangout for locals and Americans from the nearby air base. According to the calendar, the military personnel had been paid a couple of days earlier, and the younger, single ones would be looking to part with too much of their money. Several of the American units had departed the island a week or so earlier for training exercises in Korea or the Philippines—Emura couldn't remember which—and that meant a pack of bored military wives looking to dress up and have a good time. They were always such easy marks, or at the very least provided an entertaining distraction.

He was hungry, but the crew had already savaged the meager contents of the kitchen since arriving earlier this morning. Lunch was another reason to head back to town, but Emura knew that leaving now would only irritate Eiji Hazato, the group leader. There was a schedule to keep, after all. Emura looked to where the truck sat, ready to go. Another trip back to Naha was in the offing, and he knew that would likely keep him busy for the rest of the day. With luck, Hazato would let him go after that, and he could get on with preparing for some serious partying. Emura couldn't help but smile at the thought of the beautiful blond American women he would meet, with their ridiculous dancing after they had too many overpriced and watered-down drinks. Easy marks, and easy money. Emura smiled.

Finishing his cigarette, he ground the butt against the house's cinder block wall before tossing it toward the yard, which was still damp from the morning rain. He wiped his forehead with his hand, feeling the perspiration on his fingers.

It was already too hot, and would only get hotter before the afternoon sun broke for the day.

Emura was turning to head back to into the house when he caught a glimpse of sunlight reflecting off something. A look toward the cinder block wall on the house's west side obscured his view of the surrounding trees, but not enough to mask the movement of something dark. Turning in that direction, he squinted in an attempt to get a better look, and caught movement between two overgrown thickets.

"What are you doing?" called a voice behind him, at the precise instant Emura saw a figure moving around the trunk of a large tree, not twenty meters away.

• • •

"Yeager, wait!"

Jack hissed the warning just as Samuel Yeager let the first round fly, his Beretta pistol's discharge muffled to little more than a metallic snap thanks to the sound suppressor fixed to its barrel. The single shot, from at least forty feet, was on target, taking the man on the porch just above his left eye. Yeager hadn't seen the second man, who had chosen the wrong moment to step out of the house and now was a witness to the death of his companion.

"Son of a bitch." Jack brought up his own suppressed Glock and tried to take aim as the second man stumbled backward toward the house. The pistol bucked in his hands and Jack saw the bullet drill into door where the man's head had been an instant earlier. Then shouts rumbled from inside the house.

"Everybody move in," said Yeager into the walkie-talkie clipped to his equipment harness before charging out from the concealment provided by the treeline and heading for the house. It had taken the group—Yeager and his four men, along with Jack, Banovich, Rauf Alkaev, and Manish Pajari—nearly fifteen minutes to spread themselves around the perimeter. Using the surrounding trees to conceal their movements, they searched for signs of guard patrols or other watchful sentries. They had encountered no one in the woods, bolstering Jack's hope that anyone they had to face would either be in the house or the neighboring outbuilding.

Guess we're going to find out, one way or the other.

"Come on," Jack said, tapping Amorah Banovich on her shoulder as he set off after Yeager. The three of them had maneuvered into position on the house's west side, which was free of windows. The lone man smoking a cigarette had been the only sign of life, and Banovich had tried to get Yeager to just let the guy go back inside before making any attempt to advance on the house. Jack had voiced his own support of the idea. It was the better tactical play, as it preserved their element of surprise at least for a short while longer.

Yeager had ignored their advice, and now here they were, charging across open ground in broad daylight. Their targets had been alerted to their presence and were likely preparing to repel the impromptu assault.

Idiot's going to get us killed!

Staying low and utilizing the cinder block retaining wall to mask his approach, Jack ran straight for the house, sacrificing for speed any chance he might have as a moving target. Banovich ran beside him, matching him step for step while keeping more than an arm's length between them. Both of them were forced to jump over or sidestep holes or ruts in the uneven ground, and as they drew closer Jack heard more shouts of warning and confusion. He figured they had perhaps ten seconds remaining to them before someone in the house got their act together and started deploying firepower.

"Stefan! There!"

Hearing Banovich's warning and seeing her pointing toward the house at the same time, Jack noted a figure to his right, exiting the house from a rear door. Only the man's head, bald on top with close-cropped black hair on the sides, was visible over the retaining wall, but Jack also saw the barrel of a rifle aiming at an angle toward the sky. It took him only an instant to recognize it as an M16, or at least some variant of the assault rifle. Yeager saw the new threat, too, and he sprinted toward the wall away from the rear of the house, angling to keep from the other man's view.

Jack and Banovich reached the wall just as a second Okinawan man, this one more heavyset than his companion, barreled through the house's rear door and onto the back porch. In his meaty right hand was a large caliber pistol. From its shape and size, Jack figured it for a Desert Eagle, a powerful handgun that could do serious damage if its wielder had any idea what he was doing.

It was Banovich who'd opted against giving him that opportunity. Rising up so that she could aim over the top of the retaining wall, she let loose with three quick rounds from her Glock. At least two struck the big man in the chest. Jack saw his body react to the shots, and the Desert Eagle barked as the man's finger convulsed on the trigger. A .50 caliber round punched into the side of the house before he dropped facefirst onto the porch. The man with the M16 was turning in their direction and bringing the weapon around to take aim, but Jack was faster. He fired two rounds into the rifleman's head, sending him stumbling backward off the porch and collapsing into the mud.

Other shots were ringing out around the area now, and Jack could make out the suppressed weapons from the assault group, interspersed with shots coming from the house or immediately outside it. On the far side of the house, Jack caught sight of Alkaev and Pajari advancing with two of Yeager's men on the buildings. There were more shouts coming from inside the house now, and as Jack studied the structure, his eyes fell on the lines running from one corner of the house to a pair of poles at the mouth of the gravel driveway leading out of the front yard.

Damn it. How did I not see that sooner?

Had he been distracted by Yeager's premature triggering of the assault? Maybe, but that was no excuse. It was a rookie mistake on his part, one for which he would have chewed out any of his men if this were a Special Forces op. There had been time during their earlier survey to identify the power and phone lines. Of course, the plan at the time had been to approach by stealth and take out everyone in the house before any of the bad guys could react to being ambushed.

The best laid plans, and all that.

"Cover me," he said, closing his left eye as he took aim at the point where the lines connected to the house. He fired three rounds and one of the lines fell free, and a fourth shot took care of its companion.

Banovich nodded in approval. "Power and phone. Good thinking, Stefan."

"Come on," called Yeager, and Jack looked over to see the man bracing his back against the retaining wall at its far end. "We've got to hit them while they're still confused." He punctuated his remark by pushing off from the wall and stepping around it, pistol aimed out in front of him.

"Let's go." Arms extended and with both hands cradling his Glock, Jack maneuvered around the edge of the retaining wall, ignoring the sounds of gunfire from the other side of the house and searching for immediate threats. Training and experience guided his movements, ensuring he swept the area ahead with eyes and weapon and never lingering too long on any one fixed point. He forced himself to take deep breaths, not allowing the rush and stress of the moment to cloud his vision. He heard Banovich moving behind him, and as he swept from side to side he caught glimpses of her mimicking his movements.

The Glock's barrel moved past the front of the cargo truck backed up to the entrance of the outbuilding and Jack started looking for anything closer to the house. He sensed movement to his right before he saw it. Feet on the ground just behind the truck slipped in the mud, and Jack dropped to one knee an instant before the man, another Okinawan, appeared from around the vehicle's far side. He was wielding a shotgun, but its barrel was pointing at the ground when his eyes fell upon the intruders in his midst. Jack fired twice just as the man was starting to raise his weapon. Both rounds took him high in the chest, pushing him back against the truck's front bumper. Banovich's Glock coughed once, putting a bullet into the man's head and dropping him for good.

"Stefan!"

Something to his left caught Jack's eye just as Banovich snapped her warning, and he shifted to see another man charging through the house's rear door. He was holding an M16 and struggling to bring the weapon to his shoulder and take aim. Jack's first shot was just to the right as he brought the pistol around and the bullet splintered the doorjamb. It was still enough to make the man flinch, giving Jack time to adjust his aim, but before he could shoot there was more weapons fire from inside the house. The Okinawan's body twitched as rounds struck him in the back and he pitched forward, tripping over his own feet and falling from the porch.

Yeager appeared in the doorway, Beretta grasped in both hands, and put a final round in the fallen man's head. Looking up from his work, he nodded toward Jack and Banovich, his expression flat.

"Clear."

• • •

Yeager and his men were efficient enough, Jack observed. Even with the assault's rocky start, the group had made short work of the raid, dispatching eleven men in less than two minutes and suffering no casualties. A sweep of the area revealed that ten of the eleven men were dead. The lone survivor had taken a single shot to the stomach, and Jack and Banovich had attempted to dress the wound with bandages from the first aid kit on Yeager's equipment harness. Despite their efforts, Jack could see that the injury would end up being fatal if the man didn't receive immediate medical treatment.

"My guys have finished their sweep," said Yeager as he walked to where Jack and Banovich stood near the cargo truck and the outbuilding. Banovich had found a faucet and they were using its slow stream of water to wash the blood from their hands. "No sign of anybody hiding out."

"Did they find anything interesting?" asked Banovich.

Yeager shook his head. "We collected the individual weapons, IDs, and a few other things, but nothing of any real value."

Checking his watch, Jack said, "We can't stay here. Somebody had to have heard the shots."

"You're right," replied Yeager. "If someone called this in, then we've got ten, maybe fifteen minutes to be gone before the police show up."

"There's nothing in there," said Banovich, gesturing to the truck and the shed. "A couple of cases of the rifles, but that's it. If the rest of the shipment even made it out here, it's gone." She scowled. "No sign of our money, either."

Yeager rested his forearms on the magazine pouches affixed to the front of his gear belt. "We'll take whatever's left. Call it a peace offering for Jimura-san."

"What about the men?" asked Jack, wiping his wet hands on his trousers. "Are we sure they're all Kanashiro's?"

Regarding him with skepticism, Yeager asked, "What do you mean?"

Jack glanced first to Banovich before replying, "We found out this morning that the Japanese military has agents embedded within Jimura's organization. They're obviously trying to build a case against him. If what you say about Kanashiro is true and he's trying to muscle out Jimura, then it makes sense that the JSDF would have agents in his group, too."

"Why didn't you say something about this before now?"

"Because we didn't trust you," said Banovich. "Besides, I can't believe Jimura doesn't suspect moles and spies within his network. Do you trust all of your men?"

For the first time since well before the assault, Yeager smiled. "I don't trust anybody. Point taken."

After ordering his men to load whatever could be found in the cargo truck and with Banovich directing Alkaev and Pajari to help with that effort, Yeager led her and Jack back into the house, where the lone survivor of the raid lay sprawled on a couch. One of Yeager's men stood watch nearby, his pistol in his hand. The bandage Jack and Banovich had applied to the wounded man's stomach was already dark red, and blood was seeping around its edges. His breathing fast and shallow, the man's complexion had turned pale and he was sweating.

He's not going to make it, Jack realized.

"Where's the rest of the stuff?" asked Yeager without preamble as he moved to stand before the man. When the Okinawan didn't answer, Yeager kicked his foot, which elicited a grunt of pain from the man. "Where are our guns and money?"

Swallowing, the man didn't lift his head from the couch.

"Gone. Moved. Two hours ago."

"Where?"

A raspy cough escaped the man's lips, and he reached up to wipe his mouth. "North. Motobu, or maybe Nakijin."

Glancing to Jack and Banovich, Yeager said, "They're towns north of Kadena, up on the coast."

"Motobu," whispered the wounded man. "I think I heard . . . someone . . . Motobu."

Yeager nodded. "I think I know the place he means." Without saying anything else, he drew his suppressed Beretta and put two quick rounds in the other man's chest. Then, with the same casual air one might use to invite them to lunch, he turned to Jack and Banovich. "Let's go."

His eyes lingering on the dead man, Jack forced himself not to offer any emotional reaction. This situation was continuing to circle the drain, and he was no closer to finding a way to contact his CIA handlers. Were they even still looking for him, or had they written him off? Did they think he was dead, or that his cover had been blown? How much longer did he have before they pulled the plug on the operation and cut their losses?

Cohen wouldn't leave him twisting in the wind. Jack didn't know about anyone else, whether they were here on the island or back at Langley, but he was certain Abigail Cohen would not abandon him so long as there was breath in her body.

You willing to bet your life on that, Jack?

Yes. He trusted Cohen. His faith in her was absolute. The question was, did she feel the same way about him?

"Stefan," said Banovich from behind him, and Jack turned from the dead Okinawan to see her standing at the entrance to the hallway that would take them to the rear of house. "Are you coming?"

Jack nodded. "Where else do I have to go?"

So far as Tateos Gadjoyan was concerned, it was never too early to gaze upon beautiful women.

Such was the case at just past 7:00 in the morning, as he entered Zanzi, his members-only all-hours club that existed—as Gadjoyan liked to describe it—outside the realm of the world beyond its walls. The first person to greet him was Meline, one of the club's servers, who stood just inside the foyer holding a tray upon which sat his morning beverage of choice, a triple espresso. Like the rest of the waitstaff, she was a physically fit and attractive young woman in her early twenties, dressed in the standard server's uniform of a black bikini bottom that left little to the imagination. He had received many compliments from his regular customers on this particular aesthetic choice, which harmonized with the overall serene atmosphere he had worked to cultivate here.

"Good morning, Mister Gadjoyan," said Meline, smiling as she lifted the tray toward him.

Despite the troubled emotions roiling within him, Gadjoyan retrieved the cup. "Good morning, my dear. As always, you are even more dependable than the very sun itself." It wasn't the first time he had complimented her on her astonishing devotion and attention to detail, and the praise was well-earned. During her brief tenure of employment, Meline had become one of the club's most reliable workers. He didn't recall her missing even a single hour of work, and she often was among the first to volunteer for extra shifts during peak hours or special events.

"Is there anything I can do for you, sir?" Meline asked, lowering the tray.

"Just what you always do," he replied. "Take care of our guests."

Not a fool, Gadjoyan could tell from her demeanor and the way she always seemed to be within earshot even before he realized he wanted her that Meline had her own ideas regarding advancement. It was obvious she wasn't content to spend her life as a topless server, and in truth Gadjoyan thought she might well be ready for more responsibilities sooner rather than later. She would have to earn that opportunity, of course; there would be no shortcuts. Despite his appraising eye when it came to the lovely ladies in his midst, that was the limit of his admirations. He had learned at a very young age from his father that getting involved with an employee was unwise. Even without the personal entanglements, it was just bad for business.

Look, but don't touch.

Meline offered a parting smile before turning and heading off to see to some other task, leaving Gadjoyan to take in the scene as was his habit. Despite the early hour, Club Zanzi boasted a respectable breakfast audience. Gadjoyan noted several familiar faces at tables around the square pool that was the center of the room, and servers dressed in the same fetching swimsuit bottoms moved through the club, leaving no guest or request unattended. One girl was descending the stairs into the pool where a couple of regulars were already enjoying the soothing waters. Bright lamps positioned behind murals illuminated scenes of a lush tropical rain forest, and recessed speakers even provided a low-volume background audio simulation of a jungle environment in the form of animal sounds and a waterfall. The track was played on a constant loop regardless of the time of day, quiet enough not to seem intrusive. Numerous plants and ivy lattice-work clung to fake stone facades that helped to mask the room's regular square shape, adding to the illusion that one was navigating a winding path through the undergrowth.

"Mister Gadjoyan," said a male voice, and he turned to see his club manager, Jamar Lagunov, walking toward him. "It's good to see you again so soon."

Forcing a smile as they shook hands, Gadjoyan replied, "You know I can't stay away from here too long. This is my prize."

Of the three clubs he owned in Kiev, this was his favorite. Just walking through its well-guarded door was enough to ease the burdens he carried, if only for a while. Engineered so that anything beyond its walls did not intrude upon its environs to even the smallest degree, Zanzi was a luxury available to a very select clientele. It was far more exclusive even than Eros, the more conventional nightclub that occupied this building's first two aboveground floors. The fortunate few who had come to know the inside of this subterranean sanctuary harbored very particular tastes in everything from food to wine to companionship. Requests to enter this tantalizing realm were numerous and most were ignored. Every new member was approved—or revoked, as the case may be—by Gadjoyan himself, and once a membership was rescinded it was never reinstated, for any reason. Fees were expensive, no one who wasn't a member was allowed entry, and whatever transpired within these walls remained here. Penalties for violation of the club's sanctity were swift, severe, and even fatal on occasion, depending on the nature and extent of a given transgression. To that end, those who were granted admittance tended to protect that coveted status with extreme care, and Gadjoyan placed in Lagunov his trust to run the club and its attendant affairs with the same discretion and decisiveness he would employ himself. After five years as manager, Lagunov had yet to disappoint to even the slightest degree.

"I for one wish you'd come around more often," said Lagunov, and Gadjoyan watched him absentmindedly fidget with the cuffs of his dark blue silk shirt. "I miss our evening chess games. We received a new shipment of cigars and rum from Cuba, and I saved a small cache for our next rematch."

"Soon," Gadjoyan said. "Once I clear some lingering business out of the way."

Lagunov's smile vanished. "I heard about Grisha and the

others. I am sorry, Mister Gadjoyan. I know how fond you were of him."

"Thank you, Jamar." Gadjoyan offered him an appreciative nod. Even with the trust he had earned through his loyalty and work, Lagunov still insisted on formally addressing him even during their private conversations. It was his subtle way of showing unflagging respect, and Gadjoyan had long since given up trying to break him of the habit.

"It is a sad fact of our business, my friend," he said, gesturing for Lagunov to accompany him as he began a walking circuit around the pool's edge.

"Have you heard any more details?" asked Lagunov, walking to Gadjoyan's left and allowing his employer to enjoy the view closest to the pool.

Gadjoyan shook his head. "Not since last night." The satellite phone call from Amorah Banovich, Grisha Zherdev's second-in-command for the group he had sent almost a month ago on a roundabout trip from Kiev to Okinawa, had been heart wrenching, at least for a moment. He knew that his was a dangerous business, but it was still unfortunate to lose well-trained and loyal people. Disregarding any personal feelings he might have, it was time consuming to train people to fill the void left by such valuable resources.

As for Okinawa, that insignificant speck of an island in the Pacific Ocean, which his father had all but ignored during his leadership of the business, had become quite a lucrative investment of both time and money for Gadjoyan. His dealings with Miroji Jimura had been very profitable, with the elder Okinawan arms dealer able to secure the sort of American military weapons that eluded most of his competitors. His prices were reasonable, and Jimura held himself to an honor code that seemed to be common with those of his generation. Gadjoyan knew that Jimura had witnessed firsthand the United States military's invasion of his home, sweeping across the island on their way to total, final victory over Japan and an ending to the Second World War. Jimura made no secret of the fact that he held little regard for the Americans or their soldiers. He took personal satisfaction in doing anything to undermine their efforts, on Okinawa or anywhere else in the world where opportunity presented itself. It was as though the man was on a personal mission of vengeance, though Gadjoyan didn't see how such a battle could ever be won.

"Her first message was brief," he said, "in accordance with Grisha's instructions about avoiding lengthy calls to prevent being traced. Amorah thinks that a rival of Jimura's is responsible for the attack on our people, which I suppose is possible given that some of his people were killed, as well." They reached one end of the pool and he navigated the corner, nodding in greeting to one of the club's older members, who also ran what he called an "independent automotive parts acquisition enterprise." The man had proven himself a valuable ally on more than one occasion, resulting in his eventual admission to the Zanzi client list.

"Good morning, Mister Gadjoyan," the man said.

"Mister Nakovitch."

Another of the club's beautiful servers, whose name escaped Gadjoyan, was tending to Nakovitch, and he seemed most appreciative of the attention. Gadjoyan suspected that by the time he and Lagunov completed their circuit of the pool and walked past a second time, Nakovitch and his server would be gone, off to one of the private rooms where the club's menu of "additional services" was offered. Gadjoyan scoffed at the man's weakness, while at the same time welcoming the rather large sums of money paid to indulge it here on a regular basis.

We thank you for your patronage, Gadjoyan mused.

"Do you have any idea when you might expect to hear from Amorah again?" asked Lagunov.

"No." Checking his wristwatch, Gadjoyan did the math and realized it was early afternoon in Okinawa, seven hours ahead of local Kiev time. "I have to give her credit. It was her idea to approach Jimura about finding a way to salvage something of the original deal. That shows promise." He had expressed reluctance to the suggestion, at first, but Amorah had convinced him. "I always thought she was a natural for this business. She may well make a good replacement for someone like Grisha, one day."

Lagunov sighed. "Grisha will be a hard man to replace."

"Dear Grisha was like a son to me, but then again so are many who work for me." Gadjoyan shook his head. "When something like this happens, it is like a knife through my heart."

His father had tried to teach him the pitfalls of emotional investment in subordinates, but Gadjoyan had come to realize that leading an enterprise such as he did required more than simple fear to keep in line those who worked for him. People like Lagunov and Grisha Zherdev had earned unprecedented levels of trust from him, but Gadjoyan conferred such confidence on only a chosen few employees. Loyalty and respect were invaluable commodities in this line of work, and though it had taken him many years to understand the advantages and dangers of attempting to achieve such balance, Gadjoyan had found a way that worked for him.

He could be ruthless when circumstances warranted it, but he preferred to leave the more unpleasant aspects of discipline and retribution to his mid-tier leaders. Such things were far more prevalent in the lower levels of his organization, of course, but that was why his captains and lieutenants were so well paid. Even then, those sorts of incidents were rare. His managers hired good people, dealt with problem individuals quickly and quietly, and generally saw fit not to bother him with day-to-day minutiae. Gadjoyan could count on one hand the number of times he had taken direct, violent action in the past ten years against a deserving individual. Those were by a personal desire to see the proper retribution meted out by his own hand. He usually reserved such action for someone who had inflicted personal harm or emotional distress upon him.

Such would be the case, this morning.

"Where is he?" he asked.

"In the back," Lagunov replied, gesturing toward a door that led from the main floor and bore a sign marked EMPLOYEES ONLY.

"He's uninjured?"

"As you ordered." Lagunov led the way to the door. He entered a four-digit code into the keypad that was part of the door's lock, then pulled open the door so that Gadjoyan could pass through first. Once in the connecting hallway, Lagunov moved to another door marked PRIVATE and knocked twice.

"It's Lagunov," he said. "With the boss."

There was the sound of a lock disengaging, then the door opened inward and Gadjoyan stepped into the adjoining room. Holding the door was a muscular man with black hair slicked back and held in place with gel. His face and nose were flat, as though he had been pressed against a concrete wall since birth. Under his left arm, suspended in a shoulder holster worn over a taut collarless shirt, was a Makarov semiautomatic pistol, the standard sidearm for Russian military and police forces.

"This is Sero," said Lagunov. "One of our security men. He's totally reliable."

Nodding to the muscled man who closed the door behind them, Gadjoyan turned his full attention to the room's only other occupant. Handcuffed to an armless wooden chair, the man's hair and face were damp with perspiration, and his white undershirt stuck to his sweat-soaked torso. His khaki trousers were dirty, but there were no visible injuries or blood, and the man's expression was one of unfiltered terror.

"Tevan," said Gadjoyan by way of greeting, keeping his voice low and flat. "Of course, that's not your real name, though."

Drawing himself up as much as his restraints would allow, the other man said, "Mister Gadjoyan, there's been a mistake. I . . ."

Holding up a hand, Gadjoyan shook his head. "Don't. It's insulting for the both of us. I know who you are, Mister Daniel Boyce of the United States Central Intelligence Agency." Though the man might have been well trained in the art of espionage and resisting interrogation, the fleeting look of recognition and fear of discovery condemned him.

Crossing his arms, Gadjoyan stepped toward the man. "There's no need for any more lies, or for wasting any more time. Tell me what I want to know, and I promise a quick and merciful death for you. Very simply: Did you turn Grisha Zherdev against me? Did your masters pay him to be their lapdog?"

When the man said nothing, Gadjoyan held out his hand to Sero, who without need of further instruction removed the

Makarov pistol from its holster and extended it grip-first. Gadjoyan took the weapon and with practiced ease verified a round was chambered before he pointed it at Boyce's left thigh and fired.

The pistol's report was loud enough to make Gadjoyan blink but it wasn't sufficient to drown out Boyce's cry of shock and pain as a dark red stain appeared around the hole in his trouser leg and began spreading. His body jerked in the chair and his face screwed up in agony. Eyes closed, he clenched his jaw, drawing short, audible breaths.

"Of course, I already know this to be true," said Gadjoyan, raising his voice to be heard over Boyce's moans of pain. "Just as I know you are an undercover spy for your government. Who else have you infected? How many others in my family have you turned against me?" He didn't bother waiting for an answer but instead fired a second round, this time into Boyce's right thigh. Renewed cries of suffering bounced off the walls but Gadjoyan didn't care. The room was soundproofed; no one would hear Boyce's final moments.

"I loved Grisha like he was my own flesh and blood," Gadjoyan hissed, reaching out with his free hand to smack Boyce across the face. "You took him from me, poisoned his mind with your money and your whores and your filth. You overfed, pampered pigs, who look down on the rest of the world while you spend your days idolizing football players who murder their wives and send your soldiers off to die in wars your masters create for profit." Stepping forward, he grabbed a handful of Boyce's hair, jerking his head up so that he could glare into the man's eyes. "Who else have you corrupted? What about Grisha's men? Are any of them part of this?"

Even with what Gadjoyan suspected was incredible pain, Boyce said nothing. In doing so, he said everything.

There are others.

It was pointless to continue, Gadjoyan concluded. Boyce was likely too well conditioned to say anything, or perhaps he didn't know the identities of other turncoats or spies.

One final bullet through Daniel Boyce's forehead ended the interrogation. The echo of the pistol shot was still rolling across the room as Gadjoyan returned the weapon to Sero.

"What are you going to do now?" asked Lagunov.

Turning to the door and waiting for Sero to open it, Gadjoyan grunted in irritation, still stinging from the depths of this revealed betrayal. There was only one thing to do: find any other traitors lurking in his midst, and eliminate them.

"Amorah or someone with her might also be a part of this." The words tasted like acid in his mouth, deepening his anger as he marched into the hallway. "No. I couldn't possibly be so wrong about her."

Like you were with Grisha?

• • •

"We got another one."

Looking up from the reports on his desk, which were starting to blur together, anyway, Christopher Kurtz frowned at his partner. "Another what?"

"Shooting," said Jordan Aguilar, holding up a piece of paper as she crossed the squad room toward their desks. "Northeast of Naha. House in the middle of nowhere, but local law said there were reports of multiple shots for a couple of minutes, like a firefight."

Kurtz pushed back his chair as Aguilar passed him and dropped the paper in his lap on her way to her desk. "When?"

"Half hour ago, give or take." Reaching for her desk's bottom drawer, Aguilar retrieved her Beretta pistol in its holster and clipped it to her belt before shifting the weapon to her right hip. "Details are sketchy, but local law and JSDF are already on the scene." She gestured toward the paper Kurtz held. "Guess whose house it is."

His attention divided between his partner and the paper, it took him an extra second to note the address information. "Kanashiro? For real?" He lowered the report. "You thinking what I'm thinking?"

"No, you're thinking what I'm thinking." Aguilar smiled. "This is payback for this morning."

"Damned right." Kurtz had recognized the address on the

report, which he had placed on this desk atop the other files. He tapped the paper. "We've had surveillance on this place before. So has JSDF. It's a known hangout for a bunch of Kanashiro's boys. They go there to blow off steam and act stupid, apparently. Cards, hookers, campfire sing-alongs, Twister, whatever."

Aguilar wiggled her eyebrows. "Tell me more about the Twister."

"Sorry. I'm a Monopoly guy." Grabbing his own weapon from its lockbox in his desk, Kurtz secured the Beretta to his hip as he rose from his chair. "Come on. Let's go have a look." At this time of day, it likely would take them at least thirty minutes to make the transit to the crime scene. He hoped the local police and their good friends from the Japanese Self-Defense Forces wouldn't have everything bagged and tagged before he and Aguilar got down there.

"Hey, guys," said a new voice. This one belonged to Special Agent Nick Minecci, who was walking toward them and carrying a manila file folder. A short but brawny man, Minecci looked to Kurtz like a fire hydrant dressed in khaki pants and a dark blue knit shirt with the NCIS logo over the left breast pocket. His shaved scalp was as reddened as the rest of his face and his forearms, testifying to the time he had spent in the hot midday sun, but it was his dour expression that caught Kurtz's attention.

"Uh-oh," said Kurtz. "I know that look."

Minecci nodded. "Yeah, it's one of those. Naha Police found a body in an abandoned auto garage on the outskirts, down in the old industrial district that's gone all to hell? Anyway, JSDF identified the guy as one of their own." Opening the file folder, he looked at the top page of whatever document it contained. "Tadashi Enogawa."

"Enogawa?" repeated Aguilar, her eyes widening in shock. "Really?"

His expression growing even more somber, Minecci asked, "You know him?"

Kurtz nodded. "Yeah. He was working undercover inside Jimura's operation. Been in place about a year. He was part of the joint task force between us and JSDF, helping try to prove that Jimura's been trafficking in American military hardware."

A sick feeling in his stomach made him frown. "Damn. He was a good guy. One of their best agents. Even though we really don't know that much about Jimura's inner circle, whatever we do know—Enogawa fed it to us."

"Damn," Minecci whispered. "Sorry, man. I didn't know."

"His identity was a secret," said Aguilar. "Not that it matters, now."

Minecci held up the folder. "JSDF had been looking for him all morning. He was at the warehouse for the exchange, and went missing after the shootout. According to the medical examiner's preliminary report at the scene, he was found tied to a chair, and he'd been tortured before somebody executed him." He sighed. "As you can imagine, JSDF is pretty pissed."

"Let our contact over there know we're working a new lead," said Kurtz. "They're welcome to join us." There was no way he was going to tell their JSDF counterparts that they couldn't help investigate the murder of one of their own. Besides, he and Aguilar could use all the help anyone wanted to offer.

"You got it," said Minecci before heading off to his desk to make the appropriate phone calls and leaving Kurtz and Aguilar to head for the door.

"If Jimura really did call for a hit against Kanashiro," said Aguilar as she walked beside him, "we could be about five minutes from all-out war between the two camps."

"Yeah. Won't *that* be fun?" Pushing on the door leading outside, Kurtz led the way as they both walked into the midday Okinawa sun.

He had to wonder what else they were walking into.

Trouble, Kurtz mused. Nothing but trouble.

• • •

The phone rang again.

Keeping his right hand on the steering wheel and his eyes on the fast-moving traffic around him, Dale Connelly fumbled for the car phone. He almost dropped the receiver as he pulled it from the unit's carrying bag.

"Hello?" he asked, once more cursing himself for how

frightened he sounded. His mouth and throat were dry, and he couldn't seem to generate any spit. A canteen or a bottle of water would be a blessing right now, but he knew that stopping for any reason was out of the question.

"You doing good," said the voice with broken English that made Connelly's hands clench. "You know where you are?"

Connelly clenched his jaw before replying, "Yes." His gaze flickered to the car's rearview mirror, but he still saw no sign of anyone following him. Who were these people? Where were they?

"Good. You go to Camp Hansen now."

"What?" The response was past his lips before Connelly could stop it. Faking a cough, he tried to soften his reply. "I'm having a hard time hearing you. Did you say Camp Hansen?"

"Hansen, yes. You go there now."

Checking his mirrors again still revealed no signs of a tail. If he was about to drive aboard a Marine Corps base, he would be stopped at whichever gate he used. The guard posted at the entrance would check his car for the proper military vehicle identification sticker, and might even ask to see his military ID card, depending on the security condition ordered by the base's commanding officer. Any vehicle wanting access to any military installation on the island would have to submit to the same check, which meant Connelly should be able to see who was following him.

"What am I supposed to do once I get there?" he asked, almost missing the turn that would take him east from Highway 58 toward the base's main gate on the opposite side of the island.

"Do what we tell you."

Being the largest concentration of Marines on the island, Camp Hansen was home to more than six thousand military and civilian support personnel. A good number of the Marines stationed there also had families, though housing for dependents was located at Camp Courtney to the south. Most of Hansen's acreage was devoted to training areas, including live fire ranges. Any Marine requiring weapons training usually came here, as Hansen was one of the few military installations on the island where the Okinawan government permitted live fire exercises. The base was also the home of a special forces training facility and the 3rd Marine Reconnaissance Battalion, among other units. What was there that so interested his tormentors?

"I get that," he said, trying to keep his tone level. "I mean, where am I going once I get there?"

"You go to weapons bunker."

None of this made any sense. "I work in an armory. I don't understand why you'd make me drive . . ."

Drive here. To Hansen. Holy Mary, mother of God. No.

The voice said, "You go to special bunker. You know the one we mean."

"Special bunker?" He tried to think, tried to come up with something to buy time. How in the name of Hell did these people know so much?

"Stop screwing around. You know the one we mean. Underneath office building. You have access badge and code. We see you go there."

How long had they been watching him? Long enough, Connelly decided. It was obvious that whatever these people were up to, they had planned it well.

"Look, I can't just bring people in there," he said. He took his foot off the accelerator, allowing the car to slow as he entered the thickening traffic and approached the town of Kin, which sat adjacent to Camp Hansen. Like Naha and Futenma, there were numerous businesses lining the roads here, each hoping for a piece of the action from the Marines and their families venturing off the base in search of local cuisine, groceries, souvenirs, and entertainment.

"Access is tightly controlled," he continued, "and the guards have standing orders to shoot anyone who tries to breach security if they think it necessary to defend the place." The words were coming almost too fast. He was babbling. "You try to get in there, and . . ."

"Shut up. We tell you what you need to know. For now, just drive."

Connelly forced himself not to hurl the phone through the car's open window. "Let me talk to my family."

"Drive."

There was a click and Connelly heard nothing else.

What the hell were these people going to make him do? The possible answers to that question terrified him.

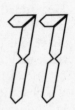

"For the love of God, Jack. What the hell are you doing to me?"

Standing before the map of Okinawa tacked to the conference room's corkboard wall, Abigail Cohen rubbed the bridge of her nose. Despite the healthy serving of aspirin from her desk drawer, it was becoming obvious that the headache growing behind her eyeballs would not be denied. It was coming, it would not be stopped, and it had a name.

Jack Bauer. You're killing me, here, you son of a bitch.

"All right, Cohen. Tell me a story."

"Once upon a time," she replied as she turned from the map, "there was a CIA agent who gave it all up to raise meerkats while moonlighting as a professional gambler in Vegas." She offered a tired, weak smile to see Mark Paquette leaning against the open conference room door, muscled arms folded across his chest. Her boss regarded her with that calm, paternal expression that often reassured Cohen but on other occasions irritated the hell out of her. This wasn't one of those times, but it had the potential to become one.

"I'd rethink the gambling thing," he said. "In case you've forgotten, your poker face sucks something fierce."

Despite her mounting irritation and general discomfort, the comment had its intended effect, and she released a small chuckle. "Thanks for the career advice."

"That's free." Pushing away from the door, Paquette allowed

it to close behind him, shutting out the sounds of the other agents and phones and typewriters and everything else, and providing the two of them with momentary privacy. "As for whatever else might be coming next? That could get expensive." He nodded toward the map. "Talk to me."

"We're still trying to figure it out. Details are sketchy, but we've got our guys monitoring police bands and picking up what they can." Cohen held up a printout she had been given by one of the team's communications analysts. "According to the Naha Police, it looks like some kind of ambush went down at a house in the middle of the sticks. Nine guys, all Okinawan, most of them inside the house but a few on the ground outside. People in the area said the whole thing couldn't have lasted more than a few minutes, and not long after that a white cargo truck and a couple of SUVs were seen leaving the area."

Paquette frowned. "A firefight? In the middle of the damned day?"

"Yeah, and this is where it gets interesting." Cohen paused for effect. "According to chatter on the police band, the house may have belonged to a guy named Edoga Kanashiro. He's apparently a rival of Miroji Jimura, though of course there's no hard evidence to back that up. There's even less to prove the house is tied to him, or that any of these idiots had anything to do with what went down this morning."

"Rival gangs going after each other." Paquette shook his head. "I know that was your theory earlier, but it's starting to look pretty good."

Cohen wasn't at all thrilled about having her initial suspicion borne out. It would have been much easier to deal with the rapidly deteriorating situation if it was just a case of Jimura's men trying to double-cross the group sent by Tateos Gadjoyan. If another player had entered the game, it would make things that much harder to keep under control.

"So," said Paquette, "what about Bauer?" He put his hands on his hips, the simple act highlighting his muscles, even those in his forearms. "Where does he fit into this, if at all?"

"And now we get to the part that's giving me a headache," said Cohen. "Naha Police has a witness who says she's sure she saw at least three or four foreigners in the vehicles leaving the area, including one woman who matches the description of Amorah Banovich. One of the males could be Bauer, but the description was pretty vague. Medium build, blond or brown hair. Hell, that could be half the Americans on the island."

Paquette snorted. "That could be half the guys in this building." He scowled, and Cohen could see him trying to fit together pieces of a mental puzzle that was fighting him at every turn. "Let's say this report is worth a damn. Why would Banovich and Bauer be mixed up in a hit on a rival of Jimura's?"

"I don't have the first clue," said Cohen, hating to have to make such an admission. "It doesn't make a lick of sense. All I can figure is that Jimura knows who put the hit on his crew this morning, and the people from Gadjoyan's crew who survived are working with Jimura to get some payback."

As though turning this idea over in his head, Paquette grimaced. "I suppose that could be it, and if that is the deal, then maybe Bauer is in too deep to get clear and call us."

"That, or he's somehow still trying to get the intel we need to hammer Gadjoyan, and maybe even Jimura." Cohen shrugged. "It'd be a nice bonus, and I bet NCIS and JSDF would thank us for the solid we'd be doing them."

Paquette grunted. "Yeah. Flowers, candy, dancing. The whole nine yards." He reached up to rub his forehead. "I think your headache's contagious. How the hell am I going to explain this to Langley?"

"Singing telegram?"

"I'm still in the doghouse for that strippergram I sent for the deputy director's birthday."

"You should probably send the girl, next time."

"Good tip."

"All part of the service." Cohen turned back to the map, her gaze locking on the small red circle she had drawn around the area where this latest incident had taken place. "Okay, let's pretend for a minute that my idea isn't crazy. Jack is maintaining his cover. He and Banovich and whoever else from Gadjoyan's crew are helping Jimura get back at this Kanashiro character. What are we supposed to do now?"

Paquette said, "Not a lot of choice. We have to put more people on Jimura and his crew. We have to do the same for this Kanashiro, but I'd never even heard of the guy before I walked in here. Then there's Bauer, assuming he's still alive as part of your pretending." He eyed her with obvious skepticism. "What are you thinking?"

"If Jack's alive, and he and Banovich and the others from their crew are hooked up with Jimura, then we need to concentrate on the known hangouts for Jimura's people. We know from experience that he's too smart to bring any business like this to his home, but it won't hurt to step up the surveillance there. We've got a list of a few houses and industrial buildings that may be his, but there's nothing concrete."

Cohen drew a deep breath, holding it for a moment and closing her eyes before exhaling. She had managed to forget about her headache for a few minutes, but now it was back. It had already been a long day, and she saw no sign of it ending anytime soon. In fact, she was sure it was about to get a lot worse, and she was about to help it along.

"I think we need to hook up with NCIS." Before Paquette could respond, she added, "I know it's a risk. Jimura has contacts within JSDF, and it's even possible he's managed to get to somebody inside NCIS."

"Right," replied Paquette, "and right now, none of those groups knows we're here on the island. At least, we're pretty sure they don't know. If we start trying to get in on their investigation, somebody's going to wonder why we're here. Gadjoyan's people won't take long to put it together, and they might even get suspicious about Jack." He shrugged. "I admit that's a long shot, but that's the thing with field ops; they can turn to crap on you in a heartbeat, when you least expect it, and at the worst possible time."

Cohen knew he was right, of course. While getting involved with NCIS and JSDF might aid in her getting a bead on Jack's location and status, she could just as easily betray him to Gadjoyan's people. Prudence and patience were still needed.

Patience. There were times Cohen loathed that word.

Like now.

• • •

The water tasted like wine. Jack drank it in greedy gulps, not caring that it was warm with a metallic tinge as it coursed through the worn, sun-baked hose. With every drink, Jack felt energy return. He drenched the front of his shirt, letting the water cool his sweat-soaked skin. The thick, humid summer air had grown stifling in the early afternoon, and he knew that they hadn't yet reached the hottest part of the day.

"Here," he said, handing the hose off to Rauf Alkaev, who along with Manish Pajari was waiting his turn. As the other man drank his fill, Jack stepped away from the side of the house to where Amorah Banovich leaned against the side of the cargo truck. The vehicle's rear door had been raised and its loading ramp extended so that it rested at an angle as it bridged the gap between the truck and the opening to the oversized storage building. Jack, Banovich, and their companions had emptied the truck, working with some of Samuel Yeager's men to unload the meager goods taken from Edoga Kanashiro's house.

"Are you okay?" Jack asked, mindful to maintain his Russian accent as he watched Banovich wipe sweat from her face.

She nodded. "Just tired. We've been going for a while now."

"Yeah." Wiping water from his mouth, Jack dried his hand on his jeans. Leaning against the side of the truck, he glanced at his watch. They had been awake more than twelve hours already, beginning with their departure from the *Konstantinov* for the exchange with Jimura's men. Jack could feel his body coming down from the adrenaline highs he had experienced since things had gone to hell, and he had already fought off the urge to steal a precious few moments to catch some much-needed sleep. He was vulnerable, and any misstep due to inattention or letting his guard down for something as simple as a catnap could be fatal. Hunger was becoming a concern again, as well. Thankfully, Banovich had said as much to Yeager, who had gone into the house in search of food.

"So," said Jack, pulling his Glock from the holster under his left arm. "What do we do now?" He dropped the weapon's magazine before sticking the pistol in his belt, then extracted a box of nine-millimeter ammunition from his jacket pocket.

Banovich shook her head. "I don't know. A couple of crates of rifles won't be enough to make Jimura happy, even with the other stuff we took. Besides, his money's still missing."

The bulk of the M16s that had gone missing during the morning shootout had either been moved from the house or else had never been there in the first place. Yeager, his men, and Banovich's group had still been able to find a few things of relative value. First, there was a healthy stash of small arms ammunition, to which Jack and the others had all availed themselves in order to recharge their personal weapons, with the rest loaded into the cargo truck. There also was a decent stash of various stolen prescription medications. That was perhaps the biggest prize, along with several crates containing hundreds of copies of bootleg musical albums on compact discs and pirated movies on VHS videotapes. Jack noted that most of the music represented popular bands and genres from the United States and England, and the videos ranged from recent blockbuster films to pornography. He knew that intellectual property piracy was rampant across Asia, particularly with American material and despite efforts by the State Department to work with the governments of various countries to address the issue. Judging by what he had seen at the Kanashiro house, Jack didn't think those efforts were meeting with much success.

Though Jack didn't see the appeal, Yeager had mentioned that the seized materials would fetch decent prices from those contacts of Jimura who dealt with such things. According to him, there were shops all over the island, usually in proximity to the American military bases, where the bootleg CDs and tapes fetched decent money. Whenever law enforcement saw fit to shut down such an establishment, two more sprouted to take its place. Then there were smaller-time dealers who sold the material out of their cars or on tables in alleys and on street corners. Yeager likened the fruitless efforts at enforcement to playing Whac-A-Mole, but without the reward of tickets used to claim prizes.

Not really your biggest problem right now, Bauer.

"We've got more money on the ship," he said as he finished

inserting new rounds into the nearly spent magazine. "Why not just work out a new deal with Jimura?" Inserting the magazine back into the Glock, Jack returned the weapon to its holster and concealed it with his jacket.

Banovich replied, "It's not that simple, Stefan. There's more at stake here than one deal, after all. Gadjoyan and Jimura have been dealing with each other for years. There's a level of trust that's hard to acquire in this business. Both men place great value on such things, and Gadjoyan will want to do whatever's possible to preserve that trust. And as we discussed earlier, Jimura also is a man of honor, though I suspect even his patience can be tested." She sighed. "I just hope that he sees our gesture as a genuine desire to make things right. Otherwise, you and I may not see tomorrow."

That had been a possibility all along, as far as Jack was concerned. He and Bill Fields had lived in constant fear of discovery from the first moments of attempting to insert themselves into Tateos Gadjoyan's organization. There remained the very real danger of someone learning or realizing that they were plants, either by virtue of some mistake he made, someone within Gadjoyan's camp uncovering the truth, or any of a dozen different other things. What he needed was a way out of here, but that required contacting Abigail Cohen and alerting her to his growing desire to be pulled the hell out of the ever-expanding circle of chaos in which he had found himself.

Phone. Maybe there's a phone in the house.

It was a long shot, at best, but Jack only needed a minute or two to relay a message to Cohen. The possibility was worth a reconnoiter of the house's interior.

"I'm going to go find a bathroom," he announced, pushing himself away from the truck. "You want anything when I come back?"

Casting a playful look in his direction, Banovich said, "A bath and a bed, and someone to share them with."

"I'll see what I can do." Jack smiled, masking his discomfort with her flirting as he walked toward the house's rear porch. A muscled Okinawan man was standing near the door, presenting the air of a soldier on guard duty, and Jack noted the visible bulge under the man's jacket and beneath his right arm. As he approached the porch and began climbing its steps, the man held up a beefy left hand.

"What you want?" he asked in fragmented English.

"Bathroom," said Jack, making a rude gesture to simulate what he intended to do upon reaching his destination. The man nodded in understanding, hooking an oversized, scarred thumb over his shoulder and toward the house. Jack offered an appreciative nod. "Thanks."

It took a few seconds to navigate the house's narrow, poorly lit central passageway, and he passed one bedroom just after stepping inside. The hallway intersected with a shorter corridor that Jack saw led to an enclosed bathroom. It was easy to see that this was a new or recent addition to the house's original configuration, and he wondered if the home had featured a separate outbuilding for toilet and bath facilities. The Kanashiro house had possessed such a setup within its adjacent building, and Yeager had mentioned that such things were common in many homes that were away from the cities and larger towns.

Whatever works.

"Please, don't."

Jack stopped at the sound of the female voice, coming from somewhere behind him. Turning from the bathroom, he saw that he was alone in the passageway. He listened in silence, and heard another voice, a man's, say something he couldn't make out, but then the female responded.

"Please. We're doing what you asked. Just leave us alone."

Walking to the turn in the hallway, Jack peered around the corner and saw the back of an Okinawan man standing just inside what looked to be another bedroom. In front of him, sitting on a bed with unmade sheets, were a Caucasian woman, a teenaged girl, and what Jack guessed was a boy of perhaps eight or nine years of age. The woman's voice carried no accent, and Jack's initial suspicion that they might be Americans was bolstered when he saw the Marine Corps emblem on the boy's green T-shirt.

A Marine's family? What the hell . . . ?

Jack's thought was interrupted as the man stepped forward

and grabbed the woman's arm, trying to pull her from the bed. She jerked back her arm, her expression one of fear, and the man responded by slapping her across the face. The sound of the strike was enough to make Jack blink, and he was already halfway down the hall before he realized he was moving even as the Okinawan grabbed the woman's arm again. This time he managed to pull her from the bed just as another man appeared from another hallway.

Jack froze as the new arrival, without a single word and almost without breaking stride, pushed the woman back to the bed before shoving the first man aside. The woman bounced on the sagging mattress and the girl and boy who had to be her children latched on to her. Meanwhile, the second Okinawan was berating his companion, his invective spewed forth at a furious rate in his native language. The first man said something that Jack interpreted as backtalk, the response accompanied by a flurry of gestures toward the other man and the woman.

Then the second Okinawan pulled a pistol from his waistband and fired once at point blank range into his companion's face. The man's head snapped back and he sagged to the wooden floor, dead even before he fell. On the bed, the woman and her children were screaming and scurrying back on the mattress in a futile effort to put some distance between them and their apparent savior.

His eyes riveted to the body on the floor, Jack almost didn't hear the footsteps running in the hall. Snapping out of the shock at what he had just witnessed, he backtracked the way he had come. The shadows infesting the dimly illuminated passageway provided some measure of concealment as another pair of Okinawan men appeared at the room's entrance, and there was more talking back and forth that Jack couldn't understand. The shooter pointed to the man he had just killed and barked something that had to be a directive to remove the body, because the two new arrivals set to lifting the dead man by his arms and legs and walking him out of the room.

"I'm sorry, Mrs. Connelly," said the man to the woman and her children. "His behavior was unacceptable. I promise that will not happen again. So long as you do what we tell you to do, you will not be harmed." Jack noted that his command of English was better than some of the other Okinawans he had encountered around the house.

"What are you doing?"

So engrossed was he in what was transpiring in the bedroom that Jack hadn't heard Samuel Yeager approaching him. Now the American stood within arm's reach, regarding him with obvious distrust.

Shaking his head and putting on the air of a man who had seen something troubling—which wasn't far from the truth— Jack made a show of clearing his throat before replying, "Sorry. I was just looking for the bathroom when that happened." He nodded in the direction of the hallway. "What's that about?"

Yeager's expression didn't change. "Not your concern."

If he pressed, Jack knew he ran the risk of triggering even greater suspicion, from Yeager and anyone else in the house. Whatever was going on, Yeager was in on it, but what could he want with this American military family? Had they been kidnapped? Were they being used as leverage against the woman's husband, who might be a service member, if the boy's T-shirt was a legitimate clue? There was no way for Jack to get answers to these sorts of questions without endangering his cover. Likewise, his chances of finding a phone and calling Cohen had likely just been flushed, at least for the time being.

"Fair enough," he said, holding up his hands. "I don't want any trouble; just the bathroom."

After using the facilities and venturing back outside, Jack found Yeager standing with Banovich next to the cargo truck. A few of Yeager's men were milling about, as were Alkaev and Pajari. Banovich appeared locked in an animated conversation with Yeager, and as he drew closer, Jack could see that Banovich didn't look at all happy.

"What's going on?" he asked.

Banovich reached up to push aside a lock of her dark hair. "Another hit. Jimura wants us to help Yeager on another ambush."

"Really?" In truth, Jack had suspected this might be coming after the relative non-success of the first hit, but that didn't alleviate his concern. "So soon? Won't Kanashiro's people be expecting that?"

Yeager nodded. "Probably, and for what it's worth I agree with you." His tone was accommodating, but Jack guessed the man was still not over the suspicion he had demonstrated inside the house. "But, I was able to confirm some of the information that last guy gave us at the other place. We've got a bead on another possible location for the shipment." He eyed Banovich. "You still want your guns, right?"

"Of course," she replied, "just as I suspect you want your money."

"Doesn't matter what I want," countered Yeager. "I work for Mister Jimura, and he's telling me to jump."

Jack said, "If we're going to do this, we need to move fast. If Kanashiro doesn't know by now that somebody hit his other house, he will soon, and he'll probably beef up security at other locations he wants to protect." He didn't like the idea of conducting yet another assault in broad daylight with minimal planning and working with people he didn't know. There were just too many things that could go wrong. On the other hand, having Yeager and his men gave the group additional options and firepower. "What do you know about where we're supposed to be going?"

"Not much," replied Yeager. "It's a warehouse about eighty kilometers north of here, near Motobu." He paused, looking around the area. "It's not like this place, or even where we did the first hit. We're going to have to watch our step if we want to avoid attracting attention. By now, Naha Police have sent advisories to the other towns and precincts, letting them know what happened this morning, and maybe even at the Kanashiro place. They'll be paying attention to anything that doesn't look right."

That did little to improve Jack's assessment of the current situation. Though he knew little about Miroji Jimura and even less about Edoga Kanashiro, he was familiar enough with the type of men they were. Both of them were sure to have informants within the various police departments in the precincts where they carried out their various dealings, to help them out of whatever sticky situations might arise. If that was the case, then it was likely someone was feeding intel to both arms merchants as the day wore on. What information of any worth did the police have, beyond eyewitness reports and other uncorroborated accounts about what had happened to this point? With luck, he, Banovich, and their people, to say nothing of Yeager and his men, were still moving a bit ahead of the police and Kanashiro.

Right. Keep telling yourself that.

"Get your people ready," said Yeager to Banovich. "We're leaving in ten minutes. We'll figure out the particulars once we're on site and get a recon of the area." Without waiting for her to reply, he turned and walked back toward the house.

"I'll get us some more ammo," said Banovich. "I think we'll need it."

Jack nodded. "Good idea." He watched her walk toward the storage building for a moment before his gaze returned to the house as Yeager climbed the steps to the porch and disappeared inside.

What about the family in there?

It was hard not to think about the apparent hostages in the house. Who where they? How much danger were they in? That someone might use his own wife and daughter against him because of his chosen line of work had long been the stuff of nightmares for Jack. His thoughts turned to Teri and Kim. How far might he go to protect them if someone endangered their lives to get to him? What rules would he break? What lines would he cross?

All of them. Every single damned one.

What was Jimura's plan for this family once he got whatever it was he wanted and for which the woman and her children provided value? Was there a way for him to help them?

Yeah. Call Cohen. Right, I know. Fat chance.

For the moment, Jack knew there was nothing he could do without compromising his cover. He would have to be patient. Sooner or later, an opportunity would present itself.

Jack just hoped he was still alive to take advantage of it.

It felt good to throw the glass. Edoga Kanashiro relished the sound it made as it shattered against the wall, scattering fragments, water, and ice in all directions. The once beautiful landscape painting that was the unfortunate target of his rage now bore a nasty gash across its center, but it could be replaced.

In fact, Kanashiro now was sure that he hated it. Grabbing the glass water pitcher from the serving table, he hurled it and its contents across the room, watching water arc through the air before the pitcher slammed into the painting and knocked it from the wall. The pitcher broke into multiple pieces and water now was everywhere, and the painting's frame had cracked upon impacting with the floor.

His hands flexing and clenching, Kanashiro looked for something else on which to inflict his wrath, but already he could feel the emotional outburst beginning to ebb. He opted to focus on that, closing his eyes and listening to his breathing. After a moment spent in this impromptu bout of forced meditation, Kanashiro's muscles relaxed and the fury which had driven him fled his body. The anger that remained was useful; it could be channeled into what must come next.

"Tell me what happened," he said, opening his eyes and turning away from the now wet wall and ruined painting to face Rino Nakanashi. His assistant stood near the door to Kanashiro's office, still dressed in the white pants and wine-colored dress shirt he had been wearing earlier, which was unusual for him. With little tolerance for the brutal summer humidity and the perspiration it evoked, Nakanashi tended to change clothes more often during these warmer months.

"It was an ambush," said Nakanashi. He appeared unruffled by what had just transpired, though with his thin reading glasses perched at the edge of his nose, he looked the part of a disapproving parochial schoolmaster. That actually made Kanashiro feel better. The sight conjured from his memory an image of one of his teachers from just such a school.

"How many men?" he asked.

Nakanashi replied, "Nine. There were no survivors. Whoever hit them did so quickly and with great skill. They were gone within minutes. We have no idea who they are, no reliable descriptions, nothing. I am waiting for our police contact in Naha to provide more information, but apparently the details of the incident are being carefully guarded."

"You tell our contact that he should work harder. He's paid well enough, but nothing says that needs to continue." It wasn't his habit to verbally threaten those in his employ, or anyone with whom his organization had even a tangential connection. Those who worked for him knew what was expected of them, and the people he put in charge of his various interests saw to it that such individuals received proper training, or else were removed from the equation before they could become a problem. It was a rare occasion for him to give voice to such a warning. Even as he spoke the words, Kanashiro realized that his earlier anger still lurked nearby, threatening to cloud his judgment, and he willed away the unproductive feelings.

"Was anything taken?" he asked after a moment, when he was certain he had regained his composure.

Nakanashi replied, "I don't know specifics, but the report from our man in the police department mentioned that the storage building behind the house appeared to have been cleaned out. Tracks from a large vehicle—likely our truck—were found approaching and leaving the house, before they reached a paved road." He paused, as though concerned about how his next words would be received. "All but a few of the weapons we collected this morning were already moved at the time of the attack, though three or four cases were left behind. There's no mention of them in the preliminary police reports so we must assume they were taken. Likewise, there were no references to drugs or media."

Moving toward his desk, Kanashiro grunted in disapproval. Losing the copied music CDs and videotapes was an annoyance, but they at least could be replaced at minimal cost. The drugs, however, were a different story.

"And we're sure there's nothing tying that house to us?"

Nakanashi shook his head. "There's no connection at all to you for the house itself, though the police might be able to link one or more of the men to us. That much depends on how well local police have been investigating you."

None of that concerned Kanashiro, at least for the moment. The police and even the Japanese Self-Defense Force had made several attempts to infiltrate his organization and build a case against him, but so far he had been able to thwart their efforts. He knew that similar efforts had been launched against Miroji Jimura and a few other competitors on the island. The bulk of that scrutiny had been aimed at Jimura, a man of enormous patience and deliberation who simply didn't make stupid decisions or undertake ill-advised actions. Kanashiro had been able to evade similar attention to this point, but were the police now keeping their watchful eye on him, as well?

"The timing of this assault isn't a coincidence," he said. Standing before his desk, he rapped his knuckles atop its smooth, polished wooden surface. "And I think we both know the most likely responsible party."

Nodding, Nakanashi said, "Jimura. Given this morning's events, it makes sense, but how would he know to suspect us?"

"No one else has the balls to do what we did." Kanashiro had been a vocal detractor of Miroji Jimura and a champion for the idea that the older man might well have passed his point of relevance in their shared business, but he hadn't gone so far as to publicly threaten Jimura's interests. None of the other, smaller rival groups had done as much, either, but neither had they ever said or done anything else which might be interpreted as hostile or even impolite. The old ways were still pervasive here on the island, and younger, hungrier challengers to the region's ever-expanding market were beginning to assert themselves. Kanashiro considered himself the leader of that pack, as did Jimura, which meant that the older man would first cast suspicious eyes on Kanashiro when anything untoward occurred.

Undone by my own arrogance? Perhaps, but only if I don't follow that arrogance with resolve, and results.

"We need to be ready to hit Jimura back," he said, beginning to pace the length of his office.

Nakanashi replied, "We are already working on that. Several of Jimura's top men are still under surveillance, carrying over from the operation at the warehouse this morning. So far, only two of our teams have reported anything interesting. It seems that Jimura has taken an interest in an American Marine from the Futenma air base. Two of Jimura's men forced their way into one of the base armories, and since then have apparently ordered this Marine to drive north while they follow him. Two of our men are following them, and they think they may be heading toward one of the bases in that direction. We'll know more when they call in."

Frowning, Kanashiro stopped his pacing. "What do they want with this Marine?"

"I have no idea, but it seems another pair of Jimura's men has kidnapped the man's family. Our team following them watched the whole thing play out on the street. They tried to follow, but lost them in traffic."

Kanashiro considered this twist to the story. "Jimura obviously wants this Marine to do something for him, and is using his family to force his cooperation."

"That's likely it," said Nakanashi, "though I have no idea who this Marine is, or what value Jimura sees in him."

It was an interesting development. Was Jimura extorting this American to steal something or carry out some other illicit task? There was no way to know. At least, not yet.

"Have our people stay on this," said Kanashiro. "I want to know what this is about, and if we can use it against Jimura."

What are you up to, you old relic?

• • •

Dale Connelly slowed his car as he approached the guard shack at Gate 1. The Marine on duty, a corporal, was dressed in camouflage utilities and wearing a green equipment belt with a holstered Beretta nine-millimeter pistol on his right hip. He stepped from the shack and approached Connelly's side of the car. The window was rolled down, and Connelly extended his right arm with his wallet opened to display his military ID card.

"Good afternoon, Master Gunny," said the corporal, recognizing the rank insignia on Connelly's collar before scrutinizing the ID. "Go on ahead." He made a sharp motion with his right hand to direct him to drive onward.

Connelly nodded as he eased the car forward. "Thanks." He checked his rearview mirror as he guided the vehicle past the checkpoint and onto Camp Hansen property, but saw no sign of a car behind him. Where was his watcher?

The bag phone rang.

"Yes," he said into the receiver. There was no point to proper greetings any longer. Who else was going to be calling him on this phone?

"You know where to go," said his tormentor. It wasn't a question.

Guiding the car onto the street that would take him toward the northwest area of the base, Connelly tried to clear his parched throat. Real fear was now beginning to assert itself, not just for his family but also for what the man on the other end of the call was going to ask of him. There could only one reason for Connelly to go to this particular building, but how did this person know about that? Where had he gotten his information?

"What do I do once I'm there?"

"Go inside. Go to secure level, open the secure door."

How do they know? How can they know about that?

"We know the door can only be opened from the inside, at the far end of tunnel. You go."

The man was correct, of course, though Connelly couldn't begin to fathom how he had this information. The underground level beneath what on the base map was benignly labeled as an "administration and logistics" building was unknown to all save a precious few trusted individuals, including him. Even the Marines under his command didn't know of its existence, and he was duty bound to never mention it in any capacity. The only reason he knew about the level was because he was one of a handful of people on the entire island trained and qualified to work with what was stored there.

This is impossible. This can't be . . .

"What are you going to do?" he asked. "I can't just let anyone in that door for no reason. There will be guards, and questions. They'll never let me get away with it."

"You find a way."

"Even if I can get the door open without somebody raising hell, this is a restricted base. They don't just let anyone aboard, you know."

The voice now had an air of irritation. "You no worry about that. Do your job. We'll tell you what you need to know. Get moving. We're watching."

The line went dead yet again, and Connelly returned the receiver to its cradle. It took him three tries to do that with his shaking hand. So distracted was he by that action that he nearly drove the car up onto a curb. He overcorrected, then finally straightened the vehicle. His pulse pounded in his throat and blood rushed in his ears as he passed Marines, American civilians, and even the odd Okinawan on the sidewalks or in the grass to either side of the road. In fact, he had passed at least a half dozen locals in dark garb tending to the lawn and landscaping since he had boarded the base. Could any of them be watching him?

Eyes were on him. Connelly could feel them. Where were they? How many were there? How many would he face if and when he ever met them?

"I can't do this," he said, to no one. "I can't do what they're asking me to do." Even setting aside thoughts of treason, which was essentially the act he was about to commit, the end result of the task he had been given carried heavy, even catastrophic consequences. What else were these people expecting him to do? What would they do once they had what they wanted?

Connelly didn't even care what they did to him. For all intents and purposes, his life would be over, one way or the other, before the end of the day, but what about Jessica and the kids? What would happen to them, particularly if he wasn't around to protect them.

You're not protecting them now, you idiot. There's only one way to do that. You don't have a choice.

"Dear God, help me."

• • •

There were bodies everywhere.

"This is becoming an annoying trend," said Christopher Kurtz.

"Nine, altogether," said Jordan Aguilar, walking past several uniformed Okinawan police officers and a host of other men and women in civilian clothes. "Four outside, the others inside. Whoever did this knew what they were doing."

Kurtz frowned. "What makes you say that?"

Gesturing toward the open fields to either side of the house, Aguilar replied, "Uniforms have found tracks in the mud from the flanks." She pointed toward the house. "No windows on the sides. They were able to mask their approach." Next, she indicated the retaining walls to either side. "The ambushers used fire and maneuver, enveloping the point of attack between them. Based on the timeline established by eyewitness statements, the whole thing was over and done in about two minutes. Witnesses said there was a single shot, followed by a couple more, then all hell broke loose for a good minute or so. That sound like a street gang to you? Or even somebody working for a guy like Jimura?"

"Nope. Sounds like somebody with military training."

"Exactly, which leads me to my next point." She pointed to the west side of the house. "Some of those tracks were made with what looks to be the Vibram soles on a pair of American military-issue boots, size ten and a half. That's about a size twenty-eight the way they measure shoes here; on the high side for Okinawan males. There's another set of tracks that could be a woman's, and a third set made with what looks to be a pretty worn pair of work boots, or maybe some other kind of military boot." She shrugged. "I'm not that big on fashion."

"Yeah," said Kurtz, "but I know what you're getting at. Some of the stragglers from this morning were in on this." They had been operating under the theory that at least a few people from the group of Americans or Europeans who had been gunned down at the Naha Port warehouses had been involved in the car chase and shootout a few hours later. Had they regrouped and set their sights on Edoga Kanashiro?

Aguilar nodded. "If that's so, then these people are getting around. What I don't get is why."

"Payback," replied Kurtz. "For this morning. Of course, that presupposes they knew who hit them in the first place. The other problem I'm having is how Jimura is in on this, if at all."

"What if Jimura and these other guys have teamed up?" asked Aguilar. When Kurtz eyed her with skepticism, she added, "Hang on. Work with me, here. Jimura's guys and these other clowns get ambushed in Naha. There are some survivors on both sides, so word gets back to Jimura that the deal went bad, but the foreigners say it wasn't them. Jimura decides it's Kanashiro, or another rival, and orders a hit in retaliation, and the gaijin pitch in to help. What do you think?"

Pondering this, Kurtz rubbed the side of his face. "I think that's a lot of maybes, in there." He waved toward the house. "We only think this house belongs to Kanashiro, but we've got no proof. Some of the bodies are guys we suspect are on his payroll, but there again we're working with no real evidence. So, everything you just said is pretty much a big wild-assed guess, right?"

"Right. So, let's start ruling out some of this crap. We've got at least some of Kanashiro's known buildings and other locations under surveillance after that shootout from this morning, right?"

Kurtz nodded as he surveyed the scene. "Yeah, but those are the legit businesses, like his nightclubs, things like that." There were other points of interest to local police, NCIS, and the JSDF, but at the moment, these buildings and other businesses had done nothing to draw any sort of overt suspicion. Like Miroji Jimura, Edoga Kanashiro was no slouch when it came to covering his movements and illegal activities, and pinning anything to him had proven difficult.

"Well, you're gonna love me for this. After we started liking Kanashiro as our leading suspect for the hit down at the port, I had Nick call our contacts at the major police precincts and have some of his uniforms do some extra drive-bys past some of those other places we think belong to him." Aguilar gestured toward their car. "I just talked to Nick and he gave me an update on that. There's a warehouse up in Motobu that they suspect belongs to Kanashiro. It's had a lot of traffic during the last couple of days. The police chief up there thought it was odd, because so far as he knows, that place's been vacant for about a year."

"That's what he said?" asked Kurtz.

"Wait. It gets better. Seems there was a white cargo truck up there just this morning." Aguilar smiled. "You're loving me right now, aren't you?"

"Little bit, I have to say." Kurtz had always liked Aguilar's ability to see a bigger picture far more quickly and with greater clarity than he could manage. While he might be the senior agent with more practical experience, she possessed superior instincts he had learned to trust. He had no problems turning her loose during a case and following wherever her gut took them. More often than not, the leads they tracked down at least served to further their investigation if not blow it right open. She was a damned fine detective, and had the commendations to prove it. Kurtz had already twice recommended her for promotion and assignment to lead her own investigation team. That would happen one day soon, of that he was certain, and on that day he would lose his best partner in sixteen years on this job.

"What are the odds that's just a big coincidence?" he asked, and before Aguilar could reply, Kurtz waved away the suggestion. "Trick question. Okay, I'm liking this theory. Let's get our people up to speed and notify JSDF. Maybe they've got something more on this location. Besides, they're still wanting in on the action after this morning."

Aguilar nodded as they started walking toward her car. "Yeah, but we should be careful. The tension's liable to be turned up a couple of degrees, you know."

"I know, but can you blame them?" Kurtz sighed. "The poor bastard was tortured and executed."

By now, news of Tadashi Enogawa's death had circulated through the NCIS office and likely was being spread to the rest of the JSDF task force assigned to this investigation as well as other units stationed on the island. Like any police force, they would be looking for answers about the slaying of their comrade-in-arms, and the desire for retribution would be strong. Still, JSDF officers prided themselves on their professionalism and accountability, so Kurtz wasn't too worried about any units working this case conducting themselves in a way that didn't adhere to their high standards. This did not mean they wouldn't be angry, though, and Kurtz was certain that he wouldn't want to be the target of their ire.

"Let's get them updated on this," he said as they reached the car. Opening the driver's-side door, he more fell than sat in the seat, reaching for the ignition and firing up the Toyota sedan's engine as Aguilar got in on the passenger's side. He gestured to the car phone between them before putting the car into first gear. "And let's get a response team geared up and heading for Motobu."

Aguilar replied, "Already on it. I had Minecci call out a team and put them on standby. They're meeting us at Futenma, and we'll take a chopper up to Camp Hansen. Minecci's taking care of the ground vehicle logistics right now, and he'll have it worked out before we land."

Unable to suppress an appreciative smile, Kurtz slammed the car into second and stomped the accelerator. "You know what? I'm loving you a lot more, right now."

"I'm really quite something."

"Except modest." Kurtz chuckled. "No one's ever going to accuse you of that."

"Modesty is for losers. Drive faster."

Sweat ran down the inside of Dale Connelly's T-shirt, and he could feel it on his head and neck. His legs felt as though they might give out on him, sending him tumbling facefirst to the deck, and his heart was pounding so hard that he was sure it was about to launch itself from his chest like the monster in those science-fiction movies. That, or he was about to spew vomit everywhere.

"Good afternoon, Top," said the Marine sergeant who had risen from his chair behind the desk upon seeing Connelly enter the building. The name tape over his pocket read ROXBURGH.

"Afternoon, Sergeant. I see you got the swing shift."

Roxburgh smiled. "Just my turn. Sixteen hundred to midnight for the next two weeks. Still beats graveyard. I am *definitely* not looking forward to that."

Connelly held out his regular military ID card and the access pass given to him by his commanding officer. Both cards carried his picture, and while his normal identification was pale green in color and bore a small black and white photo from three years ago, the access pass was red and contained a larger, color picture that was much more recent. Standing orders required the cards to be renewed every two months, and each card was fitted with a magnetic strip bearing information that would expire after that sixty-day period. Losing the card or failing to renew it in a timely manner carried harsh penalties.

The sergeant took both forms of identification and checked them, verifying each photograph against the man standing before him before running the red card through a small reader positioned next to the phone on his desk. An indicator light flashed green.

"You're good to go, Top," said the younger man, handing back the cards.

"Thanks," replied Connelly, returning the IDs to his wallet. "Have a good one."

"You all right?" asked Roxburgh. "You look kind of pale."

Caught off guard by the unexpected question, Connelly swallowed and shook his head. "Yeah, I'm fine," he said. "Pushed it a bit too hard today at PT."

"They just went to Black Flag," said the sergeant, referring to the color flag system used by Navy and Marine Corps units to alert personnel in high heat and humidity conditions about the risk of heat exhaustion or heat stroke during physical training or other demanding outdoor activities. It had been Red Flag earlier in the day during the PT run Connelly had taken with his unit, but that was typical for this time of year and all of his Marines were acclimated to the summer heat. Regulations called for the suspension of all but mission-essential strenuous activities once Black Flag conditions were declared, which usually happened in the afternoon hours this time of year.

Move your ass! They're waiting on you.

"I'll be fine," said Connelly, offering a mock salute with the camouflage cover he held in his hand. "Thanks."

The desk check at the building's front entrance was the only challenge he should have to face, at least from a living person. Unless something had changed since his last visit, there would be two secure hatches, each requiring his access card via a reader and an eight-digit code input to a keypad on the door locks. Failure to properly enter the code after two attempts would trigger alarms that would bring a reaction team of Marines armed with M16s and authorization to employ deadly force in defense of the secure level's contents.

For a moment, Connelly considered entering an incorrect code and provoking such a response. He knew from training drills just how quick and efficient the react teams could be. If he attempted to resist, even to the smallest degree, the Marines would be empowered to kill him on sight. They might even receive commendations or medals for such action.

If you do that, Jessica and the kids are as good as dead, too.

Somewhere, someday, and assuming he survived to hear the question, someone would ask why he didn't sacrifice himself—and his family—in order to protect what this building safeguarded. It was, Connelly conceded, a valid query, and one for which he would spend a great deal of time composing a response; again, assuming he lived to do so. In the meantime, the people who would put such questions to him were not here, and it wasn't their wife and children at stake. Carrying out one's duty regardless of circumstances or personal cost sounded compelling in the pages of a book or during a class lecture, but when weighing the cost of that commitment against the lives of innocents, orders and regulations that sought to provide clarity on such issues became hopelessly muddied and useless.

It's not over. You can still find a way to turn this around, and save Jess and the kids. Think, damn it. Think!

Connelly proceeded through the pair of security doors, locking each one behind him as he descended to the underground level. Once inside the secure area, he moved with brisk strides past the storage vaults, refusing to look at their doors or the signs indicating their contents, and proceeded to yet another reinforced metal hatch. This one was a larger affair, operated by hydraulic motors that would swing the door outward. The door itself was steel, five feet thick, and like the bulkhead around it could withstand a direct assault from an M1 Abrams tank. It could only be opened from the inside, but set into the metal wall next to it was a smaller hatch of equal width designed to accommodate individuals. This one also utilized a card reader and keypad, and he made his way through that hatch and into the tunnel on its far side.

From here, it was a short ride via golf cart to the far end of the tunnel, approximately one hundred yards from where he presently stood. Only now did he realize how he might be able to open the door at the tunnel's opposite end without arousing suspicion. Turning back to the door, he reached for the phone mounted on the adjacent bulkhead, lifting the receiver from its cradle. There was no dial or keypad on the phone itself. None was needed.

A voice answered after the first ring, "Operations. Gunnery Sergeant Laszlo speaking."

Thank God. Somebody I know.

"Gunny, this is Master Gunny Connelly." There was no need to identify his location. The Marines on duty in the operations office already knew that much, just by virtue of his having accessed the door locks and this phone. "My authorization is Alpha Oscar Three Nine Five Five. I've been ordered to check the outer door lock and alarm."

There was a pause before Laszlo replied, "Your authorization checks out, Top, but I've got nothing on my schedule for today."

"Son of a bitch." Connelly played up his tone of irritation, which wasn't difficult under the present circumstances. "Captain Blair said he sent the paperwork yesterday. He wants me to give everything a last look before I turn in my access card. You know I'm shipping stateside tomorrow." He had known Gunnery Sergeant Timothy Laszlo for almost two years, since the younger man had rotated to the island from his previous assignment at the Naval Weapons Station at Fallbrook, California, near the Camp Pendleton Marine base. They were not close friends, but there was a familiarity thanks to their shared work assignments that on occasion brought Connelly here from Futenma. Would that be enough for Laszlo not just to bend but to break one of the numerous rules governing the security of this facility?

Apparently, it would.

"How long do you need?" asked Laszlo.

"Five minutes, max. Everything else is battened down. I'm the only one here."

After another pause, Laszlo said, "Okay, Top. Five minutes. Less, if you can swing it. I'm sure the paperwork's in here, somewhere, and just hasn't made its way down to us yet."

Forcing himself to hold back an audible sigh, Connelly said, "Thanks, Gunny. I appreciate it."

"No problem. Call me when you're finished."

The conversation concluded, Connelly made his way down the tunnel in the battery-powered cart that had been liberated from the golf course on Kadena Air Force Base before being brought here, painted Marine camouflage, and outfitted with knobby all-terrain tires.

At the tunnel's far end was a door almost identical to the one he had left behind, though this one didn't include a man-sized alternative exit. This hatch, reinforced and set into a frame that was embedded in the rock, rested at a forty-five degree angle from upright, and the tunnel floor sloped upward to meet its threshold. Hydraulics lifted the door from its frame, allowing vehicles access to the tunnel.

Deactivating the alarm was a simple process, taking only a moment for him to punch in the correct code to the keypad next to the door. The pad's indicator light turned from red to yellow and Connelly heard the massive metal bolts holding the door closed retract into the door itself. Once that was completed the indicator turned green, and he pushed the topmost of two oversized red buttons next to the keypad. The hydraulic motor embedded in the rock wall came to life, and the door began rising upward, swinging from right to left. It took the door thirty seconds to rise to a vertical position, leaving a gap fifteen feet across.

Nothing awaited him at the door.

"What the hell?" he asked, ascending the sloped floor until he stood outside. Turning back toward the door, Connelly studied the entrance's exterior. Unlike the inside of the facility, the door looked old and rusted, though he knew that largely was a facade affixed to the hatch in order to simulate neglect, and the area around the door was overgrown with vegetation. All of this combined to bolster in deliberate fashion the illusion that the door led to nothing more remarkable than a simple bunker or underground storm shelter that had gone unused for years.

The relative silence outside the tunnel was disrupted by the sudden sound of a vehicle's engine—no, two of them, Connelly realized—flaring to life from somewhere to the east of the bunker entrance. He turned toward the sound and saw a pair of civilian panel trucks driving into view, using the dirt access path that led back to the paved street. Both of the vehicles were of the regular, everyday, nondescript sort that could be seen all over the island, including the various military bases. They were used as delivery and cargo trucks, and by civilian contractors performing construction, landscaping, or utility services around the different installations. Essentially, their ordinary appearance made them all but invisible. No one gave them a second thought.

Damn it all to hell.

The trucks slowed but didn't stop as they made the turn and proceeded into the tunnel. A male Okinawan jumped from the passenger seat of the first vehicle. His black hair was slicked back, and he was dressed in a set of blue overalls of the sort worn by maintenance and construction workers on all of the bases. Connelly almost recoiled when he saw the pistol in the man's right hand. Instead of pointing the weapon at him, the Okinawan gestured with his free hand to move back inside the tunnel.

"Close the door," the man said as he approached, the second truck passing behind him and into the bunker.

Connelly blinked once, then two more times in rapid succession as he heard the command. This was the *voice*.

"Close the damned door!" the man snapped. This time he lifted the pistol, and Connelly saw that the weapon—some model of Glock—was fitted with a sound suppressor.

Holding up his hands, Connelly offered a nervous, frantic nod. "Okay. Okay!" He checked to make sure the entrance was clear before hitting the bottom button on the control pad, and the door began to lower back into its frame. Once it was closed, Connelly reengaged the locking mechanism.

"Leave the alarm off," said the Okinawan.

"If I do that, it'll attract the guards." Connelly gestured toward the keypad. "I told them I'd only be about five minutes." Looking down the tunnel, he saw that the pair of trucks hadn't waited for him, but instead were driving toward the secure door at the passage's far end.

The Okinawan scowled. "Then you tell them something else." He pointed to the golf cart. "Let's go."

"Are you the one I was talking to on the phone?" Connelly

asked after they had climbed into the cart. He glanced at the man's pistol before turning his gaze to the front of the cart.

"Drive."

After Connelly had turned the cart around and was heading to catch up with the trucks, he tried again. "Look, I'm doing what you asked. I just need to know that my family's okay." The muzzle of the pistol was within reach, less than an arm's length from him. He outweighed the Okinawan by at least fifty pounds, and even if the other man was a trained fighter, Connelly figured he only needed a couple of seconds. The temptation to throw a fist toward the man's face was almost overwhelming, to the point that his hands began to shake on the steering wheel.

"Your family alive," said the Okinawan, in the broken English Connelly had been hearing all afternoon. "For now. Just do what we say. You be fine."

The trucks were waiting for them at the tunnel's opposite end, their engines idling. With the Okinawan directing him at gunpoint, Connelly proceeded to unlock the security door. By the time he had scanned his access card and entered his code on the keypad, he realized that the other man was no longer alone. Four men had emerged from one of the vehicles. All were dressed in similar blue overalls, and each carried what Connelly thought might be a Heckler & Koch MP5 submachine gun, fitted with an integrated suppressor. Two of the men wore satchels slung over shoulders.

"Get inside," said the Okinawan with the pistol, who Connelly now thought of as "Slicky."

The door swung inward. Connelly stepped into the large bay, and he thought his heart might skip a beat as his gaze fell upon the figure of Gunnery Sergeant Timothy Laszlo, dressed in camouflage utilities with cover. He also wore a duty belt with an M9 Beretta pistol in a holster on his left hip.

"Hey, Top," Laszlo said as Connelly came through the door. "You didn't call, so I figured I'd come. . . ." The rest of his words were lost and his expression changed, and Connelly knew the Marine had seen the people behind him. Laszlo's left hand moved for his pistol but he never got there before the room was filled with a trio of metallic snaps. Laszlo's body jerked as three red plumes erupted on his chest and the Marine fell backward. He collapsed unmoving to the deck as Connelly could only watch in helpless terror.

"You didn't have to do that!" he barked, eyeing Slicky with open contempt.

Ignoring Connelly, the Okinawan moved past him and stood over the body of the fallen Laszlo. He aimed his suppressed pistol at the Marine's head and fired twice. Then, as though having already forgotten what he had just done, he turned and faced Connelly and the other men.

"Let's go."

• • •

Connelly only had to open the second of the two inner doors leading from the secure vault level. Once they were past those barriers, Slicky's men moved as though they knew the builidng's floor plan, leaving Connelly and Slicky to follow behind. Any thoughts Connelly might have had about resisting or shouting a warning as the group proceeded down the hall were crushed by the muzzle of Slicky's pistol pressing into the back of his neck.

What the hell have I done?

He was forced to watch in mute horror as the four men made short work of the building's occupants, sweeping from door to door and dispatching anyone in the rooms with quick, cold precision. Only Sergeant Roxburgh at the duty desk stood any chance, sitting in the building's open first-floor foyer. The Marine had spotted one of Slicky's men rounding a corner in the passageway and his reactions were immediate. Rising from his desk, his right hand drew his service weapon at the same time his left hand moved to something on his desk, but the lead Okinawan wasted no time putting four rounds through the sergeant's chest, following those with a single round to the younger man's head. Connelly saw that the Marine had been trying to reach an alarm button.

Damn it!

"Lock the door," said Slicky, gesturing to one of the other men with his free hand. "Lights out."

What time was it? Connelly glanced around the room but saw no clock. It was after 1630, practically the end of the day for any nonessential personnel or those assigned to duty outside normal working hours. Someone should likely be missing him by now.

The party!

Were his Marines wondering why he hadn't yet shown up for his own celebration? Back at the armory, he had fed Sergeant Holt the story about needing to finish some lingering paperwork, but that excuse would have expired by this point. Someone had to be wondering about his whereabouts, right?

"Move," said Slicky, pointing his Glock at Connelly.

It took them less than a minute to return to the secure level and relock the reinforced doors behind them. With every step, Connelly felt as though his arms and legs had been weighed down by cement blocks. The energy had all but fled from his body, replaced by despair, guilt, and mounting hopelessness.

For the first time, Connelly noticed that one of the Okinawans still wore a picture ID clipped to one of his lapels. It was the same sort of identification issued to contractors working aboard the different American military installations around the island; the same thing he saw countless times every day.

Of course.

This was how they had been able to pull off all of this. Most if not all of these men were plants, carrying out assorted mundane tasks around the bases while keeping tabs on the comings and goings of key personnel, vehicles, and material. Many a security briefing offered by base commanders had touched on this subject, and the need for Marines to remain vigilant when moving among these civilian workers. Why contractors of this sort were even allowed on base in the first place was a subject of frequent and continued discussion. The employment of local civilians in any number of capacities was but one part of the convoluted "status of forces agreement" between Okinawa and the United States. The SOFA governed the details of the American military's continued presence on the island, as it had since the U.S. returned Okinawa and the rest of the Ryukyu Islands to local control in 1972. Security experts had warned that the contracts allowing Okinawan civilians to work aboard American military bases were fraught with risk. While the majority of those employees were trustworthy, at least some would be susceptible to coercion by local criminal elements and foreign powers.

And look where we are.

"We won't have much time," said another of the Okinawans, intruding on Connelly's thoughts, and he noted that the man's English was better than Slicky's.

"Yes," said Slicky before turning his attention to Connelly and waved his Glock at the storage vaults. "Weapons lockers. Open them."

His heart once again racing, Connelly looked to where Slicky was pointing, and only just managed to avoid releasing a sigh of relief. The vaults in question held all manner of arms and munitions. He guessed they would command impressive prices on the black market or wherever Slicky's bosses planned to sell them. The aircraft munitions alone would almost certainly go for hundreds of thousands of dollars each, if not more.

But is that really all they want?

• • •

Despite his best efforts, Jack couldn't stifle the yawn. It was loud and long, even with his hand pressed to his mouth.

"Someone needs a nap," said Amorah Banovich, who once more was behind the steering wheel as they made their way along the Okinawa Expressway. Instead of a purloined sedan, however, she along with Jack and the others were utilizing one of however many black Toyota SUVs that seemed to be assets within Miroji Jimura's organization.

Blinking away the drowsiness, Jack sat up straighter in his seat. He couldn't help a glance over his shoulder to where Yeager sat in the SUV's middle seat. Behind him, Alkaev and Pajari lounged on the rear bench, and Jack noted that Pajari had already found a way to fall asleep. Jack envied the man's easy ability to accomplish that, but there was no way he could allow himself to drift off even for a moment. For one, he didn't trust

Yeager. If the man could sell out his own country to work for an arms dealer who sold weapons to American enemies, he would have no trouble killing anyone who got in his way.

Jack guessed that Yeager had elected to travel with them in order to monitor the outsiders working with him. It displayed an interesting level of trust for the man not only to ride in the vehicle, but to essentially be surrounded by Banovich and her people. Of course, there was no reason for them to kill Yeager, assuming everything about this temporary arrangement was on the level. From what both Banovich and Yeager had said, Jimura and Tateos Gadjoyan expected this partnership to go that way. That was all well and good in some back room or while sipping tea on some back porch, but Jack took a much different view of things where bullets were flying. There was no way he was going to trust Yeager or his men for a moment.

And don't forget about Banovich and the others, either.

Of course, circumstances now called for him and Amorah Banovich to watch each other's backs, and likewise for Alkaev and Pajari, but Jack also knew that if he somehow gave them reason to suspect him of deception, then his life would be forfeit.

Long story short? He wouldn't be sleeping for a while yet.

"What can you tell us about where we're going?" asked Banovich, keeping her eyes on the road and the other two black SUVs that were part of their informal convoy.

Yeager shifted in his seat. "From what I'm told, it's something of a way station. At least, that's how it was described. Whatever goods Kanashiro's moving on or off the island go through one of about a half dozen of these places that are scattered around the island, with a couple more on one of the adjacent islands. Based on how much time's passed since the shootout this morning, the location in Motobu is the one most likely to have our stuff, but it has the potential to be a gold mine of guns, drugs, and various other illicit yet lucrative items."

"So," Jack said, trying to appear thoughtful, "if we could make a big score here, we could give all of that to Jimura."

Yeager chuckled. "You catch on quick, Voronov."

"He can have it all," said Banovich. "I just want what Gadjoyan sent us here to get. We can tie a bow on top of everything else for Jimura. Let's get in there, get it done, and get the hell out. We're on a schedule, now."

Though he said nothing, Jack agreed with her. The *Konstantinov* was due to depart Naha Port at midnight, with or without them. Banovich had told Jack, Alkaev, and Pajari that she wanted to be aboard, with their shipment for Gadjoyan, with time to spare. Going back empty-handed was out of the question. Jack checked his watch, noting that they had just over seven hours before the ship cast off. Would they make it, or would they be dead?

It was even money at this point, Jack concluded.

Of course, there were other wrinkles. Given the events of the day, it seemed impossible to him that the NCIS and JSDF agents assigned to investigate the situation wouldn't know about locations such as the one he and the others were about to assault. Taking into account the JSDF agents working undercover within Jimura's organization, Jack figured it all but likely that they knew about this rivalry between Jimura and Kanashiro, and therefore any relevant interests either man might possess.

The more pressing issue was the action they were about to undertake. Launching another assault against one of Edoga Kanashiro's interests so soon after the raid on the other house was a risky move. On the other hand, if Kanashiro had been caught off guard by the abrupt, violent nature of the ambush, he might not yet have had time to regroup and redeploy other men to protect his other buildings, houses, or whatever.

I guess we'll see.

"What about the area around this warehouse?" asked Jack, slurring his words a bit as he affected his accent. "What can we expect?" Offering another chuckle, Yeager replied, "Gunplay won't go unnoticed, if that's what you mean. This is going to be different from the house. We need to get inside and take out as many men as we can without a firefight erupting in the street, otherwise the police will be on our ass inside of five minutes. Ten, tops, and that's only if there's traffic or a parade or some damned thing."

Their success relied on too many factors that were out of

their control, making the entire mission a huge risk. Were this a military operation, there was no way Jack would go forward based on such a shaky plan. Doing so invited disaster. They would have to tread with extreme care if they were to have any hope of getting away from there undetected. Doing so after recovering Gadjoyan's weapons shipment seemed more than a tad farfetched, the way Jack saw it. Of course, all of this was predicated on them completing a second successful ambush against an unknown number of enemy combatants.

It also hinged on Yeager or another of Jimura's men not double-crossing them and Jack getting a bullet in his head.

But we might be looking at all we need to break our case wide open. Damn it, Bauer. You've got to find a way to call Cohen.

Jack knew he was living on borrowed time before somebody way above Abigail Cohen's head called it a day and left him swinging in the wind out here. Everything they needed to connect Gadjoyan and maybe Jimura to the theft of American weapons for sale to terrorists might be inside that warehouse. Here he was, in the middle of the biggest case of his multi-phased career— certainly the most far-reaching of his brief tenure with the CIA— and there was no one he could call for help.

This day just keeps getting better and better.

"We're getting ready to turn," announced Yeager.

As she guided the SUV to follow its two companions through an intersection, Banovich asked, "Where is this?"

"We're going to hump in on foot from here," replied Yeager. "We need to reconnoiter the area before we try to sneak in the back door." He smiled. "I hope you brought your walking shoes."

Feeling the eyes of her escort on her back, Jessica Connelly walked in silence from the bathroom to the room that defined the boundaries of her existence.

"Thank you," she said, both to the man walking with her and the other Okinawan, the one who had dealt with the earlier, unpleasant experience with one of the other men. He was standing at the entrance to the room, his stance communicating that he was taking custody of Brynn and Dylan while she made use of the facilities.

The man nodded. "You are welcome." Though there was no particular warmth to his reply, he was polite. This was business to him, and he was carrying out whatever instructions had been provided to him with professional detachment. He had already assured her more than once that she and the children wouldn't be harmed, so long as they remained quiet and did what they were told, and that agreement—if that was what it could be called—was reinforced when he had killed one of his own men. They were safe, for now.

The thought sounded reassuring in her head, at any rate.

Aside from the couple of trips each of them had made to the bathroom since their arrival here, Jessica and the kids had seen nothing beyond this one section of the house that was their prison. She had no idea where she was. The room in which they were being kept had but a single window that was painted over in a shade of lime green. Some feeble light was able to come through, but she otherwise was denied any attempt to look outside and perhaps get her bearings. How long had they been here? A couple of hours, she guessed. There were no clocks visible within the small section of the house she had seen, and they had taken hers and Dylan's wristwatches. There was neither a television nor a radio, at least within sight or hearing.

"Is there anything else you need?" asked the Okinawan, whose English was much better than most of his companions.

Stepping past him and into the room, Jessica paused and returned his gaze before shaking her head. "No. Thank you."

The man nodded. He appeared older than the rest of the men they had seen so far. Though looking a bit soft around the midsection, he was still intimidating thanks to his tanned, muscled arms and broad shoulders, and a thick head with a heavy brow and black hair cut short in a buzzed, pseudo-military style. He had no neck to speak of, and his jaw was big and angular. Like his friends, he hadn't deigned to offer a name, but Dylan had already taken to calling him "Frankenstein."

Taking a seat on the bed between Brynn and Dylan, she kept her gaze on the floor, not wanting to make further eye contact with either of the men outside the room. Then, as the older man began to close the door, she held up a hand.

"Wait."

Pausing, he regarded her for a moment; not with suspicion or annoyance, or any other notable emotion, for that matter. He simply stared at her for several seconds before offering a simple reply. "Yes?"

"Will somebody please tell me why we're here? Have we done something wrong? Have we made someone angry? What are you going to do with us?"

The Okinawan's features remained fixed. "We're going to keep you here, until I receive new instructions. Nothing more. Nothing less." His voice was also lower than what she had come to expect from Okinawan men, and possessed a raspy quality that seemed to indicate he was a smoker, though Jessica hadn't caught the odor of cigarettes from him.

"But I don't understand. We don't know anything, and we're

certainly not rich. All of our belongings are on their way to the United States. We're supposed to be going home tomorrow."

"I know all of this." The man's composed demeanor was almost infuriating.

And where's Dale? Is he even still alive? Had these people killed him? The very thought was like an icy spike slamming through her heart.

Fighting the urge to cry out in anger, Jessica instead allowed herself to release a loud, exasperated sigh. "Look, I'm not trying to be difficult. I'm just scared. My children are scared. You're all scaring the hell out of us. How do you expect us to react to all of this?"

"Just as you have." Pushing open the door, the man put one foot into the room. "I will be honest with you. I do not know the exact reason you are here. My employer tells me only that which I need to know to carry out the assignments he gives me. What I do know is that I have been given strict instructions that you and your children are not to be harmed, except to ensure your continued cooperation and prevent any attempts at escape. As you've been told, remain quiet and obey our instructions, and you won't be hurt." He paused, casting his gaze toward the floor for a brief moment before returning it to her. "And I promise that you won't endure any other improper behavior from any of my men, either."

His voice was soothing, noted Jessica in a flash of insane realization. The very thought almost made her shudder, and she tried to force it out of her mind. Instead, she forced an uncertain nod before exchanging glances with each of her children. She saw her fear mirrored in their eyes, and without thinking draped her arms around their shoulders and pulled them close. Tears were welling up in the corners of her eyes but she willed herself not to wipe them away. Her lower lip wanted to tremble but she ground her teeth to the point that they began to hurt.

If the Okinawan noticed or even cared about her emotional turmoil and her attempts to maintain her composure, he chose not to mention it. Instead, he tapped his fingers along the door handle he still held in his left hand, and Jessica heard the slight clink of metal on metal. A ring? Was this monster *married*?

His expression remaining flat, he said after a moment, "There is one other thing that I can promise you."

Despite the man's poised demeanor, something in his voice made Jessica's stomach twitch. "Yes?"

"If you give me a reason, I promise that I'll kill you, but not before I kill your children while you watch, and then I'll personally deliver your heads to your husband, right before I kill him, too. Do we understand each other?"

With her children covering their mouths as they pressed ever closer against her, Jessica tried to summon a response, but no words would come. Coherent thought was hopeless. She could only sit and stare, her eyes wide with horror while her thoughts provided brutal, unforgiving imagery from this man's words, as he slowly closed and locked the door.

• • •

"All right. That's the last of it. Finish loading, and get ready to move."

Whoever these men were, Dale Connelly had concluded that they were professionals of one sort or another. There was just no other explanation for the cold, ruthless efficiency with which Slicky and his band of marauders had carried out the events of the past half hour. After ordering Connelly to unlock each of the underground armory's vaults, and working from a list he had pulled from his trouser pocket, Slicky had directed the bulk of his men to select and load specific pieces of weapons, ammunition, and aviation ordnance into the pair of trucks. Slicky had known from the start what he wanted, and in what quantities, not even bothering to ask Connelly for confirmation on a particular item's location.

At first unable to understand why they were not simply cramming as much into the two trucks as could fit, it dawned on Connelly that even the weight limits of the vehicles had been taken into consideration. He watched Slicky oversee the loading of the first truck, going so far as to tell the men in what order each box or crate should be put aboard. It was a process not at all different from the embarkation training Connelly had taken years ago, in which he had learned the proper procedures for loading Marine equipment and vehicles aboard Navy vessels. Contrary to common belief, it wasn't a simple matter of dropping boxes into a cargo hold and setting sail for faraway lands. Weight distribution was a critical component of the loading process. The first truck had been loaded in a similarly efficient manner, whereas most of the material selected for the second vehicle remained positioned near its rear cargo door. Slicky was not yet ready to load this equipment, but why?

He's still looking for something, obviously.

Footsteps behind him startled Connelly just before two of Slicky's men walked past him. They were still wearing their coveralls, but he noted that they had dispensed with their weapons and tactical gear belts in favor of standard canvas tool satchels. Both men also wore identification cards clipped to their breast pockets or lapels.

"It's done," said one of the men, directing a glance at Connelly before looking at the black runner's watch on his left wrist. "We need out of here, thirty minutes." His English, though broken, still communicated an uncomfortable intensity.

Slicky asked, "That's with fifteen-minute buffer?"

"Yes."

This seemed to satisfy Slick, who then pointed to Connelly. "You come."

Is this it?

The question rang in Connelly's mind as he followed the Okinawan back to the storage vaults, with two of the men with MP5s trailing him. Had he served his purpose for them? Were they going to execute him and be on their way?

Holy God. Wait. There's got to be something. . . .

"One vault missing," said Slicky. "Where is it?"

It took an extra moment for Connelly to register what the other man was saying. When realization dawned, he once more felt weakness in his legs. He locked his knees and clenched his hands to keep them from shaking.

"I don't understand."

Without warning, Slicky slapped him across the face with enough strength to jerk Connelly's head to the right. Everything left of his nose stung and he actually had to blink away his momentary shock from the strike. Instinct took over and he took an automatic step forward, only to stop when he heard warning shouts from behind him. He froze, looking over his shoulder and seeing the muzzle of an MP5.

"You know what I mean." Slicky held up the paper in his hand for Connelly to read. It was a printed and itemized list, detailing each of the selected weapons and munitions, accompanied by the quantities loaded or staged for loading on the trucks. Almost every item on the list had a small check mark in blue ink, made from the pen in Slicky's shirt pocket. Only the last entry lacked such an indication: "B61, Qty 1."

Connelly almost threw up all over Slicky's shoes.

"Open vault," said the Okinawan, "or you die. Your family die. Do it now." To emphasize his point, he raised his Glock, the muzzle of which now hovered less than six inches from Connelly's face.

"All right," he said, his voice dry and hoarse. He raised his hands in surrender.

The entrance to the vault in question was hidden within one of the other storage vaults. To the naked eye, it appeared as nothing more than the rear bulkhead of the room Slicky and his men had just pilfered. With several crates and other large boxes removed, the outline of the hidden door now was visible. Stepping closer, Connelly opened the small access panel set into the bulkhead, behind which was another keypad.

"You understand that once I do this, my access card will be recorded upstairs." He looked over his shoulder at Slicky. "They'll know it was me."

Slicky once more raised the Glock. "Open the door."

It wasn't until he had swiped his card and entered the access code that Connelly realized he was holding his breath. He exhaled as the door's lock disengaged, then slid to one side.

"Go," prompted Slicky.

Stepping through the open doorway, Connelly fumbled on the wall to his right until he found the light switch and toggled it. Overhead fluorescent lights flickered to life, chasing away the darkness and revealing two dozen identical metal crates, each one on its own set of rollers.

God help me.

Connelly didn't know how long the stockpile of B61 variable yield thermonuclear weapons had been here. What he did know was that their very presence violated every agreement the United States enjoyed with Okinawa and Japan with respect to American military forces occupying territory in the region. They were intended for use by Harrier jets that were a major component of the Marine Corps' aviation presence at Futenma. If it was learned that the United States had violated its SOFA agreements in such an egregious manner, the harm to international relations between the American and Japanese governments might well be irreparable. Then there was the damage to the United States military's force projection capabilities into Asia, which hinged on the bases on Okinawa and the Japanese mainland.

And that's before these maniacs set one off somewhere.

• • •

Something was off. Jack could feel it.

"What's the matter, Stefan?" asked Amorah Banovich, from where she lay next to him on the ground, using part of a fallen tree for cover. Their position, twenty-five meters from the warehouse and concealed by trees and other vegetation, gave them a decent view of the surrounding area, which Jack had surveyed with the binoculars he still held before returning his attention to the building itself.

From the outside, it looked the same as hundreds of other structures he had seen since arriving on the island. It appeared composed of concrete with a sloped aluminum roof, surrounded by asphalt with gravel roads leading away from the compound toward major roads. Aside from two entry points, access from those roads was restricted. A trio of smaller buildings were scattered around the area. Samuel Yeager had identified them as additional storage and a home for the warehouse manager, who apparently worked for Edoga Kanashiro even though that fact seemed to have eluded law enforcement officials.

"I've only counted three men outside," Jack said, after

another moment studying the compound. "That seems odd, considering what we did earlier. I'd think Kanashiro would have added more security."

Lying on the ground to his opposite side, Yeager said, "Maybe they're still trying to get additional men here. This might be good for us."

"That, or it's a trap." Jack handed the binoculars to Banovich. "Are we sure this is the right place?"

Yeager nodded. "This is the address the guy gave us."

"I wish we could get a better look inside," said Jack. The three men he had spotted had exited and entered the building at different times, and there were a half dozen cars parked nearby. From what he could tell, the warehouse appeared to be only lightly defended.

And that's what bugged him.

"Even if they have a dozen more men inside," said Banovich, "we can still take them if we drop anyone outside without attracting attention." She gestured to the warehouse. "But, if that place is packed to the rafters the way Jimura thinks it is, there's no way we can truck out everything he wants with just our crew. We need more men."

Yeager nodded. "I was just thinking the same thing. We can either wait for me to get some extra guys, and risk Kanashiro beefing up security while we sit here on our thumbs, or we can take it with the men we have, and hold the fort until my reinforcements show up."

Neither plan sounded ideal to Jack. "Or, we take the place, load up what we can, and blow the rest." In truth, that was his preferred action. If the warehouse did contain stolen American military materiel, destroying it would be preferable to allowing it to be sold to terrorists and other enemies of the United States. If he could verify that Kanashiro had gotten into the same game as Jimura to traffic in such weaponry, NCIS needed to be alerted.

Frowning, Yeager said, "That wouldn't be Mister Jimura's preferred way to go, but if it keeps Kanashiro from making any money off of what's in there, he'd get over it." He turned to Jack. "I like the way you think, Voronov." He rolled over and onto his feet, extending a hand to Banovich while Jack stood.

"How do you want to do it?" asked Banovich.

Yeager gestured with a thumb over his shoulder. "Let's go get the rest of my guys, and call in for some extra hands." He nodded to Jack. "Then we'll do it like Voronov says." He pointed to the warehouse. "Take out anybody who's wandering around outside, then we split into two teams. One on the south door, the other on the northeast. We sweep toward the center, and kill anybody who's not us. Then we load up whatever we can carry out of there, and blow the rest."

"What about explosives?" asked Jack.

That prompted another of those smiles Yeager probably thought were charming. "We brought along some goodies."

It was a short walk through the forest to where the rest of Yeager's men waited with their vehicles. The trees would provide a nice cover for their approach on the warehouse, Jack decided. Waiting until dark would be better, but that suggestion had already been shot down. They apparently were going now, or not at all.

"Wait," said Banovich, holding up a hand. "Listen."

It took Jack a moment to realize what she meant, and when he heard the noise, he shifted his gaze upward.

"Helicopters."

The three of them ducked beneath the canopy of a large tree at the drone of at least two helicopters. A moment later, a pair of what Jack recognized as CH-53E Super Stallions bearing U.S. Navy markings appeared from beyond the tree line east of the warehouse, flying low and with obvious intent. This was no flyover, Jack realized.

"Son of a bitch," he breathed, almost forgetting his accent. They all crouched down as the choppers drew closer, and now Jack heard more rumbling in the distance, but not from the air.

Banovich gripped his arm. "It's a raid. It's a goddamned raid!"

Movement from one of the roads caught his attention, and Jack turned to see four black SUVs bouncing along the gravel path. Four other vehicles were approaching on the other road, but they were beginning to spread out into the open field surrounding the compound.

"We've got to get the hell out of here," said Yeager, and Jack noted that he had already drawn his pistol. "They're going to cut us off."

Nearly every door to the warehouse swung open, disgorging more than a dozen men running in all directions. Some ran for the cars parked in the compound while others just plunged headlong across the asphalt toward the surrounding trees.

"Damn it," said Jack. "We've got to get away from here right now."

"How the hell did the Navy know about this place?" asked Yeager.

"Later!" Jack pushed Banovich to her feet.

He turned back toward the warehouse, and saw that some of the men were running in their general direction, and two of the SUVs had broken off from the packs to intercept people heading for the trees.

"Split up," he said. "Get back to the cars."

• • •

The door was locked, but Corporal Ray Ferren had a key. What he didn't understand was why he had to use it.

"Hey, Roxy, you around?" he asked as he entered the foyer. The lights were off, which was unusual, and the duty desk at the room's far end was unoccupied, which was not. Checking his watch, Ferren saw that it was a bit before eighteen hundred hours, so maybe Sergeant Murray Roxburgh was taking a walking tour of the building. That would be normal for the Marine on duty. Ferren could wait.

Still, the place felt like a tomb. Listening, he heard no sounds of activity coming from any of the nearby offices. No talking or radios, or anything else. It was after normal duty hours, but that didn't prevent personnel from working into the evenings, particularly during weeknights. The last few days before payday were often a time when Marines short on cash opted to put in some extra hours at work, catching up on mundane tasks they put off the rest of the time. Ferren had done that, himself, a few times. In fact, he could not recall a night where he had come here and found no one still lurking in the building this early in the evening.

"Hello?" he called out, walking past the duty desk. "Sergeant Roxburgh? Roxy?" He checked his watch again. "If we want to get chow, we need book, man. They close in a few minutes, and I don't have cash for Burger King." He didn't want to eat junk food anyway, as he was planning a workout in the base gym later that evening. Lifting weights didn't cost money, for one thing, but he also was hoping to run into that new lance corporal from supply. Her workouts seemed to be coinciding with his lately, and Ferren figured he had stalled long enough.

"Okay, I'm leaving you. Sayonara, bro."

He turned back toward the desk, and saw the boots.

"Rox?" Ferren moved around the desk, stopping short when he saw Roxburgh's body lying facedown on the floor. A pool of dried blood flanked him, coming from the ragged hole in the back of his head.

His hand to his mouth, Ferren felt the need to vomit. He spun around, looking for the nearest trash can, when he saw the bomb. Three bricks of C-4 plastic explosive, wrapped together with black tape and fitted with a digital clock. The display was active, and Ferren's eyes widened as he read the numbers: *00:02*.

00:01.

00:00.

• • •

Jack ran.

Behind him, the black SUVs and helicopters were pouring into the clearing. NCIS agents and JSDF soldiers were swarming the warehouse, while others were forming a perimeter around the outer edges of the compound and working their way inward. There had already been weapons fire, and shouts of warning and pain. Sirens from the SUVs were everywhere, and the two Super Stallions were hovering above the entire scene. The situation had gone to chaos, at least from the perspective of anyone fleeing the warehouse, but Jack knew better.

This was planned. All of it.

Yeager and Banovich had taken off, each in different directions. Their strategy was simple: split up and run like hell, hoping to avoid the cordon that was being established around them, or at least take advantage of whatever confusion was caused by Kanashiro's men as they scattered, engaged the NCIS and JSDF agents, or ran for their lives.

"Federal agents! Freeze!"

Jack flinched at the sudden cry, halting his headlong sprint. He looked to his left, expecting to be staring down the muzzle of a rifle. Instead, he saw a man and woman dressed in black windbreakers and aiming Beretta nine-millimeter pistols at . . . someone else. Looking farther to his left, Jack caught sight of two Okinawan men, each carrying pistols. They were out of breath from running, and Jack figured they had to have been among those who had fled the warehouse.

One of the men fired.

Both agents scrambled for cover, firing on the run as the two Okinawans started shooting. The man hunkered down behind a tree while his female partner dropped below a line of vegetation. The Okinawans were advancing on the agents, trying to take advantage of having them pinned down.

Moving around a tree that blocked their view of him, Jack gripped his Glock with both hands and opened fire. His first two shots took the first Okinawan in the head and he went down. The other man spun toward the gunfire and Jack fired again, putting two rounds into the man's chest.

"Freeze! Drop your weapon!"

Jack raised his hands and held them away from his body. He let the Glock spin by its trigger guard around his finger before it fell from his hand to the ground. Turning toward the voice, he saw that both agents, NCIS according to the logos on their windbreakers, were aiming their pistols at him.

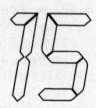

"Who the hell are you?"

Staring down the length of his Beretta pistol, Kurtz eyed the blond man standing before him. Not an Okinawan. There was an intensity in his eyes that was almost unnerving.

Still holding his hands in the air, the man replied, "My name is Jack Bauer. I'm with the CIA." He spoke with an American accent, which was to say he wasn't a Russian or European speaking poor English.

"Right," said Aguilar, "and I'm Whitney Houston. Get on your face."

"Listen," the man continued, "my name is Jack Bauer, and I'm an undercover agent. My handler is Special Agent Abigail Cohen. We're here trying to build a case against an Armenian arms dealer named Tateos Gadjoyan." He gestured back toward the warehouse. "That building supposedly contains American military hardware, that was to be sold to Gadjoyan by an Okinawan dealer named Jimura, but we were ambushed by one of Jimura's rivals. Some guy named Kanashiro."

"You were involved in that mess down in Naha?" asked Kurtz.

The man, Bauer, nodded. "Yes. Some of us got away."

Kurtz was unable to prevent a glance toward Aguilar, only to see that she was eyeing him while directing the rest of her attention to this mysterious man who was starting to say some very interesting things.

"Keep talking," said Kurtz. "Convince me."

Bauer replied, "I don't know about this Kanashiro, and all I know about Jimura is that he's a contact for the man we're investigating. I think Jimura is up to something, and whatever it is, it's going down today."

"What?" prompted Aguilar. "What's going down today?"

"I don't know. Listen, my handler, Agent Cohen, can back up everything I'm telling you, but I have to get back to the people I'm with. If they suspect I'm a plant, they'll scatter. We'll lose our case against Gadjoyan, and maybe any lead we might have to whatever Jimura's doing."

"You're investigating Jimura? I thought you just said you didn't know anything about him."

His jaw clenching, Bauer shook his head. "I'm not investigating him. I'm just following the lead to Gadjoyan wherever it takes me. Look, this guy Kanashiro is responsible for killing one of our people this morning. The only reason I know that much is because we're working with Jimura's people to get back what Kanashiro took."

"You know anything about a house shootout earlier this afternoon?" asked Aguilar. "Or a car chase down by Naha?"

"Yes. Jimura wants his money or his weapons, and so does Gadjoyan. The people I'm with are in charge of this, and they're working with Jimura's people to dish out some payback. I honestly don't care if they all kill each other, except as it relates to finding stolen American weapons."

"Assuming I buy any of this," said Kurtz, "you seem to be having a pretty bad day, and everything you try to do just digs you in deeper. Maybe the spy game's not for you."

Bauer scowled. "It's my first solo mission. The guy who died this morning was the senior agent. I've been on my own since then."

"No kidding." Kurtz was surprised to realize that he wanted to believe this clown. Some parts of his story were hard to swallow, at least without more information, but there was something about this guy that seemed to elicit trust.

Is he telling the truth, or is he just a really smooth talker?

He looked again to Aguilar. "Cuff him. We can check out his

story once we get him back to the shop."

"That's a mistake," said Bauer. "If I don't meet up with them, they'll think I'm dead or that you captured me. If we work this out and I try to get back to them later, they'll be suspicious. You have to let me go back now."

Kurtz shook his head. "Sorry, pal. Can't do it." As Aguilar holstered her weapon and extracted a pair of handcuffs from a holder at the small of her back, Kurtz stepped forward. "Now, be nice to the lady, or I'll have to put a bullet in your face."

The two-way radio he carried on his left hip chose that moment to squawk, followed by a male voice.

"Unit Two for Unit One."

Reaching for the radio, he pulled it to his mouth as Aguilar moved behind Bauer. "Go for Unit One."

"We've got it wrapped up down here. Fifteen suspects in custody. One wounded, but the medic's taking care of it. He'll live."

"We'll be there in five. Do another sweep of the compound to check for stragglers." Aguilar was behind Bauer now, reaching for his left wrist and instructing him not to move.

"Copy that."

Bauer's next move was fast, so fast that Kurtz almost didn't believe what he was seeing. As Aguilar's hand closed around his wrist and started to bring it down for the handcuffs, Bauer spun toward her, yanking her arm up and over her head. It was enough to pull her off balance as he moved behind her, his right hand pulling her Beretta from her holster and in a single fluid motion aiming it at Kurtz. He had twisted Aguilar's other arm up and over her shoulder and was pulling it back and down, and she gasped in pain.

"Don't," Bauer snapped, his right arm unwavering as he aimed the pistol at Kurtz. "Drop the weapon and the radio. Now."

Kurtz lifted his pistol's muzzle before crouching low enough to place it and the radio on the ground at his feet.

"You don't want to do this, man," he said.

"No, I don't, but you're not leaving me much choice." Aguilar started to squirm and Bauer pulled on her arm again. "Stop moving or I'll dislocate it." To Kurtz, he said, "You got cuffs?"

"Yeah."

With Bauer standing out of reach and holding Aguilar's pistol on them, she and Kurtz used both sets of handcuffs to link themselves together while they stood facefirst against a tree. Its trunk was as thick around as an average adult male, offering them enough room for some movement. Once they were secure, Bauer stepped closer, holding up the handcuff key he had taken from Kurtz, along with their NCIS credentials. Then, without a word, he placed the key on the ground near Kurtz's foot. Next, he laid both agents' weapons, radios, and IDs on the ground out of their reach. He had already retrieved his Glock and returned it to his shoulder holster.

"I'm sorry about this," he said.

Aguilar replied, "Kiss my ass."

Looking to Kurtz, Bauer said, "Agent Kurtz, remember what I told you: Special Agent Abigail Cohen. Call her when you get back."

Then he turned and ran, leaving the two agents to watch him as he disappeared into the trees.

"I'm not believing this." Aguilar was already eyeing the handcuff key on the ground. "Come on. Help me get the damned key."

Kurtz started shifting his body so they could get their linked arms down the tree. "Yeah. I really don't want the guys to find us like this."

"You think he's for real?"

"Why else would he leave us alive?"

By stretching her left hand, Aguilar was just able to capture the key between her fingers. "I don't know. Kicks?"

· · ·

More sirens screamed past the truck, muffled by the vehicle's side paneling. It was the third set they had passed in less than two minutes, according to the watch on Dale Connelly's left wrist. Sitting on the truck's wooden floor, his hands bound in front of him with duct tape, he braced himself against the wall and tried to listen to the sounds of passing traffic. Where were they? How long had they been moving? Ten or fifteen minutes, he guessed. He had tried to keep track of their direction just by turns the truck made as it left the underground bunker, or when gravel gave way to asphalt, but it was useless. There had been too many curves, turns, stops and starts for him to remember it all, though he guessed they had made their exit from Camp Hansen without incident.

"Where are we going?" he asked the pair of Okinawan men assigned as his escorts. Neither man appeared happy with the assignment, as it called for them to be stuffed into the back of the cargo truck with no ventilation. Sweat ran freely down their faces, matting their hair and soaking their shirts, and Connelly felt his own undershirt sticking to his back and chest. For the fourth or fifth time since climbing into the truck, he wiped perspiration from his forehead.

When neither man opted to answer his question, he asked, "Do you have any water?" He hadn't been minding his fluid intake during the day, and the earlier run with his unit coupled with the heat and the stress of the past few hours was starting to wear on him. A dull ache pounded in his temples, and he realized it had been hours since his last meal. Hunger pangs gnawed at him but he doubted he could eat now even if food was available.

One of the Okinawans, a short, stocky one who seemed not to be handling the heat as well as his partner, reached into a knapsack near his feet and tossed Connelly a canteen of water. It was one of those flat aluminum models with a blue nylon cover and carrying strap, and the water it contained was warm and possessed a rusty taste. Connelly drank every drop before closing its top and, being careful not to make any sudden moves, slid it back to the man.

"Thank you."

As he had more than a dozen times since being forced into the truck, Connelly regarded the oversized metal crate. It was long and thin, its wheels locked into place while the crate itself was secured to the cargo compartment's forward bulkhead. He didn't need to study the crate's markings, as he had long ago memorized such details. Although the abbreviations appeared to the untrained eye as little more than indecipherable clusters of letters and numbers, to Connelly they told a complete story. From those markings, he knew which of the twenty-three weapons hidden at the Hansen facility was nestled inside this particular crate. He could recite the serial number on the bomb's casing, and even its date and location of manufacture. The precise weight and measurements were figures at his immediate recall, and he even knew which shade of gray had been used to paint its outer shell.

Connelly also knew just how much damage this weapon could inflict, and—depending on where it was deployed—how many people it could kill. The training he had received for the care and maintenance of the bomb had been a sobering experience. The instructor had rattled off soulless strings of facts and figures to describe the B61's effectiveness. With much the same level of dedication as he had put toward learning about the use and maintenance of every firearm he had ever wielded, Connelly had listened with rapt attention to every statistic. He wrote them down, studying them and committing them to memory. If a time ever came when he was required to ready such a weapon for actual use, he wanted a complete understanding of exactly what he was doing. It was that knowledge and the respect it engendered that made him appreciate the power carried by such weapons, and the responsibility to use them with wisdom, or not at all.

And yet, you just handed one over to these guys.

Connelly didn't fight the taunting thought. Why resist the truth? He had aided these people, and in doing so committed treason. Perhaps a general or a judge might sympathize with the circumstances, but in the end, neither civilian nor military law offered provisions for personal stakes when it came to the obedience to one's duty. Assuming he lived through the day, Connelly knew he was looking at imprisonment and perhaps even execution. If his family didn't survive, then his own fate wouldn't matter to him. If by some miracle he could save them, then he could at least stand and face the consequences of his actions knowing they were safe.

Of course, what he had done to this point only raised questions about what else his captors would want from him. Why was he even still alive? The only thing that made sense was that whoever had wanted the bomb didn't possess the knowledge to arm it or otherwise deploy it. They at least had sufficient information to guide Slicky and his goons with respect to making sure the correct equipment was procured. It was Slicky who had pointed out the toolkits stored in the vault with the weapons, which were used to inspect, maintain, and prepare the bombs for use. Connelly doubted Slicky's boss had access to a Harrier jet or other plane capable of carrying the weapon, so that meant some other form of deployment.

They're going to make you arm it, you know. You're going to arm it, and then they're going to kill you.

That thought had plagued him from the moment he watched the bomb being loaded into the truck, and Connelly's fears only deepened when they hadn't simply shot him back at the bunker. He had tried to ignore the idea, but there was no escaping it. The true horror of his actions wasn't that he had handed a nuclear weapon to an enemy, but that this same enemy was going to use him to harm others.

His stomach heaved, and there was no holding back the vomit that spewed forth, staining the truck's wooden floor. Though mostly water, there also was bile and remnants of breakfast from hours earlier. Both of the Okinawans recoiled, pushing themselves away from him and toward the other side of the truck, but there was only so far they could go.

Coughing as he reached up to wipe his mouth, Connelly grimaced. "Sorry," he said. His apology was met with derisive grunts from the two men, before one said something to his partner in their native language that evoked a disdainful laugh. Connelly didn't catch it all, but he did pick up an off-color reference to female anatomy.

He wiped his hands on his camouflage trousers, then held his forearm against his nose in an attempt to hold back the odor. How much longer were they going to drive? The heat inside the truck was only making the stench worse.

Beats being dead.

Connelly wasn't so sure about that.

• • •

"Stefan!"

Amorah Banovich was the first to see him emerge from the trees, and Jack forced a smile while at the same time holding up his hands to show Yeager and his men that he wasn't carrying his pistol.

"What happened?" asked Rauf Alkaev, from where he stood behind Banovich and next to Manish Pajari. "We were starting to worry."

Jack replied, "Some of Kanashiro's men made a break for it, and NCIS sent two teams to grab them. Everybody was coming at me, so I had to find a place to hide while they sorted it out. At least one of Kanashiro's people was shot, and I think they rounded up everybody else. I was able to slip through the perimeter in all of the confusion."

His report contained as much fact as falsehood. While it was true that the NCIS and JSDF had established a cordon around the warehouse and the immediate surrounding area, he had made good time on foot getting beyond the ring's outer boundary even as the law enforcement agencies were closing off routes of escape and rounding up Kanashiro's men. His only other obstacle was a near-tragic encounter with a habu, one of only a few species of venomous snakes that were abundant all over Okinawa and the other Ryukyu Islands. From what Jack had read, the snakes were territorial, predatory, and irritable. While their venom was toxic, fatalities were rare if the victim received timely medical treatment. Given the company he was currently keeping, Jack wondered if Yeager or even Banovich might not just put him out of his misery had he suffered a bite.

Opting not to test that theory, Jack instead had shot the snake.

He wondered how long it had taken the two NCIS agents, Kurtz and Aguilar, to free themselves from the predicament in which he had placed them, and if they had yet had a chance to call Abigail Cohen.

Here's hoping.

"What do we do now?" asked Banovich, looking to Yeager.

The American shook his head. "Beats the hell out of me.

Mister Jimura's going to be pissed when he hears about this."

"This might not be all bad," said Jack. When that earned him a dubious glare from Yeager, he added, "Think about it. Thirty minutes later and it would've been us the American agents were apprehending. Kanashiro and his people are the ones who are going to be dealing with them, not us. There's no link to Jimura. Even the weapons Jimura stole, if they're in that warehouse, are going to fall on Kanashiro." He was making this up as he went, but it sounded convincing, at least to his ears.

Yeager seemed to be buying it, as well. He was silent for a moment, as though processing this scenario, then nodded. "You might just be right. Maybe you should come to work for me. You've got a good head for this, Voronov."

"Hands off, Yeager," countered Banovich. "Stefan already has a job." She glanced at him, and Jack noted her flirtatious wink.

Nice to know I have options, after the agency fires my ass.

"Come on," Yeager said, nodding toward the SUVs. "Let's get out of here."

Banovich asked, "Where are we going now?"

"I have instructions to rally at another of our safe houses." Yeager nodded toward the warehouse. "We're done here, and it'll be dark soon. Come on, let's move."

• • •

The sun was partially obscured by the trees and hills to the west, and as they approached the warehouse, Kurtz felt Aguilar slapping him on the arm.

"What the hell is that for?" he asked.

"If anybody asks, we got a flat tire."

Kurtz shrugged. "I was going to tell them we stopped for a burger."

"Whatever."

The compound outside the warehouse was awash with dozens of NCIS and JSDF agents, a good number of whom were engaged in various activities pertaining to the building itself and the fifteen Okinawan nationals who had been apprehended trying to flee the area. That much had been communicated to Kurtz and Aguilar via their two-way radios.

Standing next to a blue sedan with United States government plates was Nick Minecci, wearing a tactical vest over his dark blue knit shirt and khaki pants. The agent was talking into a mobile phone sitting in its carrying bag on the car's hood. When he spotted Kurtz and Aguilar approaching, Kurtz heard him say, "Hey, let me get back to you, all right?" After hanging up the phone, he turned to them with a curious expression. "Well, look who it is. What the hell happened out there?"

"Flat tire," offered Kurtz.

At the same time, Aguilar said, "We stopped for a burger."

Minecci's eyes narrowed. "You want to take a sidebar?"

"Yes," said Kurtz.

Aguilar shook her head. "Nope."

"What's the story?" asked Kurtz, gesturing toward the warehouse.

"Baby, we hit the mother lode." Waving for them to follow him, Minecci led the way to the warehouse's nearest door. "You're not going to believe the stash these guys had. Money, guns, drugs, electronics, bootleg movies and music. There's even knockoffs of designer purses. It's like Sears in there. Somebody somewhere is going to be six kinds of pissed when they find out they lost all of this."

They entered the warehouse, and Kurtz stopped as he beheld the stacks of crates and other shipping containers taking up space inside the building. There also were rows of storage lockers against the walls, and folding conference tables arranged in rows of ten. Various tools and equipment littered the tables, and trash cans were positioned at various points along the rows. Many of the boxes were filled to overflowing with packing materials, scrap pieces of wood and cardboard, soft drink and beer cans, food wrappers, and other junk. A handful of NCIS and JSDF agents were milling about the area, cataloging and photographing the room's contents.

Minecci said, "Now, most of this crap is garden variety bootlegging. There's a room at the far end with banks of CD burners and VCRs, and enough blank tapes and CDs to put RadioShack out of business." Then, the agent pointed to a row of boxes along the room's back wall. "That over there's the primo stuff. Drugs and guns, and guess who the guns belong to?"

"Uncle Sam," replied Aguilar.

Kurtz smiled. "Please tell me we can tie any of this to Kanashiro, or maybe even Jimura."

"That's the bad news, or at least the 'not so good just yet' news." Minecci sighed. "None of the boneheads we grabbed had any ID on them. We can do fingerprints, but it's going to take a while to see if there are any matches to known associates."

Aguilar asked, "What about the building?"

Shaking his head, Minecci replied, "No go. According to records, the building belongs to a local construction company. I've got a couple of agents going to check him out, but you know he's not going to know anything. If we're lucky, he'll have the documentation to show he's leasing the building to some other guy who ends up being a paper phantom, with no ties to Kanashiro."

"Damn it." Reaching up to rub his temples, Kurtz groaned with fatigue and annoyance. "Okay, keep poking around in here. Maybe we'll get lucky." Drawing a deep breath in an attempt to shake loose the cobwebs, he asked, "Hey, did you get the number I asked for?"

Snapping his fingers, Minecci reached into his pants pocket and withdrew a folded piece of paper. "Not an easy lady to find."

"That's why I put you on it." Kurtz had relayed the request over his radio as he and Aguilar were walking to the warehouse from the little obstacle the man named Jack Bauer had fashioned for them.

Outside, Kurtz and Aguilar availed themselves of the phone from Minecci's car, and Kurtz dialed the number on the paper. There was a pickup after two rings, followed by a female voice.

"Special Agent Cohen."

"Yeah, my name's Special Agent Kurtz, with the Naval Criminal Investigative Service here on the island. I've got a message for you: Jack Bauer says hello."

• • •

Brigadier General Leslie Timmons looked at the smoking ruins of his building.

Standing in silence, he watched as Marines and civilian emergency response teams moved around the perimeter of the collapsed structure. The fires scattered across the rubble had been extinguished and water ran from the piles of concrete, metal, wood, and whatever else had gone into the building's construction, but plumes of smoke still drifted skyward. Fire trucks, both from the base and the neighboring town of Kin, were scattered around the scene. Timmons noted with satisfaction that the response to the incident had been exceptional.

"Do we have any idea what the hell happened?"

Standing to his left and a pace behind him, Sergeant Major Ronald Hanagan replied, "Nothing official, General, but we've already got people coming from all over the base saying it was an explosion. It blew out windows in buildings within fifty meters, and we're even getting reports from out in town about people being rattled. It could take days to find out what really happened."

Timmons tried not to dwell on the implications that evoked. "What about casualties? Any word on that, yet?"

"Not yet, sir. We've got the unit commanders verifying their rosters and letting us know about anyone who's not accounted for." The grizzled, veteran Marine paused, clearing his throat. "I know how this sounds, General, but we were lucky, sir. If this had happened in the middle of the day . . ."

Timmons could appreciate Hanagan's meaning, having seen firsthand the results of a bombed building when it was fully occupied. More than a decade earlier, in October of 1983, he had lost three good friends on what should have been a mundane Sunday morning. A truck packed with explosives had destroyed a barracks and killed more than two hundred U.S. Marines assigned to a peacekeeping mission in Beirut, Lebanon. Fifty-five French paratroopers fell victim moments later to a second truck delivering a similar attack at their own base. Timmons had been a lieutenant colonel then, and by happenstance was at the Marine compound's opposite end when the first truck broke through the barricades and delivered its deadly cargo. The images of that day, and the days that followed as bodies of friends and fellow Marines were pulled from the wreckage, haunted him to this day.

"How many civilian responders are on scene?" he asked.

Hanagan replied, "Seventeen, sir, all from units based in Kin. The rest are our people. There actually wasn't much to the fire, and it only took one unit to bring it under control. Right now, they're checking for hot spots."

"You know we need a secondary sweep," said Timmons, eyeing his aide with a deliberate look.

"Already on it, General."

The sergeant major made a small gesture toward the remains of the destroyed building, where two Marines dressed in typical firefighters' protective clothing complete with helmet, oxygen tank, and mask were making a slow circuit of the building's far end. Clipped to the first Marine's equipment harness was a device that could pass for a regulator or some other gauge on his respirator equipment, but Timmons recognized it as a compact, field portable Geiger counter. After a few moments, the Marine stopped to study the device before looking around the area. When his eyes settled on Timmons and Hanagan, the Marine offered a thumbs-up signal.

Thank God.

Timmons' authority as the commanding general of Marine Corps Base, Camp Smedley D. Butler extended not to a single base but instead almost every Marine installation and tenant organization on Okinawa, all of which fell under the Camp Butler command sphere. The lone exception was the air station at Futenma, but the two commands made frequent use of each other's facilities and resources.

Like the one right in front of you.

He was responsible for the health and well-being of every Marine, military dependent, or civilian employee at each of the bases under his command. The list of resources, missions, and ongoing support duties he oversaw was staggering, including several that fell under a security umbrella. The destroyed building before him was one such responsibility.

Upon his arrival on Okinawa—his third tour here, as it

happened, and the second duty assignment to the island he had undertaken with his family in tow—and assumption of duties as Camp Butler's commanding general, Timmons was stunned to be briefed into one particular piece of classified information. Learning that the United States was storing two dozen nuclear weapons on the island, in direct, unflinching violation of agreements with the Japanese and Okinawan governments pertaining to such arms, had shaken him for several days after the revelation.

He understood the original justification given for the storing of the weapons. They were a contingency against the Russians in the event of conflict between the two superpowers at the height of the Cold War. Now that the Soviet Union had imploded, however, that threat had faded, to be replaced with "rogue states" and terrorist cells. Timmons had come to realize over the course of a twenty-nine-year career that, in political circles, it was always preferable to have a new threat. There needed to be new adversaries America could point at and use as a reason to remain ever vigilant, prepared, and continually churning out new weapons of unimaginable power. That this occurred while funneling astonishing amounts of money into the pockets of the military-industrial complex, upon which many a presidential or congressional candidate tended to pin their futures, was of course a pleasing happenstance for many a Washington political crony. This knowledge often conflicted with Timmons and his genuine desire to serve and protect his country in honorable fashion, and there were days when resolving the two sides of the issue was all but impossible.

Two more years until retirement. Two more years.

Meanwhile, there were twenty-four questions for which he needed answers, and all of them were buried under the rubble of this building.

"Once we get the civilian responders out of here," said Timmons, "I'm going to want another sweep, just to be sure. I also want people on hand as they start recovery operations." Even that would be a more convoluted operation than normal, he knew, owing to the need to protect from prying eyes the secrets that lay beneath this building. He also would have to apprise NCIS and perhaps even the Japanese Self-Defense Force, depending on what cause was determined for the blast. Was this a deliberate act of sabotage, or simply a tragic accident?

Les Timmons desperately hoped it was the latter.

With every punch, the bag shuddered and swung. Edoga Kanashiro watched its leather shell fold and wrinkle. He reveled in the sound of the rope suspending it creaking and groaning in protest, along with the wooden beam holding the bag above the floor. He was lashing out as fast as the bag would return to him, pummeling it ever harder with each successive strike. Even with the padded gloves, there was shooting pain in his knuckles, and he was certain he felt the moisture of his own blood seeping between his fingers.

He didn't care. Kanashiro ignored the pain, and the sweat seeping into his eyes. Through stinging, blurred vision, he hit the bag harder, snarling and growling with each new blow until patience ran out and he drove his right foot forward in a thrust kick. The impact was powerful enough to snap the rope from its beam, sending the bag arcing to the floor before it skidded into the waist-high wall of his open-air exercise area.

Standing in the middle of the exercise mat, Kanashiro held his mouth shut and forced himself to breathe through his nose, willing his respiration to subside. He felt the rivulets of perspiration running down his shirtless torso, helping to cool him in the early evening air. Only when his breathing returned to normal did he move from his stance, and for the first time used his forearm to wipe sweat from his face.

He sensed someone behind him, knowing only one person

would dare disturb him in this private space.

"Tell me," he said.

"It is not good," replied Rino Nakanashi. "Not good, at all, Kanashiro-san."

Using his teeth to loosen the Velcro fasteners securing his gloves to his wrists, Kanashiro turned to face his trusted assistant. "I didn't ask for your feelings on the matter. What happened?"

"The warehouse in Motobu was raided by the Americans and Japanese forces. I am still attempting to learn what drew them there in the first place. According to lookouts I have surveying the scene, the authorities are still there, inventorying everything."

As he removed his gloves, Kanashiro blew out his breath. "Everything."

"That's correct, including the balance of the consignment we . . . liberated from Jimura's people this morning."

Kanashiro closed his eyes, tossing away the gloves and forgetting them on the padded training mat. Satisfied that his anger was sated for the moment, he moved to a water cooler standing against the exercise area's far wall. "That's unfortunate, for several reasons. If the Americans are involved, then they will keep digging and scratching their way from house to house, hole to hole, until they find those who are stealing their weapons." Dispensing water from the cooler into a paper cup, Kanashiro drank the entire portion before refilling it. "Tell me we are insulated from this."

"I don't know that I can do that, in all honesty," replied Nakanashi. "So far as I know, none of the men working there carried identification, and of course none of them have any direct ties to you. That does not mean the Americans or local police won't strive to make such a connection."

Nodding in reluctant agreement, Kanashiro finished the second serving of water and threw the empty cup into a trash can next to the cooler. "What of the building itself?"

"My sources tell me the American agents are already verifying its ownership. They have tracked it to the construction company we use as a front, but that should lead them to nothing." Nakanashi smiled. "We endeavor to keep you well away from such easy traps, Kanashiro-san."

Not of a mind to listen to his assistant's smug self-confidence, Kanashiro said, "And yet, the Americans walked right in and confiscated an entire warehouse. Do you think it was a random selection, Rino? You may wish to revisit your methods, and soon."

"Yes, Kanashiro-san." Nakanashi bowed, appearing duly chastised.

Returning to the exercise mat, Kanashiro picked up the punching bag and sat it on its end against the nearby wall. He took a towel from a stack on an adjacent table and began wiping his bare and still damp chest, arms, and shoulders. "This cannot continue. It's obvious Jimura's not going to let this morning's events pass, and he no longer seems content to wait for me to come to him. He's bringing the fight to us." He could appreciate and perhaps even admire such audacity, but only to a point. "What of these trucks of his?" he asked, wiping his face with the towel. "The ones that came from the American Marine base."

Nakanashi shook his head. "We do not know what, if anything, was in those trucks, Kanashiro-san, but have you seen the news?"

"Yes." A report aired just before he had come to exercise, highlighting an explosion at Camp Hansen, one of the Marine Corps bases on the island's northern half. According to the reports, the blast had leveled an entire building. Casualties were feared, but so far, no bodies had been recovered.

"It's impossible that this is coincidence," said Nakanashi.

Kanashiro nodded, slinging the towel over his shoulder. "I agree. It looks like he really is going after the Americans, as our source told us. What I don't understand is how or why he chose to do so in such blatant fashion." It would be a bold move for any of them to attempt—but Jimura? It was unheard of. Had Jimura's hatred of Americans in general and their soldiers in particular finally robbed him of his senses? The afternoon's actions implied that he was losing the edge that had always made him such a formidable rival. These brazen attacks were a way of communicating that he had run out of patience, and now was willing to do whatever was required to secure what he wanted, regardless of the risk.

Or, was it something else?

"Those rumors," said Kanashiro after a moment. "Jimura, supposedly sick. Has that ever been confirmed?"

Nakanashi shook his head. "Not confirmed, no, but the rumors persist. We know he has had doctors come to visit him, and he tends to conduct business from his house rather than one of his offices. It's possible that he suffers from the usual sorts of maladies that affect the aged."

"Perhaps," said Kanashiro, but he wasn't convinced. "Find out what you can. If Jimura is suffering from something more serious, that might well be affecting his judgment, and if he's making decisions as a result of some impairment, that makes him even more dangerous." He would be not unlike a rabid dog, and there was only one way to deal with such a problem, but at what cost? Kanashiro had already lost too many men and resources today, for which he had nothing to show. How best to proceed from here?

Nakanashi said, "I think you should consider relocating to one of the safe houses that are not known even to most of your employees."

Kanashiro glared at him. "You want me to hide?"

"No, merely give yourself an opportunity to regroup, and to plan next steps. Today has been . . . a trying day. Perhaps some fresh thinking is in order."

To Nakanashi's credit, the idea made a certain sense to Kanashiro. In addition to this, his primary home, he also possessed two other houses, each with its own dedicated staff, to which he could retire with little notice and remain in seclusion until this situation was resolved. If things deteriorated to the point that he needed to leave the island, each safe house contained sufficient resources to support such a move. He could disappear to practically anywhere in the world, and set everything into motion with but a phone call.

"We need to extend this idea of yours," he said. "Let's make sure our inner circle people are aware of what's going on. As for the people in the outer circles, I leave it up to the department leaders to decide who should be informed."

For years, almost from the beginning, Kanashiro had organized his operation in what he liked to think of as concentric circles. At the center was himself, and a very small, select group of trusted individuals. Next came the inner circle, which were the men he entrusted with running the various facets of the organization, where the fruits of labor and deal making were harbored. The outer circles consisted of employees in numerous capacities, most of whom were oblivious to the true nature of their employer. Recruitment from these outer circles into the inner realm happened only on rare occasions, and Kanashiro was very particular with respect to such selections. It was a variation on a classic arrangement that had worked for generations, insulating him from anyone looking to do him harm, such as law enforcement or a rival.

It also gave him an idea.

Smiling, he turned to Nakanashi. "So, the Americans have opted for direct action. Fine. Let's give them something on which to act."

"What are you suggesting?" asked Nakanashi.

"I'm suggesting that if the Americans begin raiding some of Jimura's houses and businesses the way they seem intent on coming after mine, this will give him fewer directions to run, both himself and his goods. The trick is seeing to it that Jimura is left with only certain hiding places: ones we know about, but the Americans do not."

"You propose alerting the Americans to Jimura's safe houses?" Nakanashi's eyes narrowed. "That is unprecedented. There are those who will see it as dishonorable."

"We were planning to replace or remove those people, anyway," replied Kanashiro, "starting with Jimura."

Pondering this for a moment, Nakanashi asked, "Why not just alert the Americans to all of Jimura's safe houses? Let them do your work for you?"

"Because, Rino, there's no sport in that. I will take Jimura myself, tonight."

I will carve the withered heart from your chest, old man.

• • •

Jack reckoned this house was even more run-down than the last one.

"I can see what you're thinking," said Samuel Yeager as he climbed out of the SUV's front passenger seat. "It's a unique fixer-upper opportunity."

Opting not to reply, Jack studied the house's dilapidated exterior, with its chipped, fading paint, rusted metal roof, overgrown weeds and shrubs around the foundation, and rotting wooden porch that might double as a booby trap. His instinctive response was that they might be better served by setting the house on fire and roasting hot dogs over it, but he opted for silence. Disparaging the home of one's host was considered rude in most cultures, after all.

"Is there a bathroom?" asked Banovich, emerging from the vehicle's rear seat.

Pointing toward the house, Yeager replied, "Around the back, past the barn. Enjoy the view."

As the rest of Yeager's men, Alkaev, and Pajari unloaded from the SUVs, Jack gestured toward the house, which was dark save for dim lights in two windows. "Any water in there?"

"Yeah, there should be big bottles inside."

"Thanks." Jack started toward the house, following several of Yeager's men, but stopped at the sound of approaching vehicle engines. Looking in the direction of the sound, he saw headlights moving through the trees, following the winding dirt path that connected to the main road.

"Relax, Voronov. They're ours."

The headlights belonged to a pair of white cargo trucks, and Jack watched them as they drove to the mouth of the dirt path, maneuvering past the house and toward the larger barn behind it.

"Hey, Voronov," said Yeager, and Jack turned to see him gesturing toward Alkaev and Pajari. "Take your men back to the barn. My guys brought some treats for you."

Exchanging wary glances with the other two men, Jack forced himself not to draw his pistol as the trio made their way beyond the house and toward the barn. Jack heard a motor start from somewhere in the barn, and a moment later an oversize light over the structure's door flared to life. Additional lighting came on inside the barn itself, and from three more of the larger lamps on poles positioned around the area of yard between the barn and the house.

The trucks were positioned so that their rear cargo doors faced the barn, and more Okinawan men were climbing out of both vehicles. Jack noted that three of the men huddled together and spoke in hushed tones before two of them, each armed with what he recognized as an H&K MP5 submachine gun, ran toward the trees in the general direction of the road. Were they sentries? Jack had seen no one who might be a guard on their way in toward the house, but he supposed he could have missed someone observing from a concealed position in the near darkness.

"What's going on?" asked Banovich as she joined Jack and the others.

Alkaev replied, "Yeager sent us back here. He says there's something for us."

"Oh, yeah, there is," said the American as he walked toward them from the house. He waved to one of the trucks. "Take a look."

Using a flashlight to peer into the truck's rear cargo compartment, Banovich played the beam over several crates. Standing next to her, Jack recognized from the markings on several of the containers that they held M16A2 rifles. Beyond those containers were other boxes, each of them labeled with some other type of American military weaponry, if the markings were to be believed.

"For Mister Gadjoyan." Yeager nodded toward the truck. "From Mister Jimura, and courtesy of the United States Marine Corps."

"Where did you get these?" asked Banovich, running her hand across the top of one of the crates.

Yeager shrugged. "Let's just say there was something of a fire sale. I'm told that this should cover the consignment lost this morning. You're free to verify that, of course."

Banovich nodded. "Please pass on my thanks to Mister Jimura. This is unexpected, and very generous."

"Don't get too excited just yet," replied the American.

"We've still got unfinished business."

"Understood," said Banovich, "and we're not leaving until that's concluded." She gestured toward the truck. "However, we need these loaded to our ship in Naha before midnight. That's when it's supposed to depart the port, and if there's a delay, somebody will get suspicious."

Yeager replied, "There's still time. Don't worry. You'll make it."

"Don't forget about the Americans," said Jack. When both Yeager and Banovich turned toward him, he added, "It's obvious they're on to Kanashiro, and probably Jimura, too. We shouldn't stay here too long."

"Nobody knows about this place," said Yeager. Then, his expression changed and he looked in the direction of the road. "Well, almost nobody. Either way, we're not going to be here that long."

Jack was about to say something else, but then his attention was drawn to a man emerging from the second truck. He was an American male, dressed in a camouflage uniform and with his hands secured before him with gray duct tape. From the man's haircut and the way the sleeves of his uniform top were rolled, Jack could see that he was a Marine. When the man stepped down from the truck, he turned to face one of the Okinawan men escorting him, and Jack was able to make out the letters on the embroidered nametape above the man's right breast pocket: CONNELLY. It took Jack an extra second to recall where he had heard that name.

Son of a bitch.

It was a huge piece of the puzzle Jack had been trying to fit together all day, with a picture he couldn't yet see. Jack said nothing as the man was escorted into the barn, leaving Jack with all manner of questions. This man, Connelly, was being used by Jimura somehow, with his family being held in order to force compliance. Who was he? What of value did he possess, or was he able to access?

Though she also was curious about the new arrivals, Banovich kept her attention on Yeager. "We're moving again?"

"That's the name of the game today," replied Yeager, waving

toward the trucks. "My instructions were to meet up with the trucks, then proceed on to another staging area. One thing about Mister Jimura: He likes to keep things moving, and I don't just mean figuratively. Nothing stays in one place too long. We move goods in and out as fast as possible, and any standing inventory is kept squirreled well away from prying eyes. Even I don't know where everything is. Anyway, my point is that Mister Jimura plans ahead, and not just a few moves. He's not usually worried about the game you're playing right now; he figured it out a while back, and he's working on how to beat you three or four games down the road."

To Jack, Miroji Jimura was sounding more and more like the sort of person on which the CIA should be keeping a closer eye. This business with Gadjoyan might have put the Okinawan arms dealer on their radar, but it seemed like he was overdue for the sort of intensified scrutiny that only Langley's finest could provide.

I'll be sure to put that idea in a memo, assuming I live long enough.

That line of thought was interrupted by the sounds of rushed footsteps. From the dirt path leading out to the road, the two men Jack had seen taking off into the woods were returning, only now they were not alone. At gunpoint, they were guiding two other Okinawans toward the barn. Both of the new arrivals were walking with their hands raised, and while one man carried himself with defiance and even contempt, his companion's face was a mask of fear.

"Well, well," said Yeager. "What've we got here?"

One the men carrying the MP5s replied, "We spotted them tailing us. We think they have followed us from the base."

Base?

Jack frowned at that. What base? A Marine base? Is that where they had found their prisoner, Connelly?

Yeager nodded toward the man who was eyeing him with open disdain. "I know this guy. He works for Kanashiro. Isn't that right, Hachiro?" For the benefit of Jack and the others, he said, "This is Hachiro Jiroku. He's a relatively low-level courier type, but he at least knows the real deal, rather than just being some lackey who fills out one of Kanashiro's fronts." He looked to the other man, who was avoiding eye contact. "Don't know much about this guy, though."

As though reaching into his pocket for a cigarette or a stick of gum, Yeager drew his pistol and aimed it at the first man, pulling the trigger from a distance of less than a foot. The single round went through the man's forehead and his body jerked backward before falling lifeless to the ground. Even Jack was unprepared for the sudden, brutal action.

The man's partner hadn't seen it coming, either, and his immediate reaction was to scream in horror as his stared at the body of his dead friend. His scream only grew louder when Yeager put a round through his leg. He collapsed on the ground, reaching for his leg while his escorts stepped back to give Yeager room. The American moved closer and knelt beside the now-terrified man.

"Okay, then. Let's you and me have a little chat."

• • •

If there was one thing Kurtz hated in this business, it was an anonymous tip.

"Please tell me we're taking this with a ten-pound bag of salt," said Aguilar. Standing at her desk, she had disassembled her Beretta pistol and was giving all of its components a once-over. Lying next to the weapon was a tactical vest, a radio, and other accessories she was planning to take with her.

Kurtz, in the midst of double-checking his own, similar collection of gear, replied, "Don't worry. Minecci's checking out everything. We don't move until he gives the all-clear."

The evening had taken an interesting turn when the NCIS duty desk fielded a call from someone wishing to remain unidentified. Speaking in native Okinawan, the caller had imparted what Minecci described as "salacious tidbits" regarding Miroji Jimura and three separate locations that the NCIS, JSDF, and local police believed were safe houses or otherwise of interest to the suspect arms trafficker.

Having finished wiping down the Beretta's various parts,

Aguilar was beginning the process of reassembling the pistol. "Okay, so anybody want to place bets? We know it's probably not just a concerned citizen, so are we talking informant, or somebody from inside Jimura's camp trying to set us up?"

"Either one works," said Kurtz, as he dropped two replacement magazines for his own pistol in a nylon pouch he could fix to his belt. "The guy knew about the hit in Naha, and the hit on the house, and our warehouse raid." What hadn't come up during the call was any mention of the explosion at Camp Hansen, which had leveled a building. Though no one had come out and mentioned any connection between that incident and everything else that was going on today, Kurtz had been doing this long enough to know that the odds of these events not being related in some fashion were rather thin.

"Yeah," said Aguilar. "Well, I'm still going with 'too good to be true,' for the moment, if it's okay with everybody." With her Beretta now reassembled, she racked the weapon's slide to make sure it was functioning properly. Inserting a magazine into the pistol's grip, she chambered a round and engaged the safety before returning the Beretta to its holster on her hip.

Kurtz nodded. "Yeah, I hear you. We can wait on Nick." Now with actionable intel on which to move, Minecci had already deployed teams to each of three locations given by the caller. The teams would recon two houses and a commercial building just south of Naha, in the hopes of finding something that would lead NCIS and JSDF to Jimura.

Stifling a yawn, Kurtz glanced at his watch. It was well past the end of their normal duty day, but today had evolved way past anything resembling "normal." He had consumed a sandwich from one of the vending machines in the break room, doing his best to swallow without actually tasting whatever meat-like substance lurked between the slices of soggy bread, but hunger was announcing itself yet again.

"I need food," he said. "Or, a reasonable facsimile thereof, and coffee. Want anything?"

Aguilar replied, "A margarita the size of my head."

"I'll see if they've restocked the machines." Kurtz turned to head for the break room, fumbling for change in his pants pocket, when he realized he was about to run into someone standing in his way. Looking up, he saw a woman dressed in faded jeans and a green satin top beneath a black windbreaker. She had "federal agent" all but tattooed on her forehead.

"Special Agent Kurtz?" she asked.

"Yeah?"

The woman held out her hand. "Abigail Cohen."

Kurtz nodded as they shook hands. "We've been expecting you, Agent Cohen." Directing her back to his and Aguilar's desk, he made introductions and said, "Your boy Bauer's been having himself quite a day."

"Well, it's just the latest in a string of long ones," replied Cohen. "He's been undercover inside Gadjoyan's organization for a while now, and he and Agent Fields were on the verge of catching a big break before everything went to hell this morning." She paused, and Kurtz got the sense that she was still dealing with the death of her fellow agent, William Fields, during the Naha shootout.

That emotional wavering lasted only a brief moment, though, before she returned her full attention to the topic at hand. "Since then, Bauer's basically been trying to keep his head above water. We haven't heard from him since this morning, and based on what he told you, we're thinking he's doing whatever he can to maintain his cover long enough for us to make our case against Gadjoyan. That it's managed to dovetail with your investigation into Miroji Jimura and this other player, Kanashiro, seems to be a fortunate accident."

"Accident's a word," said Aguilar.

Cohen replied, "Look, I get you're not happy about Bauer, but the simple fact is that your guy, Kanashiro, set off a grenade in the middle of what was supposed to be a pretty uneventful arms deal." She rolled her eyes. "As uneventful as you can be when we're talking about selling American weapons to potential terrorists, that is. This Kanashiro character has apparently decided it's time to stir the pot around here. What that means for Jimura and every other scumbag on the island, I don't know or care, except that it's obviously playing into my case."

She crossed her arms. "I know our bosses like to dance

around each other, but I honestly don't give a damn about that today. I've got a man twisting in the wind and a case to bring against Tateos Gadjoyan, and you could probably use some extra help with your investigation. I say we team up, piss off all our bosses, and get something done. You in?"

Kurtz found her plea compelling, and it was a refreshing change from the wall of silence that was the usual response whenever NCIS or anybody else who wasn't a part of the Central Intelligence Agency requested help from the boys and girls of Langley, Virginia. It was obvious that Cohen was putting the well-being of this other agent, Bauer, ahead of her mission and quite possibly her career. He could damn well respect that.

"Yeah," he said. "We're in."

Aguilar asked, "Did you give this speech to your higher-ups?"

"I've got approval from my direct supervisor," replied Cohen. "Everybody else can read the after-action report."

"You want to back up?"

Brynn Connelly crossed her arms and offered her best condescending teenaged girl expression at the man standing outside the bathroom. He had been lurking just a bit too close to the door when she opened it, and she had no reservations about communicating her disapproval.

Perv.

The looks she and her mother had received from the various men since their arrival here had been uncomfortable at first, but by now Brynn realized the leering was very likely as far as things would go. That much had been made clear with the man who had tried to paw her mother. There was still blood on the floor of their room where he had fallen after the other man shot him.

Brynn could still hear the pistol shot and the thud of the man's body collapsing to the floor. It was the first time she had ever seen anyone die right in front of her, let alone in such violent fashion, and she knew she would carry that image with her for a while. Her brother, on the other hand, hadn't reacted well. The shock of the killing had shaken Dylan to the point that their mother had been forced to rock him to sleep, and now that he had awakened from a fitful nap he was sitting in the corner of the bed, pressed up against the wall with his knees pulled to his chest. He had said nothing, and his eyes seemed vacant, as though he were a zombie. Any offers of food or water had been ignored, and Mom had spent the past hour trying to comfort him, to no avail.

Meanwhile, Brynn found reason to rebel.

"Stop staring at me," she snapped at the man who was her escort from the bathroom back to the room she shared with her mother and Dylan. From the looks of his eyes, he had been drinking, and that made Brynn worry. Alcohol had a tendency to bring out the worst in people. If someone was already a lowlife to begin with, how much worse could booze make a situation?

Right.

The guard's only response was to widen the smile he directed at her. She could feel his eyes on her as they walked back to the bedroom, listening to his stumbling, even uncertain footsteps. Was he that drunk?

She hugged herself in a vain attempt to ward off the chill coursing through her. It was getting later in the evening, just based on the quick looks she had snagged from windows in other rooms as she made her way back and forth along the hallway. She had no idea what time it was, but there were fewer people here at the house than there had been earlier in the day. The man who had killed the guard being a jerk to her mother had left a couple of hours earlier. It seemed that with the boss gone, some of the employees were starting to relax.

Brynn didn't like what that might mean.

Why were they still here, anyway? Why bring them here in the first place? None of this made any sense, and their captors had made no effort to alleviate that confusion. How much longer would they be here? It was the one question that gave Brynn pause, because she didn't want to contemplate answers to the question which logic demanded would come next.

What's going to happen to us?

"Wait," said the guard behind her. When she turned, she saw that his attention was on something inside the room they had just passed. He gestured for her to step back toward him as he more stumbled than walked into the room, and when she moved to the door she saw an unmade single bed pushed against the far wall.

"Don't even think about it," she said, hoping the man didn't hear the tremor in her voice.

Casting a scornful glance over his shoulder, the guard shook his head before reaching for a small refrigerator next to the bed. It was a model similar to the one in her hotel room. This, of course, reminded Brynn that she hadn't eaten in a few hours, and now she was hungry.

There was no food in this refrigerator, but instead several cans of what she suspected was beer. The kanji text on the can confirmed her guess, and she offered silent, sarcastic thanks to her high school Japanese language teacher.

With another leer, the guard offered her a can. She was tempted to take it just to see what he would do, but thought better of that idea. The last thing this guy needed was anything he could interpret as an invitation. Instead, she kept her expression set on "judgmental," even when he tripped over the lip of the ragged throw rug in the center of the room, dropped his beer, and kicked it across the floor.

Well, she almost did that. Instead, she giggled.

Damn it.

That was definitely not the way to go, as evidenced by the way the guard's features reddened and his mouth devolved from a smile to a snarl. His hand started to move to the pistol stuck in his waistband, but then he refrained from drawing the weapon in favor of taking a few wobbly steps in her direction and extending a hand toward her.

Do it. Do it now.

Just as she had learned in self-defense classes taught at the base gym, and as her father had shown her, Brynn stepped toward the guard. She used her left hand to sweep his arm up and out of the way before driving the heel of her other hand into his jaw. It was just like in the classes. The man's head snapped back and he grunted in pain, but then the alcohol clouding his judgment and slowing his reactions kicked in and he tumbled backward, falling heavily to the floor.

Run!

After four trips to the bathroom, Brynn knew the location of at least one exit. Trying to keep as quiet as possible, she jogged the length of the hallway toward the bathroom, then turned right at the corner and plunged headlong toward the door at the end of the shorter passage. Behind her, the first shouts of alarm were echoing through the house, but then her hands were on the door. She expected it to be locked but instead it opened with no resistance, as did the screen door beyond it. Then she was out of the house, leaping from the porch to the ground. Stumbling on the landing, she pitched forward and almost planted her face in the dirt. She threw out her hands, fingers sinking into the soft soil before pushing off like the sprinter her track coach was teaching her to be, running full out along the dirt path away from the house.

The voices in the house were louder but already fading as she kicked into high gear, dashing down the path. She stayed to the narrow road's right side, avoiding the trench running along the opposite flank and keeping her eyes on the dirt ahead of her, watching for ruts or holes that might prove hazardous.

Somewhere behind her a car's engine started, followed by another. Brynn pushed herself even faster. In the distance were lights filtering through the trees. Help lay in that direction. Should she stay on the path, or take her chances across fields or through the nearby tree line? She didn't like the idea of being in the woods after dark, in an area unfamiliar to her. The house couldn't be too far from a main road or highway. Maybe she could flag down a passing car. Better still, maybe someone could help her find a police officer.

The engines were louder, now, and the first flickers of headlights played across the trees to her right. Her lungs were starting to ache, but Brynn knew she could keep going, even longer if she had a chance to slow her pace. She just needed to get some distance, and maybe hide long enough for them to miss her in the dark. Then she could figure out what to do next.

Like a hunted animal, Brynn Connelly ran.

• • •

Another warehouse.

Jack was getting pretty tired of warehouses, and he would be content never to see another such structure again; at least not for a year or two. Could that be asking too much?

Okay, longer.

As with several of the other houses and buildings he had seen throughout the course of the day, this warehouse looked to have been converted from something else, as it seemed too small to be of practical use for a large inventory or any individual items of size. He studied the structure, illuminated as it was by the streetlights arrayed around the asphalt lot in which it sat. It looked to have been converted from two adjacent yet separate and similar structures, with a new section built to connect them. The giveaway was in the roof, which showed a visible seam at the midpoint between the two original buildings, and the hue of the sand-colored clay shingles didn't quite match. It made Jack wonder about the person who had chosen to make such a modification, and for what purpose.

Maybe you can take a guided tour. You're tired, Jack. You're starting to lose focus. Pull it together, man.

"Where are we?" asked Manish Pajari as he walked alongside Rauf Alkaev.

Banovich, who had approached Jack from the SUVs in which they had arrived, replied, "Just east of Kadena, in Okinawa City. The American air force base is not far from here."

Knowing that it played host to CIA operations based out of Okinawa, Jack also was aware of Kadena Air Force Base by name and reputation. For years, the installation had been the origin point for hundreds of high-altitude reconnaissance flights over the former Soviet Union, thanks to the squadron of SR-71 Blackbirds maintained in their own special hangars on the base. According to gossip in military and intelligence circles, the Air Force had continued to deny the very existence of the top-secret aircraft for years, even long after civilians captured the plane on film and while local merchants in the neighboring towns sold T-shirts, posters, postcards, models and other toy replicas of the plane. The SR-71 even held the nickname "Habu" here on the island, a tribute of sorts to the deadly species of snake that called Okinawa home.

"A little too close for me," said Jack. Looking around the warehouse's parking lot, he noted that they were mere yards away from what looked to be a main thoroughfare, with two lanes each traveling east and west. There were cars parked along the street and in a parking garage across the road, which sat adjacent to a large, bawdy-looking pachinko parlor that he knew was basically the Japanese equivalent of a casino. The gaming establishment attracted a lot of traffic, which could be good or bad, he thought, depending on how one wanted to view it.

I'm going with bad.

Smiling, Banovich swiped at his arm. "You scared, Stefan?"

At least, that was what he figured Stefan Voronov would think. On the other hand, he was quite happy with the idea. How far was he from the CIA field office on that base? Where was Abigail Cohen? She should at least know he was alive, if that NCIS agent, Kurtz, had done as asked. Jack figured he made that call, to satisfy curiosity if nothing else. Cohen was out there, now, looking for him and—more importantly— looking *out* for him.

"All right," called Samuel Yeager as strolled out of an open bay door set into the side of the building. He gestured to the cluster of his men standing next to the two cargo trucks. "Start unloading like I told you I wanted it. And let's make it quick, okay? I don't want us here any longer than we have to be."

Jack tried not to watch with too much interest as the Marine, Connelly, stepped from the rear of the second truck and was hustled inside. The man looked not only exhausted but also dejected, if not broken. That made sense if he was being extorted to cooperate with these people out of fear for his family's safety, but what could Jimura want from him? From the man's collar insignia, he was a senior enlisted Marine, E-8 or E-9, as Jack recalled from the rank charts. That implied a certain level of leadership and responsibility, but how far did that go? Did Connelly possess classified information or materials, or access to something sensitive or otherwise valuable to Jimura? Of course, it could be something simpler, like just needing him to get aboard one of the bases, but that didn't quite track. Access to military installations on Okinawa, though restricted, wasn't airtight. Someone with the proper skills and resources could gain entry under any number of guises. The legions of civilian workers, both Okinawan and American, doubtless provided countless opportunities just by themselves.

"Banovich," said Yeager, waving toward one of the trucks. "We're putting your cargo back in the truck. It'll be ready in about ten or fifteen minutes to head to Naha."

"Excellent," replied Banovich. "Thank you."

Yeager shrugged. "Just holding up our part." Next, he pointed toward the warehouse's far end. "There's a kitchen down that way, with sandwiches, rice, fruit, stuff to drink, and whatever else we could scrounge up. Knock yourselves out, but don't wait too long. My guys'll eat this place down to the foundation."

The thought of food and a break was a welcome one. Jack was fast approaching being awake for twenty-four hours, and the first tendrils of fatigue had long since taken hold. He had been operating on adrenaline and—yes—a portion of fear since well before dawn. The latter had ramped up in the wake of losing Bill Fields, the worry that his cover might be blown at any second, and the uncertainty of his handlers. Were they still supporting him, or had they pulled the plug and faded into the night? His gut told him that even though he might be alone right here, Cohen or somebody out there was at least trying to watch out for him.

Yeah, but the question is whether any of these bozos are watching me, too.

They were still standing in the lot next to the trucks when Jack caught sight of an elderly Okinawan man lurking just inside the warehouse door, observing them. He was dressed in dark clothes that allowed him to blend with the shadows. His thin, white hair accented his head with no sense of direction or style, and he wore a pair of small, circular eyeglasses that sat perched on the tip of his nose. He was stoop-shouldered, but there was an intensity about him that belied his advanced age.

Jack had no doubts that he was looking at Miroji Jimura.

Playing dumb, he looked to Yeager before indicating the warehouse. In a low voice, he asked, "Is that who I think it is?"

"Yes, it is indeed George Burns."

He almost acknowledged the poor joke, but at the last possible instant Jack realized to do so would very likely be out of character for someone like Stefan Voronov, a former foot soldier with little to no access to the entertainment fodder of the imperialist Americans. Offering a confused expression, he asked, "Who?"

"Never mind." Yeager then nodded. "Yeah, that's the boss. You should be honored. He usually prefers to remain apart from the everyday business of his various 'enterprises.' Seeing him out in the open like this is a lot like spotting Bigfoot."

If I was paranoid, I'd swear this jackass is trying to trip me up with this pop culture crap.

Yeager's comments did offer him a new thought. Jack had to wonder why Jimura was here, now. Did it have something to do with the Marine, or perhaps the large box on wheels, shrouded beneath a tarp, that had been rolled out of one of the trucks? Were those two things somehow related?

If that was the case, then what the hell was under the tarp?

• • •

Miroji Jimura watched the group of gaijin talking among themselves while waiting for Samuel Yeager to separate himself from the conversation and join him inside the warehouse.

"*Konbonwa,* Jimura-san," said Yeager, offering a formal bow. "How may I be of assistance?" When Jimura stifled a cough, the American's features darkened. "Are you all right? Can I get you anything?"

Jimura, tired from the long and stressful day and with still so much to do, was in no mood to be coddled. "I am not a child or a wayward pet, Mister Yeager. Is everything still on schedule?"

"For the most part, yes." Yeager cleared his throat. "There've been some hiccups today, sir, but we're managing, considering the obstacles. If that warehouse in Motobu is any indication, NCIS and JSDF are starting to move against at least some of Kanashiro's businesses and other interests. We can't be sure they won't be coming for you next."

It was a logical deduction, and one Jimura had already made. That the authorities might finally have found their spines if not their honor and elected to confront him directly was amusing. It would make a nice change from their usual cowering in the shadows, waiting for him to do their work for them by making some pitiful mistake. As always, their efforts would come too late to be of any real consequence. After all, time was on his side, no matter how one looked at it.

Another dry cough racked his body and he placed his hand to his mouth. It had come with such force that he now felt lightheaded. Yeager saw this and reached out to steady him, and when Jimura looked into the man's eyes, he saw genuine concern. Samuel Yeager's loyalty had never been in question, dating back to his first days working for him. It had been an unusual step for Jimura to hire a gaijin for any reason, but Yeager had proven his trustworthiness time and again. Still, he was gaijin, and therefore Jimura would never feel any real fondness for the man. He could, however, respect his devotion to duty, even if that dedication was driven by a love of money and the excesses it permitted.

"Are you sure I can't get you anything?" asked Yeager. "Water, something? Maybe you should sit down."

Jimura waved away the suggestion. "Later." He realized it was an interesting choice of response. Later, none of this would matter. "Where is the Marine?"

Taking him by the arm, Yeager led him deeper into the ware-house to an area separated from the rest of the floor by storage crates. Within this small perimeter was the metal box Jimura had seen unloaded from one of his trucks. Long and thin, it sat on wheels attached to a frame. Standing behind it were two of his men, flanking the American Marine, Connelly. To his credit, Connelly was doing his best to put forth a brave front, but there was no mistaking the fear in his eyes.

Jimura pointed first to the Marine, then the box. "You know what this is?"

The American swallowed a nervous lump before nodding. "Yes."

"You know how to maintain it, to care for it?" Jimura took a step closer to the crate. "To arm it?"

Closing his eyes as though summoning a prayer, Connelly nodded again. "Yes." It was obvious to Jimura that the man had determined on his own the reason for his presence here, and why he hadn't just been killed earlier in the day after helping his people obtain the weapon. Whatever internal conflict he was waging with himself, he seemed on the verge of losing control over it.

"Good." Now close enough to touch the metal container, Jimura laid a weathered hand atop its surface. It was cool beneath his skin. "You will do so, now. Arm it so that it can be detonated with a timer we provide you."

For the first time, the Marine's resolve appeared to falter. "Sir, I don't understand what this is about. Please, if you just let my family go, we can . . ."

"We can . . . what?" Jimura eyed the man with pity. "Talk? Take my grievances to your government? I'm afraid that's not possible." He tapped the metal container with the nail of his right forefinger. "You see, my grievance *is* your government. Your military. Your culture. Your desecration of my home."

"My family," said Connelly. His eyes were wet, Jimura noticed.

"No. I have no grievance with your family, except that they are content to wallow in ignorance, oblivious to the legacy they bear: a vile heritage that began the day after your people declared victory over mine, and then stayed to ensure we never forgot our defeat. Every day I look into faces like yours, and every day I see the faces of those who ran roughshod over my people. I see those who destroyed our homes and our villages, and who shot at us with no regard for the fact that we were not combatants, but civilians caught between armies. You took everything from us, and then you stayed like the conquerors you were. I watched what was left of the village where I was born buried beneath the base you now call home."

His eyes wide, Connelly tried to speak, and it took him three attempts before he said, "But, the Japanese, they killed your people. Raped them, forced them into service. I'm not saying Americans were saints, but . . ."

"I have my own issues with Japan, as well, but it was your soldiers, and those who came after, who took everything from me and my people." Jimura raised his hand and leveled a finger at Connelly. "Now, I will take some of it back."

Turning to Yeager, he said, "I want it armed within the hour, or kill him, and his family."

As he gave the order, Jimura watched the Marine and saw the shock, disbelief, and horror etched into his face. This was good. Now the man understood, even if on some meager, superficial level, what Jimura's own family had endured, from the moment the first American ships were sighted on the horizon, until their very last breath.

Live in fear, gaijin.

Crouching next to a large tree, Brynn Connelly watched a pair of headlights and a trio of flashlights crisscrossing the massive field between her and the house. She had already ducked and hidden three times to avoid being spotted, and the speed with which the men launched their frantic hunt had forced her to abandon her headlong flight along the dirt path to evade the continuing pursuit.

All of the lights were now on at the compound, illuminating the house and the storage building behind it. She could see two men moving about in frantic fashion, searching and re-searching all of the same potential hiding places. How many men were there? Nine, she thought, of which at least four or five were outside, looking for her. That left one in the house to guard her mother and Dylan.

Why had she not kept running? Because there had been no sign of a paved road, for starters. The dirt path twisted and turned through the woods, leading her away from the lights she could see in the distance. That left running through those areas of jungle overgrowth where housing, farming, and other development hadn't yet encroached, but she wasn't keen on scrambling through the undergrowth at night. Who knew what was out there?

Should I go back?

No, Brynn decided. Her mother would want her to escape,

to find help. Of the three of them, she was best suited for fleeing on foot. The only way Mom and Dylan would have a chance is if they could get their hands on a car.

A car.

She looked back toward the house, seeing the sedan and the SUV that were not being used in the ongoing search for her. The SUV in particular would make a great getaway car, right? It was big, and fast. Once it got up to speed, it wouldn't stop for anything. Brynn was certain she could drive it. She had only obtained her license a few months ago, but she could drive enough to get them away from here.

The lights from the other vehicles were more distant. They were expanding their search. For them to be going to this much effort, did it mean losing her would make someone mad? Mom had been told by the one man that they wouldn't be harmed as long as they cooperated, but how far did that really go? Brynn was sure she didn't want to put that to the test.

Another car engine revving up made her turn to see the SUV backing away from the storage building and turning around. She could see two figures in the vehicle's front seats. That was enough to make her decision. Run back to the house, get Mom and Dylan, get the car, and go. How she would get past the one man still in the house—assuming he was alone— was something she hadn't yet worked out.

Something cracked behind her and Brynn flinched. She jerked her head around in time to see a dark figure approaching her from between the trees, less than ten feet away. The man had a gun, and he muttered something under his breath as he realized his mistake. As he drew closer, she saw it was the man from the house; was it her imagination, or was his jaw swollen where she had attacked him? What was quite real was the look of menace in his eyes.

Go!

Brynn was already running before the man lunged toward her. She darted between trees, searching for a clear path and praying she didn't catch a root or a hole. She heard the man lumbering after her, his footfalls heavy and uncertain in the faint moonlight filtering through the jungle canopy. Behind and to her left, she saw the SUV driving down the path and in her general direction. Any chance of them not seeing her went to hell as the man chasing her turned on a flashlight and began yelling and waving for attention.

Damn!

If she broke out onto the open ground now, they would catch her within moments. Brynn knew her only chance was to stay in the trees, but she was already running into trouble. Her feet were slipping or starting to get bogged down in mud, and it was getting harder to see. Something dark loomed in her vision and she ducked to pass under the tree branch. Her slighter build gave her that advantage, at least.

Then that benefit was gone as her foot caught on something she couldn't see and she tumbled forward. She was able to keep from sprawling out on the wet ground, but the fall had cost her time and distance. She looked over her shoulder to see the man behind her, reaching out to push aside the branch under which she had just passed.

Something on the branch moved, and then the man screamed.

As though forgetting about her, he stumbled to one side, holding both hands to his face as he tripped over an exposed tree root.

"What?" yelled a new voice, just before a flashlight beam washed across her face, and Brynn raised her hands to shield her eyes. "What is it?"

"Habu!" said another voice, and then Brynn saw the snake coiling on the ground beneath the tree branch. It had to be three or four feet in length, its mottled green-brown skin shining in the glare of the flashlight. She knew it was poisonous and would strike if threatened, but she was too terrified to move.

The man with the flashlight wasted no time. Brynn flinched at the sound of two metallic snaps, and the snake jerked and flipped as the sound-suppressed bullets tore through its flesh. A third shot was enough to take off the habu's head.

"Get up," said another voice before Brynn felt a rough hand on her arm, yanking her to her feet. She looked to see the man with the bite still writhing on the ground, holding his face and crying in pain. Recalling what she had read about the habu, Brynn knew the snake's venom was toxic, but not fatal if treated in time. What she didn't know was what a bite to the face meant so far as the potential danger.

"He needs a doctor," she said.

The man with the flashlight replied, "Yes, he does." He then aimed his silenced pistol at his companion's head and fired. Two more bullets ripped through the man's skull and he stopped moving. The Okinawan man with the gun turned to Brynn, who stood in front of the man's partner, trying not to tremble.

"We'll send someone out to take care of him in the morning." He stared at her for another moment, seething, and for the first time Brynn was certain she was going to die. Then, the man growled in restrained anger before walking past her and back to the dirt path.

"Get her back inside."

• • •

It was a nice house. Kurtz almost felt bad about breaking into it.

Not really.

"This guy definitely lives pretty good," he said, crouching next to the house's front door opposite Aguilar, who had taken up similar position. Behind each of them were three NCIS agents in full tactical gear. While Kurtz and Aguilar had donned bulletproof vests, both of them had opted to keep their service pistols rather than upgrading to the MP5 submachine guns employed by the response team.

Both hands gripping her Beretta pistol, Aguilar replied, "There are perks to being the boss's go-to guy."

"Yeah, tell me about it."

Samuel Yeager's home was a standout in this area of Okinawa City, perched on a rise overlooking a street corner. Constructed from concrete rather than wood, its exterior was finished with an off-white stucco paint and was illuminated by an array of spotlights and recessed lamps. To the casual observer, it appeared no different than the other affluent homes to be found in this neighborhood, with nothing to give away the fact that it was owned by an American rather than a local. There even was a set of large *komainu* sitting atop the retaining wall to either side of the front gate. Often called "temple dogs" by American military personnel who bought smaller versions as souvenirs, they were commonplace on Okinawa, guarding the entrances to shrines, temples, and homes.

The side street running north was on a steep incline, flanked by an eight-foot retaining wall. Stairs led through a gate from the sidewalk and up a curved ramp that wound through a garden to the front door. Recon of the area prior to Kurtz's arrival had told him the garden continued around the sides of the house to a stone deck in the back, which encircled a kidney-shaped swimming pool. The square footage of the deck and pool were bigger than the apartment Kurtz rented just off the main gate of Kadena Air Force Base.

Looking to his right, Kurtz nodded to Hiro Ashagi, the agent in charge of the special weapons group from the Fleet Intelligence Command department of the Japanese Self-Defense Force, where he had taken a knee on the sidewalk just off the porch, facing the door.

"You ready?"

Ashagi nodded. "Say the word." Behind Ashagi were five officers, all dressed in their own version of SWAT gear and carrying Heckler & Koch G3A4 battle rifles. Although NCIS was the lead agency with respect to the joint task force and their current assignment, Kurtz had opted to let Ashagi take point when it came to conducting any raids on civilian targets. Such deference would help smooth any ruffled feathers when it came time to argue over who got credit for anything turned up by the operation, or to assign blame.

Let's think positive, huh?

"Remember," he said in a low voice, turning his head so everyone could hear him, "recon teams weren't able to confirm that the house is empty. Yeager's not supposed to be here, but he's got a girlfriend who lives here, too. She shouldn't be inside, but she's not dangerous. So, proceed accordingly, and if she's in there then detain her for questioning." Yeager's significant other was a dancer at a popular city nightclub. Scouts had verified her as being at work and not expected back for hours, but Kurtz wasn't taking chances.

With another nod to Ashagi, Kurtz said, "Go."

Removing his firing hand from his rifle, the Okinawan signaled behind him and one of his team members stepped around the column. He was wielding a black metal breaching ram, and in one fluid motion he climbed the stairs to the door's porch and swung the ram at the door, making contact just below the handle and dead-bolt lock. The door swung inward and the man stepped back and to the side in what was an obvious practiced maneuver, clearing the way for Ashagi and his team to enter the house. Once the first six men were inside, Kurtz followed, with Aguilar behind him and the rest of their response team shadowing them.

Ahead of him, Kurtz watched Ashagi and his team fan out in methodical fashion, checking and clearing each door and corner. The hallway leading from the front door opened up into a high-ceilinged main room with a sunken floor. A U-shaped couch faced glass windows overlooking the backyard, deck, and pool. Glancing to the ceiling, Kurtz saw a slot that likely held a retracting projection screen, and a look behind him revealed a three-lens projector mounted to the ceiling.

"Clear," reported Ashagi, who had moved farthest into the house. Other members of his team repeated the declaration as they fanned out to cover the rest of the house.

Behind Kurtz and to his left, Aguilar said, "Clear," as she and one of their response team backed out of the white-tiled kitchen. Kurtz was moving up a short hallway, followed by two more of his team. There was but a single, open door here, and from his current position a pair of tall bookcases was visible. As he drew closer, the muzzle of his Beretta leading the way, he saw a desk with an Apple computer, a trio of file cabinets behind the desk, and more bookshelves lining the walls. Mementos from Yeager's military service and travels littered the walls and bookshelves. The man was a reader, it seemed, and his library boasted hundreds of books representing a broad range of interests in fiction and nonfiction. Kurtz observed that a significant percentage of the books bore kanji script on their spines.

"I wonder if there's anything in the files or on the computer," he said to no one in particular. "Let's get it all bagged and tagged."

Lowering his weapon, Kurtz moved behind the desk, and saw a green light attached to something on the front of one of the file cabinets. It was a motion sensor and he had just tripped it. The light changed from green to red.

You've got to be shi—

"Everybody out!" he shouted, his voice echoing through the house. "Now!"

• • •

His hands trembling as he fitted the final connections, Dale Connelly sat back in the chair, nodding to the American who had been standing at a distance and watching him work.

"It's done."

The other man, his arms crossed as they had been since Connelly had begun his work, regarded him with suspicious eyes. "You're sure?"

Connelly, all but numb, nodded. "I'm sure." When the man—he hadn't given his name—stepped closer, he turned the small case with which he had been working around so his observer could better see it. The case contained a testing unit normally used for checking and verifying the settings of various components within the bomb's casing. Using the instructions he had been provided and his own expertise, he had converted it to act as an arming trigger, and added a digital timer to the bomb itself. The component he had been given by the American was at first unfamiliar to him, but Connelly was able to figure out that inside its own shell was a newer model of commercial alphanumeric pager with a digital readout.

"Like you wanted, it's not armed." That was true for the moment, but now that this other component was connected to the arming mechanism, it could be triggered either via remote paging or by entering a code via its compact keypad. Now that Connelly's work was completed, the entire improvised contraption could be strapped to the bomb's casing.

After a moment of scrutiny, the American nodded. "Good." He called out for two of his men, his voice echoing in the warehouse, and a moment later two Okinawan males appeared around the stacks of cargo crates. The American pointed to the bomb.

"Get it on the truck."

Remaining silent, Connelly could only imagine where the weapon would soon be headed. One of the white cargo trucks was gone, loaded down with at least a portion of the weapons taken from the underground bunker at Camp Hansen and bound for Naha Port. Had somebody discovered the carnage in that building by now? Would they be checking to make sure the armory was secure? How long would it take them to figure out who had allowed access to the bunker's contents? Come to think of it, had no one yet missed him?

Who gives a damn about you? Where the hell are Jessica and the kids?

"All right," said the American, gesturing to him. "You're done. Let's go."

"Go where?" Connelly couldn't help the question, but at this point, of what possible other use was he to these people? Was this finally it?

His fears only deepened when the American chose not to answer him, leaving him with his own tortured thoughts as Connelly contemplated not his own death, but that of his wife and children.

He had failed them.

I'm so sorry.

• • •

"This is Jack Bauer. I need to speak with Special Agent Abigail Cohen, right now."

His eyes on the door, Jack listened to the person on the other end of the phone stumble and fumble over whatever response he would give under normal circumstances at this hour of the evening. He gave the man, who sounded all of fifteen or sixteen, exactly three seconds to pull it together, then his time was up.

"Listen, I don't have time for this. I need Cohen, now."

Using the phone in this office, particularly with the lights off, was an enormous gamble, but Jack didn't see that he could pass up the opportunity. Letting Cohen or someone else know that Jimura was up to something—something big—was too important now. Jack had to pass on as much information as possible, in the event something happened in the next few hours, or in case he never got another chance to contact Cohen. At least now, assuming the kid on the other end of the line didn't faint or something, others would be in the loop.

"Agent Bauer! We've been looking for you all day. It's been crazy around here. Agent Cohen is in the field right now, but. . . ."

Bauer grunted his disapproval. "Then patch me through to her."

"No can do, sir. Look, where are you? I was told that if you called we should . . ."

"Shut up, and start writing. I'm somewhere east of the Kadena air base. I don't know exactly where, but it's a warehouse with a red sign on top and signs along the sides that make it look like some kind of plumbing supply place. It's across the street from one of those huge pachinko parlors with all the neon, called Omega. I think you can see the damned building from orbit." Taking a survey of the area around the warehouse had been as simple as explaining to Banovich that he was stretching his legs and trying to clear his head. It had been a long day, after all, and everyone was starting to feel run down.

He paused, holding the receiver against his jacket as he listened. Had he imagined footsteps outside the office?

"Okay, I've got it," said the kid. "Do you want . . . ?"

"No. Look, there's something big going down here. Jimura is here. He's acquired American military weapons from somewhere. From what I've overheard, he got them today. I don't know how, but he's planning something." Once more, Jack paused, ignoring the kid's request for more information as he listened. Were his ears screwing with him, or not?

"Agent Bauer?"

"Yeah, look, I can't stay here long. Jimura has hostages: a

Marine and his family. They're holding the family somewhere else, and I think Jimura's trying to get this Marine to do something for him. The guy's last name is Connelly." Jack spelled the name before adding, "He's either a master sergeant or a master gunnery sergeant, and he has a wife, a teenage daughter, and an eight-or nine-year-old son. He was wearing camouflage, so I can't tell you anything about awards or ribbons or whatever. Find out who he is, and why Jimura might want him."

The kid replied, "Okay, but I . . ."

"And get a response team over here, along with NCIS or JSDF or whoever, and take this place down. Jimura's prepping to leave, and I have no idea where he's going."

"I'm on it," said the kid. "Is there anything . . . ?"

Jack hung up the phone, moving to the left of the office's door to avoid being seen as it opened and a hand reached for the adjacent light switch. It was one of Jimura's men, but from the other crew who had brought cargo trucks to the warehouse. An Okinawan of slender build, he appeared distracted, and didn't notice Jack until he had closed the door and turned toward the desk.

There was, Jack knew, only one option here.

The man's eyes widened in surprise just as Jack struck him in the throat with the edge of his hand. It was a disabling attack, designed for the quick silencing of a sentry or other opponent so they couldn't cry out. The man staggered backward from the force of the blow, coughing while trying to defend himself. Jack grabbed his shirt, holding him upright and keeping him from falling against the door. With his other hand, he punched at the man's head but the Okinawan was rallying.

He parried Jack's attack and tried to get in one of his own, and Jack sensed from his movements that the man had at least some unarmed combat training. He was trying to push away, perhaps to kick, but Jack held him close, rabbit punching the side of the other man's rib cage. The man's coughing now was laced with grunts of pain, and he swung a fist at Jack's head. It was an easy attack to avoid, and Jack used the opportunity to drive his knee into the man's gut.

When all the air went out of his opponent's lungs, Jack

moved behind him, hooking his head in the crook of his left elbow and pushing with his right hand. The man was struggling and trying to break the sleeper hold but Jack had him. Within seconds, he felt the man's body going limp and his arms fell to his sides.

Unable to risk letting his opponent recover and sound an alarm, Jack exercised the one option available to him, and broke the other man's neck.

His breathing was ragged from the brief exertion, and he realized his fingers were shaking. He had already killed several men today, but he hadn't taken a life in such personal, brutal fashion since his last Special Forces mission. It required several seconds for him to bring his breathing and muscles under control.

Okay, you've killed him. Now what?

There were precious few places in the office to hide the man's body, but a quick check showed Jack that the couch along the room's far wall had an angled back, such that it created a void between it and the wall itself. It was just enough to lay the man behind it before pushing the couch back against his body. The corpse likely would be found tomorrow at the latest, but if all went according to plan then Jack knew he should be well away from here by then.

That, or he would be dead.

Sirens blared and the entire block was awash in the flashing lights of police and fire vehicles. The first units had responded within five minutes of the explosion and more cops, firefighters, and emergency medical personnel were arriving every few minutes.

Kurtz watched the scene while drinking water from a plastic bottle and sitting on the hood of a black Toyota sedan that was the unfortunate recipient of a piece of concrete shrapnel. The car's windshield had been the target, and its safety glass had been unable to prevent the chunk of cinder block from dropping into the driver's seat. Kurtz figured the vehicle's owner was getting off easy, at least compared to the repair bill Samuel Yeager would be facing.

A burning shell was all that remained of the house. The explosions—all three of them—had occurred in rapid succession, starting with one at the center of the structure before a pair on either end chimed in. They had to have been small devices, utilizing limited amounts of explosive that Kurtz figured was C-4 or some other, similar material. The blasts and resulting damage largely were contained within the house itself. Despite these precautions, various pieces of debris were scattered around the surrounding yards and homes, and a few vehicles parked on the street. What remained of the house had burned or was still burning, but firefighters already had most of it under control.

"You know, I was thinking some of the roof shingles were looking a little ragged," said Aguilar as she walked toward Kurtz. "And it could probably use a new coat of paint." She was carrying a bottle of water that was a parting gift from the EMT who had cleaned and bandaged the two-inch gash in her forehead, just beneath her hairline. Other than that and a layer of dust to match his own, she was uninjured.

"I wonder if he hated the light fixtures as much as I did," said Kurtz before draining the last of his water.

The explosions had come within ten seconds of the sensor in Yeager's office being triggered, giving Kurtz and the NCIS agents with him just enough time to put a chair through the office window and take their chances with gravity. He had just hit the ground and rolled over a small retaining wall cutting across the hill on that side of the house when the first charge detonated, tossing glass and chunks of wood and concrete everywhere. One of the agents who had been with him had taken shrapnel in his leg, while the other had escaped injury. As for the rest of the team, everyone had gotten out of the house before the first explosion, but there were a variety of cuts, punctures, and even a broken ankle, but no deaths.

After tossing the empty bottle through the hole in the car's destroyed windshield, Kurtz leaned back on the hood. "Well, what do you think?"

Aguilar replied, "I think his neighbors are going to kick his ass the next time they see him."

"Yeah, but what if he wasn't planning on coming back here?" Kurtz shrugged. "You think he'd torch his own place?" He shook his head. "I'm not buying it."

"Me neither." Aguilar leaned against the damaged car. "There was too much money sunk into that house, and that's before we start talking about all the crap he had in it. Hell, if I was a bookworm like he seems to be, I'd have packed all of those first. Also, I'm not seeing him as the guy who risks killing his girlfriend. She was supposed to be back later tonight, remember?" She shook her head. "I'm liking Kanashiro for this."

Kurtz replied, "Same here. This is getting out of hand. We need to lower the boom on both him and Jimura."

"I like the way you think."

Both agents turned to see Abigail Cohen walking toward them. Wearing her own tactical vest complete with a Glock pistol in a holster on her chest and a police-issue stun gun clipped to her belt, the CIA agent appeared ready to take on all comers.

"Glad to see you both are all right," she said, "and I'm sorry about the injuries to your people and Agent Ashagi's team. I'm just happy it wasn't any worse."

Aguilar said, "Amen to that." Pausing to drink from her water bottle, she asked, "So, you think this is Kanashiro, too?"

"I don't know him like you do, but from where I sit, it plays into everything else he and Jimura have been doing to each other all day."

"Kanashiro's supposedly been planning to push out Jimura for a while now," said Kurtz. "We think that's what the ambush this morning in Naha was about."

Running footsteps made the three agents turn to see a young man in khaki pants, a dark shirt, and a vest like Cohen's running toward them. He was carrying a mobile phone and as he drew closer, he extended the unit to Cohen.

"Call from the office," said the man, while slightly out of breath. "Jack Bauer made contact."

Cohen grabbed the phone. "This is Cohen." Kurtz and Aguilar watched in silence as the agent conferred with whoever had seen fit to track her down in the middle of a field operation.

"You're jerking me," she said, earning her raised eyebrows from Kurtz. "Where? Repeat the address. Okay, got it. Can we get eyes on that location?"

Aguilar said, "I get the feeling we're going on another field trip."

"That area's congested as hell this time of night," said Cohen into the phone. "We're going to have to watch our step. Right. I'll hook up with him once we're on site. Thanks."

Hanging up the phone, she turned to Kurtz and Aguilar. "We've got a location on Bauer, Jimura, and a bunch of American military hardware. Feel like making a visit?"

• • •

The door to the room that was their prison opened with enough force for the doorknob to leave a divot when it hit the wall. It also startled Jessica Connelly to the point that she almost jumped from the bed. Brynn pushed back against her as though trying to put distance between her and the door, and even Dylan looked up in surprise.

Standing in the doorway was "Frankenstein," as her son had taken to calling him. The older Okinawan with the military-style brush cut who was the apparent leader of this group responsible for detaining her and her family. His expression was cold and fixed, but there was no mistaking the controlled fury bubbling just beneath the surface of his emotional veneer.

"One of my men is dead," he said.

Jessica nodded. "I know. I'm sorry about that."

"Don't be. He was an idiot." The Okinawan shook his head. "He was drinking and he let his guard down and he apparently had . . . intentions . . . toward your daughter. I don't mourn his loss." His expression seemed to turn even darker. "What I'm concerned about now is your demonstrated willingness to defy my instructions."

Pulling Brynn and Dylan closer to her, Jessica replied, "She was scared of your man. We're all scared, of all of you. Is that really so hard to understand?"

The man's eyes narrowed and it was obvious he didn't appreciate her comments. For a moment, Jessica was almost sure she had succeeded in finding the line she couldn't cross without expecting some form of retribution, but then the man's expression softened. It was clear he was waging some sort of internal conflict between what he wanted to do and whatever orders he had been given.

"His actions were inappropriate," he said after several silent, tense seconds, "and I apologize for that, but you must not try to escape again. I have already pledged that you will not be harmed, and now I expect that you will not cause me any further trouble."

He can't hurt us.

Jessica had been considering this notion all afternoon and into the evening, wondering if this man was simply trying to keep her and the kids quiet and cooperative with only the fear of harm to keep them in line. According to the chilling warning he had given them hours earlier, Brynn's escape attempt should have been more than enough to bring retribution down upon them all. It seemed apparent by his entrance that he was hoping to instill an even greater level of fear in the hopes of maintaining the illusion that he had any real power over them.

And that's why he's mad. He can't really do anything to us. At least, not yet.

"If your men behave, then so will we," she said. Despite her suspicions, Jessica knew she was taking a chance that this man would simply decide whatever punishment awaited him was worth disobeying his instructions. She watched his jaw clench, and knew then that her suspicions were correct. Someone else was pulling this man's strings, and whoever it was, he was someone to be feared.

Of course, he's the same man who ordered you kidnapped.

"Very well," he said after another long pause.

Now operating with a bit more confidence, Jessica asked, "How much longer are we going to be here? You can't keep us forever. People will be missing us by now."

For the first time, the Okinawan smiled. "You are correct. We cannot keep you here forever."

He then backed out of the room, pulling the door closed with him.

"That guy gives me the creeps," said Dylan, speaking for the first time in hours, and Jessica felt him press even closer. She tightened her arm around his shoulders, hugging him to her.

"They're all creeps," added Brynn. "Do you think they've got Dad, too?"

It was an unpleasant thought that had plagued Jessica all day, but she hadn't said anything for fear of further frightening her children. Of all the reasons for them to be abducted and then held like this with no explanation, it was the only one that made sense. Was he mixed up with these people, somehow? No, that was impossible. Did he have something they wanted? Was he being coerced into doing something, while she and the kids were being held as a way to force his cooperation? That had to be it, but it also begged the question: What could Dale possibly have or do that was of any use to these men?

Damn it, Dale. Where the hell are you?

• • •

It was the cigarette butts that gave them away.

At first, Jack thought he was just being paranoid when he had caught sight of two figures sitting in a car across the street from the warehouse, parked outside the pachinko parlor. Other people had been doing the same thing for a while now. However, only one car had three cigarette butts lying on the asphalt beneath its driver's side door. Only one had been there when Jack and the others arrived at the warehouse; he was sure about that. Still, conscious that fatigue might be playing tricks on him, he kept a furtive eye on them as he moved about the lot. Pretending not to notice anything amiss, he divided his attention between the car and watching Jimura's men. They had loaded the half dozen additional cargo trucks, which had appeared as if from the very air to be filled with inventory from the warehouse. Now he was sure the men were not just giving the warehouse the occasional casual glance. Instead, they were observing.

So, who the hell are they?

Thanks to the headlights from passing cars, Jack saw that both men were Okinawan. Could they be Kanashiro's men? Worse, what if they were local undercover police or JSDF or even NCIS agents? The image of Tadashi Enogawa's agonizing final moments flashed in Jack's mind. He couldn't allow that to happen again.

Glancing over his shoulder at the sound of approaching footsteps, Jack saw Amorah Banovich walking toward him. Like him, she looked tired, though he was forced to admit that even now, after being awake for nearly twenty-four hours, she still managed to look both attractive and dangerous, all at the same time.

"Hi," he said, falling back into his Stefan Voronov identity. "Everything okay?"

Banovich nodded. "Yeager just got a call from the port. Our

truck has arrived and the shipment's being loaded. Barring anything unexpected, the *Konstantinov* should be able to depart on schedule at midnight."

"What about payment?" asked Jack.

"Jimura's driver is bringing that back, drawn from the reserve funds we had on the ship. Grisha was very thorough in his planning."

Jack nodded. "That he was." Grisha Zherdev had covered nearly every base so far as his planning for this trip to Okinawa. He had always been a methodical man who considered a problem from multiple angles and always seemed to think four or five moves ahead of those around him. In some ways, it was good that he was dead. Jack was sure that, given time, the man likely would have discovered the truth about him and Bill Fields.

"Think they'll run into any problems at the port?" he asked.

Banovich shrugged. "I guess we'll know soon enough, but I doubt it. I suspect Jimura has everything taken care of."

"Probably." From his direct if fleeting observations of the man, Jack knew Miroji Jimura left little if anything to chance, and it was obvious that he trusted Samuel Yeager to carry out his instructions without need for oversight. Once the loading of the cargo trucks had begun, Jimura had departed the warehouse. Where he was going was anyone's guess, but it was obvious he had put his plan into motion.

Jack at first had wondered how a transfer of such illicit materials might be handled without attracting the attention of port security, local police, or anyone else. Then, he reasoned that a man like Jimura would have resources and contacts anywhere and everywhere he needed in order to keep his business interests proceeding without interruption or other hassles. There doubtless were at least a few workers at the port on his payroll who could see to it that anything Jimura wanted moved was handled with the proper care. It was likely he had the ear of at least a handful of police officers, and perhaps even a contact or two within the JSDF.

There's a comforting thought.

"Are we going to make it down there in time?" he asked.

Frowning, Banovich replied, "I can't see how, but if not,

then we have a contingency plan for that, as well."

This was the first time Jack had heard about this, though it made sense given Grisha Zherdev's meticulous planning. He had to remind himself that his admittedly low position not just in Tateos Gadjoyan's organization but also Zherdev's team meant that he wasn't always privy to every little detail. He suspected that the only reason Banovich shared as much as she had about other aspects of the assignment was because of her ulterior motives regarding him and her bed. If letting her think such a tactic could work served to provide him with information he might not otherwise have, he was content to play along.

"Banovich. Voronov."

The voice came from behind Jack, and he turned to see Yeager exiting the warehouse onto the elevated loading dock, a bottle of water in his hand. Jack tried not to appear startled or nervous as he regarded the other man. For whatever reason, the American had taken an interest if not an outright liking to both Jack and Banovich as the day had worn on, and Jack was trying to figure out if it was professional respect, or simple suspicion. He suspected the latter.

Banovich said, "Yes?"

Gesturing with the bottle to Jack, Yeager replied, "You strike me as a pretty observant guy." His eyes flickered toward the street, then back. "Anything out there bug you?"

His eyes narrowing, Jack asked, "Is something bugging you?"

"Yep." Yeager sipped from his water. "Well?"

"There are two men in a car across the street. They've been there a while, and I think they're watching us."

Nodding in approval, Yeager asked, "Know who they are?"

Banovich frowned. "Perhaps they work for Kanashiro."

"That, or they're the law." Finishing his water, Yeager crimped the bottle and threw it into a nearby trash receptacle. "I think we should go ask them."

"I think you're right," said Jack.

Yeager turned back to the warehouse. "Good. Come with me."

This caught Jack by surprise. "Are you sure you want us to

go with you? I would've thought you'd prefer your own men for something like this."

"I've watched you two," replied Yeager. "You know what you're doing. You're what I want for something like this."

Could Yeager be testing them, somehow? Jack's thoughts swirled with the possibilities. It had been obvious from the beginning that Jimura's point man missed very little, and Jack had been unable to shake a feeling of uneasiness from their earlier meeting in the house where Connelly's family was being held. It made perfect sense for Yeager to be suspicious of anyone he didn't know, given his line of work. Still, if this was some kind of setup, then what was the endgame?

On the other hand, Jack now had a reason to accompany the other man to investigate the potential spies in their midst without having to ask. If they were members of law enforcement surveilling Jimura, then he could be in a position where he would be forced to defend them from Yeager or any of his men, at the risk of blowing his cover. Jack had already vowed that he wouldn't allow for a repeat of Tadashi Enogawa's death, regardless of the cost.

That's just the way it goes.

Looking to Banovich, Jack asked, "What do you think?"

She shrugged. "Whoever they are, if they're watching this place, then we're probably in as much danger as anyone else here." To Yeager, she said, "We're in."

"Excellent," said the other man, indicating for Banovich and Jack to follow him. "Let's go see who's so interested in us."

• • •

Aside from two sedans, each with varying degrees of dents and rust, and a newer model SUV that looked to have just been washed and detailed, the parking lot was empty. That was to be expected at this time of night. The retail businesses in this part of Futenma had closed hours earlier, and the lone nearby restaurant had shut its doors an hour earlier. There would be no one to take notice.

Arata Gisuji navigated the cargo truck toward a section of

the parking lot that wasn't visible from the road, tucked into a corner where two buildings met. Once he had determined the best placement for the vehicle, Gisuji backed in so that the truck's rear bumper was almost flush against the building's brick wall. The task was made more complicated by the lack of a sideview mirror on the truck's passenger side, which had been broken off at some point earlier in the day. Gisuji had commented on this back at the warehouse, but no other trucks were available, so he was forced to make do without it. He put the vehicle's manual transmission into neutral and applied the parking brake, then jumped down from the driver's seat to examine his handiwork. The gap between the wall and the back of the truck was so small that no one could squeeze through.

Gisuji nodded in satisfaction. This was exactly what Jimurasan had wanted. He had been explicit with his instructions, relaying them directly rather than passing them down through the American who served as his assistant. To Gisuji, this only served to communicate just how important his employer considered this assignment. To be given this task was an honor, and to disappoint Jimura-san to even the smallest degree was unthinkable.

This did not mean that he had no questions, of course. What was inside the truck? Gisuji had seen the large crate with its own wheels loaded into the vehicle and knew it had to be something of value to Jimura-san, but he had no idea what it might be. When he had asked Yeager, his employer's American assistant, the other man had responded that it was a secret; a sensitive matter pertaining to a longtime client, and discretion was of paramount importance. Gisuji had been surprised by that answer, but he figured it made a sort of sense. After all, he was a low-level employee, not entitled to know every detail of Jimura-san's business dealings. Perhaps in time, he would advance within the organization to the point where such information was shared with him.

One day, perhaps.

Turning off the truck's engine, Gisuji locked the doors to the truck's cab before pocketing the keys. After one last look around the parking lot and the alleys leading to it between the surrounding buildings, he concluded that the truck wasn't visible from the street, and even if someone happened into the alley, a pair of commercial trash receptacles helped to obscure the vehicle's appearance. Satisfied with what he had done, Gisuji made his way down one of the side passageways on his way back to the street. When he emerged from the alley, a black Toyota sedan was waiting by the curb. Gisuji moved to the car and got in. As the driver guided the car away from the curb and back into traffic, Gisuji smiled to himself.

His work here was done.

Using the pachinko parlor's glaring neon façade to mask his movements, Jack walked close to the building, approaching the car from behind until he was clear of the driver's sideview mirror. Glancing over his shoulder, Jack saw Banovich across the street, standing beneath the awning of a tailor shop that possessed no lighting over its front door. Ahead of him, Samuel Yeager was standing at the far side of the parlor, all but lost amid the building's pulsating light show.

It had taken them several minutes to move from the warehouse to a point down the street from the car they had targeted, with Jack and Yeager moving along the alley behind the parlor and adjacent buildings. Jack was the first to emerge onto the street, while Yeager moved past the parlor in order to take up his position ahead of the car. From there, he was able to monitor pedestrian and vehicle traffic and wait for an opportune moment for Jack and Banovich to move in. Now, it was just a matter of timing, and Jack was thankful that activity outside the parlor was slowing down. A young couple represented the only other pedestrians on this side of this street, and he had counted only three cars passing since he and the others had moved into their positions.

The car's driver-side window was down and the man sitting behind the wheel was letting his arm hang out while holding a lit cigarette. Below him and scattered on the sidewalk and in the street next to the front wheel were four other cigarette butts. These guys had been here a while, and Jack now saw the vantage point of the warehouse they had enjoyed. They were able to observe the cargo trucks being loaded and unloaded, though from this distance Jack was sure they wouldn't have been able to determine what was being moved. As far as he could tell, neither man had left the car since his first noticing it. Did they have a mobile phone in order to relay updates and other information, and who was on the other end of such calls?

He couldn't ignore the gnawing fear that had gripped him since spotting the car. This idea of Yeager's to confront their would-be observers carried risks that had nothing to do with any actual altercation. If it was timed poorly and somehow managed to attract local police officers, that could bring the hammer down as authorities moved in. Jack worried this might set off Jimura to do whatever it was he was planning that involved the Marine, Connelly.

As for the guys in the car, what if they were law enforcement officers? Was he about to aid and abet their interrogation or even their possible torture and death? Not if there was anything he could do to prevent that, of course, but what if there were other observation teams positioned around the area? Would taking these two out of the game bring down the rest of whatever operation might be in play? If that was the case, were Agents Kurtz and Aguilar involved? What about Abigail Cohen? It was possible that she also was a part of whatever operation was being put into play against Jimura.

Of course, Jack knew that if this was being pushed by Edoga Kanashiro, then all of his concerns were unfounded. On the other hand, that possibility only served to highlight a wholly different set of issues, chief among them whether Kanashiro was preparing to mount an assault on Jimura here, tonight, as retribution for the day's earlier events.

You can ask them about it later. Let's do this, already.

His hand moving inside his jacket to draw his Glock pistol, Jack looked to Yeager, who held out his thumb in their prearranged signal. Relaying that signal to Banovich, Jack started moving toward the car. To his left, he saw Banovich crossing the street, her right hand held low against her thigh while gripping her own weapon. He crouched low, coming in under the driver's line of sight until he was at the window, then dropped to one knee next to the car door and shoved the Glock's suppressed muzzle into the driver's right cheek.

"Don't move."

Banovich mirrored his movements on the car's passenger side, but the driver's friend made the mistake of reaching for something, and she fired. Her suppressed pistol coughed inside the car and the back of the passenger's head exploded. The move was so sudden and so vicious that Jack almost flinched, but he maintained his position as Banovich shifted her aim to the driver's head.

Yanking open the car door, Jack gestured for the man to get out. At the same time, Banovich was pushing the passenger's body down across the driver's seat, hopefully out of sight to anyone who might happen by. Once he was out of the car, the Okinawan raised his hands. He was all but shaking. To Jack, there was no way this guy was a trained professional or even cannon fodder of the type he had encountered throughout the day. This was a simple errand boy, sent to watch the warehouse and report whatever he saw.

"Put your hands down." Jack glanced in Yeager's direction and saw him maintaining his position, watching for possible trouble. The coast was clear for the moment, but Jack was certain they already had to be pressing their luck. He gestured toward Banovich. "Follow her."

There was no one in view to hamper their getting the man across the street and back to the warehouse. Jack noted that all six of the cargo trucks that had been in the process of being loaded were now arranged single file at the entrance to the lot, as though their drivers were awaiting further instructions.

"Are we leaving?" asked Banovich as they hustled the Okinawan into the warehouse.

Yeager replied, "Something like that." He led the way between rows of cargo crates, and Jack noticed that one section of the floor had been cleared of such containers, which now resided in the trucks parked outside. There was no need to guess at what might be in those boxes—he knew. The only questions of any importance involved where the crates were going, and to what purpose their contents might be put.

Once beyond the rows of cargo containers, Yeager turned on the Okinawan, who was so startled that he staggered backward before Jack stopped him. "Okay, listen up. I don't have time to screw around, so I'm going to make this easy. Tell me what I want to know, and you walk out of here. Otherwise?" He shrugged. "I'll let you fill in the blanks. So, easy question to start: Do you work for Edoga Kanashiro?"

To Jack's total lack of surprise, the man nodded, then began babbling in his own language, which only stopped when Yeager held up a hand.

"Shut up." Before Jack could react, the American drew his pistol and fired a single shot into the man's head. He dropped in a lifeless heap to the floor, but Yeager was already turning and heading back toward the front of the warehouse. Still reeling from the Okinawan's execution, Jack ran after Yeager with Banovich following close behind.

"Yeager!" Jack shouted. "What is it?"

Instead of replying, Yeager was yelling at other men in the warehouse, shouting orders for them to get their weapons and to take up defensive positions. For the first time in over an hour, Jack saw Connelly, the Marine still being held captive. Like everyone else, he was looking about in confusion as Yeager continued to bark instructions.

"Banovich," said Yeager. "You and your people get ready to move out with us. We need to get the hell out of here."

Moving to stand next to Jack, Banovich asked, "Kanashiro?"

"Yeah," Yeager replied. "He said they've been making regular updates. They've got a phone in their car, or something, so we're bugging out." To Banovich, he said, "You all are with me, same as before. We'll regroup and figure out what Jimura wants us to do next."

Jack asked, "What about the trucks?" He cast a glance over his shoulder to where Connelly was being guarded by two Okinawans. What was Yeager's plan for him?

"We've got that covered." The American was walking as he

talked, and Banovich and Jack had to hurry to keep up. "They know where they're supposed to go."

Whatever he might say next was lost when all of them heard a faint shout of alarm. It was followed by another cry, but this time from another direction. Jack and Banovich exchanged knowing glances at the same time Yeager turned and started running toward the warehouse's far end.

"They're here!" he was shouting as he weaved between a set of cargo containers and disappeared from sight.

"Son of a bitch," Jack said, pulling his pistol from its shoulder holster. "Amorah, we've got to get out of here, right now. Whoever it is, they're after Jimura, and they don't give a damn about us." If it was Kanashiro launching some kind of counterattack, Jack was content to let both sides kill each other, so long as he wasn't caught in the crossfire.

Banovich, her weapon already in hand, nodded. "Right. Let's find Alkaev and Pajari and get out of here."

"Where?" asked Jack, dividing his attention between her and the rest of the warehouse.

"Naha. We're leaving. We've done our part to make things right. This is between Jimura and Kanashiro now."

Connelly!

Jack knew he couldn't leave the Marine to his fate, regardless of the personal risk. Whatever the man had done, it didn't warrant abandoning him to what might well be escalating into some sort of civil war between the Jimura and Kanashiro clans. There had to be a way to get him out of here.

Movement to his left caught his attention and Jack saw a pair of Okinawan men he didn't recognize emerge from behind a row of cargo crates, each carrying an H&K MP5 fitted with a sound suppressor. Any doubts that they may have been Jimura's men vanished when they saw him and Banovich and began bringing up their weapons.

Jack and Banovich were faster. Banovich was the first to shoot, her initial round going off as Jack took aim. The first Okinawan was already dropping to the floor when Jack fired twice at his companion, taking the man in the chest. His body jerked and he collapsed facefirst to the concrete.

"Yeah," said Jack, gripping his Glock in both hands and advancing on the two assailants to verify they were dead. "Time to get the hell out of here." Holstering his pistol, he retrieved one of the MP5s and tossed it to Banovich before claiming the second submachine gun for himself. A quick frisk of both bodies turned up four additional magazines for the weapons, two of which he gave to Banovich.

"There's going to be a lot more of them," he said. "We should split up. It'll be faster finding Alkaev and Pajari, and then we get clear of here."

Banovich seemed to weigh this before nodding. "Okay, but don't take too long. We've got less than an hour before the ship's supposed to leave. If you miss it, head for the backup rally point in Naha." She had provided Grisha Zherdev's secondary meeting site in the event they were unable to make it back to Naha before the *Konstantinov* left port at midnight. According to the plan, the cargo ship would wait off the coast for twelve hours, giving Banovich and the others an opportunity to secure some kind of boat they could use for a rendezvous.

What could possibly go wrong with that plan? Besides everything, that is.

"Okay, go," said Banovich. "Good luck, Stefan."

He watched her disappear among the crates, and for a second he realized he was worried about her safety in the same way he would feel about Bill Fields or any other trusted colleague. The stresses of the day had almost made him forget that from the beginning, Amorah Banovich had been his partner in a very real sense. Their lives had depended on one another from the moment the first shot was fired in Naha hours earlier.

If she knew who you were, she'd put a bullet through your brain. Focus, Bauer.

Hearing voices ahead of him, Jack made his way down another row of cargo crates, trying to trace back his steps. Three heads were visible over a large container ahead of him, one of which could only belong to an American. Jack heard at least two voices arguing, but it was in Okinawan so he couldn't understand. As he came around the side of the crate, one of the men, armed with a revolver, was pushing at Connelly. Despite his bound hands, the Marine resisted and now was raising his arms to defend himself as the Okinawan lifted his weapon.

Jack took aim with his MP5 and fired. The suppressed submachine gun snapped off three quick rounds, two of them taking the Okinawan in the head. His companion, stunned by the sudden shots, turned toward Jack in time to be struck in the chest by another trio of bullets. Both men were dead in seconds, leaving Connelly startled and trying to back away from Jack.

Lowering his weapon, Jack held up his left hand. "Wait," he said. "I'm not going to hurt you." For the moment, he was maintaining his Russian accent. When that made Connelly stop in his tracks, Jack closed the distance and grabbed the Marine by his arm. Seeing the frightened man's face, Jack knew there was only one thing he could do. With a folding knife he pulled from his pants pocket, he cut the tape binding Connelly's hands. He then handed the Marine one of the Okinawans' MP5s.

"Come on."

Scowling in confusion, Connelly asked, "Where are we going?"

"First, we're getting the hell out of here," replied Jack, dropping his accent. This prompted a look of surprise from the Marine.

"Who are you?"

Jack said, "I'll explain everything once we're out of here. Now, let's go."

With Connelly following him, Jack led the way through the warehouse. He could hear the sounds of gunfire and other fighting in other sections of the building. Approaching a window, he looked out at the parking lot and saw at least a dozen figures running through and around the pools of light from the streetlamps and other lights arrayed around the building's exterior. It appeared Kanashiro's men had come prepared to conduct what they at least had planned as a covert assault, employing as they were suppressed weapons, but now Jimura's men were responding in kind. Jack knew that the noise and gunplay would soon attract every police officer within the area, and maybe even the local equivalent to a SWAT or rapid response team. He needed to be gone before police could set up perimeters and blockades and drop the proverbial net on this entire neighborhood.

Bullets chewing into the top of a crate to his right made Jack recoil, ducking away from the window and pushing himself against the side of the container. He caught sight of the bobbing heads of at least three people on the other side of the row. Connelly was behind him, crouching next to the crate and holding his MP5 with its muzzle pointing toward the ceiling. More bullets tearing into the box's flank made both men flinch.

"You know how to use that thing?" asked Jack.

Connelly nodded. "It's no M16, but I know which end to point where."

Gesturing up and over the top of the crate, Jack said, "Wait for my signal, then cover me." He pushed himself to his feet, keeping his head below the top of the container as he moved toward its end. Footsteps on the concrete floor ahead of him made him stop just as a man in dark clothing stepped into view. Jack let loose with the MP5 and five rounds stitched across the man's chest, throwing him against the crate behind him before he slid to the floor.

"Now!" Jack shouted, and seconds later heard the bark of Connelly's MP5 as the Marine stood and fired the submachine gun in rapid bursts of four or five rounds. Using that distraction, Jack maneuvered around the crate and saw two more Okinawan men ducking to avoid Connelly's cover fire. With the MP5 tucked into his side, Jack released another barrage, catching both men in the chest and head and sending them both tumbling to the warehouse floor. Looking back toward the crate, he waved for Connelly to follow him.

"Come on!"

As he moved to fall in behind Jack, Connelly said, "You're working with that other guy, the American."

"Hell no, I'm not working with him. It's a long story."

Reaching the warehouse's far end, Jack recalled the building's layout along with the surrounding parking lot and adjacent properties. He pushed open the door that led out to the driveway and saw no potential threats. Whoever was attacking Jimura's men seemed to be occupied elsewhere, and there were no more reports of weapons fire. Now was the time to run for it.

With Connelly tailing him, Jack headed across the asphalt and toward the alley between two neighboring buildings, vanishing into the darkness.

• • •

The muffled gunfire had moved from somewhere outside the house to what Jessica Connelly thought was the living room. Cries of pain echoed along the hallway outside the bedroom's locked door. Having pulled Brynn and Dylan with her, Jessica now hunkered in the room's far corner, hearing heavy footfalls advancing up the corridor.

"What's going on?" asked Brynn. "Is it the police?"

There was no way to know, but Jessica suspected this was something else. The three of them had heard the initial shots from outside mere minutes earlier, if indeed even that much time had passed, but none of them had heard any sirens or other obvious indications that this house was being raided by police officers. So, if not the authorities, then who was attacking the house and these men?

Jessica's thoughts were hijacked by the sound of the doorknob jiggling. She watched it move as someone outside tested its lock before the door was kicked inward with such force that its top hinge ripped from the frame. A bald, muscled man Jessica didn't recognize and carrying a shotgun stepped into the room, and leveled the weapon at her and the kids, both of whom cowered ever closer to her.

"No!" she shouted. "Please!"

The man's surprise and confusion was evident as he beheld them, and he raised the shotgun so that its muzzle pointed away from Jessica and the kids. He yelled something over his shoulder, most of which went over Jessica's head.

"He just told someone that he thinks we're Americans," said Brynn, and Jessica heard the tremor in her daughter's voice. Her words also caught the man's attention, and he glared at the three of them. "He thinks we're prisoners of some guy named Jimura."

Who was Jimura? Jessica had never heard the name, but it

was the first clue toward understanding why they had been brought here. The Okinawan was glaring at her now, and the shotgun's muzzle was starting to aim again toward her and the kids. Dylan pushed in close to her, burying his head beneath her arm. He was mumbling something she couldn't understand.

Another Okinawan appeared in the doorway. He was of smaller build than the first man and wore his dark hair in a short ponytail, and seemed to be the one in charge. He snapped something at the larger man even as he regarded Jessica and the kids with cold, calculating eyes. Stepping past the man with the shotgun, the new arrival fixed Jessica with an unflinching gaze.

"Why you here?" he asked, in broken English.

Jessica shook her head. "We don't know." She repeated the answer twice more as he repeated the question, and her responses didn't seem to sit well with him. "They brought us here earlier today. We've been trapped here since this morning. We don't even know who brought us here."

When the two men exchanged words with one another, Brynn translated, "Something about a lot of stuff in the building out back. Guns, drugs, videos. The one guy's confused about us, but his partner is saying that if we're here, then someone named Jimura really wants something from us."

"Stop talking!" snapped the second Okinawan. He made a motion for them to follow him from the room.

"What are you going to do?" asked Jessica.

The man scowled before barking, "Move!"

After another round of chatter between the two men in their native language, Brynn said, "They're moving us to another room with a door to keep us out of trouble. They keep talking about somebody named Kanashiro. He must be their boss, and they think he'll want us alive." She paused before adding in a lower voice, "For now, anyway. The one guy said something about if Jimura thinks we're important, Kanashiro will, too."

What the hell was going on? Jessica's mind reeled as she considered these new arrivals. Were they gangs, or factions of something like a gang? Had she and the kids been caught up in the middle of some kind of territorial dispute? If that was the case, then Jessica knew their own personal situations would mean nothing to these men. They had to find a way out of here, before someone just decided that keeping her and her family alive served no active purpose.

Hustled into another dingy bedroom, Jessica and the kids could only watch as the bald Okinawan who escorted them pulled the door shut. There was an audible click as the door's lock was engaged, and they were alone in the room. Unable to stop her own body from shaking, Jessica held Brynn and Dylan tightly.

"Mommy," said Dylan. Jessica felt his body trembling. "What are they going to do to us?"

"I wish I knew, sweetheart," replied Jessica, gripping her children to her. "I wish I knew."

Surveying the scene around him, Edoga Kanashiro was unimpressed.

He walked past a group of his men who were taking charge of the cargo trucks Miroji Jimura's people had been so thoughtful to load for him. Checking his watch, Kanashiro knew they already were working on borrowed time, and needed to be out of here in the next few minutes. He heard no police sirens piercing the night air, which was puzzling all by itself. Surely, the actions of Jimura's men, careless as they were to fire weapons not fitted with sound suppressors, had attracted the notice of nearby residents? Kanashiro found it unfathomable that someone hadn't alerted local law enforcement to the brief yet intense firefight that had occurred here.

"Get the trucks moving," he said, pointing to one of his men who stood at the head of the half dozen cargo vehicles positioned outside Jimura's warehouse. His men had already confirmed that the trucks were loaded with all manner of goods that would fetch respectable prices from his various clients. Checking his watch, he added, "I want to be out of here in two minutes."

"Kanashiro-san!"

The new voice was coming from behind him as he walked along the loading dock outside the warehouse, and he looked to see another of his men, Yoshiaki Gahara, waving at him.

"What is it?" he asked as he walked toward the other man.

Gahara replied, "We have the American."

Kanashiro allowed his underling to lead him into the warehouse, where he saw three of his men standing around another, much taller and more heavily muscled man. He had brown hair that was thinning on top and along the sides, and he wore a black shirt stretched across his broad chest and tucked into black, military-style cargo pants. Kanashiro immediately recognized him.

"Mister Yeager. It's a pleasure to finally meet you."

Despite a defiant gleam in his eyes, Yeager was doing a poor job of hiding his concern. Was he afraid? He seemed to be waging some sort of internal conflict.

"Same here," he said, after a moment. His insincerity was evident, which Kanashiro could appreciate, given just how many of his and Miroji Jimura's men had been killed in the last few minutes.

Kanashiro made a show of looking around the inside of the warehouse. "Where's your employer?"

"He's safe."

Smiling, Kanashiro said, "You mean to say he's abandoned you." He shook his head. "It seems obvious to me that he has very little regard for anyone, even his most trusted associates. Perhaps you should consider a career change."

"You should probably stop wasting your time talking to me, and think about getting the hell out of here." Yeager cleared his throat as he cast glances toward the three men guarding him. "If I were you, I'd start hauling ass north, and fast."

"What are you babbling about?" asked Kanashiro. Then, he nodded in understanding. "I see. Jimura-san's mysterious plan. Is that why you stole American military weapons earlier today?"

Yeager seemed surprised to hear this, and despite trying to maintain his composure, Kanashiro saw through his attempt.

"Yes," he said, nodding. "I know about your theft. Quite brazen, I must say, but to what end? Surely, Jimura-san cannot believe he will elude the American military forever."

"He doesn't want to," replied Yeager, his gaze never wavering. "He doesn't have to. By the time the military figures out what's going on, it'll be way too late."

Feeling his ire beginning to rise, Kanashiro said, "It's already too late. I've been patient, but Jimura-san's stubbornness shows no signs of fading, and it's well past time for a change."

To his surprise, this prompted a chuckle from Yeager.

"This amuses you?"

"Yeah. You could say change is coming, all right. In a big way."

Stepping closer, Kanashiro asked, "What is Jimura-san doing?"

Yeager shook his head. "Sorry. All I can tell you is that it's in all our best interests to be the hell away from here, and pretty damned soon."

A bomb, thought Kanashiro. Something large enough to make Yeager want to flee, but what could Jimura be targeting? The Americans, most likely, but how? Had he managed to get some kind of explosive device onto one of the military bases? There was a time when Kanashiro would have thought such a feat impossible, but Jimura had already demonstrated at least twice today that he was able to penetrate the security in place for those installations.

"The Americans," said Kanashiro. "It has to be. Everyone knows Jimura-san hates them. He's spent the last fifty years protesting their presence here, or assisting others to stage such protests. But, are you saying he's finally summoned the courage to attack them directly? Why now?"

Even when Yeager said nothing, his expression betrayed him, and then Kanashiro started to see some pieces of this strange puzzle beginning to fit into place.

"Jimura-san *is* sick, isn't he?" asked Kanashiro. When that question made Yeager's eyes widen, he stepped closer. "What, is it something incurable?"

Casting his gaze toward the floor, Yeager nodded. "Cancer."

He's going to die, thought Kanashiro. *He's going to die, and wants to make some kind of last statement against the Americans before he goes.*

Even now, that old man was continuing to surprise him, but where had he gone? Surely, a man facing his own demise wouldn't run and hide in some hole after going to such trouble to bring about whatever it was he was planning against the Americans. Instead, Jimura would want to watch his plan carried out. Only then would he be satisfied with dying here on the island of his birth, which had become polluted and infested after war and five decades of occupation and marginalization at the hands of gaijin.

"What's Jimura-san's target?" asked Kanashiro. When Yeager didn't answer, he pressed, "You said we should head north. Does that mean he's going after one of the southern bases?" The two most important American installations were close; Kadena Air Force Base and the Marine Corps air station near Futenma. Both were critical components of the United States' ability to project air power toward East Asian points of concern such as China and North Korea. Even though the Russians were doing their best to destroy themselves from within, the Americans still flew routine reconnaissance missions over the former Soviet Union in the hopes of monitoring the Russian military's enormous stockpile of nuclear weapons. Many of those arms were believed to be at risk of being stolen or otherwise acquired by terrorists or other rogue elements. Kanashiro was forced to admit that he found such a prospect troubling. After all, American targets on Okinawa were of keen interest to enemies of the United States, regardless of the threat potential to civilians living here on the island.

Once more, Yeager refused to answer, and this time Kanashiro slapped him across his face. The force of the blow was sufficient to snap the other man's head back, and when he recovered, there was a new fire in his eyes.

Excellent. Kanashiro could appreciate and respect courage.

"Where is Jimura-san?"

Yeager shrugged. "I don't know."

"Liar." Drawing from his waistband a Walther PPK semiautomatic pistol, Kanashiro thumbed the weapon's safety and placed the muzzle against Yeager's forehead. "Tell me."

The sounds of shouting from somewhere outside made him look toward the door, and it was to see several of his men running past. Then one stopped in the doorway as though laying eyes on something unpleasant and changed direction, and Kanashiro was stunned to see the man drop his rifle and continue running without stopping to retrieve the weapon.

"Listen!" said one of the men guarding Yeager. "Do you hear, Kanashiro-san?"

He did hear it. Many of the shouts he heard were commands and other instructions being barked by Americans.

"Sorry," said Yeager. "Guess you'll be hanging around a while."

Kanashiro pulled the Walther's trigger and the single bullet tore through the other man's forehead, making his escorts flinch. Yeager's head snapped back and he dropped like a felled tree to the concrete floor.

"Freeze!"

The command came from somewhere behind him. His arm still raised and extending the pistol, Kanashiro turned his head to see at least ten men dressed in dark tactical clothing complete with helmets and body armor swarming into the room.

• • •

General Leslie Timmons wasn't afraid to admit that there were times during his life when he had been scared. Recruit training, carried out what seemed like centuries ago. His first week in Vietnam, and most of the weeks that followed until he left that hellhole behind. That awful Sunday morning in Beirut.

Today was also one of those times.

"You're absolutely sure about this?" he asked, directing his gaze to the Marine captain, Timothy French, who was wiping sweat from his face and neck after he had removed the hood of his yellow hazardous materials suit.

"Yes, General," replied French. "We verified it three times. There's one missing."

The captain didn't need to specify what he meant by "one." Timmons knew exactly what his report entailed, and even as he listened to French's clarification, he could feel his blood running cold as he attempted to come to terms with the frightening reality he now faced.

Nearly five hours had passed since the explosions that had

brought down the building. In that time, Timmons had conjured all manner of horrendous possibilities while he waited for confirmation on the status of the twenty-four B61 nuclear bombs stored in the supposedly secret, allegedly secure underground bunker. Following the initial search of the rubble that was all that remained of the building sitting atop the hidden armory, Timmons had called in excavation equipment. The operators of the bulldozer, backhoe, and crane dispatched from the 9th Engineer Support Battalion were given a single, simple mission: to create an access point to the sections beneath the building.

Working under Timmons' personal supervision while the area was cordoned off to keep away unwanted eyes, the engineers had managed to clear a shaft through the rubble to the secure level. That was when Captain French and his assistant, a staff sergeant whose name Timmons couldn't remember, climbed down to survey the scene firsthand. It had been a task fraught with risk, with the possibility of the entire building coming down upon the two men at any moment. Neither Marine had balked at the orders, and it had taken them only minutes to confirm Timmons' worst fear: Twenty-three of the twenty-four B61s had been counted. One of the nuclear weapons was missing.

Empty quiver.

It was one of several nightmare scenarios that had become ever more likely in the years following the collapse of the Soviet Union, with its military in disarray and so many of its assets lacking critical oversight. Contingency planners at the Pentagon and various government think tanks had devised a number of imaginary situations in which a nuclear weapon was stolen from either a Russian or an American arsenal. Most of these setups involved detonating or attempting to detonate the stolen device on United States soil. For a number of years, as these sorts of possibilities were downplayed to the public, strategic minds in the halls of American political and military power fought an ongoing battle to anticipate just such an event. They operated under a simple, driving idea: It wasn't a matter of whether it might occur, but where and when it would happen.

And with what device, Timmons reminded himself. The

magnitude of what had taken place here today now settled upon his shoulders. There was no escaping it. Determining how the B61 had been taken would be the subject of innumerable meetings, hearings, and perhaps even courts-martial, starting with his own, but Timmons couldn't be concerned with any of that. For now, there was only the mission of finding out the weapon's location, and doing everything in the power of the United States to secure its safe return. Starting that process required him to contact the small cadre of people beyond the confines of the island who were aware of the facility's existence, almost all of whom lived and worked in Washington, D.C.

"What about the others?" asked Timmons. "Are they secure?"

French replied, "As secure as we can make them, General. We've also verified every radiation reading. Everything's green in that department, sir."

"Small favors, I suppose." Reaching up to rub the bridge of his nose, he sighed. "Continue the search sweep, Captain. You're in charge here until I get back. I need to start making some phone calls."

Two years to retirement, Timmons mused. *Two lousy years.*

• • •

"So, you're Edoga Kanashiro," said Christopher Kurtz. "You know, you look taller in our surveillance photos."

The raid on the warehouse had been a near pitch-perfect operation, with Agent Hiro Ashagi and his team from JSDF leading the charge. Kurtz, Jordan Aguilar, and their response team from NCIS had assisted, covering the property's southern perimeter as Ashagi and his people converged from the north. Both teams had provided coverage of the flanks, enveloping the dozen or so Okinawan men who had seen fit to try resisting them. That action had proven futile, but it was only when Kurtz had entered the warehouse and saw Kanashiro with his own eyes that he realized the size and value of their prize.

"You should be happy to see me," said Kurtz, studying Kanashiro, who had said nothing since being taken into custody.

"My partner wanted to sit back and watch you all shoot each other to hell, but she started getting impatient."

Standing between two NCIS agents dressed in tactical gear and with his hands cuffed behind his back, Kanashiro remained silent. There was no mistaking the raw hatred in his eyes, which glared at Kurtz.

"You think you're mad now," said the agent, "just wait until you taste the food in our prisons. Word of advice? Ketchup helps."

A recon team dispatched to the warehouse thanks to the tip from Jack Bauer and relayed by CIA Agent Abigail Cohen had reported the aftermath of the ambush conducted by Kanashiro's men. It had been well planned, taking Jimura's men almost completely by surprise. It was unfortunate that Jimura himself hadn't been on site, as it seemed he had fled at some point after Bauer's call to Cohen. Kurtz was irked about that, cursing the slowness with which the approval had come for NCIS and JSDF to carry out their own sweep of the warehouse. Those in charge were still feeling the sting of the operation at Samuel Yeager's house, and had wanted to proceed with caution despite Kurtz's contention that time and speed were of the essence.

"There's no sign of Bauer," said Abigail Cohen as she entered the warehouse and began crossing toward Kurtz and Aguilar. "And other than the dead guy, Yeager, there are no foreigners anywhere in the building."

Kurtz had seen Samuel Yeager's body in another part of the warehouse, executed by Kanashiro mere seconds before JSDF found him standing over the American's dead body. "Bauer and the rest of Gadjoyan's people must have gotten away somehow."

Gesturing to Kanashiro, Aguilar added, "Likely during this bonehead's party crashing."

"This bonehead?" asked Kurtz, jabbing a thumb in Kanashiro's direction. "You mean the guy we've got for cold-blooded murder, right here?" He offered a mock frown of disappointment. "That's some bad luck you've got there, my man."

Kanashiro glared at him, and before Kurtz could say anything else, the Okinawan jerked away from the agents holding his arms and lunged forward. Even cuffed, his strength and speed were amazing. Kurtz had just enough time to register the attack before Kanashiro drove a shoulder into his chest, sending them both toppling to the floor. Shoving his arm up under the man's throat, Kurtz tried to push himself away but Kanashiro was like a man possessed. The agents along with Aguilar were moving in to help, but then Kanashiro's body spasmed and jerked, and Kurtz heard a rhythmic popping sound. It lasted only a couple of seconds, after which Kanashiro's body went limp, sagging across Kurtz's chest.

"Get this asshole off of me!" he snapped, and the two junior NCIS agents each grabbed an arm and pulled the now disoriented and docile Kanashiro away from him. Looking up, Kurtz saw Cohen standing near his feet, her stun gun in her right hand.

"I never get to use this thing," she said, thumbing the device's power button and smiling as blue electricity arced across the stun gun's spark gap. She gestured with the weapon to Kanashiro before returning it to her belt. "He'll think about that for a few minutes."

Aguilar said, "Fifty thousand volts? Yeah, that'll make you pause for reflection." She looked to Kurtz. "You okay?"

"Yeah." Wiping his hands on his pants, Kurtz then waved toward the still dazed Kanashiro and said to the two agents, "Find a holding cell for this idiot." As the prisoner was led away, Kurtz shook his head. "I don't even want to think about the paperwork we'll have to do to get rid of that asshole."

Cohen smiled. "We can probably help with that."

"Why does that sound scary?" asked Aguilar.

"Agent Cohen!"

One of the junior agents Cohen had brought with her was running toward them across the warehouse floor. He was carrying a mobile phone in its padded case under his left arm, and Kurtz likened him to a running back with the football sprinting for the end zone.

"It's a call from the office," the man said, holding out the phone. "They've got Jack Bauer."

• • •

The voice on the other end of the phone was the best thing Jack had heard all day.

"It's damned good to hear your voice, Jack," said Abigail Cohen, through the phone's loudspeaker. "We've been worried as hell about you."

Jack breathed a small sigh of relief. Although he might not be out of the woods, things were better than they had been just moments ago. "It's good to hear you, too, Abby. It's been a hell of a day." He was tired, and it was starting to show. It had taken him three tries to recall the correct phone number he had memorized for the Okinawa CIA field office.

Sitting in the small silver pickup truck he and Dale Connelly had commandeered after they had escaped Jimura's warehouse, Jack leaned into his seat's headrest. The events of the past twenty-four hours were catching up to him. He needed sleep and a decent meal, but he knew he was likely to get neither for a while yet, if at all.

"You need to come in, Jack," said Cohen over the mobile phone that was the main reason he had selected this vehicle to steal. "This whole situation's gone completely out of control. We've got Kanashiro in custody. Thanks for that, by the way, but Jimura's still out there. We need to regroup and figure out what to do next."

"Abby, listen. There's no time for that. We've got big problems. Jimura hasn't just been stealing conventional arms from American military bases here. He's gotten his hands on a nuke."

There was a distinct pause, before Cohen replied, "Jack, that's impossible. It's illegal for us to have any nuclear weapons on Okinawa or in Japan."

"Well, somebody didn't get a memo," replied Jack. "Jimura sent men to Camp Hansen today, and they took one out of a secret armory that's underneath one of the buildings there. They kidnapped a Marine's family and used them to force him to help them acess the building and the bunker where twenty-four B61s are stored."

Cohen pressed, "Jack, I'm telling you that couldn't have happened."

Nodding to Connelly, Jack indicated for him to talk to her,

and the Marine leaned closer to the phone.

"Ma'am, this is Master Gunnery Sergeant Dale Connelly. I'm an aviation ordnance chief with MAG-36 down at Futenma." He stopped, and Jack saw the guilt washing over his expression. "Agent Bauer is correct. I . . . I helped them get their hands on the weapon, and then I helped them arm it."

"Did you just admit to treason, Master Gunnery Sergeant Connelly?"

Wringing his hands as they rested in his lap, he said, "I did, Agent Cohen." His voice was trembling. "They have my wife and children."

"Jesus." Jack heard Cohen draw a deep breath. "A nuke? You said you helped him arm it. What's Jimura planning to do with it?"

Connelly replied, "I don't know, but he definitely hates Americans. He wants us all gone from the island, forever. Apparently, he lived through the battle here. His parents were killed in the midst of the fighting."

There was a pause, and Jack heard other voices farther from Cohen's phone before a new voice filtered through the unit's speaker, "Agent Bauer, this is Agent Kurtz with NCIS."

"Agent Kurtz," said Jack. "Glad to hear you're okay. I'm sorry about earlier. I hope you understand I was just maintaining my cover."

The agent replied, "I'll get over it. Listen, we've just received confirmation on this. The Marines' commanding general has verified that we've got a nuke missing. He's already been on the horn with the Pentagon and a response is being put into action to retrieve the weapon, but it's not like we can broadcast this on the news. We're not supposed to have nukes here, remember."

Jack was aware of the agreements with Okinawa and Japan made by the United States with respect to the storage of nuclear weapons here. Someone else would have to worry about the political fallout from this incident. He and the other agents here on the ground had bigger things to worry about just now.

"This thing is armed," said Jack. "Connelly can disarm it, but only Jimura knows where it is. We have to find him."

"We're on it, Jack," replied Cohen. "We're locking down the

airports and the ports, so there's no way he's getting off the island. We've got Marine assets in on this, too, and we're hitting every building or other location we think belongs to or involves Jimura, but it's a lot of places to look."

It was then that Jack felt Connelly's hand on his arm, and he saw the Marine's pleading expression. "Yeah, about that. Abby, I need a favor."

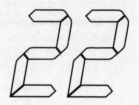

Captain Areg Markovic stood at the window, watching as the bow of the *Konstantinov* cut through the waters of the East China Sea. Checking his watch, Markovic saw that it had been just under thirty minutes since the ship cleared the inlet and maneuvered away from the island on its way to open waters.

Behind him and receding into the distance were the lights of Naha. At this time of night, the city and its neighboring coastal regions were beautiful, making the island seem like a living thing. Markovic had traveled to many ports around the world, but the Pacific had always been his favorite region to sail. Though its narrowness made Naha Port one of the trickier inlets to navigate, he had traversed it a few times in recent years, so the area was familiar. Departing just after midnight also had given the *Konstantinov* the advantage of being the only traffic in the channel.

"Set course two seven zero," Markovic said, nodding to his chief mate, who was overseeing the ship's navigation. "Make your speed ten knots. We're not in a hurry."

The other man replied, "Making our course two seven zero, speed ten knots."

Markovic didn't have to consult any navigational charts to know where the ship was heading. The *Konstantinov* would proceed on course for two hours until it reached a set of preselected coordinates. Once there, the ship would hold position until 1200 hours, local time, or until Grisha Zherdev or one of his people made contact, at which time rendezvous arrangements would be made. It was an odd set of instructions under which Markovic was operating, though not all that unusual, given his employer. Working for people like Tateos Gadjoyan often called for a great deal of flexibility and adaptability, and Gadjoyan's people always made the effort financially worthwhile. After all, it wasn't every cargo ship captain who owned a home in the Cayman Islands. Markovic longed for the fine sandy beach and azure blue water that was mere steps from the house to which he retreated for six months out of each year. Being divorced for more than a decade allowed him to partake of everything the island had to offer, and he had embraced the easy, carefree Caymanian lifestyle. As was always the case when he set sail, thoughts of rum, fishing, and tanned island women filled his head.

Soon, Areg. Soon. First, there is the work.

The contingency plan under which he currently was operating had been put into play when midnight arrived and none of Grisha's people had yet returned to the ship. Markovic had overseen the loading of a consignment into *Konstantinov*'s cargo hold, though he knew nothing about the shipment's contents and was paid well not to ask questions. It had been Zherdev himself who had given Markovic the instructions prior to his disembarking the ship, with strict orders to maintain the schedule as it was known to the Naha Port authorities. Under no circumstances was anything to attract unwanted scrutiny. If necessary, Zherdev or one of his people would make contact with the *Konstantinov* via satellite phone after the ship's departure, at which time Markovic would receive further directions. If twelve hours passed without contact, he was to set course for Kiev and deliver the consignment to its intended destination. Markovic knew that the shipping company operated by Tateos Gadjoyan would be waiting for the ship's arrival, and an on-time delivery promised a nice bonus on top of the already generous fee Markovic and his crew received. The journey would take weeks, after which he would be on a plane to Grand Cayman, assuming everything went to plan. It was this thought that made him smile.

Home.

Reaching into his shirt pocket, Markovic extracted a pack of cigarettes and book of matches and held them up for his mate to see. "I'm going outside."

The aft hatch led to an observation platform that encircled the wheelhouse and afforded him a view of the *Konstantinov*'s main deck. Ahead of him was nothing but the blackness of the ocean, and behind the ship he saw the lights of Naha growing ever smaller and fainter. As he lit a cigarette and inhaled deeply from it, Markovic wondered what had become of Zherdev and the people who had accompanied the ship into Naha. He had heard news reports of supposed gunfights at different locations around the island during the day, and wondered if his passengers might have been involved in those incidents. He was no fool; he knew the sort of business his employers conducted, and was aware of the dangers one faced in such a line of work.

Despite the money he earned for his silence and discretion, that didn't mean he was immune from curiosity. Of course, he had never acted on such impulses, and so had never inspected any cargo belonging to Gadjoyan. Still, he wondered about the people who often traveled with him, and what else they might be doing rather than playing simple escort for a shipment.

In eleven hours, you will know, Markovic reminded himself. *Or, you won't.*

Such was the nature of this business, he knew.

Shaking his head, Markovic smoked his cigarette and thought of white beaches and brilliant blue water.

• • •

The satellite phone rang less than a minute after Amorah Banovich tossed it into her bag.

Setting aside the bottles of water and other food items she was about to pack, she reached for the phone and saw in its compact digital display a familiar number. She extended the unit's antenna and keyed the button to take the call.

"Hello?"

"Amorah." The voice on the other end of the phone was unmistakable.

"Mister Gadjoyan," she said. "It is good to hear your voice."

"And yours, as well, my dear." As always, Gadjoyan adopted a paternal tone when speaking to her, a privilege enjoyed by very few people in his employ. "You are safe?"

"I think so. The ship was scheduled to leave an hour ago, and I can confirm that the shipment is aboard, but we were unable to get there before its scheduled departure. We are proceeding according to the alternate plan."

Gadjoyan replied, "I never doubted you, Amorah. What of the others?"

"We had to separate," she said. "Kanashiro launched an attack on Jimura, and we were caught in the middle. I didn't want to leave, particularly as we had pledged to help Jimura, but it was becoming too dangerous. I can't believe the police haven't swarmed in there by now." Since departing the warehouse, she hadn't heard from Stefan, Alkaev, and Pajari. She could only hope they were safe, and following the plan to rendezvous in Naha. "I know of your relationship with Jimura, and I didn't wish to disrespect it."

"You've done more than was expected, Amorah. I will not forget your efforts throughout these trying times, and neither will I forget your loyalty." His voice had taken on an odd tone.

"Mister Gadjoyan, is something wrong? Have I done something . . . ?"

"No," he said. "No, my dear. You've done nothing less than all I've ever asked of you. That means a great deal to me, particularly today. I only wish that I could say the same for others I've trusted."

Frowning, Banovich said, "I'm sorry, sir. I don't understand."

The sigh from the other end of the line seemed even heavier, routed as it was through the satellite network and across thousands of miles and numerous time zones. "Grisha. It was Grisha, Amorah. They turned him against me."

What? Grisha Zherdev, a traitor? How was that possible?

"You're certain?"

"I am. The CIA corrupted him, turned him into a spy. He

has been helping them for months. They are close to being able to move against us all, Amorah. You must be careful."

Banovich was still struggling to comprehend how someone like Grisha Zherdev, whose devotion to Gadjoyan had always been steadfast, could be turned against the man who had raised him as one of his own sons. What had the Americans promised him? Perhaps they had threatened him in some manner. That at least would make some sense.

"There are others, Amorah. Levon Sarkisian was an American spy. He's the one who turned Grisha against me. No, against *us*."

Unable to stifle the gasp that escaped her lips, Banovich covered her mouth with her free hand. "Not Levon."

"An undercover agent," said Gadjoyan. "A plant, all along. This has given me cause to question everything and everyone around me. You are one of the few people I know I can trust."

It was true. Tateos Gadjoyan had looked after her since childhood, acting as something of an uncle to her following the accidental death of her father while he was in Gadjoyan's employ. Gadjoyan had never mistreated her or used so much as an unkind word, and she knew he looked on her as he would a daughter. She would walk through fire for him.

"Mister Gadjoyan, I am so sorry. I don't know what to say."

"No words are necessary, but I do need you to do something for me."

"Anything. You know that."

Another sigh reverberated through the phone, before Gadjoyan said, "I know, and because I know, I can ask you to do this for me, even though it will be difficult for you. There is another spy in our midst, Amorah. He was working with Levon, and you must kill him. You must kill Stefan Voronov."

So great was her shock, that Banovich almost dropped the phone. "Stefan? How can that be? He's saved my life more than once today."

"It is verified, Amorah. You must kill Stefan Voronov. He's an American intelligence agent, and his real name is Jack Bauer."

• • •

Every fiber of his being was telling Christopher Kurtz to run. Being on an island made that problematic, of course, but that didn't stop him from thinking it.

"Jimura could be anywhere by now," he said, sitting behind the desk of a vacant office inside the arms dealer's warehouse and looking with disgust at the cup of coffee in his hand. It had gone cold while he sat contemplating what life on Okinawa might be like in a few hours after a significant portion of it was irradiated. His next, impertinent thought was that at least such a blast would reheat the swill in his cup, and perhaps even make it taste better.

On the other side of the office, Jordan Aguilar sat on a couch, leaning forward and with her elbows resting on her knees. Like Kurtz, she had consumed her fill of whatever unidentified substance the NCIS response team had dredged up from some well and poured into a coffee cup. Fatigue had long since taken hold in both agents and a good number of their colleagues working the scene. Aguilar was so tired that she hadn't even balked when one of the junior agents told her a body was found stashed behind the couch she had claimed.

"According to Bauer," she said, "that Marine, Connelly, adjusted the yield on the bomb to its lowest setting. Should I get my hopes up and think that Jimura doesn't really want to blow a giant hole in the middle of the island?"

Pacing between them, Abigail Cohen was rubbing her temples. "Even at point three kilotons, that's still enough to level at least a significant portion of any city on the island, and we can't forget about the EMP or the fallout. Every electronic component in the blast radius will be fried. Winds from the west should take care of most of the fallout in short order by blowing it out to sea, but anywhere up past, say, Kinbu Bay could be trouble for the northern half of the island. If he sets it off somewhere like Naha or Nago, or Okinawa City, the death toll will be in the thousands like that." She snapped her fingers to emphasize her point.

Setting aside his coffee, Kurtz leaned back in his chair. "There were only five of Jimura's men still alive here by the time we showed up. NCIS and JSDF are raiding each of his properties, but most of his senior people are in the wind. The ones we've rounded up either know nothing at all, or else they don't know the important stuff, like where he planned to use the thing."

"We've got all of the military bases sealed off," said Aguilar. "Nobody in or out. High value targets are on lockdown, and we've got teams sweeping those areas looking for anything that looks out of the ordinary. We're searching for a white cargo truck, but there's like ten billion of those things on the island. Finding a white truck or car around here is about as hard as finding the ocean."

Cohen sighed. "Okay, so we need to start narrowing things down. This is where I'm hoping Jack can help us."

"I have to tell you," said Kurtz, "your guy Bauer is some piece of work. I don't know whether to admire him or shoot him on sight the next time I see him."

"His methods are unorthodox," replied Cohen, "I'll give you that, but that's exactly why we recruited him. His Special Forces and unconventional warfare experience give him the makings of a superb field agent."

Aguilar said, "Yeah, but he's still pretty rough around the edges."

"It's my job to smooth those edges, but right now I like him just the way he is. The only reason we know as much as we do about what's been going on today is thanks to him. Not too bad for a junior agent who got thrown into the meat grinder."

In truth, Kurtz's initial feelings about Bauer had already subsided. Given the bind in which the CIA agent had found himself, Kurtz tried to imagine what he might do when faced with similar circumstances. While he might quibble with the other man's tactics, when setting those aside, it was apparent that Jack Bauer was doing his best to complete his rather dangerous mission to the best of his ability. Other than some small assistance just in the past few hours, Bauer had been working on his own, improvising and adapting to a fluid, chaotic situation.

"Any word from him?" asked Kurtz.

Cohen shook her head. "Not since that last call."

During that previous conversation and after updating them

on the situation with Jimura and the nuke, Bauer had informed Cohen that he was attempting to assist the Marine, Connelly, to rescue his wife and children. The man's family was still being held after being abducted earlier in the day, and Bauer had apparently visited their location at some point during the intervening hours. He had called for assistance from anyone who could provide manpower to support a raid on the house where the hostages were believed to be. That might also prove helpful in learning Jimura's whereabouts and plans. Even though Bauer had acknowledged that as a remote possibility, Kurtz escalated the request.

"Part of me wants to see Connelly hang," said Aguilar, "and part of me feels sorry for him. I'd like to think it's the second part that's the right one."

"He aided and abetted an enemy of the United States," replied Cohen. "It doesn't get much simpler than that."

Kurtz said, "I get the rule books, and officially I agree with you, but all I'm saying is that if it's my wife and kids, I'd nuke the White House. Twice." He shook his head. "It was an impossible choice, either way." It was all but certain that Connelly himself had ended his career and could even face execution for assisting Jimura's people to steal and arm the nuclear device taken from Camp Hansen. Whatever his eventual fate, the man's family didn't deserve whatever Jimura or his men might have in mind for them.

"Well, here's hoping we can help him," said Cohen. "It's all up to Bauer now."

• • •

This was the place. Jack was certain of it.

Scanning the house and surrounding area through his monocular from what he guessed was a distance of less than fifty meters, he recalled its layout and other features, and tried to imagine them in daylight rather than by the illumination of the moon that was partly obscured by clouds. The orientation of the front of the house to the access road and to the separate outbuilding behind it was right. The fields to the west of the house also looked familiar, though Jack was forced to admit that he had only seen it from the viewpoint of a car window. He thought he recognized one or two of the vehicles parked in the open area between the house and the other storage building, but he couldn't be certain.

"Are you sure about this?" asked Dale Connelly from where he lay on the grass next to Jack. In the crook of his left arm, he rested the MP5 submachine gun Jack had given him back at the warehouse. He had rolled down the sleeves of his camouflage uniform top, as much for concealment purposes as to provide a meager defense against the mosquitoes that were beginning to make their presence known.

"Everything's where I remember it from earlier today." Jack had been confident enough to make another call to Abigail Cohen, alerting her to the house's address and location using a map he had found in the glove compartment and the notes he had scratched out on a scrap piece of paper.

Finding the house had proven difficult at first, owing to Jack's general unfamiliarity with the island. Even with that limitation, he remembered landmarks and other points of interest along the routes they had taken to and from the house. One of those had presented itself while Jack and Connelly were exploring the area in their stolen pickup, and once Jack had oriented himself to the terrain, it became a simple matter to find the smaller, one lane road and the access path leading to the property. They had left the truck back on the paved road and made their way up the path on foot, stopping at regular intervals to look and listen for sentries. So far, the coast was clear.

He covered his mouth to suppress a yawn. Weariness had snared him in its grip, and he was exhausted from the events of the seemingly unending day. Adding on the time spent preparing for the weapons exchange before leaving the *Konstantinov* once the ship had reached Naha Port, Jack had now been awake for well over twenty-four hours. If this kept up much longer, fatigue would begin to affect his judgment and his reaction time, both of which could prove fatal during a shootout.

"I can't thank you enough for this," said Connelly after a

moment. "I know I don't deserve anything but a prison cell and maybe a firing squad, but . . ."

Jack nodded. "I get it. I do. If I were in your shoes, I can't say I wouldn't do the same thing." That meant little, of course. Charges of treason tended to leave little room for personal stakes or other nuance. "I'm no expert in this sort of thing, and I definitely can't make any promises, but if you can help us find and disarm the bomb, that'll probably go a long way toward reducing any charges they throw at you."

"I'll do anything to make this right," replied the Marine. "I just don't want my family to pay for my mistakes. If they hurt Jessica—if they hurt Brynn or Dylan—I'll never forgive myself. Help me get them back, and I'll take whatever punishment I've got coming."

Regardless of everything else, Jack had definite sympathy for Connelly in this regard. "Fair enough."

Movement caught his attention, and Jack once more raised the monocular to his right eye. "We've got activity outside the house." Almost without thinking, he tried to press himself even lower toward the ground, doing his best to think of himself as just a log in the grass. He watched as two men, each armed with what looked to be civilian shotguns, stepped down from the house's front porch while escorting a woman.

Bingo.

"That's her," said Connelly, watching as the guards guided their prisoner from the house toward the outbuilding. Jack saw no cars in that direction, and a sudden knot of alarm made itself known in his gut.

Damn it.

"We need to move," he said, pocketing the monocular and reaching for his own MP5 which, like Connelly's rifle, was fitted with a sound suppressor. "Now."

"What about backup?" asked Connelly. "The agent you called and the NCIS response team?"

"There's no time." Using the rifle's sling, Jack positioned the weapon so that it hung by its stock along his right hip, allowing him to raise it from that carry position without becoming fouled on his clothing. Looking to Connelly, he asked, "You up for this?"

The Marine nodded. "Yeah. It's been a while, but I remember the basics."

"It's easy," said Jack. "Just kill anybody who's not me or your family."

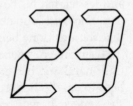

Jessica Connelly stumbled on a rock or something else she didn't see, but managed to keep herself from falling. She cast a derisive glare over her shoulder at the man who had pushed her and received a scowl in return. Her gaze shifted to the shotgun the man carried, its muzzle pointed toward the ground but easily lifted to aim at her.

"Where are you taking me?" she asked. "I want to go back to my children."

"Shut up," said the Okinawan with the ponytail, one of the two men who had been their guards to this point.

Ahead of her was a large storage building that might have been a barn in some rural town back in the States, though there was no sign of livestock anywhere on the property. Why were they being moved from the house? What was waiting for them here? Jessica's imagination began to swirl with every manner of unpleasant scenario. She didn't realize she was slowing her walk toward the barn until she felt a hand between her shoulder blades.

The force of the push jolted her off her feet. She tumbled forward, wincing as her hands scraped on hard, sun-baked soil in her desperate bid to keep from slamming facefirst into the ground. Feeling rage bubble up within her, she pushed herself to her knees and examined her hands in the weak moonlight. Her palms stung from the fall, and she could see scratches already welling up with thin lines of blood.

"Get up," snapped the Okinawan, whom Jessica simply thought of as "Ponytail."

His companion, the larger, bald man, stepped toward her, and Jessica felt his hand on her arm before he jerked her to her feet. The man spun her around, and she decided at that moment that she was done being nice.

Using the momentum from her turn, she lashed out with her right hand and her nails caught the man's face. She felt two of her fingers slip between his teeth and the inside of his cheek and she yanked downward. The man's immediate reaction was to howl in pain as his head was pulled to one side, before he backed away and reached for his mouth. Fury burned in his eyes and Jessica saw him reaching for the pistol tucked into his belt.

"No!" snapped Ponytail, holding up his hand to stop his partner, but the other man was beyond reason. He pulled the pistol free and raised it so that it was a mere arm's length from Jessica's face. Her entire body froze as she stared down the weapon's barrel, which seemed to swallow everything around it. There was no time to say anything, or even to offer a desperate prayer.

The bald man's body jerked and Jessica heard three distinct metallic snaps before she saw something dark and wet erupt from his head. He pitched forward, his body limp as he fell without protest to the dirt. His pistol dropped from his hand, bouncing and sliding across the ground toward her.

Realizing what was wrong, Ponytail reached for whatever weapon he had tucked beneath his shirt. He was turning to where he thought the deadly shots had come from before Jessica heard four more snaps and a quartet of dark plumes broke out across the Okinawan's chest. He stumbled and tripped over his own feet, falling with a heavy thud to the dry soil.

Jessica backed away from the scene of carnage, her hands covering her mouth as she caught sight of two men running toward her. Both were carrying rifles of some kind, and one of the men was wearing a camouflage uniform.

It was Dale.

• • •

Jack sighted down the MP5's barrel, tracking the second man to the ground after releasing another barrage of rounds from the submachine gun. Once he verified the Okinawan was down, he adjusted his aim toward the storage building's open doorway, searching for other threats.

"Dale!"

Jessica Connelly shouting out her husband's name, made Jack wince. He turned in a full circle, hunting for new targets but seeing nothing. Out of the corner of his eye, he saw Connelly running to his wife, and though he was relieved that the woman wasn't hurt or injured, they were a long way from being out of danger.

"Keep it down!" he hissed, pushing the words between his teeth as he continued sweeping the area. Backing toward the storage building, he turned and inspected the structure's interior, but saw nothing.

"Jack!"

Turning at the sound of Connelly's hoarse whisper, Jack looked past the Marine and his family and saw a figure stepping onto the porch. As far as he could tell, the man was unarmed. There was the momentary flash of fire as he ignited a cigarette lighter, but he froze as his eyes fell on the intruders standing twenty meters in front of him. He started to yell, the first syllable of his warning dying in his throat as Jack dropped him with a burst from the suppressed MP5.

If the man's cry hadn't attracted attention, the sound of his dead body sprawling across the porch steps would do the job. Jack could already see shadows moving past lights inside the house from various windows, and it was obvious he had done exactly what he had hoped to avoid.

"Where are your kids?" he asked, already moving toward the house. "The same place you were earlier today?"

The woman, Jessica, replied, "No, they moved us. It's closer to the front of the house."

Recalling what he could of the structure's interior from his brief visit earlier in the day, Jack nodded. "Okay. Stay with her. Find some place to stay low and out of sight. I'll be back."

Connelly hissed, "I'm coming with you."

"I need you out here in case any of them try to cut me off."

Ignoring whatever else the Marine might be saying, Jack advanced on the house. He stepped to his right, removing himself from direct line of sight of the front door as he heard footsteps clomping down the hallway's wooden floor. He saw a shadow darken the entry before the screen door swung open and a man stepped out, leading with the muzzle of a shotgun. He caught Jack from the corner of his eye and started turning toward him but he was far too slow. Jack unleashed another salvo from the MP5, tracking bullets across the man's torso and throwing him against the doorjamb. He fell against the screen door, tearing it from its hinges before he slid to the porch.

Jack heard other voices from inside the house, and used them to his advantage. This was the mission at its most pure, with no diplomacy or the intricacies of building a case against an international arms dealer. There was only killing the enemy and securing the objective, something Jack understood perhaps better than anything else. He might never make a polished, prim, and proper CIA agent who could wear a suit and tie and spend years at a desk analyzing data, or glad-handing political officials and other visitors from countries who may or may not be allies of the United States. What he did know, what he believed without doubt, was that he was the sort of tool those people sent out when the time for diplomacy and sensitivity had passed.

Jack was fine with that.

Let's get this over with.

With the doorway now clear, he stepped over the two men he had just killed, aiming the MP5 through the entry. Another Okinawan appeared from a doorway leading off the house's main hallway, a large-caliber semiautomatic pistol in his hand, and Jack dropped him with two bullets from the submachine gun, hearing the bolt lock to the rear after the weapon fired its last round. Those last two shots were enough, as the man lay unmoving in the house's front room.

Jack dropped the MP5's spent magazine and pulled a new one from his jacket pocket, slamming it home and chambering a round. He was bringing up the weapon when someone was suddenly at the door, weapon in hand. An Okinawan man fired a wild shot as Jack ducked to his right, the bullet digging into the ground where he had been standing. Dropping to one knee, Jack took aim but he never got the chance to fire before six bullets tore into the man's chest and head. The Okinawan staggered to his left before collapsing with a resounding thud to the wooden porch.

Looking over his shoulder, Jack saw Connelly lowering his own MP5 from his shoulder. His wife stood behind him, and then the couple was heading for the storage building. It was then that Jack realized he could hear something in the distance. He recognized the thrum of two distinct helicopters, getting louder as they drew closer.

Here comes the cavalry.

Knowing he couldn't wait for their arrival, Jack pushed himself to his feet and continued his approach to the house.

Five down. Who knows how many to go.

He was inside the house before the next target presented itself. The man emerged from the kitchen, wielding a revolver and a large butcher knife. He hurled the knife and its blade buried itself in the wall to Jack's left. Jack responded by shooting him in the face, but the man still managed to squeeze off a round from the pistol before dropping to his back in the hallway.

The helicopters outside were louder as Jack advanced into the corridor. The first door on the left, leading to a small kitchen, was clear, and he pivoted to his right to clear the next room. Something long, thin, and dark swung at him from the doorway as he came abreast of it, and it was all he could do to parry the blow aimed at his head. Jack brought up the MP5 and blocked the crowbar. Its wielder was swinging it like a bat—or maybe a sword—and Jack was forced to backpedal to stay out of its reach. The Okinawan, big and muscled and sporting tattoos on his bare chest and arms, adjusted his grip on the crowbar, holding it like a rifle at port arms and ready to swing or thrust.

Still recovering his balance, Jack realized he was giving his opponent too much time to attack. Before he regained his footing, he aimed the MP5 from the hip and pressed the trigger, holding it down as the submachine gun unleashed the remaining bullets in its magazine. At least eight or nine ripped through the burly Okinawan, pushing him against the wall. He sagged to the floor, eyes wide and unseeing.

Jack dropped the now useless MP5 as he heard footsteps from the corridor, and unlimbered his Glock. It was still fitted with its own suppressor and he was bringing it up as yet another gunmen appeared around a corner at the hallway's far end. This one seemed better prepared than his companions, and he had ducked to one knee before leaning into the passageway. He fired without aiming, spraying rounds from an AK-47 fitted with a pistol grip. The weapon's recoil pushed its barrel up and away from its intended target and the man was forced to use his other hand to keep the rifle under control.

This was enough for Jack, who moved up the hallway with his Glock gripped in both hands. Two quick shots to the man's chest were enough to make him tumble off his one knee and onto the floor, and Jack put another round through the shooter's head.

Almost there.

Recalling the house's layout, Jack maneuvered down the hallway, clearing rooms as he went. He passed the bathroom he remembered from earlier in the day and made the turn in the corridor. The first door on his right was closed and he kicked at it, forcing it open. When no one stood ready to confront him, Jack drew a deep breath and stepped through the doorway, aiming his Glock at the room's far corner.

An Okinawan stood there, the muzzle of the pistol in his hand pressed to the side of Brynn Connelly's head. His free hand was holding her brother, Dylan, next to her, and he was using both of their bodies to shield himself. Jack leveled the Glock at the man's head, a bit more than half of which was just visible behind Brynn and to her left. It would be a tricky shot, even from this close distance.

"Put gun down!" the man shouted. "Drop it, or . . ."

Jack fired.

The single shot drilled through the Okinawan's forehead just above his left eye. His head jerked backward, his chin pointing toward the ceiling. Brynn and Dylan dropped to the floor as the man's finger convulsed on his pistol's trigger, sending a shot into the wall to the man's left. Jack shot him again, putting two more rounds into the man's chest. The Okinawan fell against a shoddy, scarred armoire and toppled onto the bed before sliding to the floor.

"Jack!"

The voice from the hallway was accompanied by heavy footfalls seconds before Dale Connelly appeared in the door, MP5 in hand. Upon seeing his children, he dropped the weapon and ran to them, collapsing to his knees as both daughter and son threw their arms around him.

Only then did Jack Bauer allow himself a well-earned sigh of relief.

• • •

"You didn't leave us much to work with, Bauer."

Swallowing the last of a bottle of water, Jack wiped his mouth with the back of his hand as he regarded Christopher Kurtz and Jordan Aguilar.

"You're welcome."

Around them, NCIS and JSDF agents and at least two dozen United States Marines were sweeping the house and surrounding property, searching for stragglers Jack may have left behind. Portable field lights had been erected around the perimeter of the compound between the house and the storage building, which now served as a temporary base of operations while the agencies conducted their investigation. Jack was happy to let them do the cleanup work.

"I meant that as a sincere compliment," said Kurtz as he handed Jack a second water bottle. "I've never seen anything like what you just did here."

"I told you he was good," said Abigail Cohen from where she stood next to Jack. Looking at him, she offered an approving nod. "Not bad, Bauer. Not bad at all. Bill would've been damned proud."

Feeling a twinge of regret as he considered the untimely death of his friend and mentor, Jack twisted off the bottle's plastic cap. "Did you find Jimura?"

Aguilar shook her head. "No dice. If he was ever here, he's long gone."

"Damn it!" Jack hurled the water bottle to the ground. "All of this is for nothing if we don't find him."

"There's no way he's getting onto any military bases," said Kurtz. "They were locked down even before we knew Jimura had the weapon. General Timmons had already started taking protective steps from the moment he found out one of the bombs was missing."

Jack had been told about the report filed by the commanding general of all but one of the Marine Corps installations on the island. The Pentagon was on alert, and a Nuclear Emergency Support Team had been dispatched in response to the Empty Quiver event now unfolding here. The pieces were coming together to deal with the current situation, but they lacked one vital ingredient: Where to start looking.

"Jimura's people are useless," said Cohen. "If any of them know anything, they're not talking. About the only thing we can do is start pulling fingernails or waterboarding suspects."

Though he considered those sorts of interrogation methods despicable, Jack found it hard to discount the possibility of their usefulness here and now. He had seen such tactics employed against prisoners and other high-value enemy combatants. While there were occasions when they proved useful, as often as not they resulted in the tortured person simply telling his interrogators what he thought they wanted to hear. He also had seen more than one person take too much satisfaction from the pain they were inflicting on others, which made him resent the practice even more. He preferred to go his entire life without having to witness such a distasteful event ever again.

"There has to be a way to narrow down the possibilities," he said. "Jimura wants to make a statement. Connelly said he hates Americans, and has all his life; since the battle here during World War II."

"Futenma," said Aguilar.

Kurtz shook his head. "No way. That base is locked down. Armed guards at every gate, roving patrols, a curfew. Nobody's moving there, or on any base."

"Not the base." Aguilar was waving her hand. "He doesn't need to be right on the base, anyway. We're talking about an area weapon, remember?"

Jack scowled. "Why Futenma?"

"It's his home," said another voice. It was Connelly, standing at the doorway leading from the storage building. He looked tired, and ashamed, and embarrassed even to be in their midst. Jack noted the cool expressions the Marine received as he stood at the door, waiting. Behind Connelly were his wife and children, all of whom looked worn out from their ordeal, yet grateful to be free.

"Master Gunnery Sergeant Connelly," said Cohen, her voice level, "this probably isn't the place for you."

Connelly replied, "Just slap the damned cuffs on me and get it over with. I know what I did. You can hate me all you want, but my family's alive and free of that psychopath. I'd do it again if it meant saving them. I just wish I could've done more for Tom Wade and everyone else he killed today."

"You'd betray your country?" asked Aguilar.

"I gave my country twenty-six years. I'd have preferred not to end things this way, but that's the way it goes. Now, you can throw me *under* the jail for all I care, but first you need to listen to me. Jimura hates us. Every last damned one of us. He watched as we laid concrete over the town where he grew up. The base at Futenma was built by us after the war, as part of a massive land grab from the Okinawan people once the United States moved in to take over. Jimura would rather see his home go up in smoke than have it desecrated for one more day by Americans. You should have seen him when he was talking to me. He's obsessed."

"There may be something to this," said Kurtz. "According to the bio information we have, Jimura was born and raised in Ginowan, which got the hell kicked out of it during the American invasion of the island in 1945. Most of what was the old village was taken over during the American occupation after the war, and became the air station at Futenma. There have been protests for years for the United States to reduce or eliminate its presence on the island, and locals are supposedly gearing up for a huge rally next year when the fiftieth anniversary of the battle is celebrated."

Aguilar replied, "Except Jimura won't be around for that." She tapped the side of her head. "Cancer, remember? He's a goner within a couple of months at the outside."

"Son of a bitch," said Jack. "That has to be it. He wants to drive Americans from the island, so he sets off an American nuclear weapon on Okinawan soil. He doesn't care what happens to him, because he'll be dead, anyway." He frowned as he considered the outlandishness of this idea. "Is he really that far gone?"

"Well, we're talking about a guy who stole a nuke and had it armed," said Cohen, "so I doubt he's all that well adjusted. Still, there's only one way to find out. We need to go to Futenma."

• • •

The truck was precisely where Miroji Jimura wanted it.

Stifling a wet, sickly cough, he studied the vehicle with great interest. There was no need to look inside the truck's rear cargo area. He knew what it contained. Its placement also was perfect. From the street, it was practically invisible. Unless someone was actively searching for the vehicle, it was unlikely to be found.

Turning from the truck, Jimura gazed across the small parking lot behind the retail establishments and peered down an alley between two buildings. Beyond the district in which he stood and across the highway, he could see streetlamps illuminating the familiar curved roofs of the hangars. For decades, he had peered at them from his home in Ginowan, in the small house he had purchased which wasn't too far from the land on which his parents had built their home.

That house and the land on which it once sat were gone, of course, consumed by the American military machine. That process had begun in 1945 when naval gunfire had devastated numerous inland targets ahead of the amphibious assault and ground invasion of the island. Later, after the war's end and the military occupation of Okinawa was underway, he had lived with friends from Ginowan, watching the American military construct what eventually would become the Futenma air base. Never mind that the villages such as his own were the homes of Okinawa's people for uncounted generations. The conquerors had come to stay.

No more.

Jimura would have preferred to carry out his plan next year, when the base and the community observed the fiftieth anniversary of the battle that had brought the Americans here. Such an event would carry with it that much more notice. Alas, the ongoing pain in his head and the obstruction in his lungs were reminders that his time in this life was limited. Therefore, his mission would have to be launched now, if he was to live long enough to see it.

Pausing, he smiled at his own unintentional irony. There would be nothing for him to see, of course.

He removed the pistol from his waistband. It was one of the few American items he had allowed into his house. Recovered from a wounded Marine he had found in the ruins of what had been his village, the Colt .45 was the personification of all he loathed about the American military. His first act upon taking possession of the weapon was to use it on its former owner.

From then until today, he had cared for it in order to maintain its operation. He had used it only sparingly during the decades that had passed, and he only used it on Americans who somehow managed to incur his wrath. Though he didn't expect to need it here today, he had lived his life by obeying a simple maxim of never leaving anything to chance. Preparedness was the ally of the successful, he believed, and that mindset had presided over everything he had ever done. Why should today, his last day on this Earth, be any different?

My last day.

He had come to terms with this notion, and he wasn't afraid to die. On the other hand, he was worried that he might die before doing all he could to ensure that one day, Americans were driven from this island, never to return. That he wouldn't be here to witness that glorious triumph didn't make him sad.

Instead, he was content to die here, today and on his terms, rather than waiting to succumb to disease.

Miroji Jimura was done waiting.

No more.

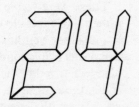

Below him, Jack likened the ramshackle collection of streets and buildings to a sprawling maze. In some ways, that seemed an apt comparison, given how lost he was just now, while searching for a way out of their current predicament.

"Do we know where he lived?" said Jack into his headset's microphone. Even with his ears covered, he was still able to make out the steady rhythm of the UH-1N helicopter's rotor blades.

Across from him in the Huey's cabin, Agent Kurtz nodded. "It's east of Futenma, up on a hillside in Ginowan City. He can probably see the air station from his house."

Something about that comment made Jack point toward the town below them. "He might want to put the bomb somewhere close like that, to do as much damage as possible to the base instead of the surrounding town."

Sitting next to Kurtz, Jordan Aguilar said, "Maybe, but if he set the bomb to its lowest yield, that doesn't really track."

To Jack's left, Abigail Cohen added, "Someplace close, then? Great. That only narrows things down to the entire town."

"Start with anything close to the base perimeter," said Jack. "We can work out from there."

Shifting in his seat, Jack eyed Dale Connelly. The Marine's expression remained somber, his gaze fixed on the deck of the helicopter's passenger compartment.

"If we find this thing," said Jack, "are you sure you can disarm it?"

Connelly nodded. "Yeah. If there's enough time, or he hasn't booby-trapped it."

These were viable possibilities, but Jack chose not to dwell on them. They would either succeed, or fail.

The Huey's circuit of Ginowan City and the neighboring air station was being conducted in a clockwise fashion, so that Jack could lean through the open hatch on the helicopter's right side. At this time of night, huge portions of the town were cast in darkness, with streetlamps and exterior lights affixed to buildings and houses providing the only illumination. Finding Jimura's cargo truck in this situation was a tall order. The Huey was fitted with a spotlight, which the helicopter's copilot was aiming at the ground below. Jack noted the increased presence of police vehicles on the streets. They were maneuvering through town without lights or sirens, moving past buildings and parking lots in deliberate fashion.

"Wait," said Connelly, and Jack felt the Marine's hand on his arm. "Back to the right. I think I saw something." It took a moment for the Huey's pilot to act on the course change, and Jack and the others waited as the helicopter banked back around the way it had come before orienting itself to the area that had aroused Connelly's interest.

After another minute, the Marine tapped Jack on the arm again, and now he was pointing. "There! See that truck? The one with no mirror on the passenger door?"

Using binoculars, Jack examined the white cargo truck tucked into a small parking area behind a trio of buildings arranged in a horseshoe formation. The truck had been positioned so that its rear door was almost flush against the brick wall of the building behind it, and he noted the damage to the vehicle's passenger doorframe from where the mount for the sideview mirror had been torn away.

"Are you sure?" he asked.

Connelly replied, "I remember it from the warehouse. That has to be the one."

• • •

They agreed to split up and approach the truck from multiple angles. While Jack didn't expect Jimura to have enticed anyone to remain with him to carry out this insane act, he fully expected to find the elder Okinawan somewhere nearby. Would Jimura be armed, or might he have accepted the inevitability of his death as a consequence of being apprehended before the bomb could go off? Jack tried to put himself in the mindset of the other man.

If I'd come this far, I'd want to go out with guns blazing.

Followed by Connelly, who was armed with a Beretta M9 pistol given to him by Agent Kurtz, Jack made his way through the narrow alley between two brick buildings. Behind him and to the northwest, across Highway 330, was the perimeter fence of the Futenma air station. Raising the threat level had put the base on full alert. The flight line and neighboring buildings and hangars were lit up, and even from this distance Jack could see people and vehicles moving about the area. The base's commanding officer had ordered a full sweep of the installation as they continued to search for signs of pending attack.

Jack emerged from the mouth of the alley, sweeping the area in front of him with his Glock. There were no signs of activity in the parking lot, but there also were several areas and corners where shadows concealed far too much. Stepping to his right, Jack turned to see the front of the cargo truck. It was parked in such a manner that it couldn't be seen from the street, with a pair of trash Dumpsters positioned between it and the alleys leading back to the front of the buildings.

To his left, Connelly stepped from the alley, the Beretta held before him in a two-handed grip. Like Jack, the Marine surveyed the parking lot, starting from his left and panning the pistol to the right until he and Jack eyed one another.

The single shot echoed in the enclosed space.

Connelly cried out in pain, one hand reaching for his midsection as he dropped to one knee. Jack turned to where he had seen a muzzle flash from the corner of his eye, but he was too slow. Another shot rang out across the parking lot and Jack felt something punch him in the left shoulder. The force of the bullet was enough to spin him around and he tripped over a concrete parking stop before tumbling to the worn asphalt. It was an awkward fall, and Jack lost his grip on the Glock as he hit hard on his injured shoulder. The pain was excruciating and he pressed his right hand against the wound, feeling blood seeping between his fingers.

Movement to his right made him turn his head and Jack saw Miroji Jimura emerge from the darkness in the parking lot's far corner. The aged Okinawan was moving slowly but with purpose, aiming what Jack saw was a Colt .45 pistol of the sort issued to American military personnel for decades. Despite the weapon's size, which appeared even larger in Jimura's slight hand, the man's arm was unwavering as he aimed the pistol at Jack's head. He said nothing as he moved closer, until he stood just to Jack's left, looking down at him over the .45's barrel. Behind Jimura, Connelly was squirming on the ground, holding both hands to a wound in his side. The stain on his camouflage uniform top was already big, and getting bigger.

"One thing you gaijin have always done well," Jimura said, gesturing with the pistol, "is create ever better ways to kill. If you weren't so good at that, I might have had to find other work."

"I know you're angry," said Jack, wincing at the pain in his shoulder, "and for all I know, you have every right to be, but this isn't the way to make things right. Think of the innocent people who will die if you let that bomb go off."

Jimura replied, "There are no innocents. My people abandoned their identity to serve at the feet of our conquerors. We've accepted our fate like some household pet, rather than standing up to fight for what belongs to us. The Japanese gave us that much, at least until they started killing us, too."

When Connelly released another moan of pain, Jimura looked in his direction. Jack watched the .45 move from him toward the wounded Marine, but before Jimura could pull the trigger, Jack lashed out with his right foot. He caught the elderly man just below the knees, taking his legs out from him. The .45 barked as its muzzle aimed upward, its report echoing off the nearby brick walls. Jimura fell, striking his head on the asphalt.

Rolling to his right, Jack pushed aside the agony in his shoulder and scrambled to retrieve his Glock. Jimura was whimpering now, one hand reaching for the back of his head, but he retained enough of his senses to point his pistol at Jack. Another shot rang out and Jack flinched, sensing the bullet whipping past his left ear. With a single motion he aimed his Glock at Jimura and fired twice. The elder man's body twisted as the bullets ripped through him. There was a final gasp before Jimura settled onto the asphalt, his lifeless eyes staring up at the sky.

"Jack?"

Running footsteps made Jack turn to see Kurtz and Aguilar emerging from the alley behind him. Both agents had their weapons drawn and moved with deliberate haste toward Miroji Jimura's body.

"I'm fine, I think," replied Jack. Holstering her weapon, Aguilar moved to him and checked his shoulder.

"Looks like it went through," she said. "We've got an ambulance and a couple of corpsmen coming from the base. They'll patch you up."

Jack shook his head. "The bomb."

• • •

Accessing the truck's rear compartment was as simple as breaking the driver's side window to unlock the door before putting the vehicle in neutral so a squad of Marines could push it out from the side of the building. With the truck's cargo door open, Jack got his first look at the B61, still sitting atop its transport cart and strapped down to the inside of the truck.

His face ashen, Dale Connelly stood over the bomb, his hands shaking as he removed the protective cover on the shell's outer casing to expose the weapon's innards. Sitting next to the bomb itself was a large, boxlike unit that connected to some of the weapon's internal components.

"Are you all right?" asked Abigail Cohen, as she and Jack watched the Marine work. The wound Connelly had sustained from Jimura's pistol was serious, but a Navy corpsman had treated him and said that transport to a hospital could be delayed for a short time. That was enough for Connelly, who had insisted on helping to defuse the bomb.

"I'll be okay," Connelly said, still gripping a screwdriver

from the tool kit he had brought with him on the helicopter. "Are they getting people away from here?"

"They're trying," said Cohen, "but it's a lot of people, and we're on an island. There are only so many places for people to go. You're our best bet, Marine."

"What can I do?" asked Jack. His own shoulder wound also had been treated and his left arm placed in a sling. The bullet had passed through without hitting any bones, so while he would be sore for a while, there would be no permanent damage.

Lucky me.

Connelly had removed a cover that Jack suspected wasn't part of the bomb's original equipment, exposing a digital timer with wires running from it to the green box outside the weapon's casing. The clock was counting down, showing that more than an hour remained until it reached zero.

"See that number pad on the arming box?" Connelly asked, gesturing with his head to the device connected to the bomb.

"Yeah," said Jack.

"Punch in zero zero six, then press the pound key." Connelly used his sleeve to wipe his forehead. "It's a diagnostic command. Enter that, and the trigger is suspended while the box performs a self-check. Once that starts, I can disconnect it from the bomb itself."

"That's it?" asked Cohen.

Nodding, Connelly replied, "That's it. However, the bomb won't really be disarmed until we disconnect the box. After that, it can't detonate unless it's readied for aerial deployment, or we go through this again."

Wary, Jack entered the code.

The numbers on the digital clock increased the speed at which they were counting down. Within seconds, the time remaining fell below one hour, and was continuing to dwindle.

"Oh, damn," said Connelly, his gaze shifting between the bomb's interior and the box. "This shouldn't be happening. I did everything according to the instructions!"

Moving closer, Jack eyed the counter. "Son of a bitch. Jimura must have done something after you armed it. Changed the commands, scrambled the codes, whatever." Jack possessed only basic knowledge about disarming explosives, and nothing about the internal workings of nuclear weapons. Out of his element, he looked first to Connelly, then Cohen for guidance.

"What can we do?" asked Cohen, and Jack heard the tension in her voice.

Using his hands to steady himself against the cart, Connelly closed his eyes and took several deep breaths. "Let me think. Maybe we can interrupt the signal between the box and the bomb's internal wiring." He seemed wobbly, as though his knees were weakening, and when he started to fall backward Jack caught him.

"Connelly," he said, helping the Marine to sit on the floor of the truck. "We need you. Tell us what to do."

"Interrupt. Signal." Connelly's breathing was growing shallow. "Has to be fast."

"We're halfway gone, Jack," said Cohen. "Timer's under thirty minutes. I think it's speeding up."

Looking to Connelly, Jack saw that the wounded man's eyes were closing. He was out of it. "Damn it!" He lowered Connelly to the floor of the truck before shuffling over to the bomb. Slipping his wounded arm from its sling, he grimaced at the stab of pain in his left shoulder as he grabbed the arming box. He turned it over in his hands, looking for a means of opening it to access its internal parts. On its bottom was a recessed panel, which he was able to open with a screwdriver from Connelly's tools. Jack peered into the compartment, seeing three sets of dual in-line package switches. Arranged in groups of eight, the switches were set in varying combinations of ON or OFF.

"Any of that make any sense to you?" asked Cohen.

"No." He looked toward the truck's open rear door. There was no time to drive the bomb to another, perhaps safer location. Even the ocean, mere minutes away, was out of reach. Evacuating was a useless idea at this point, Jack knew. The bomb would detonate well before they made it to any safe distance.

"What did Connelly mean?" he asked. "Interrupt the signal, but it has to be fast." From his limited experience defusing other, more conventional bombs, a disruption of the electrical current between the weapon's timer and trigger usually resulted in detonation. Booby-trapping the trigger mechanism also was a popular hobby for those who specialized in these sorts of things. Even if Connelly hadn't been coerced into adding such a feature, it was entirely possible that Jimura had done so.

"We're at fifteen, Jack," said Cohen. "It's definitely moving faster, now."

"To hell with it." There wasn't time for anything else. Jack reached for the wires running from the arming box to the bomb.

Cohen stuck out her hand. "Wait! What are you doing?"

Ignoring her, Jack took up the slack in the wires, readying to pull them. He turned to Cohen to say something—exactly what, he had no idea—and saw it.

"Son of a bitch."

"What?"

He grabbed the stun gun from Cohen's hip. Without thinking, he jammed it into the arming box until he felt it make contact with the circuit board. Drawing a deep breath, he pressed the stun gun's power button.

"Jack!"

Blue electricity flashed inside the box and every diode on the timer display flared to life. The box spat out a series of beeps and Jack smelled burning plastic. Smoke rose from the arming box's open panel before the counter went dark.

"It's out!" shouted Cohen.

"Now! Pull the wires!" Jack snapped.

Cohen obliged, reaching for the wires connecting the box to the bomb and yanking them free of the smaller and less directly lethal device. She and Jack held each other's gaze, waiting for the detonation, but it never came. When they both realized that they apparently were going to live, Cohen rolled her eyes and sank to the floor.

"Holy shit, Bauer. Are you insane?"

"No, but I can see where it might come in handy." Blowing out his breath, Jack dropped the stun gun and all but collapsed against the cart, forgetting for a moment just what it held. He winced at the pain shooting through his shoulder and returned his wounded arm to his sling. "Agent Cohen, this is my official notice that I've had enough fun for one day." He looked to Connelly, who was unconscious. "We need to get him to a hospital."

"I know." Cohen pushed herself to her feet and was moving toward the rear of the truck when she stopped and placed a hand on Jack's uninjured arm. "Damn fine work, Jack." After a moment, she sighed. "I'd love to put you on the first plane home, but there's one more thing you need to know about."

• • •

Even with dawn more than an hour away, Amorah Banovich saw signs of increasing activity in this section of Tomari Fishing Port. Though the larger cargo and passenger vessels in Naha Port to the south were always busy even at this early hour morning, it was here that the real work was being done. At least, that was the way she preferred to think of it. Small ships coming in from the sea would soon be selling their fresh catches, while others would be heading out for days or even weeks of fishing or crab hunting.

At this time of morning, several fishing boats were moored in slips along the port's immense concrete dock. A wide, pitted and cracked sidewalk separated the dock from a row of small buildings, vehicles, and storage tanks. Most of the buildings were dark, but Banovich saw light coming from a few windows. With luck, they'd be able to conclude their business and be away from here.

"He may not come," said Rauf Alkaev. He, along with Banovich and Manish Pajari, stood in the darkness between two dilapidated buildings situated across the dock from where a group of five boats were moored side by side. "If what Gadjoyan says is true, he may already be on his way home to the United States."

Banovich said nothing. Her mind still reeled from the information Tateos Gadjoyan had given her about Stefan.

No. His name is Bauer. Jack Bauer.

It was unthinkable that she had been so taken by the American spy; that he had been so convincing in his undercover role. She had trusted him, and he had saved her life. How deep into the lie had Bauer allowed himself to fall, that he could so easily conceal his true identity?

And you thought the two of you might . . .

So great was her anger that Banovich didn't even realize she was clenching her fists until they started to tingle and ache. Blinking several times, she loosened her hands and shook them to restore proper feeling.

"Are you all right?" asked Pajari.

"I'll be fine once we deal with Stefan."

Bauer. Stefan is dead. He never existed. Only Bauer remains, for now.

Pushing aside the bitter thoughts, Banovich focused on the boats ahead of them. The one on the far end, to her left, was the vessel that would take them from the island. There was light coming from the windows of the boat's bridge, and Banovich saw the occasional shadow of someone moving about on deck. She checked her watch, noting that a little more than an hour remained until the boat's scheduled departure time of 5:00. It was something of a late start for a fishing crew, but she knew that this had been yet another of Grisha Zherdev's fallback preparations for this assignment.

Indeed, it was Grisha's fondness for such planning that was giving Banovich second thoughts about Bauer. Gadjoyan's instructions had been for her to eliminate the American using any means she deemed appropriate. This had surprised her, given her employer's preference for personally addressing matters of this sort. He took particular relish in exacting revenge for betrayal, but it was likely he also knew of her fondness for the man who had been Stefan Voronov. Perhaps Gadjoyan was allowing her this gift of retribution, and it made sense for Banovich to dispatch Bauer with all due haste before rendezvousing with the *Konstantinov* and heading home.

Now, however, she had something else in mind.

"We don't kill him. I want him alive. We're taking him with us."

Alkaev said, "But Mister Gadjoyan wants . . ."

"Gadjoyan left the decision to me," hissed Banovich. She paused, drawing a deep breath and ensuring her anger was under control. "It's a long trip home. Plenty of time to make Bauer tell us everything he knows." If she could extract any useful information from the spy, it might mitigate at least some of the losses Gadjoyan had suffered today. He would want to know if other traitors lurked among his loyal people, after all, and he would be very appreciative of Banovich's efforts to bring him that information.

As for Bauer? The long journey would also provide her opportunities to wring other means of satisfaction from him. Banovich contemplated the weeks it would take for the *Konstantinov* to make the transit to Kiev, and how she could inflict ever greater levels of suffering upon Jack Bauer with each passing day.

Her thoughts dissolved as a voice called out from the darkness.

"Amorah."

• • •

To their credit, Alkaev and Pajari were faster than Banovich. Jack saw their hands reaching for their weapons even as they spun around to face him. Pajari was a touch quicker than Alkaev, the gun in his hand rising to aim in Jack's direction. Holding his Glock in his right hand while his left arm rested once more in its sling, Jack put two bullets through the man's chest before turning his pistol on Alkaev. The silenced weapon snapped another pair of rounds and the man dropped to the ground, leaving only Banovich facing him, her own pistol in her hand but aimed uselessly at the ground in front of her.

"Don't," warned Jack, aiming his Glock at her chest.

Banovich's expression was ice. "So, it's true. You truly are a spy."

"That's right, and your boss is an arms dealer brokering weapons to people who want to attack my country." He gestured with the Glock toward her weapon hand. "Drop the gun, Amorah." Behind her, Jack now saw Abigail Cohen and the two NCIS agents, Kurtz and Aguilar, weapons drawn and moving into view and toward Banovich. They were advancing to flank her, staying out of Jack's direct line of fire. Kurtz looked ready to pounce, but Jack shook his head signaling for the agents to halt their advance.

For her part, Banovich ignored the new arrivals. "Yes, I know all about you, Mister Jack Bauer of the Central Intelligence Agency, and your friend, Agent Fields. How long have you been spying on us? Months? I have to say, no one ever suspected a thing. You played your role as one of us very well. Perhaps a little too well, I think." Her eyes were flat and cold. "I liked you better with the accent."

She was trying to rattle him. That much was obvious, but Jack wasn't falling for it. "It was my job, nothing more."

"Was turning Grisha against us, and making him betray a man who treated him like his own flesh and blood part of your job?"

Grisha? Jack hadn't even known the agency had turned Grisha Zherdev. He glanced at Cohen, whose expression revealed nothing.

Thanks for nothing, Abby.

"And what of our friendship?" continued Banovich. "You saved my life today. That also was your job?"

"Yes." Seeing that she hadn't dropped her pistol, Jack took a step forward. "Don't make me regret that." Behind Banovich, Cohen tensed, her own gun aimed at the woman's head.

"If I am the enemy, then why not kill me?"

Jack was tempted to do that. It would be easy, but Abigail Cohen's orders still rang in his ears. With Grisha Zherdev and Bill Fields dead, his own cover blown, and his returning to Tateos Gadjoyan now out of the question, Amorah Banovich had become a valuable asset. She represented a dangling thread that might still allow the CIA to unravel the tapestry of Gadjoyan's organization. The trick, of course, was convincing her to betray the man who had raised her like his own daughter. Could such deep loyalty be overcome? Jack was skeptical, but it was Cohen's call.

"There's a chance for you to get away from all of this," he said. "You don't have to go back to Kiev. You don't have to live this kind of life, anymore."

Banovich expression turned to disbelief. "You can't be serious. He'd hunt me down if it took him the rest of his life."

"We can protect you," said Cohen. Banovich tensed at the sound of the agent's voice, but did not move. The pistol in her hand remained pointed toward the ground.

"No one hides from Gadjoyan," said Banovich, her gaze still locked on Jack. "Not forever. Not me, and certainly not you, Mister Bauer. One day, he'll find you. Do you have a family? A wife or a child? He'll find them, too. You'll die, but not before he makes you watch him cut them into pieces. I'm just sorry I won't be there to see it."

Her arm jerked. The pistol rose, its muzzle aiming at his face, and Jack fired. Two bullets punched through Amorah Banovich's chest, followed by a third to the center of her forehead. Her eyes wide in shock, her body collapsed to the ground.

"Jack!"

It was Cohen, moving with Kurtz and Aguilar to cover Banovich's unmoving form. Aguilar kicked away the pistol which had fallen from the dead woman's hand. Jack watched it all with his Glock still trained on Banovich. Only when his teeth started to hurt did he realize how hard he had clamped his mouth shut.

"Damn it," said Cohen, holstering her weapon. "She was our last solid lead to Gadjoyan."

Lowering his pistol, Jack continued to stare at Banovich, his gaze locking on her lifeless eyes. "She was never going to betray him."

"Maybe not, but we might still have been able to get something out of her."

Jack flinched at the momentary stab of pain in his wounded shoulder. "I didn't feel like getting shot again." Tearing his attention from Banovich, he glared at Cohen. "You could've told me about Zherdev."

Cohen shrugged. "Need-to-know, Jack. He was a high-value asset, and you were a junior agent. Not so junior, anymore, though, I think."

"What happens now?" Jack returned the Glock to his holster. "What do we do about Gadjoyan?"

"I'm no expert," said Aguilar, "but I'm guessing having your cover blown and capping this charming minx puts a crimp in your future plans."

"That's one way to put it," replied Cohen. "The Navy is sending a ship out to intercept the *Konstantinov*. It'll be impounded and its cargo seized. It might not be enough for us to take a shot at nabbing Gadjoyan, but Edoga Kanashiro and whoever's left from Jimura's organization are about to have some really bad days."

Kurtz tipped his finger to his forehead in a mock salute. "And we can't thank you enough for that, Jack. I know you didn't start out the day with this in mind, but you ended up pushing our cases ahead several months. Kanashiro's going to be in prison for the rest of his life."

"What about Connelly?" asked Jack. "What happens to him?"

Kurtz shook his head. "There's going to be a court-martial. There's no getting around that. The best we can hope for is mitigating circumstances and the role he played in helping us recover the weapon." He gestured to Jack. "You'd make a hell of a character witness."

"Done," replied Jack. "Just tell me where and when. Anything else?"

Aguilar chuckled. "You brought down two international arms dealers, and maybe a third. You looking for an encore?"

He hadn't yet had time to process everything that had transpired since his arrival on Okinawa. It was hard to believe that so much had taken place over the course of a single day.

Let's try not to make this a habit.

Months of undercover work to get to this point, and now it was over. He was exhausted, but already Jack could feel the weight and stresses of this assignment lifting from his shoulders. All he wanted now was to go home to Teri and Kim. It had been far too long since he had last seen them. They didn't deserve to endure these prolonged separations, even if they understood the reasons.

"I think you've earned a vacation," said Cohen. "A short one, anyway."

"Short?"

Cohen smiled. "It's a big world, Jack, with lots of bad guys in it. We've still got a lot of work to do." Her smile faded. "Besides, I'm going to need a new partner."

Nodding in understanding, Jack couldn't help thinking of Bill Fields, who had trained him so well and been a true friend. Cohen was right, of course. There were many threats out there; some familiar, and others as yet unknown. Such threats wouldn't wait for them to mourn brave men like Bill Fields, or for Jack's own injuries to heal. Jack had sworn an oath to keep his country safe, and in doing so he kept his family safe. Teri and Kim might never know the truth about his job, but he hoped they understood why he did it and would continue to do it. There was never any end to such fighting. There was only the occasional pause.

Jack Bauer would pause, for now. He had earned that much.

Tomorrow was another day.

ACKNOWLEDGMENTS

Many, *many* thanks are due to Melissa Frain, my editor at Tor/ Forge. This novel marks my first time working with Melissa, and she's been absolutely wonderful throughout the rather interesting development and writing of this novel. Her enthusiasm for *24* and these novels was infectious from the start, and I'm thrilled that she decided to bring me on for what I consider an actual, honest-to-goodness Dream Job.

Thanks also to my good friend Marco Palmieri. Formerly my editor at Pocket Books before finding a new home at Tor, Marco's remained a mentor and confidant for years, and it was he who recommended me to Melissa all those many moons ago.

To my friends and fellow word pushers, James Swallow and David Mack, I raise my glass. They plowed the road ahead of me with their own top-shelf Jack Bauer tales and were there every step of the way if I had a question to be answered or just needed to share a bit in the fun we all had writing our respective books. More than anyone, they know just how excited I was to be offered this project.

To you, the reader: Thank you for taking a chance on me. If you've made it this far, then you're probably as much a fan of Jack Bauer as I am. I can only hope I did him justice in your eyes.

ABOUT THE AUTHOR

DAYTON WARD has been modified to fit this medium, to write in the space allotted, and has been edited for content. Reader discretion is advised.

Visit Dayton on the Web at

www.daytonward.com.

24: DEADLINE

James Swallow

"Stay out of my way, and I'll be gone within 24 hours. You'll never see me again. Come after me… and you'll regret it." The time is 5:00 PM. One hour ago, federal agent Jack Bauer was declared a fugitive. With his ex-colleagues in CTU now dead, under arrest, or shut down, Jack has no resources to call upon. Hunted by the FBI and a Russian covert operations unit, Jack must face old friends and enemies in a desperate race to stay one step ahead.

This tie-in novel to Fox's groundbreaking TV show *24* answers the question of what happened to CTU agent Jack Bauer after the thrilling final moments of the eighth season.

24: ROGUE

David Mack

Jack Bauer is a man without a country, a fugitive hunted
by the most powerful nations in the world. He lives
on the run, survives by his wits, and finds purpose in
his exile by waging a one-man war against those who
profit from the deaths and sufferings of others. On a
self-imposed crusade to destroy the criminal empire of
international arms dealer Karl Rask, Jack has infiltrated
the crew of one of Rask's freighters. But his mission
is disrupted when the ship is hijacked by a band of
suspiciously well-informed pirates off the coast of
Somalia. As Jack fights to free the ship, he discovers a
deadly secret hidden in its hold: a prize the pirates were
hired to steal and that could be used to ignite a world
war—unless Jack captures it first.

An all-new Jack Bauer adventure by *New York Times*
bestselling author David Mack.

THE KILLING
UNCOMMON DENOMINATOR

Karen Dionne

When firefighters respond to a suspected meth
explosion at a trailer park, they discover a man's body
in a neighboring trailer, unburned but with terrible head
wounds. The meth cooker lies in critical condition, and
undercover narcotics officer Stephen Holder feels a
kinship with the child the man leaves behind.

Then another man's body is discovered in a shipping
container at the Port of Seattle, shot execution-style.
For homicide detective Sarah Linden, two cases soon
become one, and she must unravel a complex web of
addiction, greed, and betrayal to reveal a killer.

A brand-new prequel novel based on the AMC series.